image comics presents

CHEW

The Last Suppers

created by John Layman & Rob Guillory

written & lettered by
John Layman

drawn & colored by
Rob Guillory

Color Assists by Taylor Wells

CHEW, VOL. 11: THE LAST SUPPERS. First printing. May 2016. Published by Image Comics, Inc. Office of publication: 2001 Center Street, Sixth Floor, Berkeley, CA 94704. Copyright © 2016 John Layman. Contains material originally published in single magazine form as Chew #51-55 & Chew/Revival One-Shot. All rights reserved. CHEW™, its logos, and all character likenesses herein are trademarks of John Layman, unless expressly indicated. Image Comics® and its logos are registered trademarks and copyright of Image Comics, Inc. All rights reserved. No part of this publication may be reproduced or transmitted, in any form or by any means (except for short excerpts for review purposes) without the express written permission of John Layman or Image Comics, Inc. All names, characters, events, and locales in this publication, except for satirical purposes, are entirely fictional, and any resemblance to actual persons (living or dead) or entities or events or places is coincidental or for satirical purposes. Printed in the USA. For information regarding the CPSIA on this printed material call: 203-595-3636 and provide reference #RICH–676540. For international rights, contact: foreignlicensing@imagecomics.com. ISBN: 978-1-63215-681-5

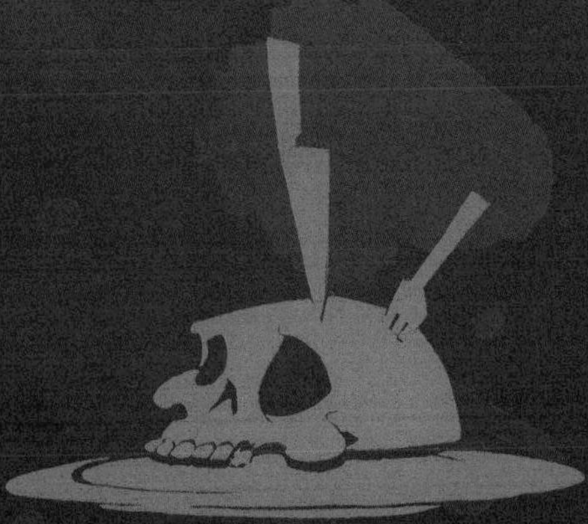

Dedications:

JOHN: To Caterina Marietti, with love.

ROB: For Andy Kuhn, who gave me my very first portfolio review.

Thanks:

Taylor Wells, for the coloring assists.
Drew Gill, for the production assists.
Tom B. Long, for the logo.
Comicbookfonts.com, for the fonts.

And More Thanks:

Tim Seeley, Mike Norton, Jenny Frison, Mark Englert, Crank!, Ross Thibodeaux, the sweet angel Joshie Williamson, April Guillory, Carter Layman, Kim Peterson, and Kathryn & Israel Skelton. Plus everybody at Image, especially Eric, Jonathan, Emily, David, Corey, Kat, Sasha, Meredith, Randy and Branwyn.

CHEW #55 cover inspired by Quentin Tarantino

Chapter 1

THEY LIE.

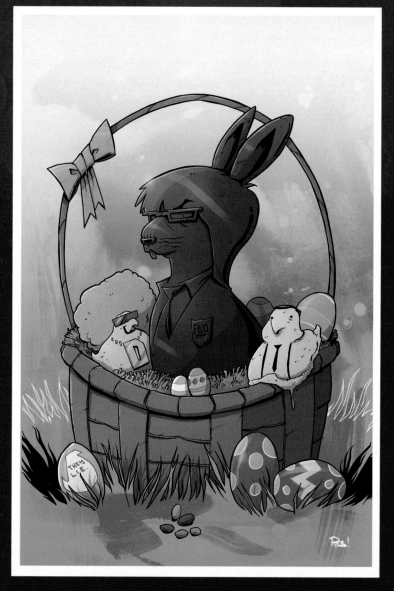

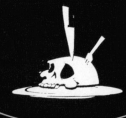

TWO YEARS LATER

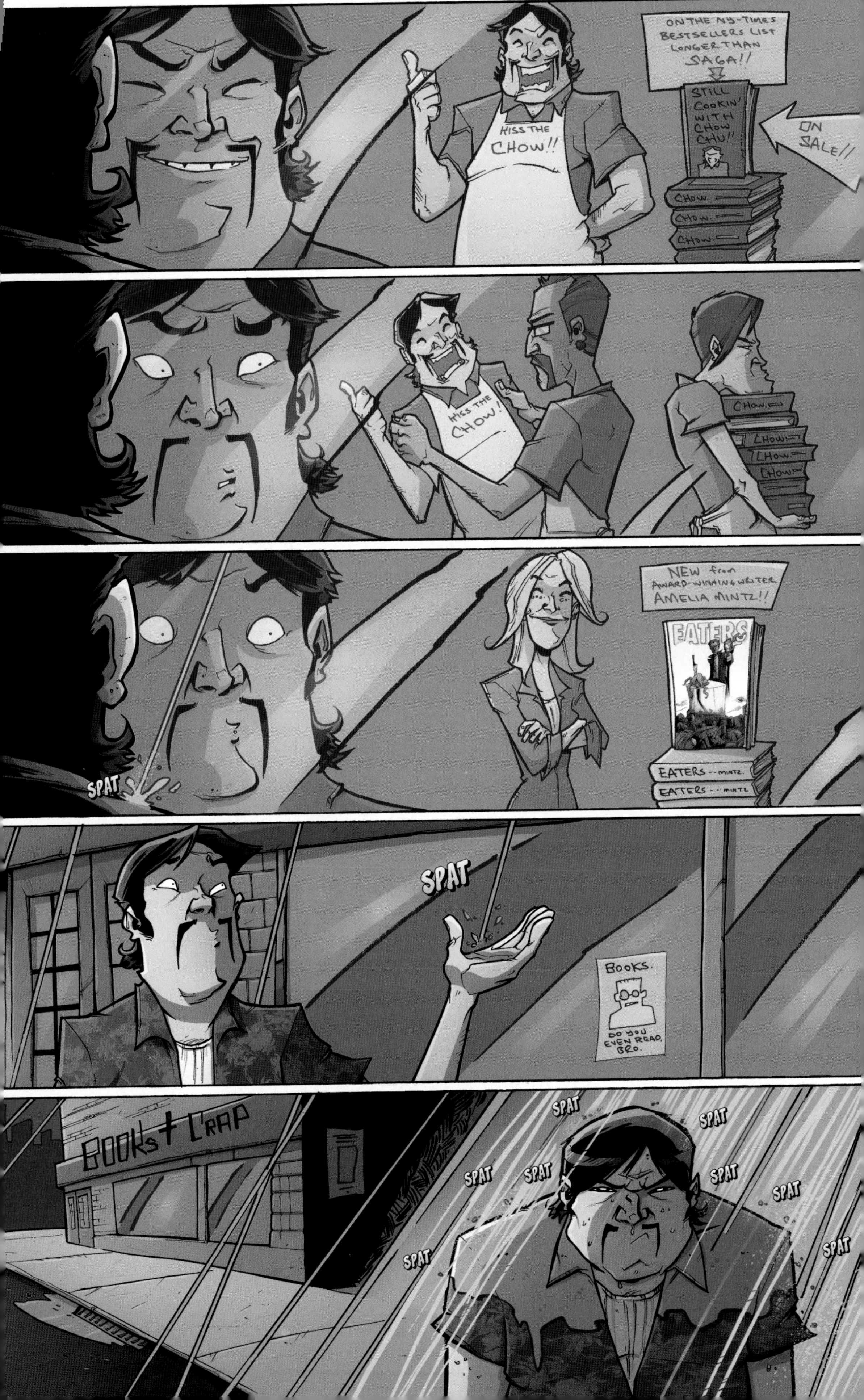

ON THE NY-TIMES BESTSELLERS LIST LONGER THAN SAGA!!
STILL COOKIN' WITH CHOW CHU!!
KISS THE CHOW!!
ON SALE!!
CHOW.
CHOW.
CHOW.
KISS THE CHOW!
CHOW.
CHOW.
CHOW.
CHOW.
NEW from AWARD-WINNING WRITER AMELIA MINTZ!!
EATERS
EATERS -- MINTZ.
EATERS -- MINTZ
SPAT
SPAT
BOOKS.
DO YOU EVEN READ, BRO.
BOOKS + CRAP
SPAT
SPAT
SPAT
SPAT
SPAT
SPAT
SPAT
SPAT

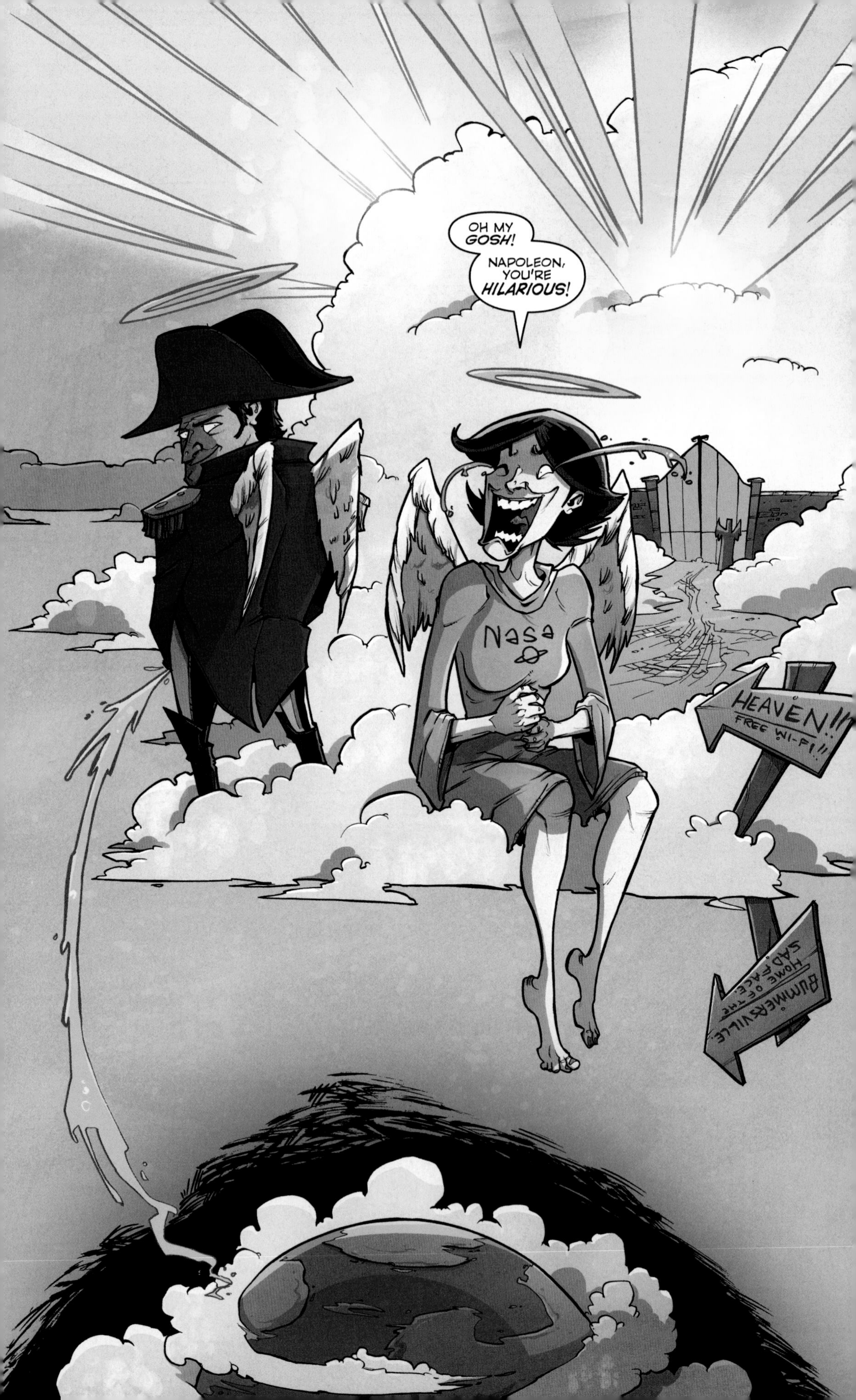
OH MY *GOSH!*
NAPOLEON, YOU'RE ***HILARIOUS!***
NASA
HEAVEN!!
FREE WI-FI!!
BUMMERSVILLE.
HOME OF THE SAD FACE.

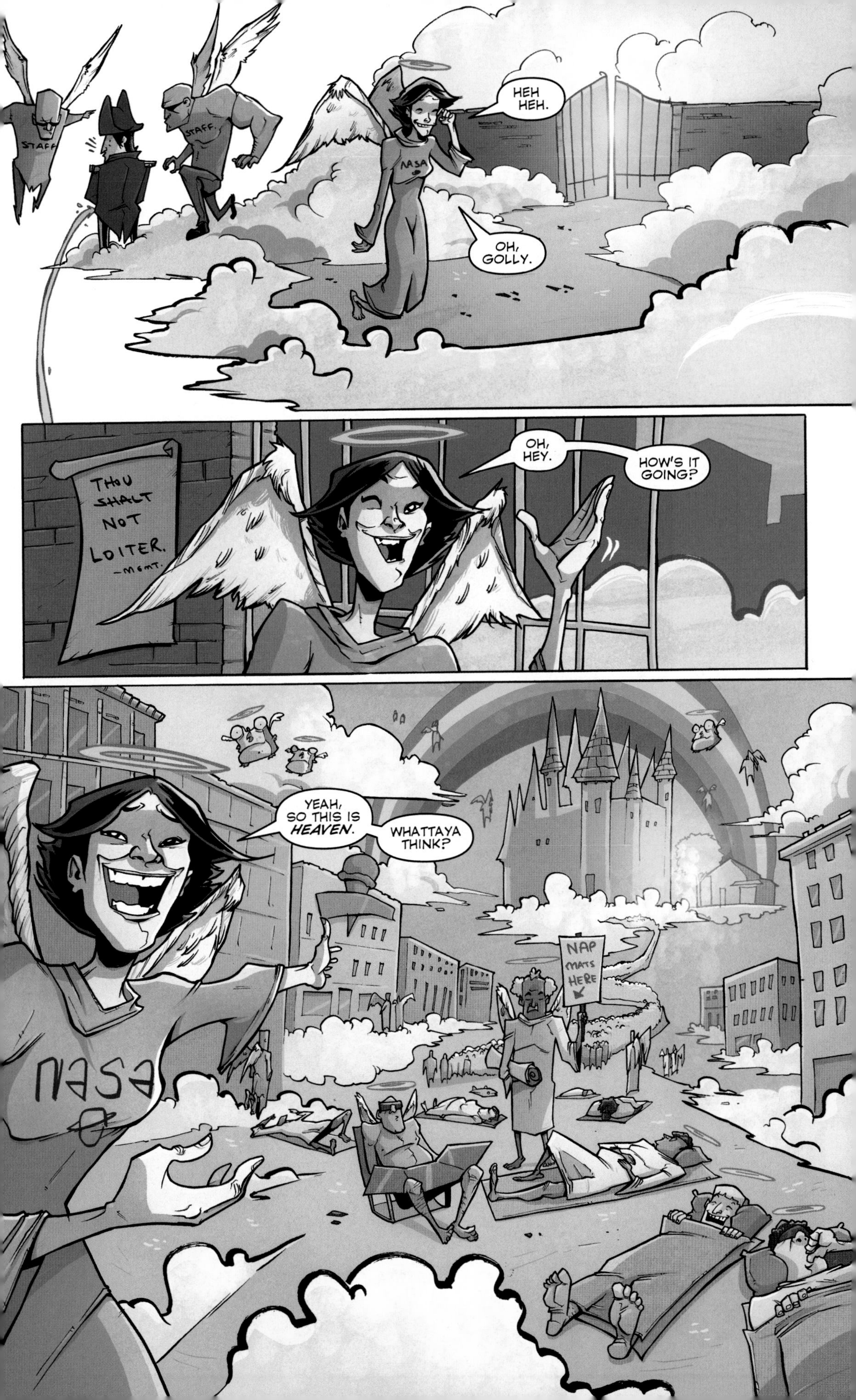
STAFF
STAFF
HEH HEH.
OH, GOLLY.
THOU SHALT NOT LOITER. -MGMT.
OH, HEY.
HOW'S IT GOING?
NASA
YEAH, SO THIS IS *HEAVEN*.
WHATTAYA THINK?
NAP MATS HERE

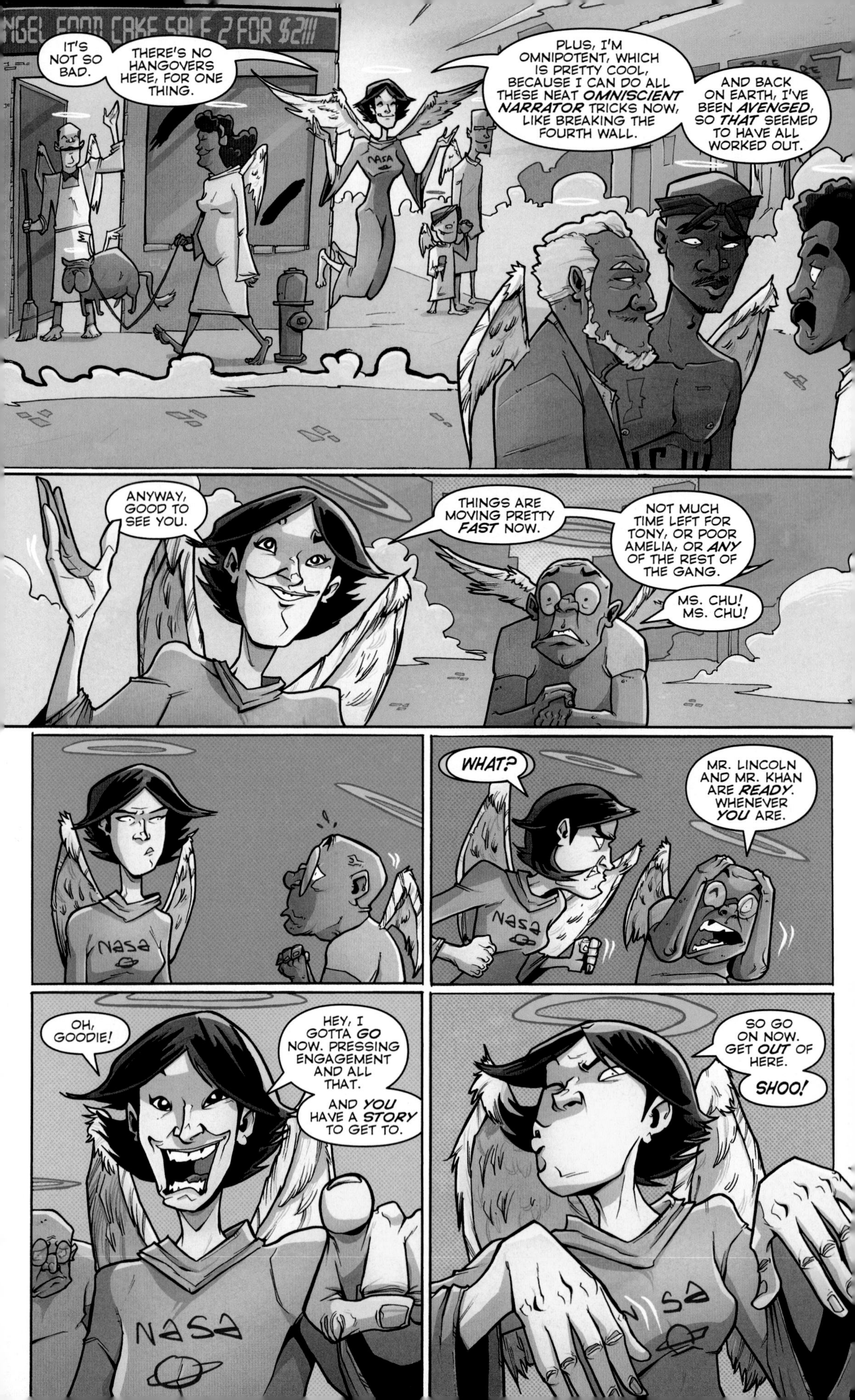

NGEL FOOD CAKE SALE 2 FOR $2!!!
IT'S NOT SO BAD.
THERE'S NO HANGOVERS HERE, FOR ONE THING.
PLUS, I'M OMNIPOTENT, WHICH IS PRETTY COOL, BECAUSE I CAN DO ALL THESE NEAT OMNISCIENT NARRATOR TRICKS NOW, LIKE BREAKING THE FOURTH WALL.
AND BACK ON EARTH, I'VE BEEN AVENGED, SO THAT SEEMED TO HAVE ALL WORKED OUT.
ANYWAY, GOOD TO SEE YOU.
THINGS ARE MOVING PRETTY FAST NOW.
NOT MUCH TIME LEFT FOR TONY, OR POOR AMELIA, OR ANY OF THE REST OF THE GANG.
MS. CHU! MS. CHU!
NASA
WHAT?
MR. LINCOLN AND MR. KHAN ARE READY. WHENEVER YOU ARE.
OH, GOODIE!
HEY, I GOTTA GO NOW. PRESSING ENGAGEMENT AND ALL THAT.
AND YOU HAVE A STORY TO GET TO.
SO GO ON NOW. GET OUT OF HERE.
SHOO!

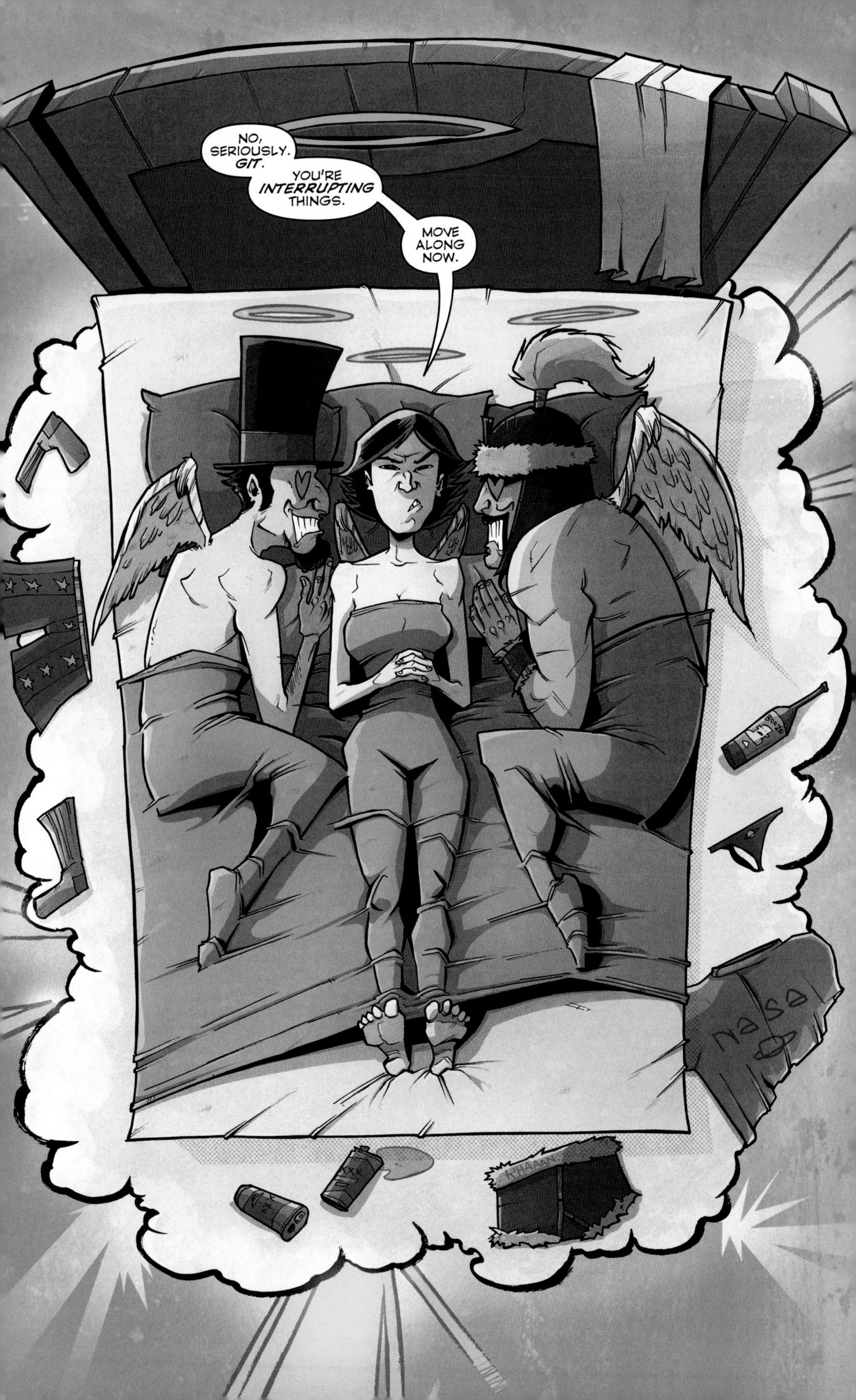
NO, SERIOUSLY. *GIT*.
YOU'RE *INTERRUPTING* THINGS.
MOVE ALONG NOW.
BOOZE
NASA
KHAAAN

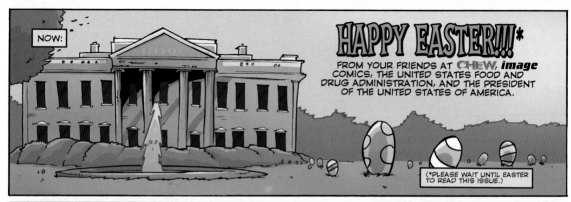

NOW:

HAPPY EASTER!!!*
FROM YOUR FRIENDS AT CHEW, image COMICS, THE UNITED STATES FOOD AND DRUG ADMINISTRATION, AND THE PRESIDENT OF THE UNITED STATES OF AMERICA.

(*PLEASE WAIT UNTIL EASTER TO READ THIS ISSUE.)

AND WELCOME TO THE WHITE HOUSE EASTER EGG ROLL, WHERE, ON THE EAST LAWN, IT'S BEEN HELD ANNUALLY FOR ALMOST 150 YEARS--

--WITH THE PRESIDENT HOSTING HUNDREDS OF CHILDREN FROM ALL AROUND THE COUNTRY FOR AN AFTERNOON OF FESTIVITIES AND HOLIDAY FUN.

AND JOINING US AGAIN THIS YEAR, A MORE RECENT BUT NO LESS BELOVED HOLIDAY TRADITION, IS THE EASTER PLATYPUS--

--THE EASTER MASCOT WHO REPLACED THE EASTER BUNNY AFTER THE TRAGIC AVIAN BIRD FLU RESULTED IN THE PROHIBITION OF CHICKEN EGGS AND OTHER POULTRY-RELATED PRODUCTS.

AND, AS HE'S DONE EVERY YEAR SINCE, THE EASTER PLATYPUS WILL BRING JOY, DELIVERING CANDY, CHOCOLATE EGGS, AND EVEN THE OCCASIONAL PLATYPUS EGG, TO EASTER CELEBRANTS ONE AND ALL.

WELL... ALMOST ALL.

ASSUME THE POSITION. DROP TROU, SPREAD 'EM WIDE--

--AND GET READY FOR THE LONG ARM OF THE LAW!

SNAP!

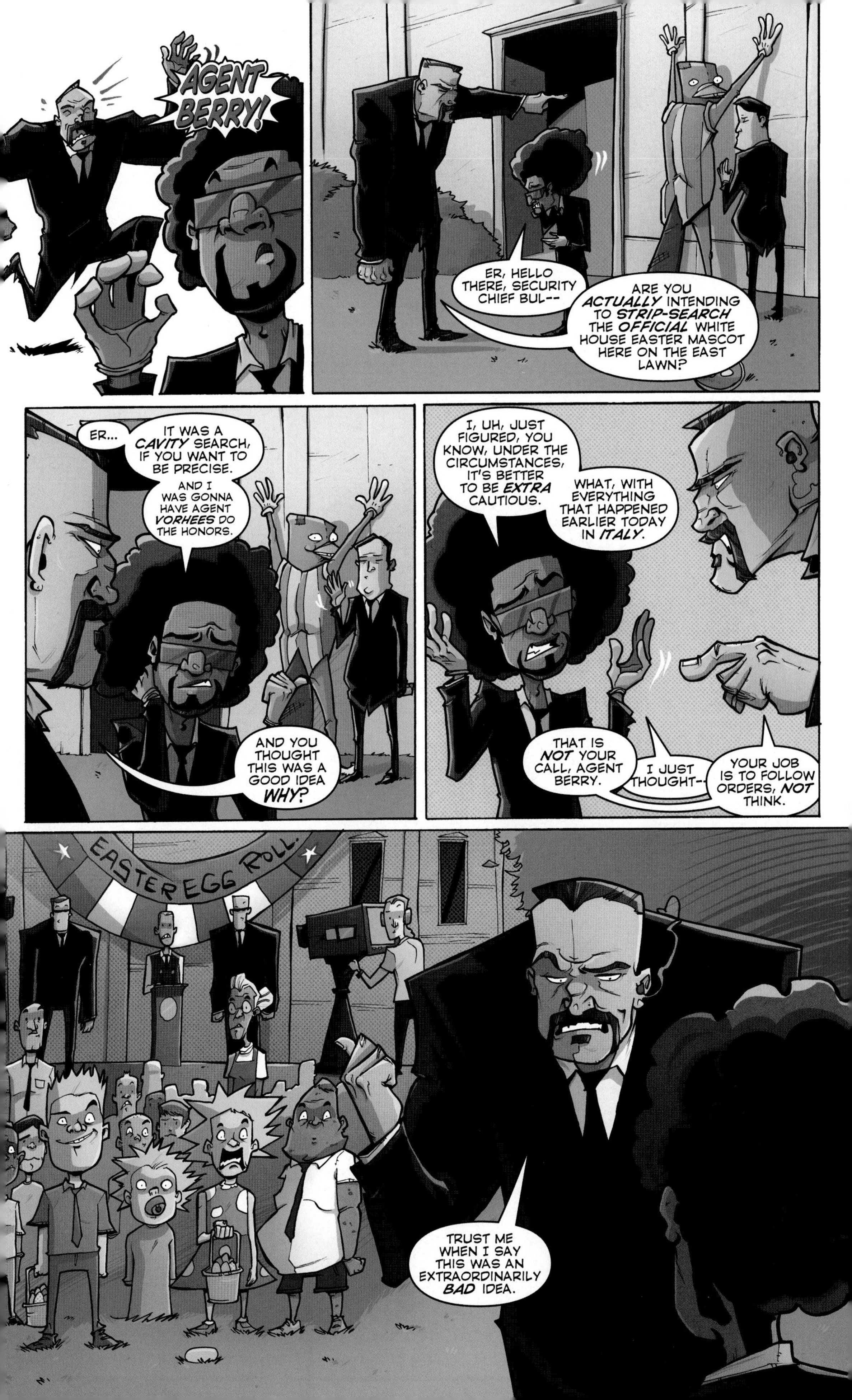
AGENT BERRY!
ER, HELLO THERE, SECURITY CHIEF BUL--
ARE YOU ACTUALLY INTENDING TO STRIP-SEARCH THE OFFICIAL WHITE HOUSE EASTER MASCOT HERE ON THE EAST LAWN?
ER...
IT WAS A CAVITY SEARCH, IF YOU WANT TO BE PRECISE.
AND I WAS GONNA HAVE AGENT VORHEES DO THE HONORS.
AND YOU THOUGHT THIS WAS A GOOD IDEA WHY?
I, UH, JUST FIGURED, YOU KNOW, UNDER THE CIRCUMSTANCES, IT'S BETTER TO BE EXTRA CAUTIOUS.
WHAT, WITH EVERYTHING THAT HAPPENED EARLIER TODAY IN ITALY.
THAT IS NOT YOUR CALL, AGENT BERRY.
I JUST THOUGHT--
YOUR JOB IS TO FOLLOW ORDERS, NOT THINK.
EASTER EGG ROLL.
TRUST ME WHEN I SAY THIS WAS AN EXTRAORDINARILY BAD IDEA.

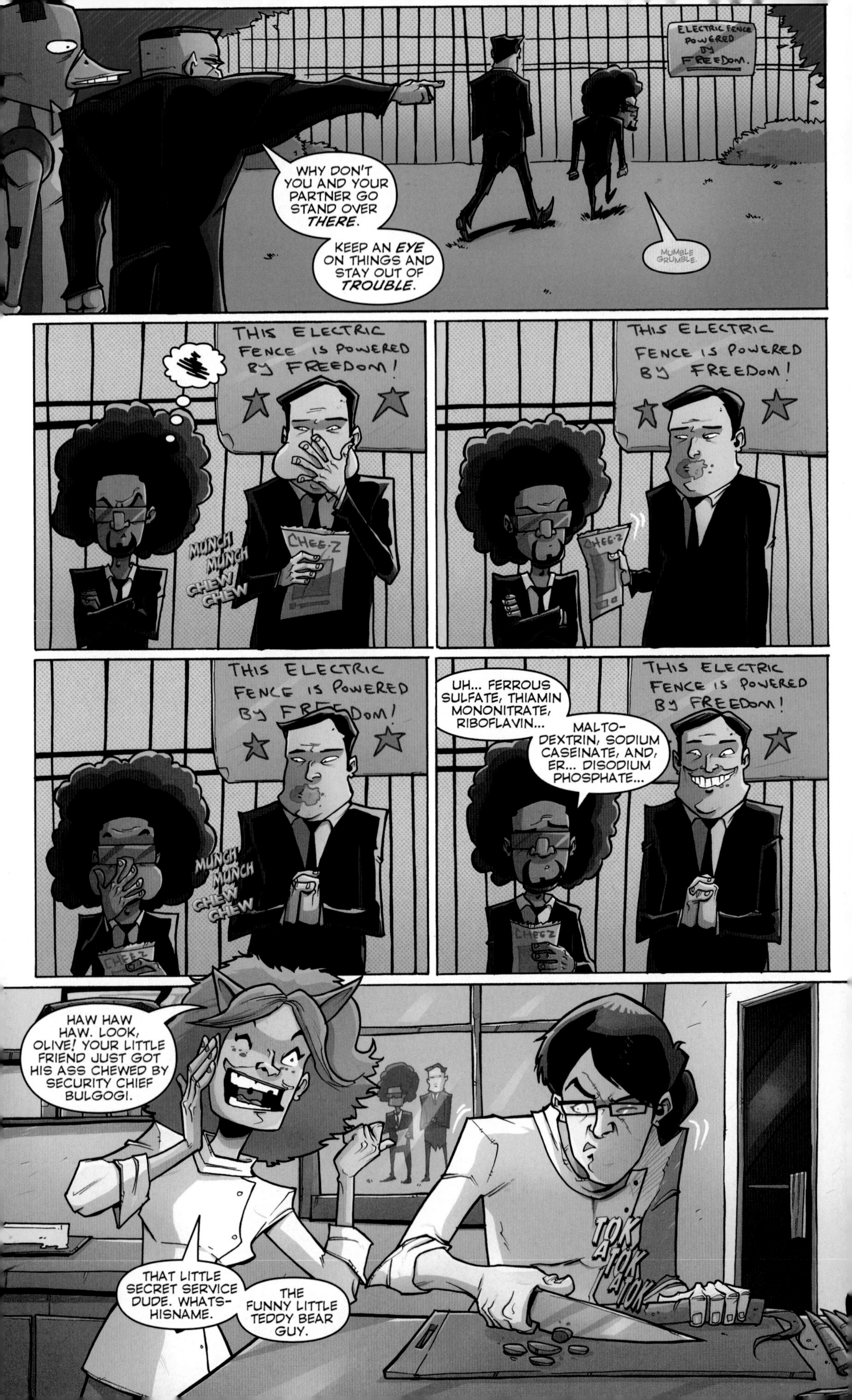
ELECTRIC FENCE POWERED BY FREEDOM.
WHY DON'T YOU AND YOUR PARTNER GO STAND OVER THERE.
KEEP AN EYE ON THINGS AND STAY OUT OF TROUBLE.
MUMBLE GRUMBLE.
THIS ELECTRIC FENCE IS POWERED BY FREEDOM!
CHEE-Z
MUNCH MUNCH CHEW CHEW
THIS ELECTRIC FENCE IS POWERED BY FREEDOM!
CHEE-Z
THIS ELECTRIC FENCE IS POWERED BY FREEDOM!
MUNCH MUNCH CHEW CHEW
CHEE-Z
UH... FERROUS SULFATE, THIAMIN MONONITRATE, RIBOFLAVIN...
MALTO-DEXTRIN, SODIUM CASEINATE, AND, ER... DISODIUM PHOSPHATE...
THIS ELECTRIC FENCE IS POWERED BY FREEDOM!
CHEEZ
HAW HAW HAW. LOOK, OLIVE! YOUR LITTLE FRIEND JUST GOT HIS ASS CHEWED BY SECURITY CHIEF BULGOGI.
THAT LITTLE SECRET SERVICE DUDE. WHATS-HISNAME.
THE FUNNY LITTLE TEDDY BEAR GUY.
TOK A TOK A TOK

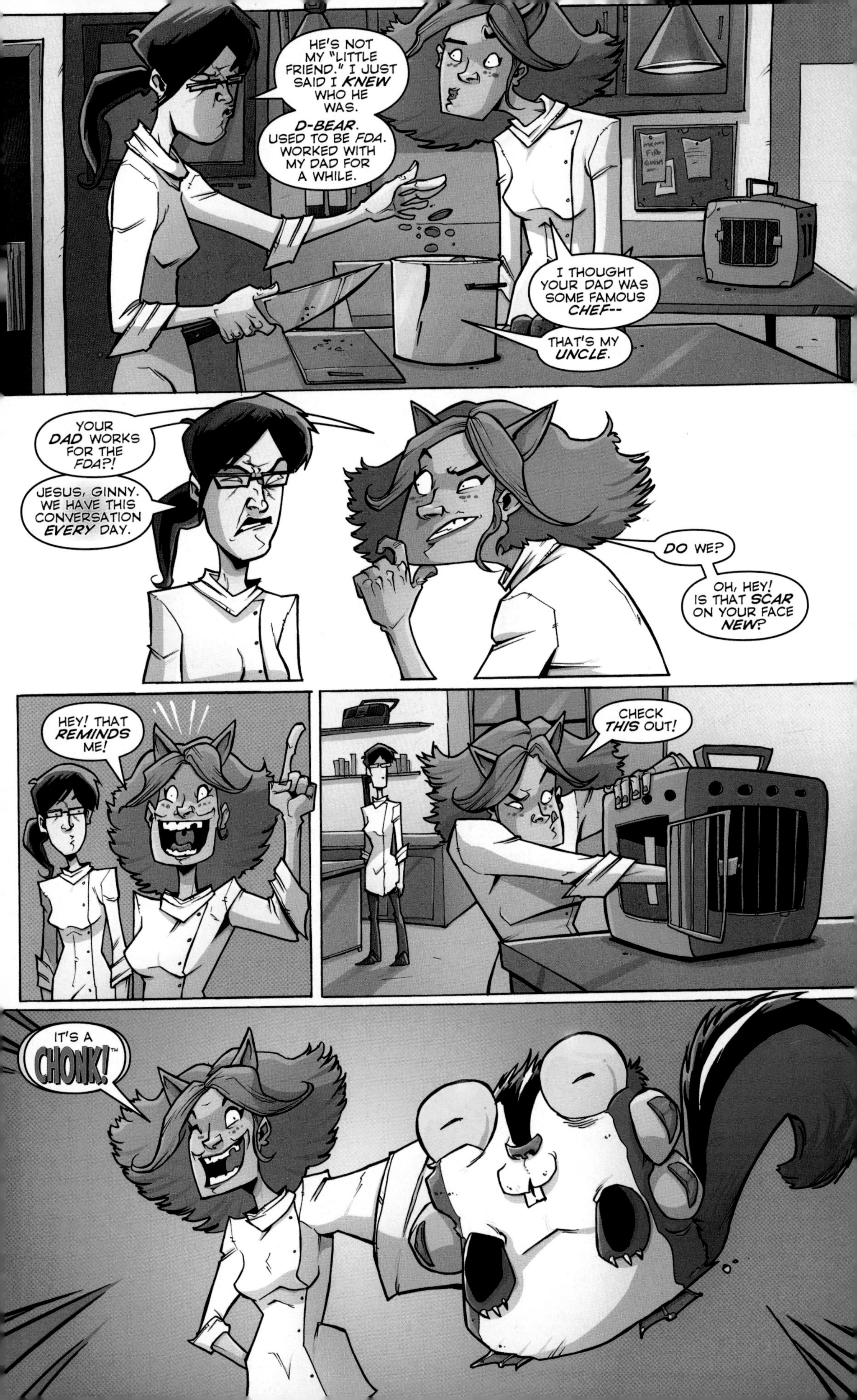
HE'S NOT MY "LITTLE FRIEND." I JUST SAID I KNEW WHO HE WAS.
D-BEAR. USED TO BE FDA. WORKED WITH MY DAD FOR A WHILE.
I THOUGHT YOUR DAD WAS SOME FAMOUS CHEF--
THAT'S MY UNCLE.
YOUR DAD WORKS FOR THE FDA?!
JESUS, GINNY. WE HAVE THIS CONVERSATION EVERY DAY.
DO WE?
OH, HEY! IS THAT SCAR ON YOUR FACE NEW?
HEY! THAT REMINDS ME!
CHECK THIS OUT!
IT'S A CHONK!™

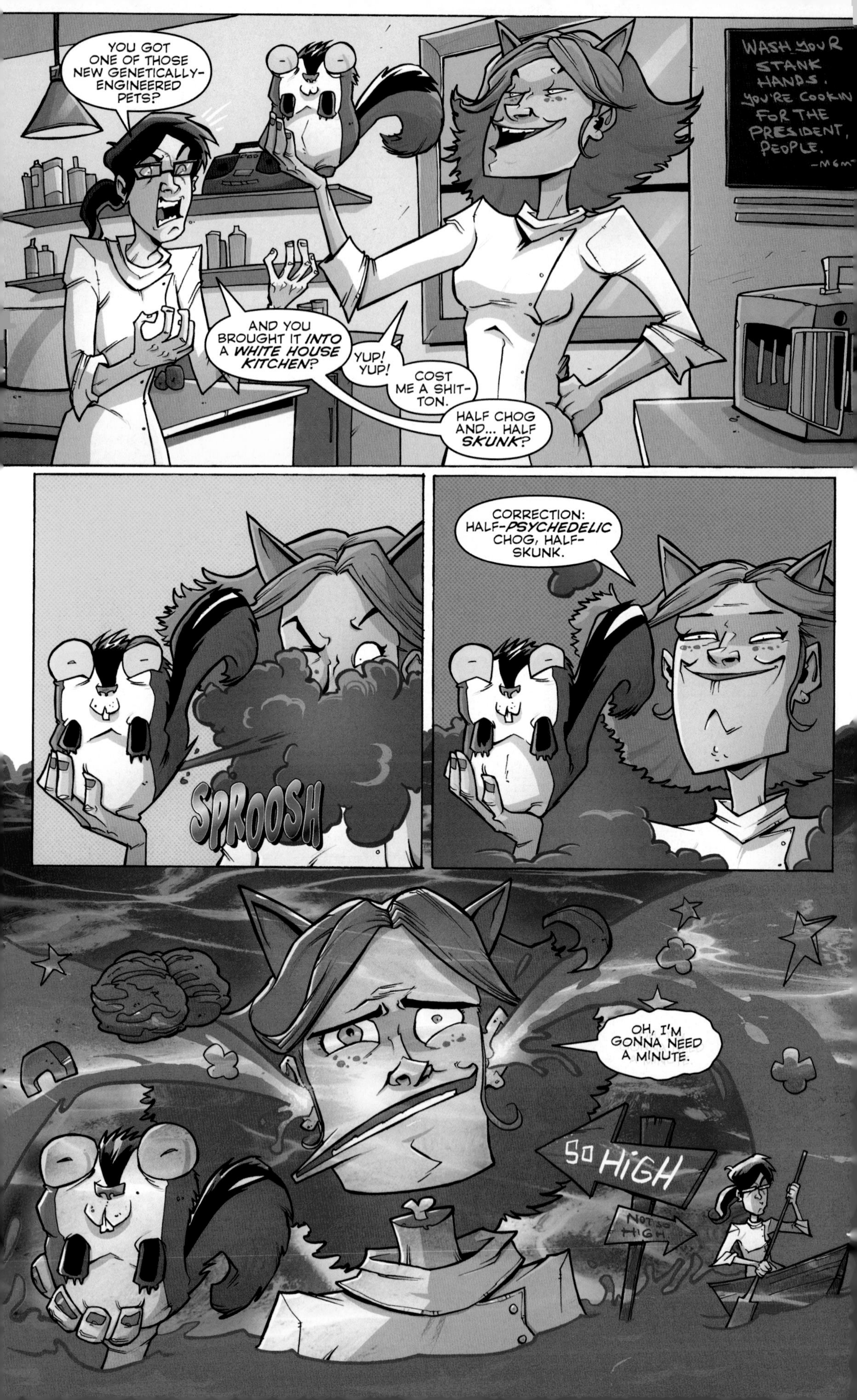
YOU GOT ONE OF THOSE NEW GENETICALLY-ENGINEERED PETS?
WASH YOUR STANK HANDS. YOU'RE COOKIN FOR THE PRESIDENT, PEOPLE. -MGM
AND YOU BROUGHT IT INTO A WHITE HOUSE KITCHEN?
YUP! YUP!
COST ME A SHIT-TON.
HALF CHOG AND... HALF SKUNK?
SPROOSH
CORRECTION: HALF-PSYCHEDELIC CHOG, HALF-SKUNK.
OH, I'M GONNA NEED A MINUTE.
SO HIGH
NOT SO HIGH

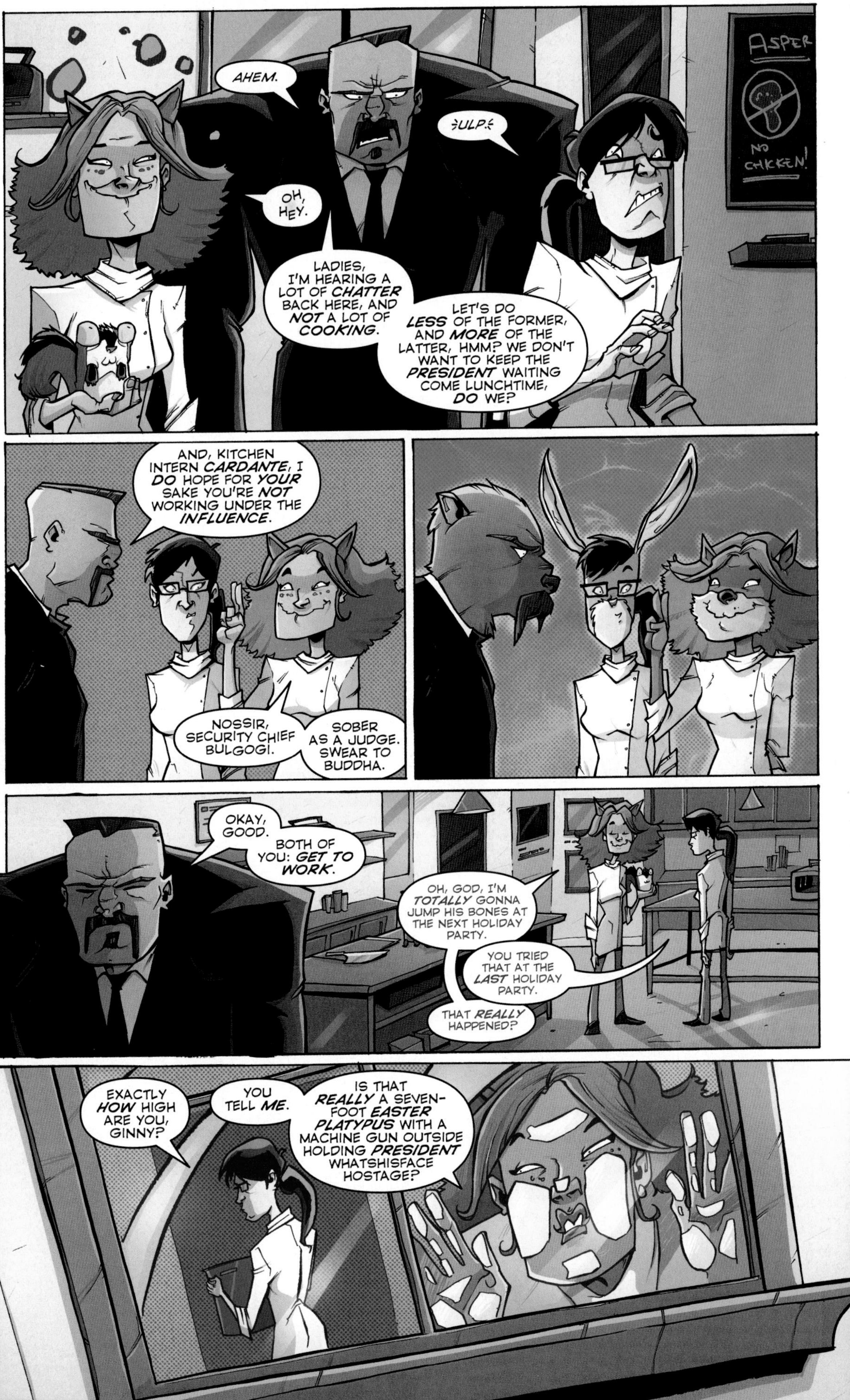
AHEM.
ULP.
OH, HEY.
LADIES, I'M HEARING A LOT OF CHATTER BACK HERE, AND NOT A LOT OF COOKING.
LET'S DO LESS OF THE FORMER, AND MORE OF THE LATTER, HMM? WE DON'T WANT TO KEEP THE PRESIDENT WAITING COME LUNCHTIME, DO WE?
AND, KITCHEN INTERN CARDANTE, I DO HOPE FOR YOUR SAKE YOU'RE NOT WORKING UNDER THE INFLUENCE.
NOSSIR, SECURITY CHIEF BULGOGI.
SOBER AS A JUDGE. SWEAR TO BUDDHA.
OKAY, GOOD.
BOTH OF YOU: GET TO WORK.
OH, GOD, I'M TOTALLY GONNA JUMP HIS BONES AT THE NEXT HOLIDAY PARTY.
YOU TRIED THAT AT THE LAST HOLIDAY PARTY.
THAT REALLY HAPPENED?
EXACTLY HOW HIGH ARE YOU, GINNY?
YOU TELL ME.
IS THAT REALLY A SEVEN-FOOT EASTER PLATYPUS WITH A MACHINE GUN OUTSIDE HOLDING PRESIDENT WHATSHISFACE HOSTAGE?

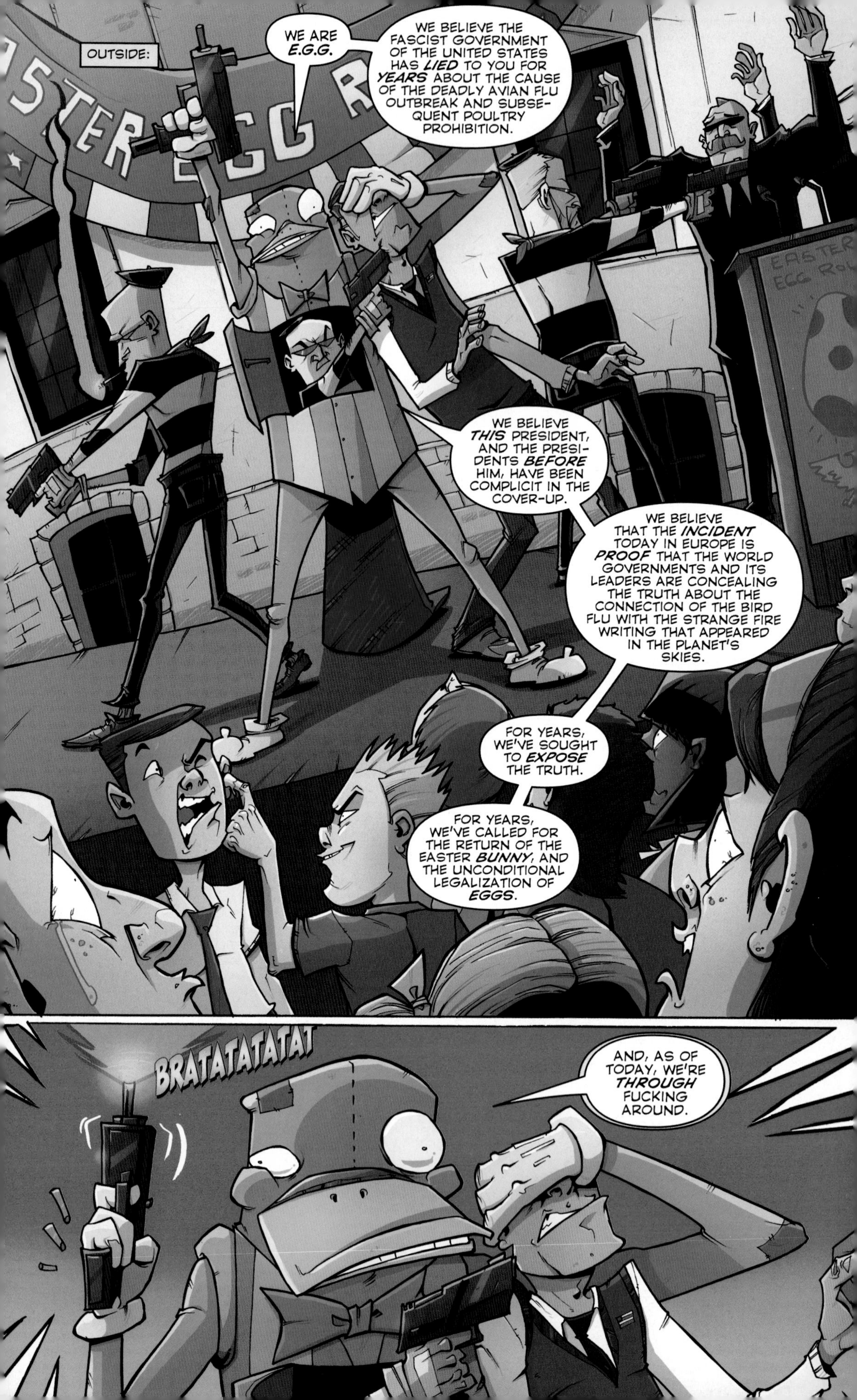
OUTSIDE:
WE ARE *E.G.G.*
WE BELIEVE THE FASCIST GOVERNMENT OF THE UNITED STATES HAS *LIED* TO YOU FOR *YEARS* ABOUT THE CAUSE OF THE DEADLY AVIAN FLU OUTBREAK AND SUBSEQUENT POULTRY PROHIBITION.
WE BELIEVE *THIS* PRESIDENT, AND THE PRESIDENTS *BEFORE* HIM, HAVE BEEN COMPLICIT IN THE COVER-UP.
WE BELIEVE THAT THE *INCIDENT* TODAY IN EUROPE IS *PROOF* THAT THE WORLD GOVERNMENTS AND ITS LEADERS ARE CONCEALING THE TRUTH ABOUT THE CONNECTION OF THE BIRD FLU WITH THE STRANGE FIRE WRITING THAT APPEARED IN THE PLANET'S SKIES.
FOR YEARS, WE'VE SOUGHT TO *EXPOSE* THE TRUTH.
FOR YEARS, WE'VE CALLED FOR THE RETURN OF THE EASTER *BUNNY*, AND THE UNCONDITIONAL LEGALIZATION OF *EGGS*.
BRATATATATAT
AND, AS OF TODAY, WE'RE *THROUGH* FUCKING AROUND.

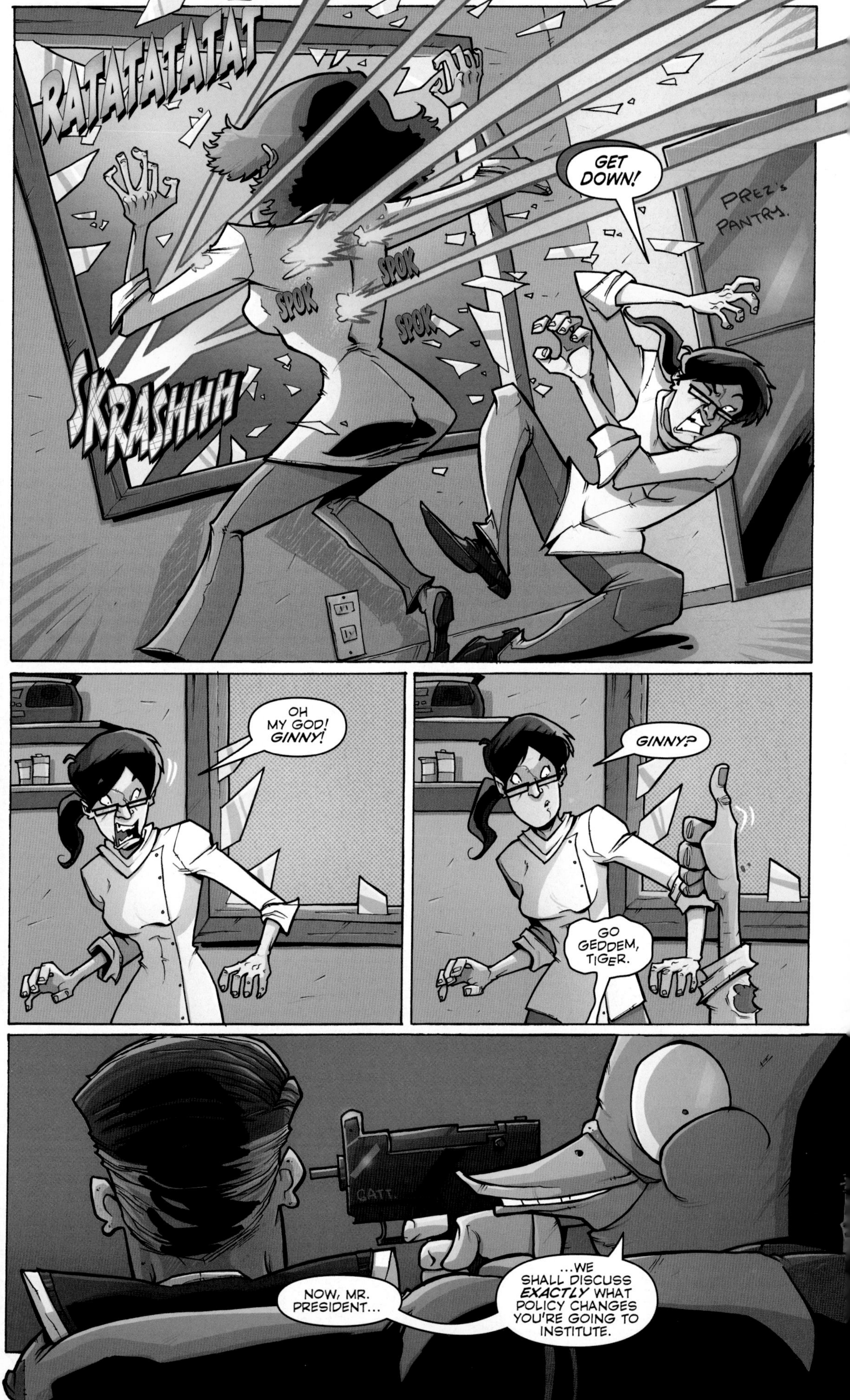
RATATATATAT
SPOK
SPOK
SPOK
KRASHHH
GET DOWN!
PREZ'S PANTRY
OH MY GOD! GINNY!
GINNY?
GO GEDDEM, TIGER.
GATT.
NOW, MR. PRESIDENT...
...WE SHALL DISCUSS EXACTLY WHAT POLICY CHANGES YOU'RE GOING TO INSTITUTE.

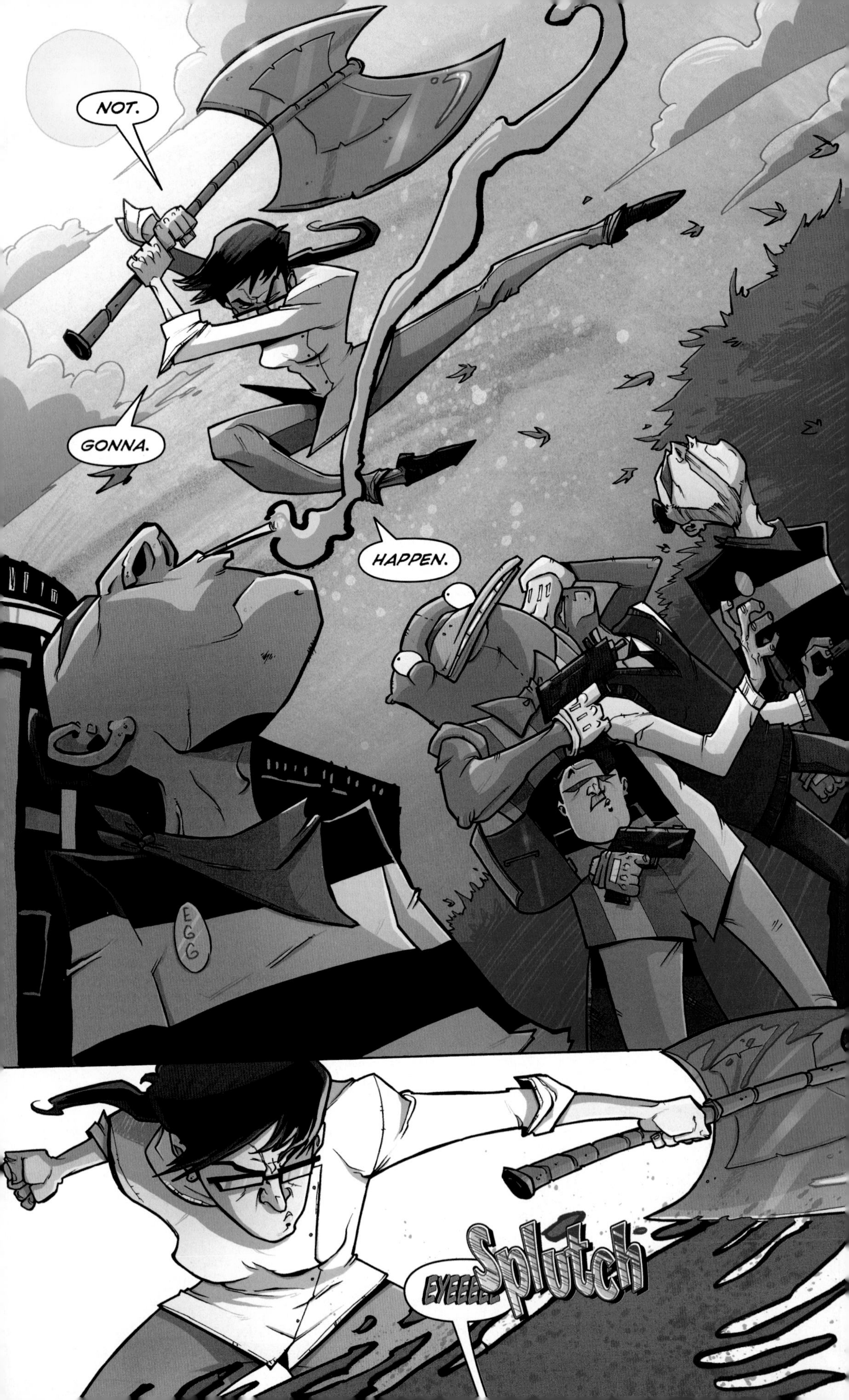
NOT.
GONNA.
HAPPEN.
EGG
EYEEEE
Splutch

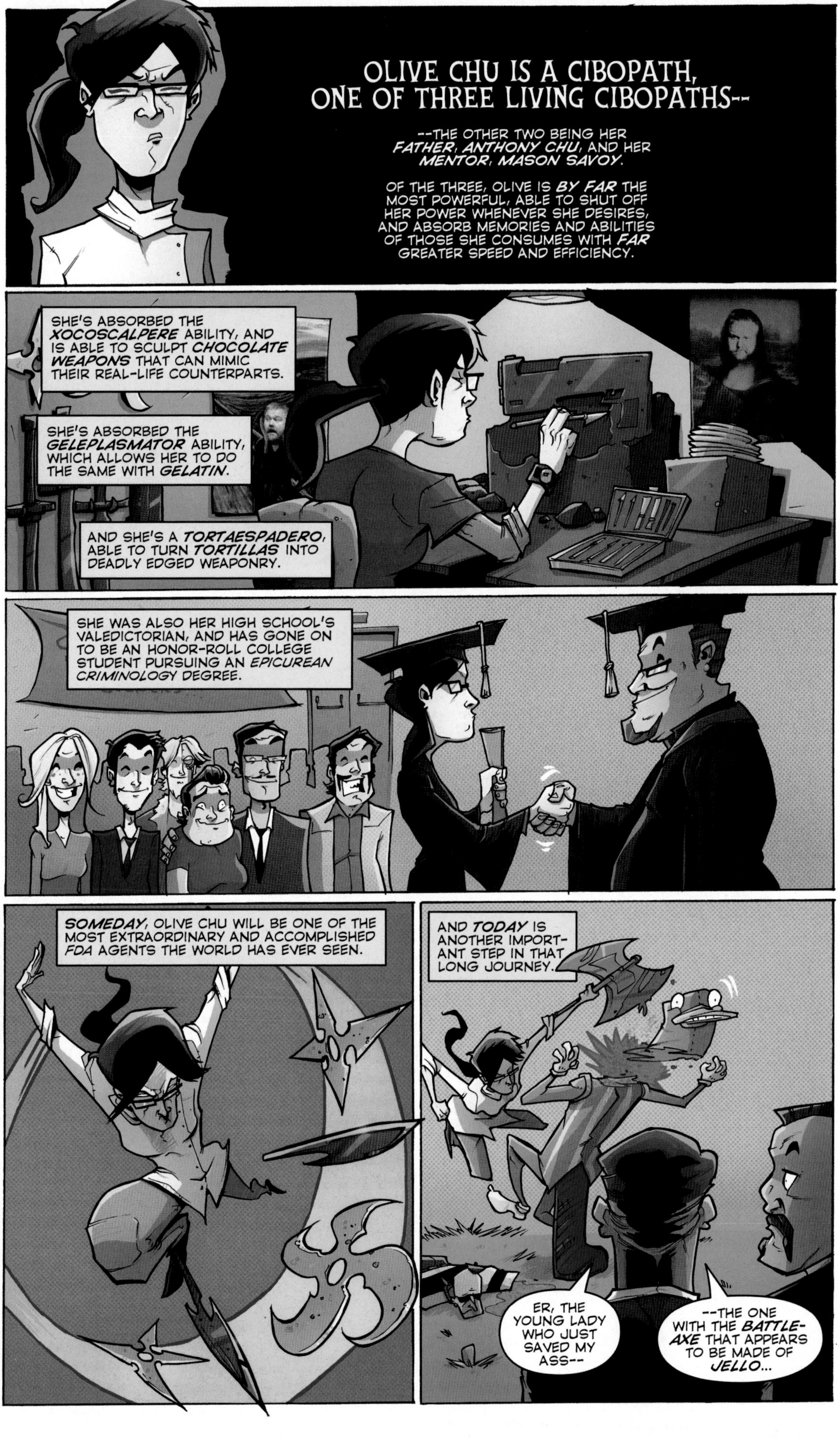

OLIVE CHU IS A CIBOPATH, ONE OF THREE LIVING CIBOPATHS--
--THE OTHER TWO BEING HER FATHER, ANTHONY CHU, AND HER MENTOR, MASON SAVOY.
OF THE THREE, OLIVE IS BY FAR THE MOST POWERFUL, ABLE TO SHUT OFF HER POWER WHENEVER SHE DESIRES, AND ABSORB MEMORIES AND ABILITIES OF THOSE SHE CONSUMES WITH FAR GREATER SPEED AND EFFICIENCY.
SHE'S ABSORBED THE XOCOSCALPERE ABILITY, AND IS ABLE TO SCULPT CHOCOLATE WEAPONS THAT CAN MIMIC THEIR REAL-LIFE COUNTERPARTS.
SHE'S ABSORBED THE GELEPLASMATOR ABILITY, WHICH ALLOWS HER TO DO THE SAME WITH GELATIN.
AND SHE'S A TORTAESPADERO, ABLE TO TURN TORTILLAS INTO DEADLY EDGED WEAPONRY.
SHE WAS ALSO HER HIGH SCHOOL'S VALEDICTORIAN, AND HAS GONE ON TO BE AN HONOR-ROLL COLLEGE STUDENT PURSUING AN EPICUREAN CRIMINOLOGY DEGREE.
SOMEDAY, OLIVE CHU WILL BE ONE OF THE MOST EXTRAORDINARY AND ACCOMPLISHED FDA AGENTS THE WORLD HAS EVER SEEN.
AND TODAY IS ANOTHER IMPORTANT STEP IN THAT LONG JOURNEY.
ER, THE YOUNG LADY WHO JUST SAVED MY ASS--
--THE ONE WITH THE BATTLE-AXE THAT APPEARS TO BE MADE OF JELLO...

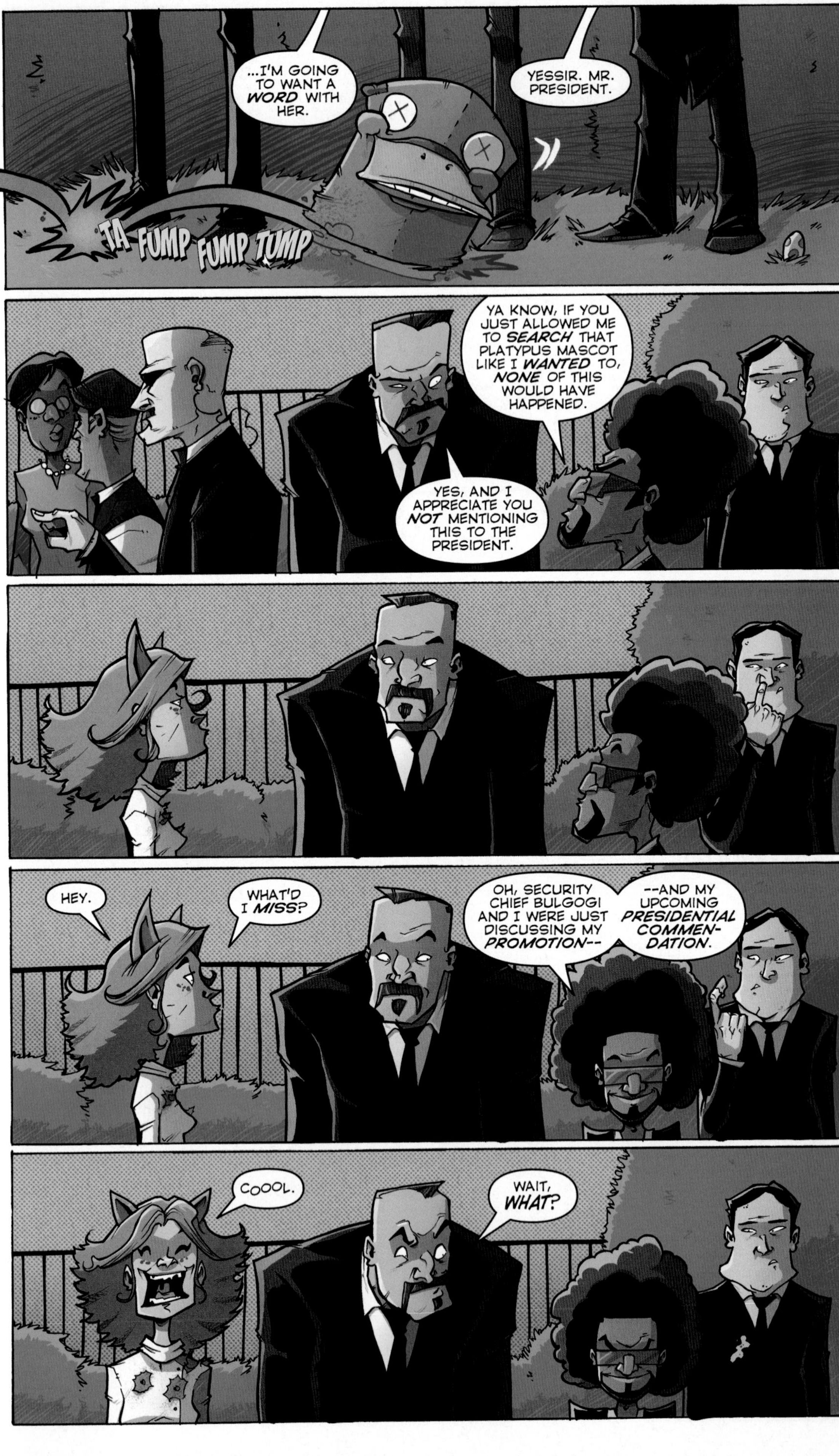
...I'M GOING TO WANT A WORD WITH HER.
YESSIR. MR. PRESIDENT.
TA FUMP FUMP TUMP
YA KNOW, IF YOU JUST ALLOWED ME TO SEARCH THAT PLATYPUS MASCOT LIKE I WANTED TO, NONE OF THIS WOULD HAVE HAPPENED.
YES, AND I APPRECIATE YOU NOT MENTIONING THIS TO THE PRESIDENT.
HEY.
WHAT'D I MISS?
OH, SECURITY CHIEF BULGOGI AND I WERE JUST DISCUSSING MY PROMOTION--
--AND MY UPCOMING PRESIDENTIAL COMMEN-DATION.
COOOL.
WAIT, WHAT?

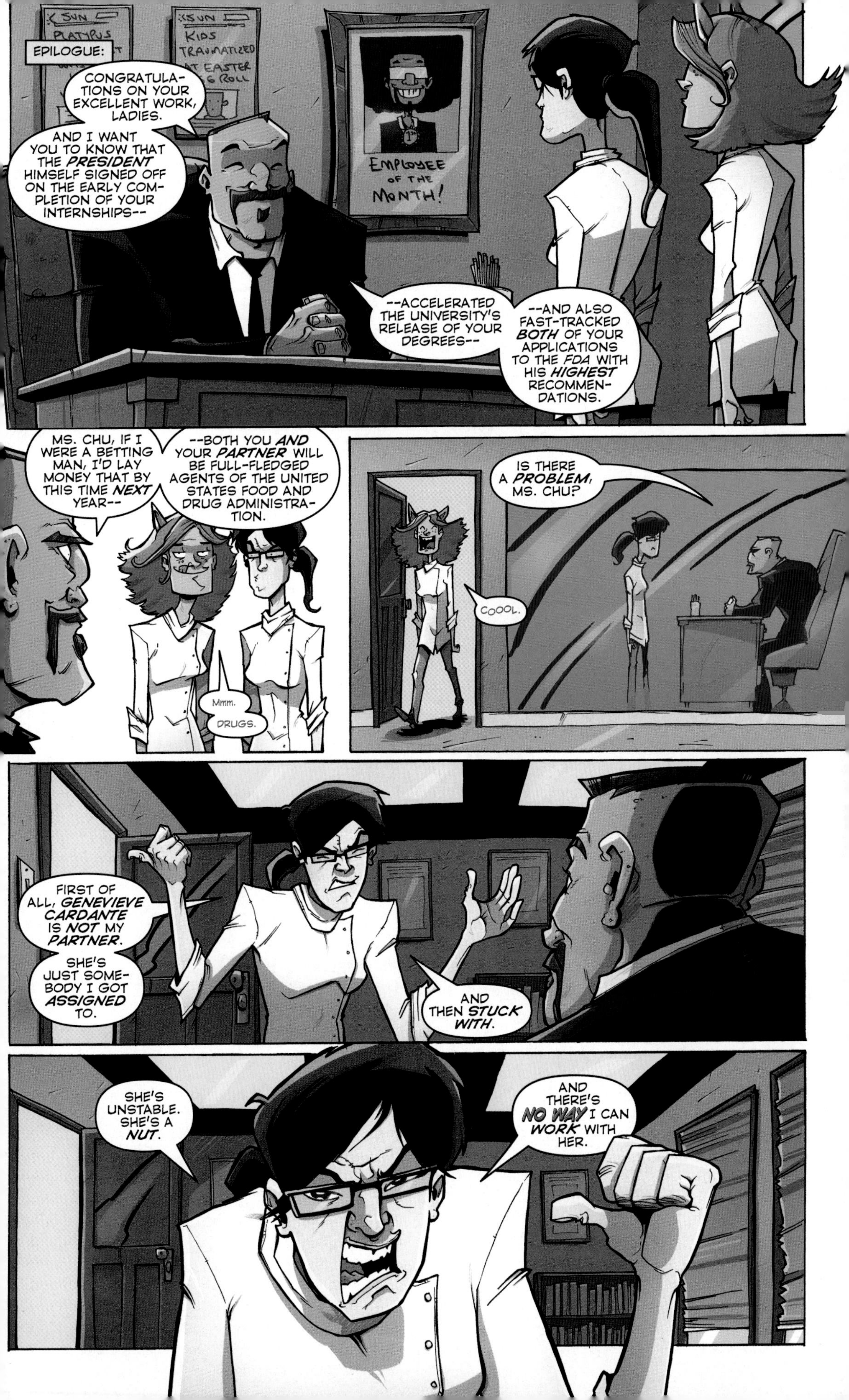
SUN PLATYPUS
SUN KIDS TRAUMATIZED AT EASTER EGG ROLL
EPILOGUE:
CONGRATULATIONS ON YOUR EXCELLENT WORK, LADIES.
AND I WANT YOU TO KNOW THAT THE PRESIDENT HIMSELF SIGNED OFF ON THE EARLY COMPLETION OF YOUR INTERNSHIPS--
EMPLOYEE OF THE MONTH!
--ACCELERATED THE UNIVERSITY'S RELEASE OF YOUR DEGREES--
--AND ALSO FAST-TRACKED BOTH OF YOUR APPLICATIONS TO THE FDA WITH HIS HIGHEST RECOMMENDATIONS.
MS. CHU, IF I WERE A BETTING MAN, I'D LAY MONEY THAT BY THIS TIME NEXT YEAR--
--BOTH YOU AND YOUR PARTNER WILL BE FULL-FLEDGED AGENTS OF THE UNITED STATES FOOD AND DRUG ADMINISTRATION.
Mmm.
DRUGS.
COOOL.
IS THERE A PROBLEM, MS. CHU?
FIRST OF ALL, GENEVIEVE CARDANTE IS NOT MY PARTNER.
SHE'S JUST SOMEBODY I GOT ASSIGNED TO.
AND THEN STUCK WITH.
SHE'S UNSTABLE. SHE'S A NUT.
AND THERE'S NO WAY I CAN WORK WITH HER.

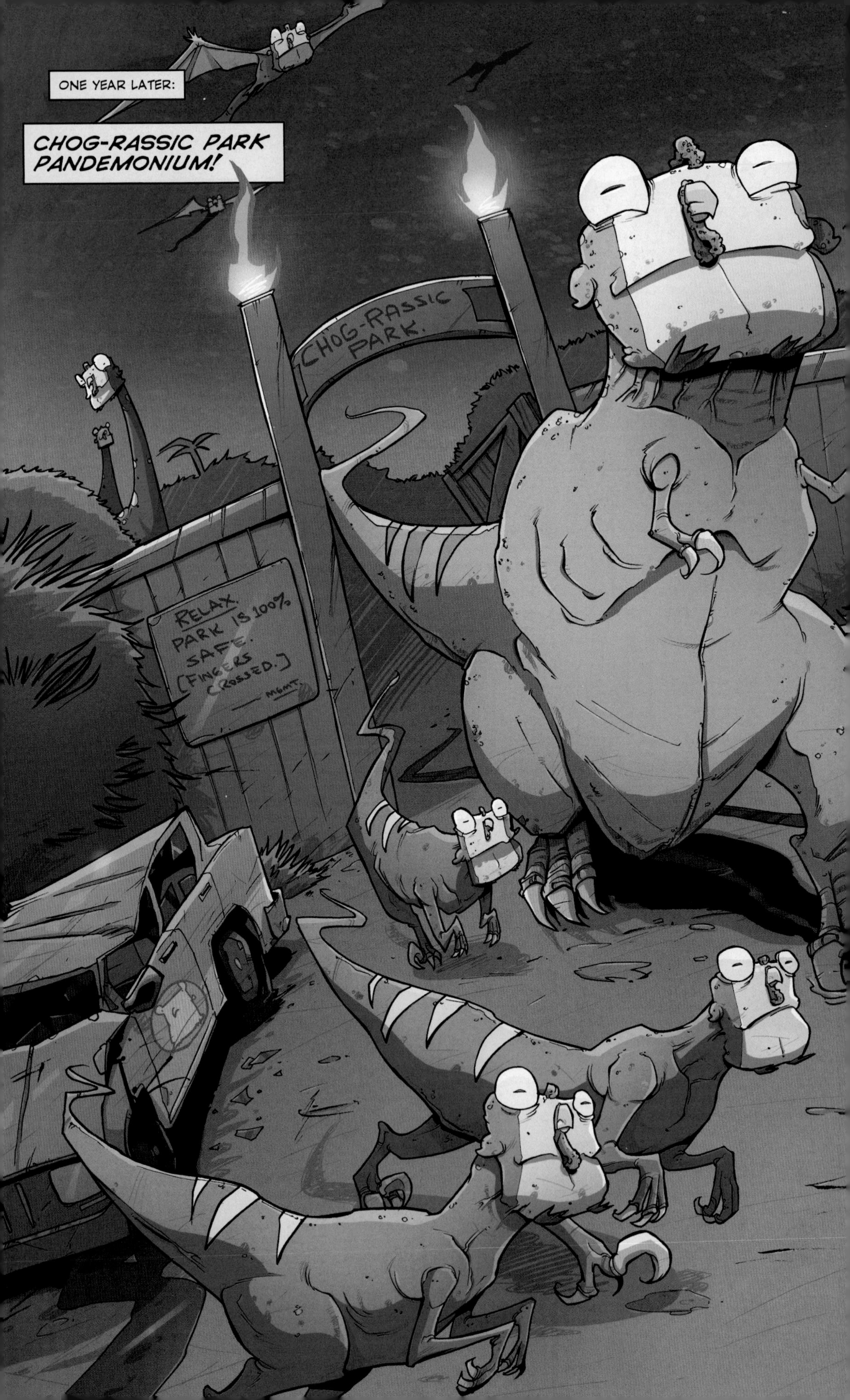
ONE YEAR LATER:
CHOG-RASSIC PARK PANDEMONIUM!
CHOG-RASSIC PARK.
RELAX. PARK IS 100% SAFE. [FINGERS CROSSED.]
— MGMT.

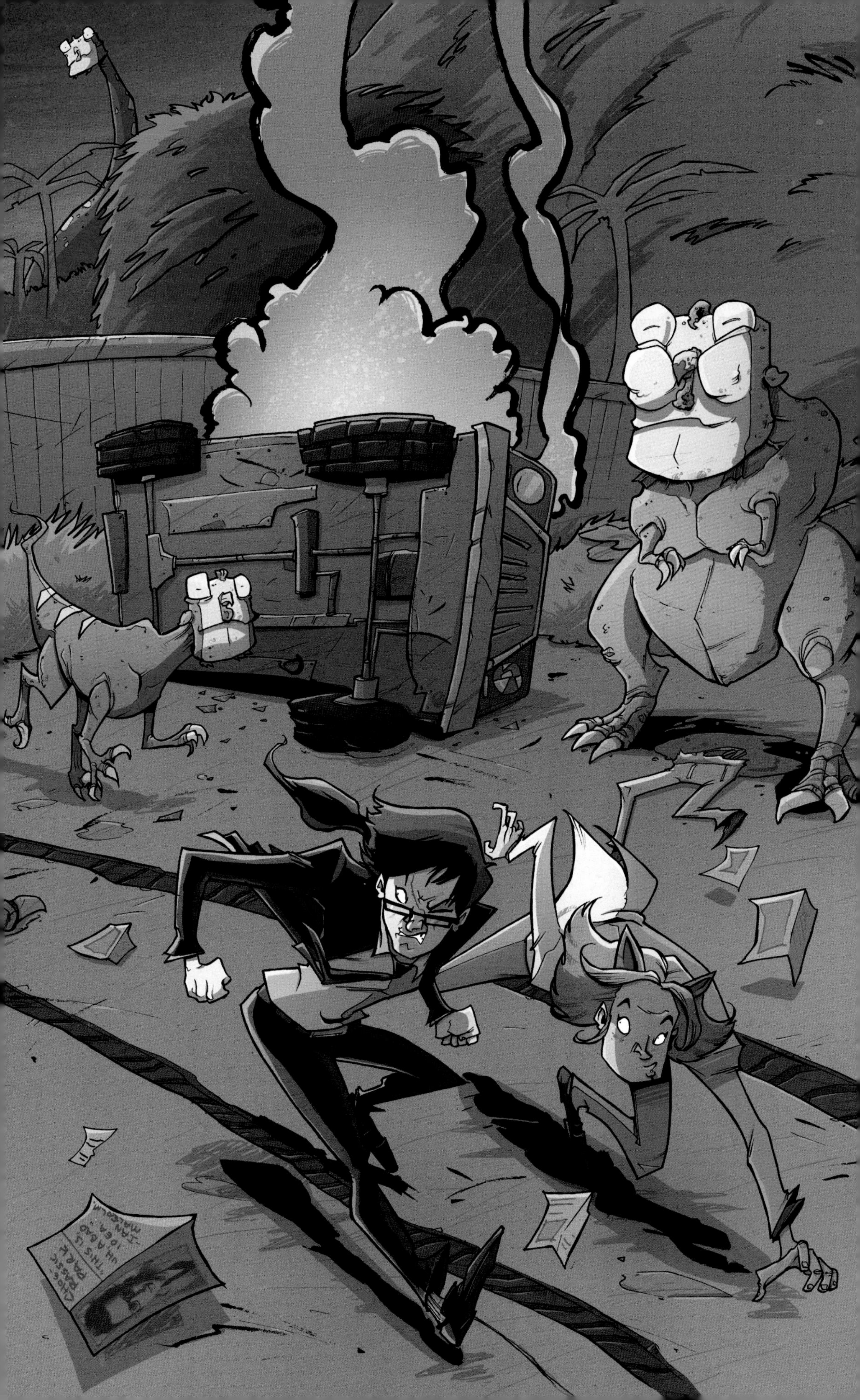
CHAOS-RASSIC PARK
"THIS IS, UH, A BAD IDEA."
-IAN MALCOLM

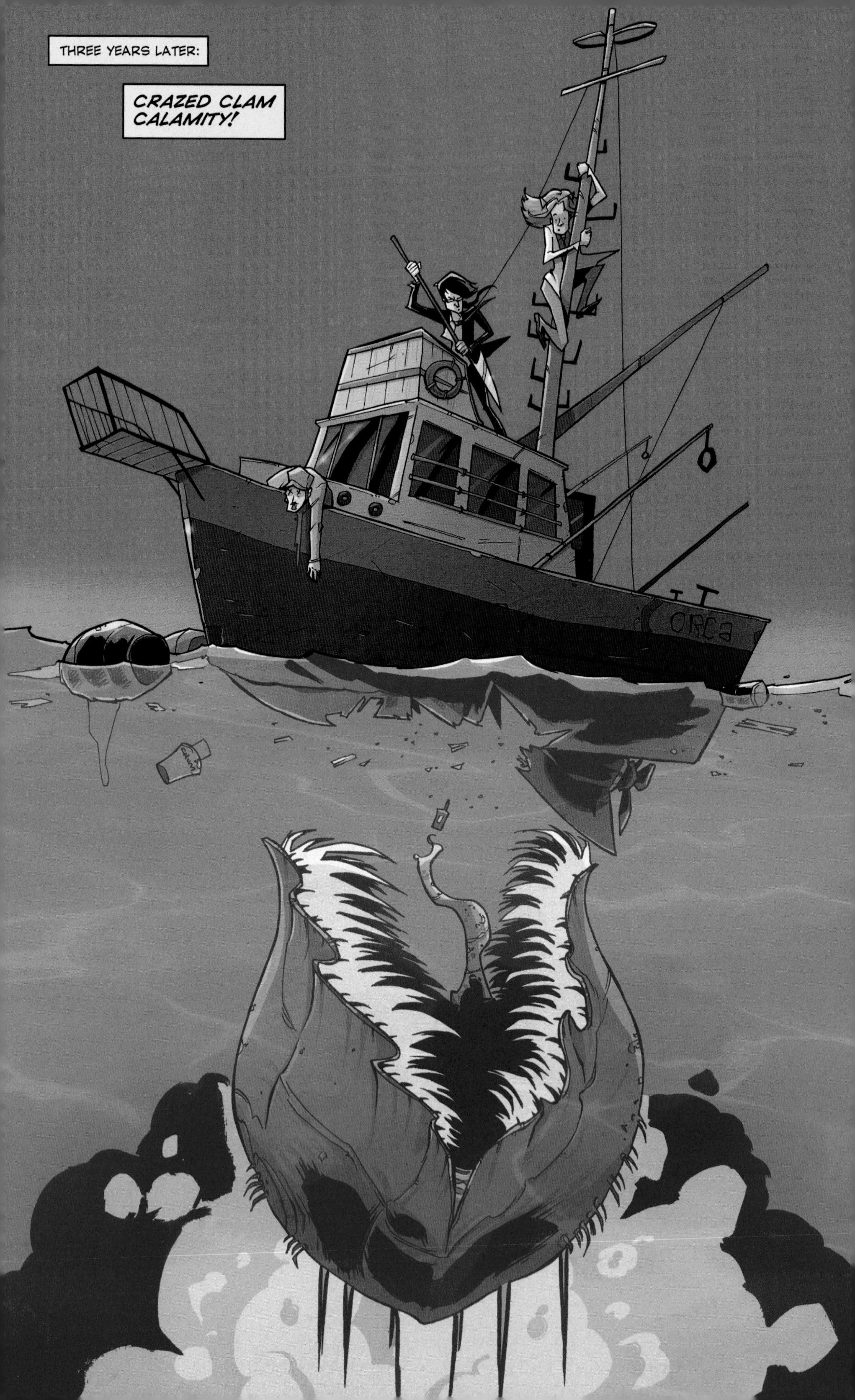
THREE YEARS LATER:
CRAZED CLAM CALAMITY!
ORCA

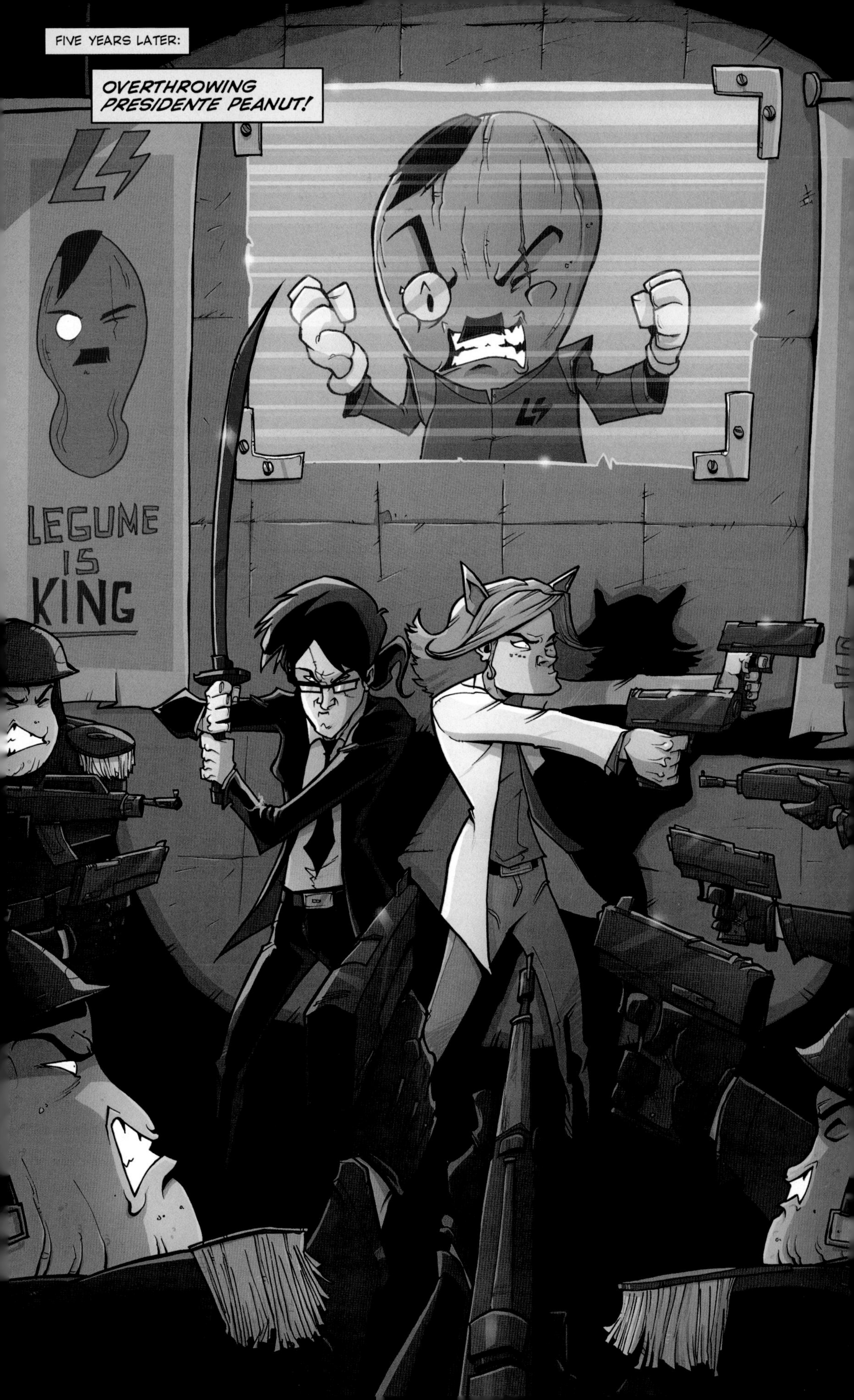
FIVE YEARS LATER:
OVERTHROWING PRESIDENTE PEANUT!
LS
LEGUME IS KING
LS

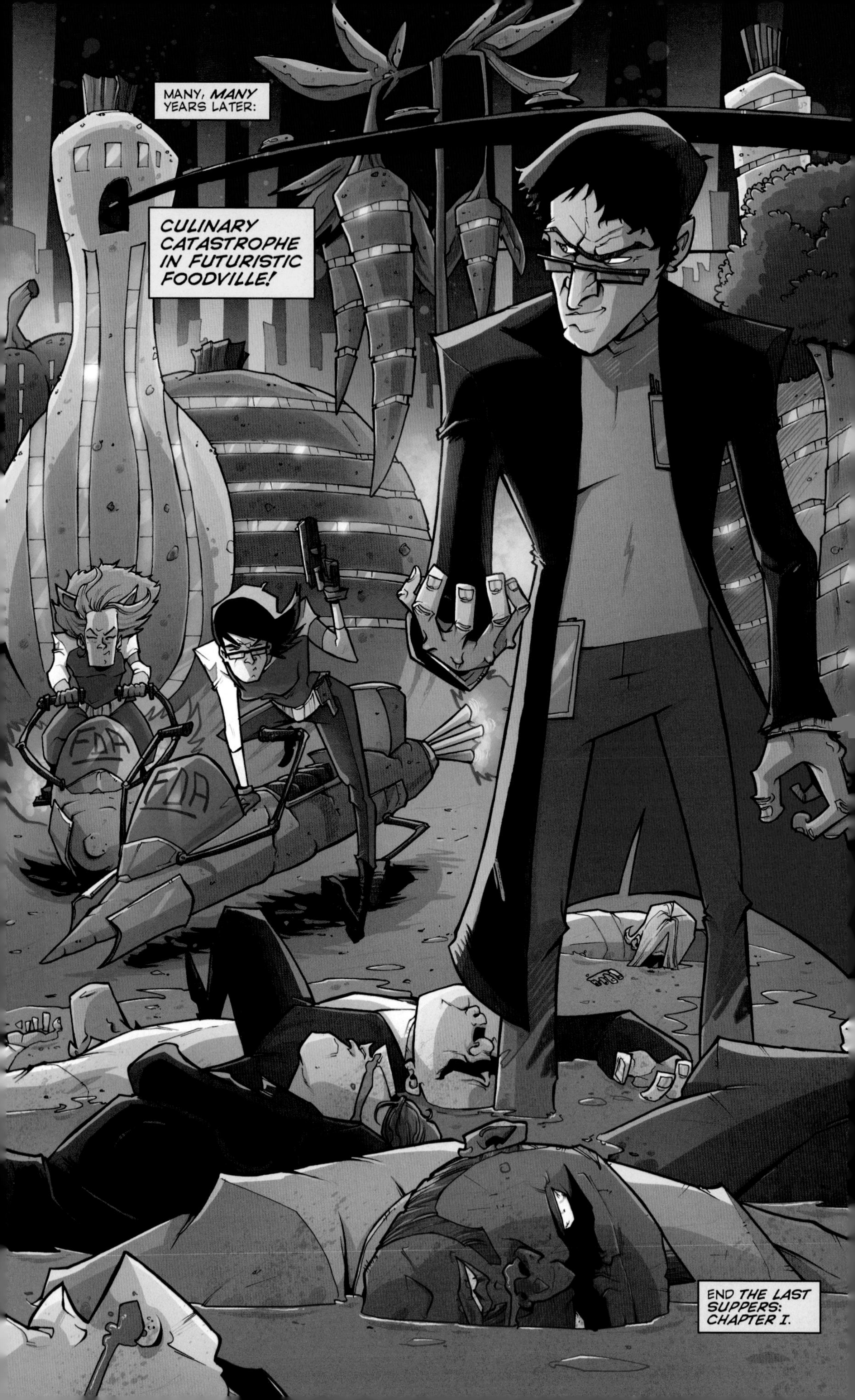
MANY, *MANY* YEARS LATER:
CULINARY CATASTROPHE IN FUTURISTIC FOODVILLE!
FDA
FDA
END *THE LAST SUPPERS: CHAPTER I.*

Chapter 2

ROB!

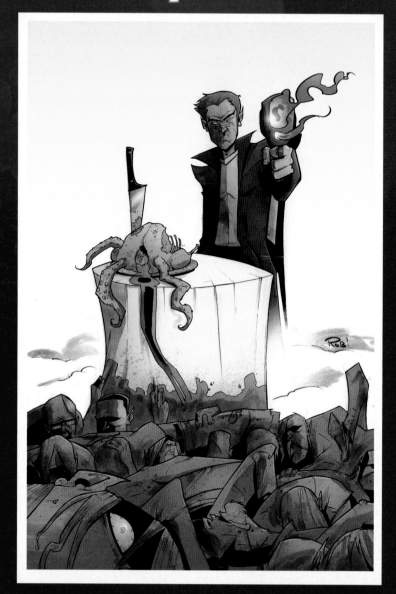

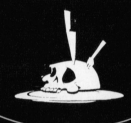

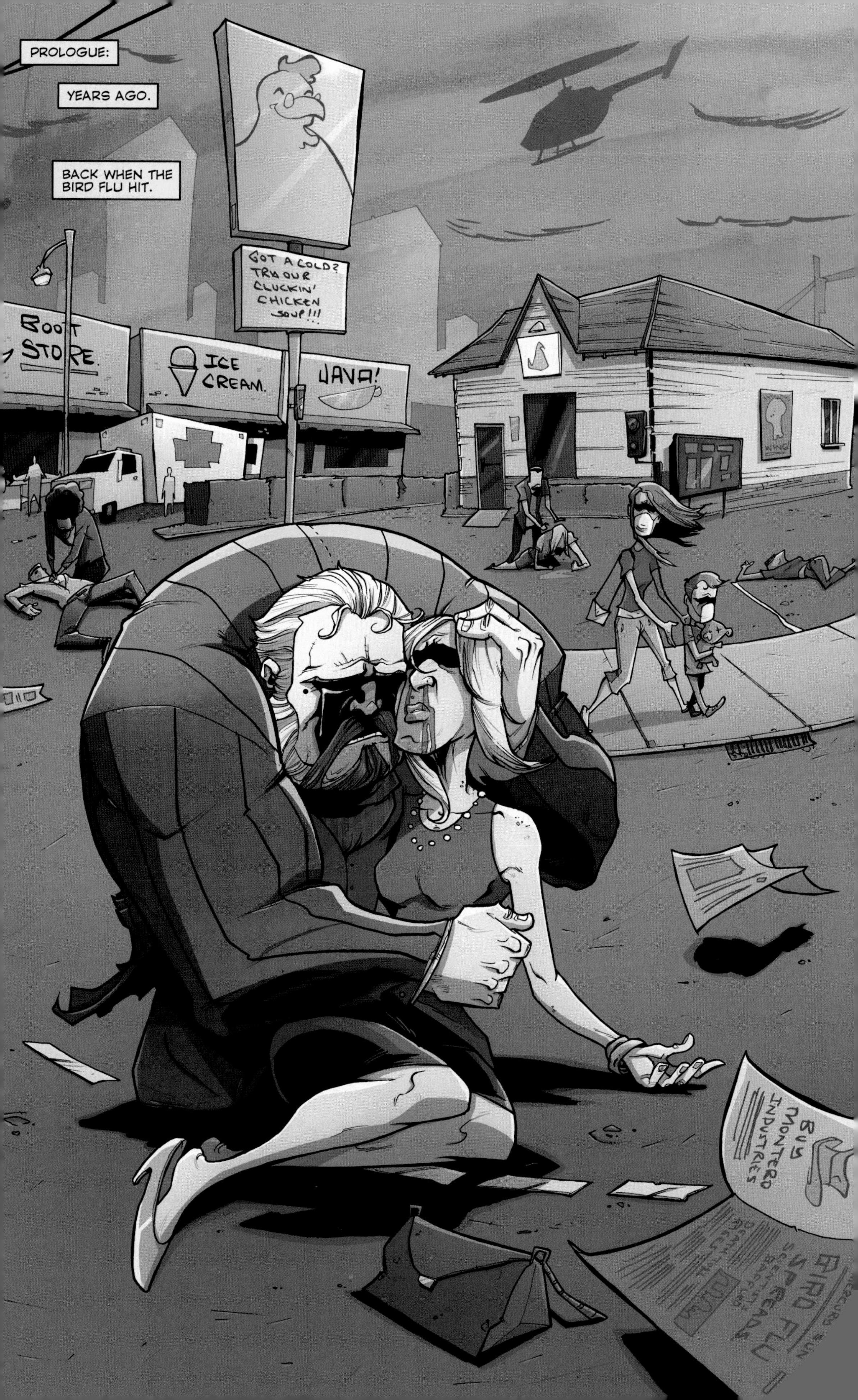
PROLOGUE:
YEARS AGO.
BACK WHEN THE BIRD FLU HIT.
GOT A COLD? TRY OUR CLUCKIN' CHICKEN SOUP!!!
BOOT STORE
ICE CREAM
JAVA!
BUY MONTERO INDUSTRIES
MERCURY SUN
BIRD FLU SPREADS
DEATH TOLL RISES

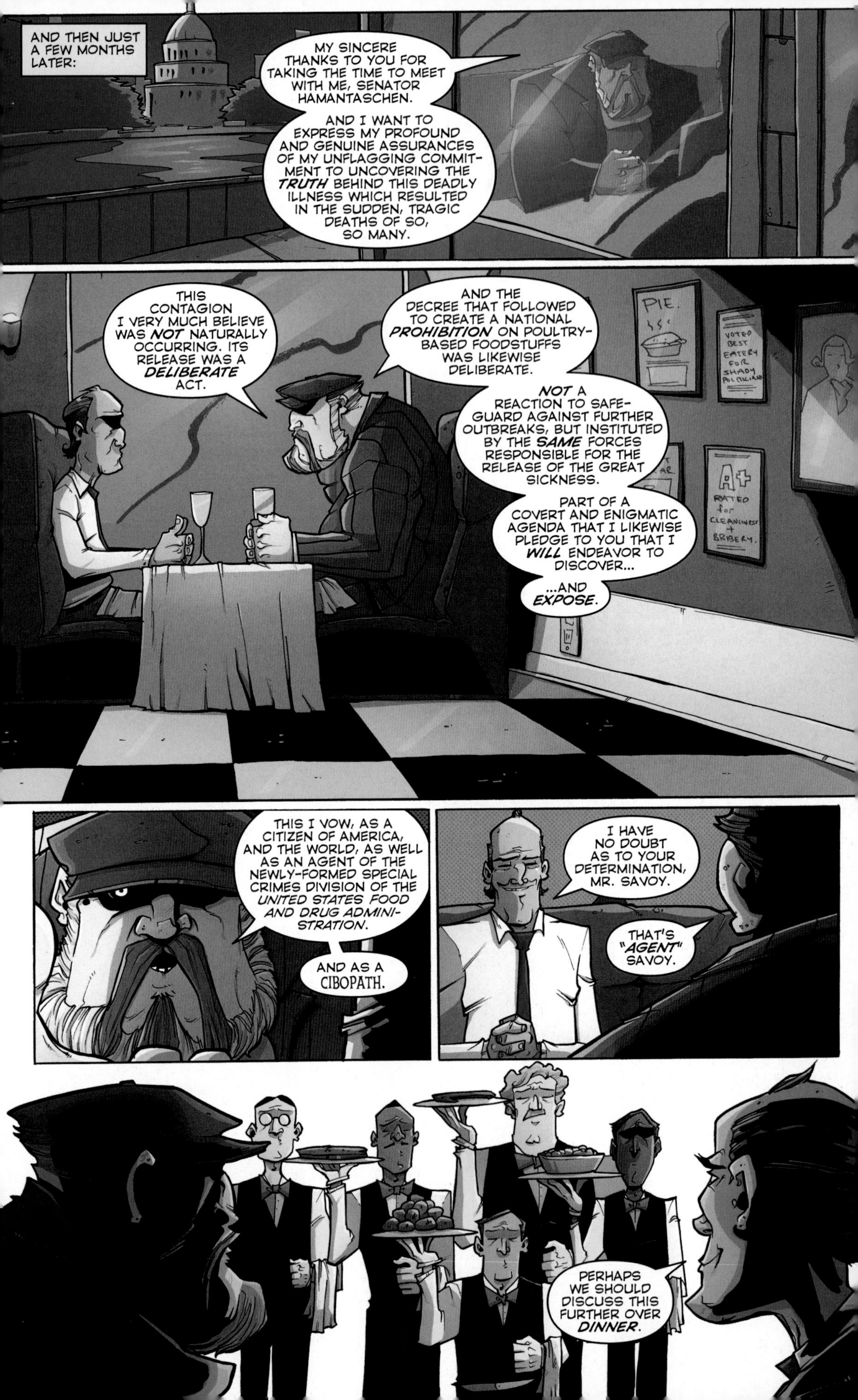
AND THEN JUST A FEW MONTHS LATER:
MY SINCERE THANKS TO YOU FOR TAKING THE TIME TO MEET WITH ME, SENATOR HAMANTASCHEN.
AND I WANT TO EXPRESS MY PROFOUND AND GENUINE ASSURANCES OF MY UNFLAGGING COMMITMENT TO UNCOVERING THE *TRUTH* BEHIND THIS DEADLY ILLNESS WHICH RESULTED IN THE SUDDEN, TRAGIC DEATHS OF SO, SO MANY.
THIS CONTAGION I VERY MUCH BELIEVE WAS *NOT* NATURALLY OCCURRING. ITS RELEASE WAS A *DELIBERATE* ACT.
AND THE DECREE THAT FOLLOWED TO CREATE A NATIONAL *PROHIBITION* ON POULTRY-BASED FOODSTUFFS WAS LIKEWISE DELIBERATE.
NOT A REACTION TO SAFEGUARD AGAINST FURTHER OUTBREAKS, BUT INSTITUTED BY THE *SAME* FORCES RESPONSIBLE FOR THE RELEASE OF THE GREAT SICKNESS.
PART OF A COVERT AND ENIGMATIC AGENDA THAT I LIKEWISE PLEDGE TO YOU THAT I *WILL* ENDEAVOR TO DISCOVER...
...AND *EXPOSE*.
PIE.
VOTED BEST EATERY FOR SHADY POLITICIANS
A+ RATED for CLEANLINESS + BRIBERY.
THIS I VOW, AS A CITIZEN OF AMERICA, AND THE WORLD, AS WELL AS AN AGENT OF THE NEWLY-FORMED SPECIAL CRIMES DIVISION OF THE *UNITED STATES FOOD AND DRUG ADMINISTRATION*.
AND AS A CIBOPATH.
I HAVE NO DOUBT AS TO YOUR DETERMINATION, MR. SAVOY.
THAT'S "*AGENT*" SAVOY.
PERHAPS WE SHOULD DISCUSS THIS FURTHER OVER *DINNER*.

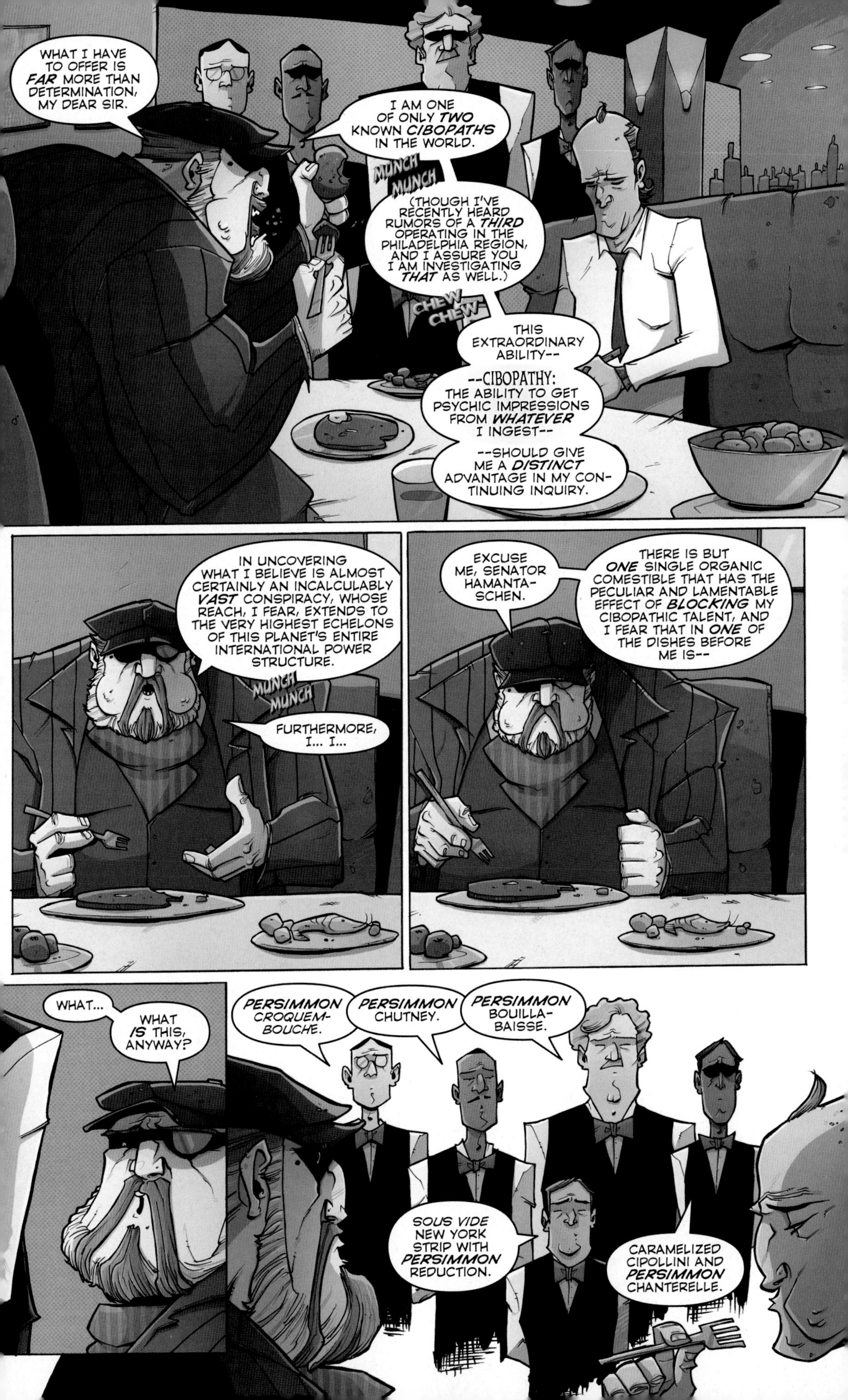
WHAT I HAVE TO OFFER IS FAR MORE THAN DETERMINATION, MY DEAR SIR.
I AM ONE OF ONLY TWO KNOWN CIBOPATHS IN THE WORLD.
MUNCH MUNCH
(THOUGH I'VE RECENTLY HEARD RUMORS OF A THIRD OPERATING IN THE PHILADELPHIA REGION, AND I ASSURE YOU I AM INVESTIGATING THAT AS WELL.)
CHEW CHEW
THIS EXTRAORDINARY ABILITY--
--CIBOPATHY: THE ABILITY TO GET PSYCHIC IMPRESSIONS FROM WHATEVER I INGEST--
--SHOULD GIVE ME A DISTINCT ADVANTAGE IN MY CONTINUING INQUIRY.
IN UNCOVERING WHAT I BELIEVE IS ALMOST CERTAINLY AN INCALCULABLY VAST CONSPIRACY, WHOSE REACH, I FEAR, EXTENDS TO THE VERY HIGHEST ECHELONS OF THIS PLANET'S ENTIRE INTERNATIONAL POWER STRUCTURE.
MUNCH MUNCH
FURTHERMORE, I... I...
EXCUSE ME, SENATOR HAMANTASCHEN.
THERE IS BUT ONE SINGLE ORGANIC COMESTIBLE THAT HAS THE PECULIAR AND LAMENTABLE EFFECT OF BLOCKING MY CIBOPATHIC TALENT, AND I FEAR THAT IN ONE OF THE DISHES BEFORE ME IS--
WHAT...
WHAT IS THIS, ANYWAY?
PERSIMMON CROQUEMBOUCHE.
PERSIMMON CHUTNEY.
PERSIMMON BOUILLABAISSE.
SOUS VIDE NEW YORK STRIP WITH PERSIMMON REDUCTION.
CARAMELIZED CIPOLLINI AND PERSIMMON CHANTERELLE.

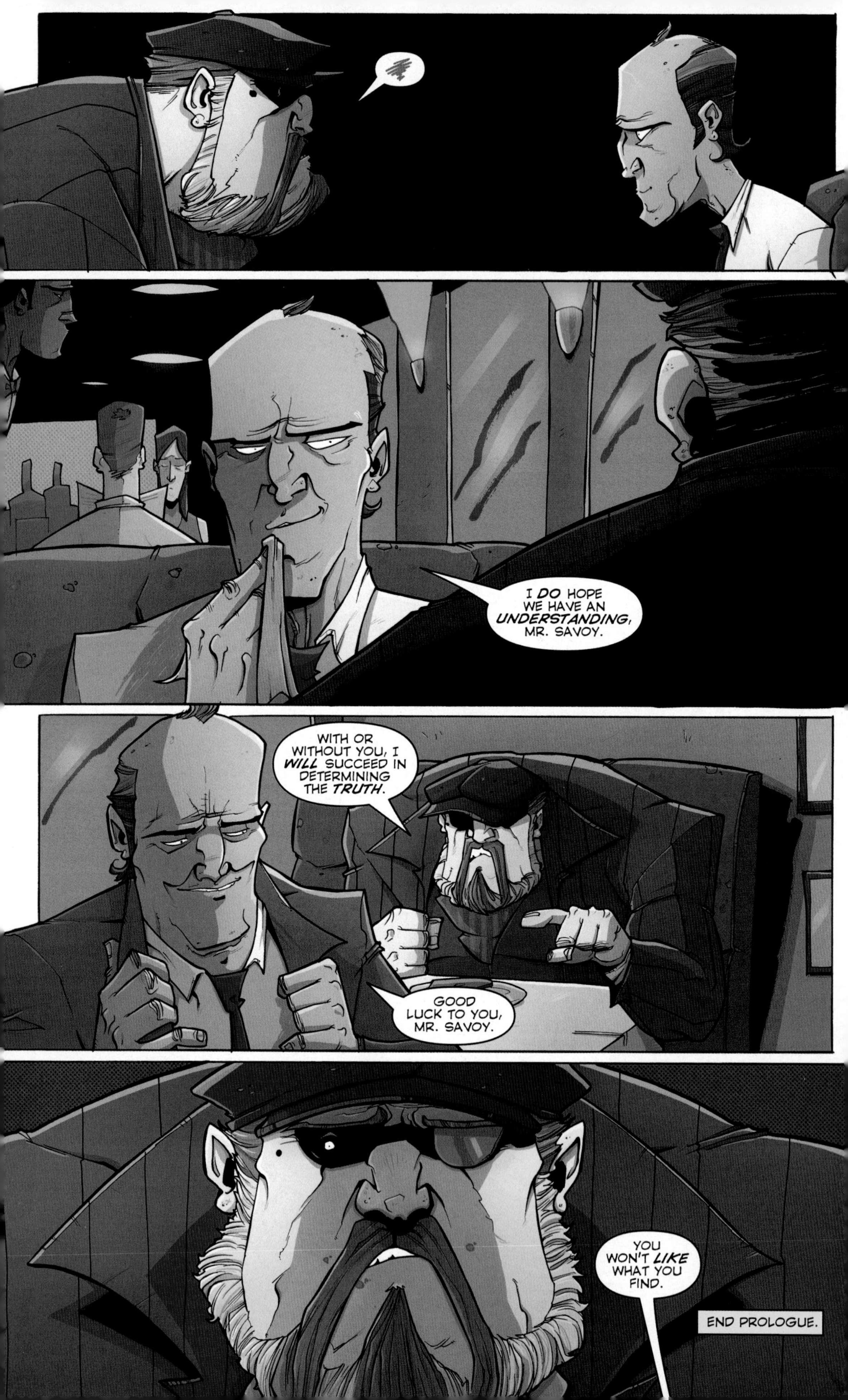

I DO HOPE WE HAVE AN UNDERSTANDING, MR. SAVOY.
WITH OR WITHOUT YOU, I WILL SUCCEED IN DETERMINING THE TRUTH.
GOOD LUCK TO YOU, MR. SAVOY.
YOU WON'T LIKE WHAT YOU FIND.
END PROLOGUE.

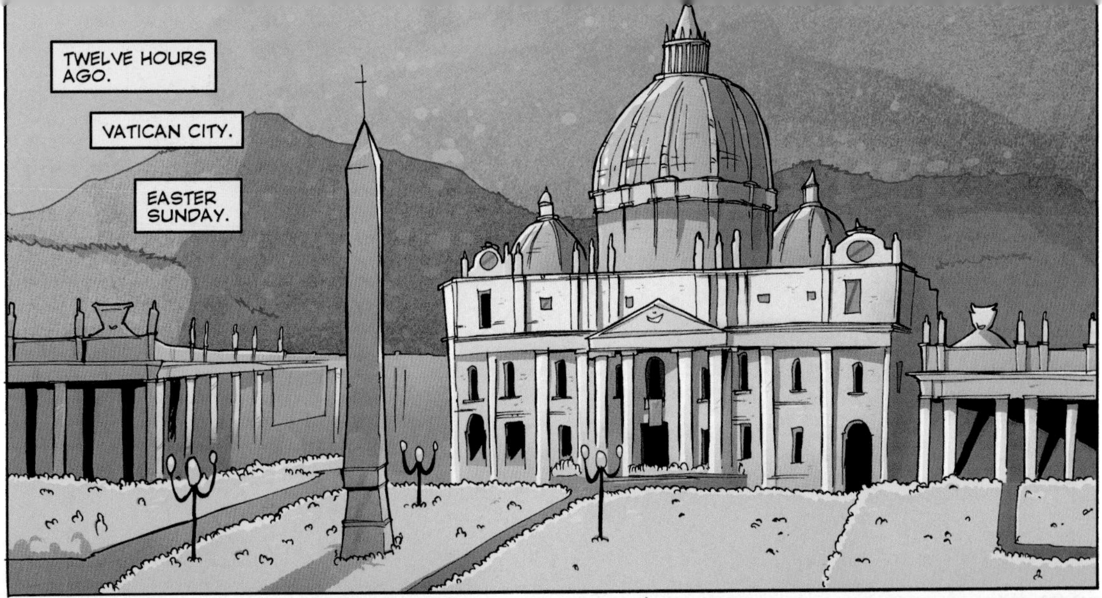
TWELVE HOURS AGO.
VATICAN CITY.
EASTER SUNDAY.

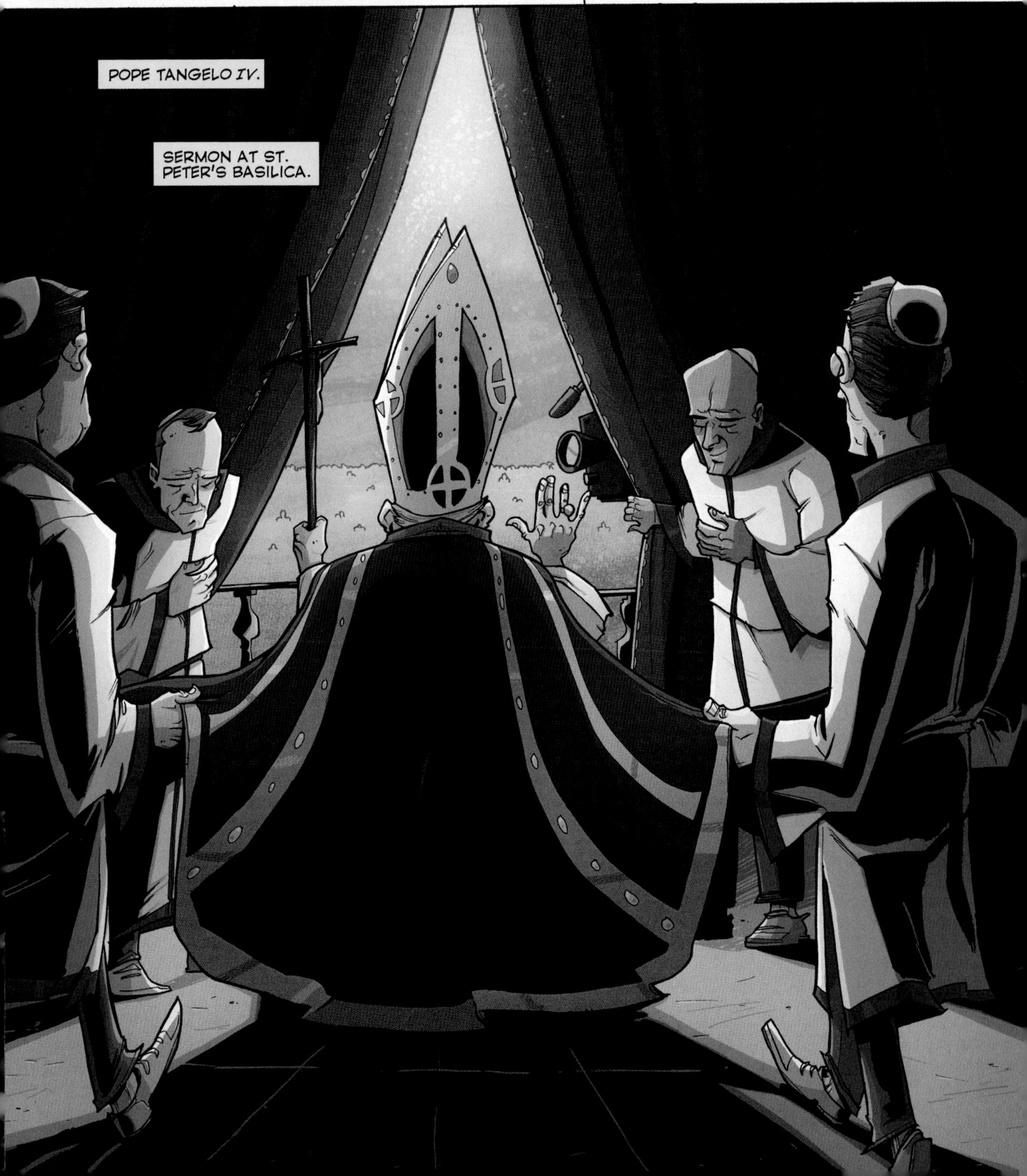
POPE TANGELO IV.
SERMON AT ST. PETER'S BASILICA.

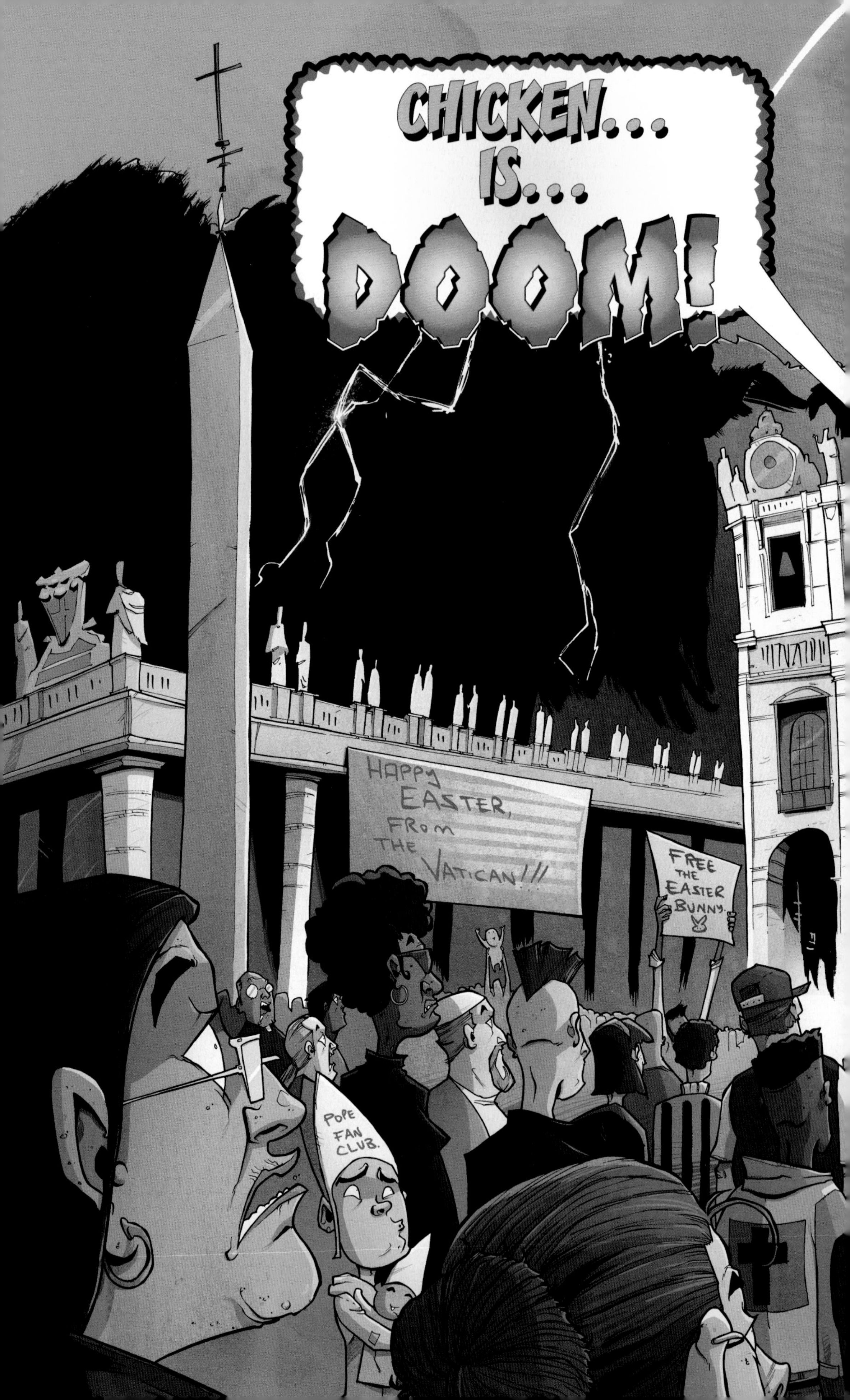
CHICKEN... IS... DOOM!
HAPPY EASTER, FROM THE VATICAN!!!
FREE THE EASTER BUNNY.
POPE FAN CLUB.

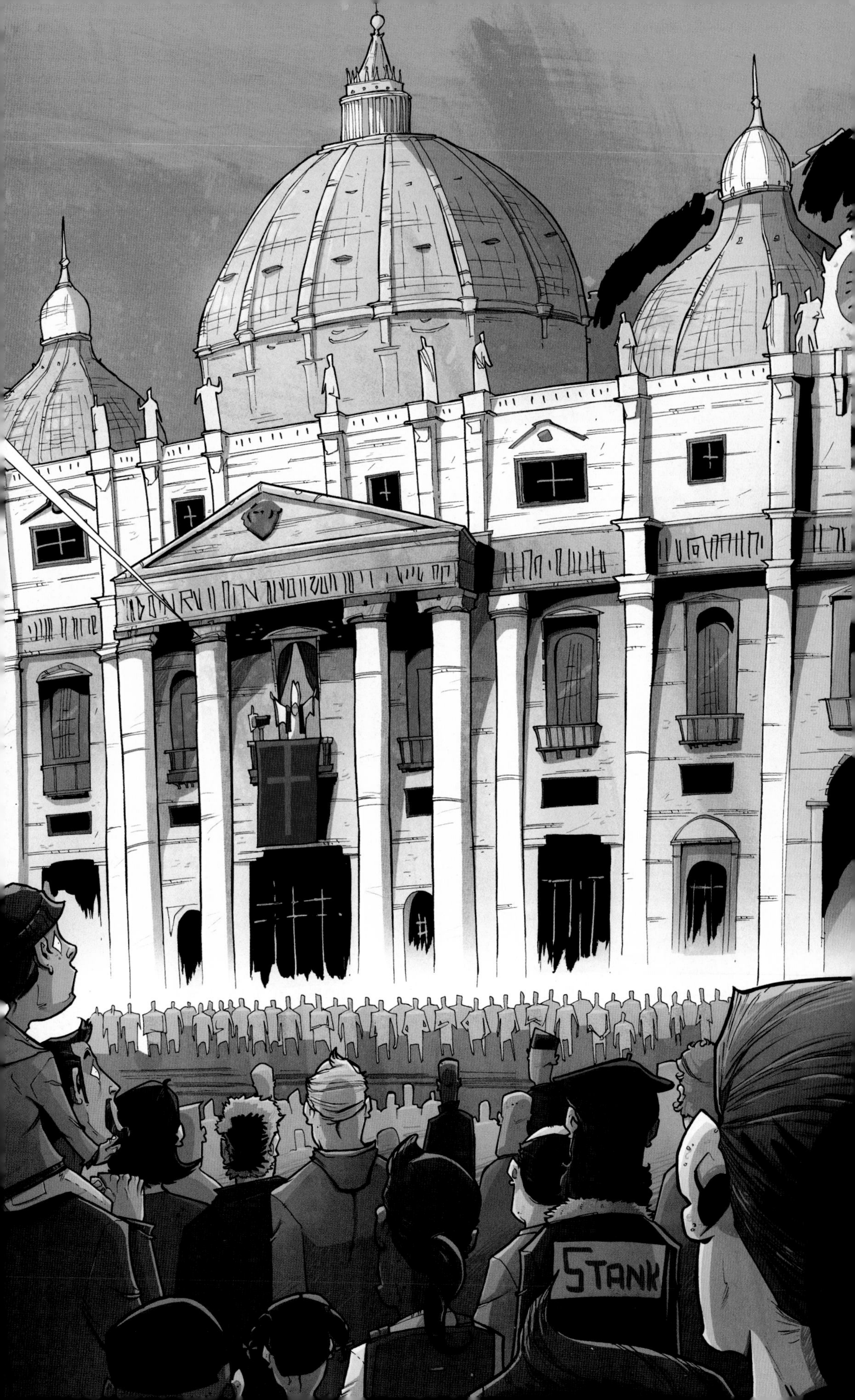
STANK

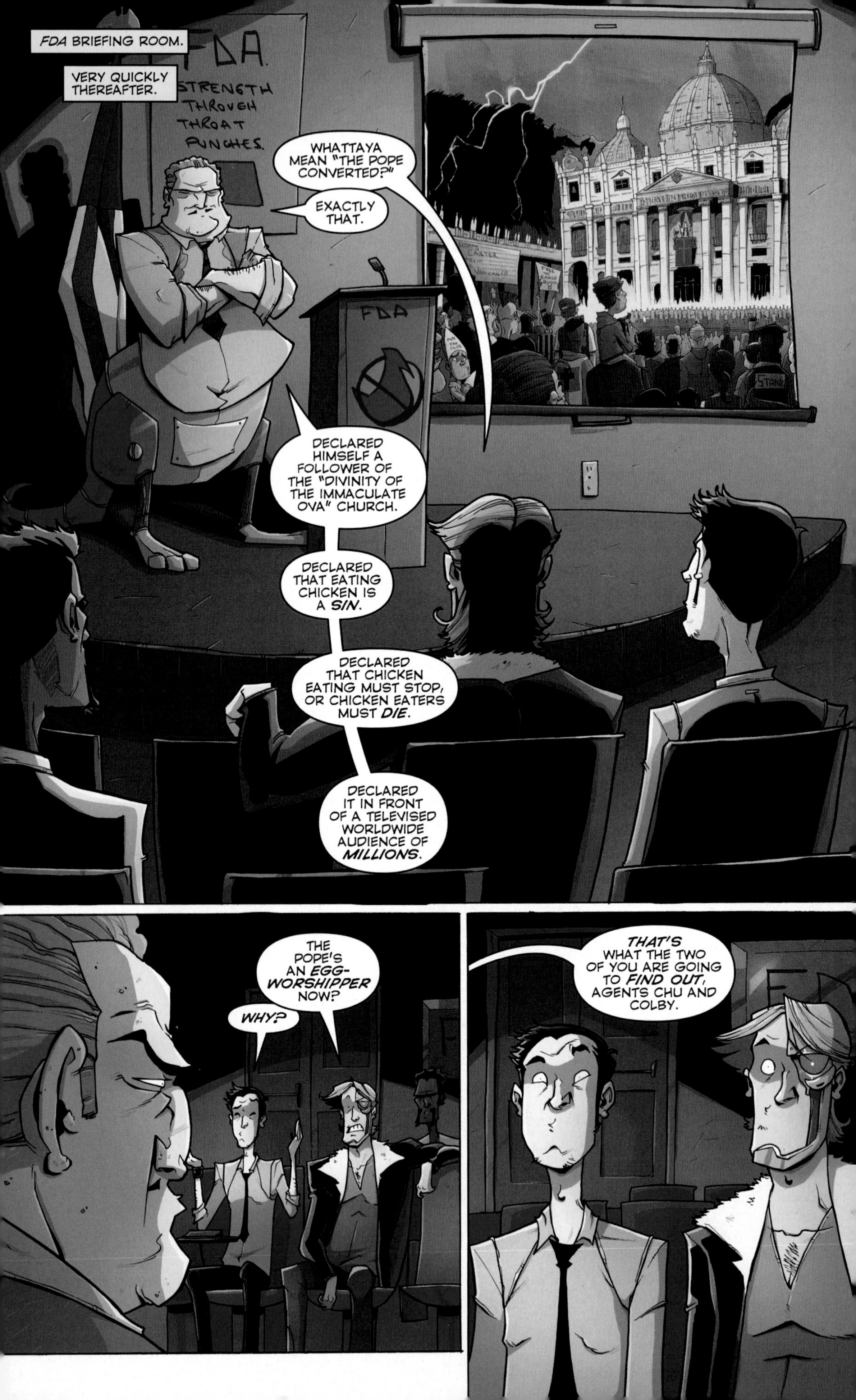

FDA BRIEFING ROOM.
VERY QUICKLY THEREAFTER.
FDA.
STRENGTH THROUGH THROAT PUNCHES.
WHATTAYA MEAN "THE POPE CONVERTED?"
EXACTLY THAT.
FDA
DECLARED HIMSELF A FOLLOWER OF THE "DIVINITY OF THE IMMACULATE OVA" CHURCH.
DECLARED THAT EATING CHICKEN IS A *SIN*.
DECLARED THAT CHICKEN EATING MUST STOP, OR CHICKEN EATERS MUST *DIE*.
DECLARED IT IN FRONT OF A TELEVISED WORLDWIDE AUDIENCE OF ***MILLIONS***.
THE POPE'S AN ***EGG-WORSHIPPER*** NOW?
WHY?
THAT'S WHAT THE TWO OF YOU ARE GOING TO ***FIND OUT***, AGENTS CHU AND COLBY.

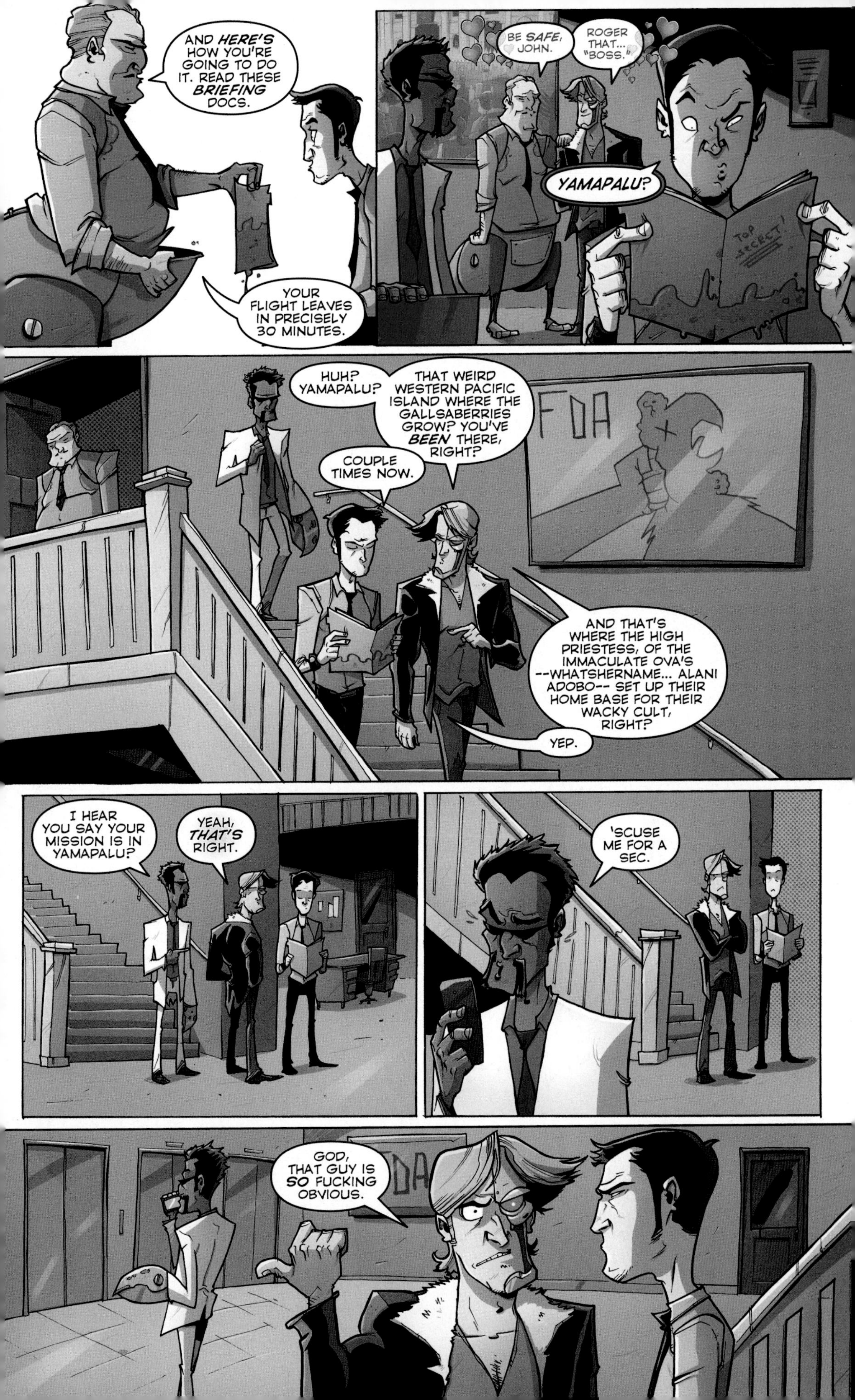
AND HERE'S HOW YOU'RE GOING TO DO IT. READ THESE BRIEFING DOCS.
YOUR FLIGHT LEAVES IN PRECISELY 30 MINUTES.
BE SAFE, JOHN.
ROGER THAT... "BOSS."
YAMAPALU?
TOP SECRET!
HUH? YAMAPALU?
THAT WEIRD WESTERN PACIFIC ISLAND WHERE THE GALLSABERRIES GROW? YOU'VE BEEN THERE, RIGHT?
COUPLE TIMES NOW.
FDA
AND THAT'S WHERE THE HIGH PRIESTESS, OF THE IMMACULATE OVA'S --WHATSHERNAME... ALANI ADOBO-- SET UP THEIR HOME BASE FOR THEIR WACKY CULT, RIGHT?
YEP.
I HEAR YOU SAY YOUR MISSION IS IN YAMAPALU?
YEAH, THAT'S RIGHT.
'SCUSE ME FOR A SEC.
GOD, THAT GUY IS SO FUCKING OBVIOUS.

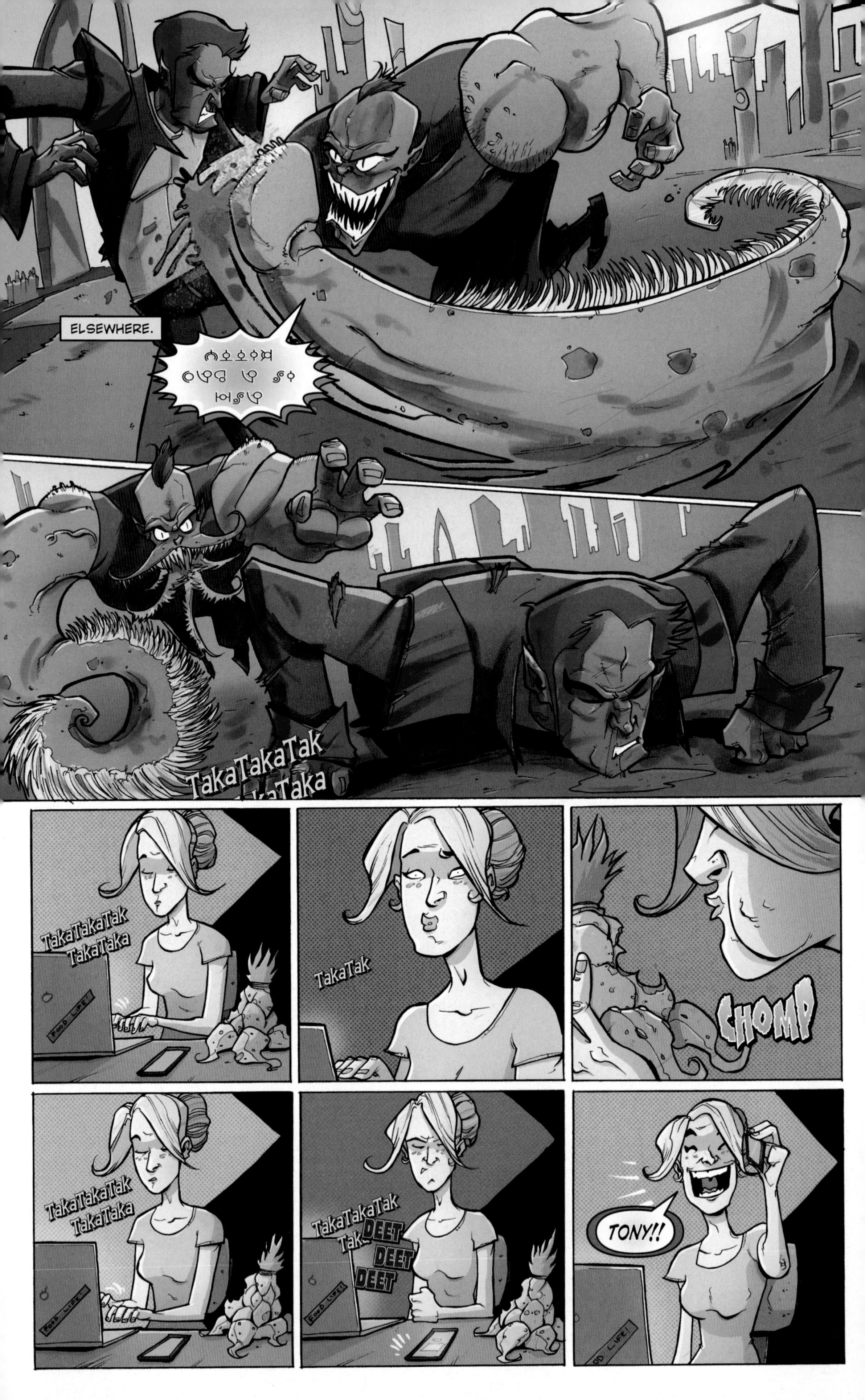
ELSEWHERE.
TakaTakaTak
TakaTakaTak
TakaTaka
FOOD LIFE!
TakaTak
CHOMP
TakaTakaTak
TakaTaka
TakaTakaTak
Taka
DEET
DEET
DEET
TONY!!

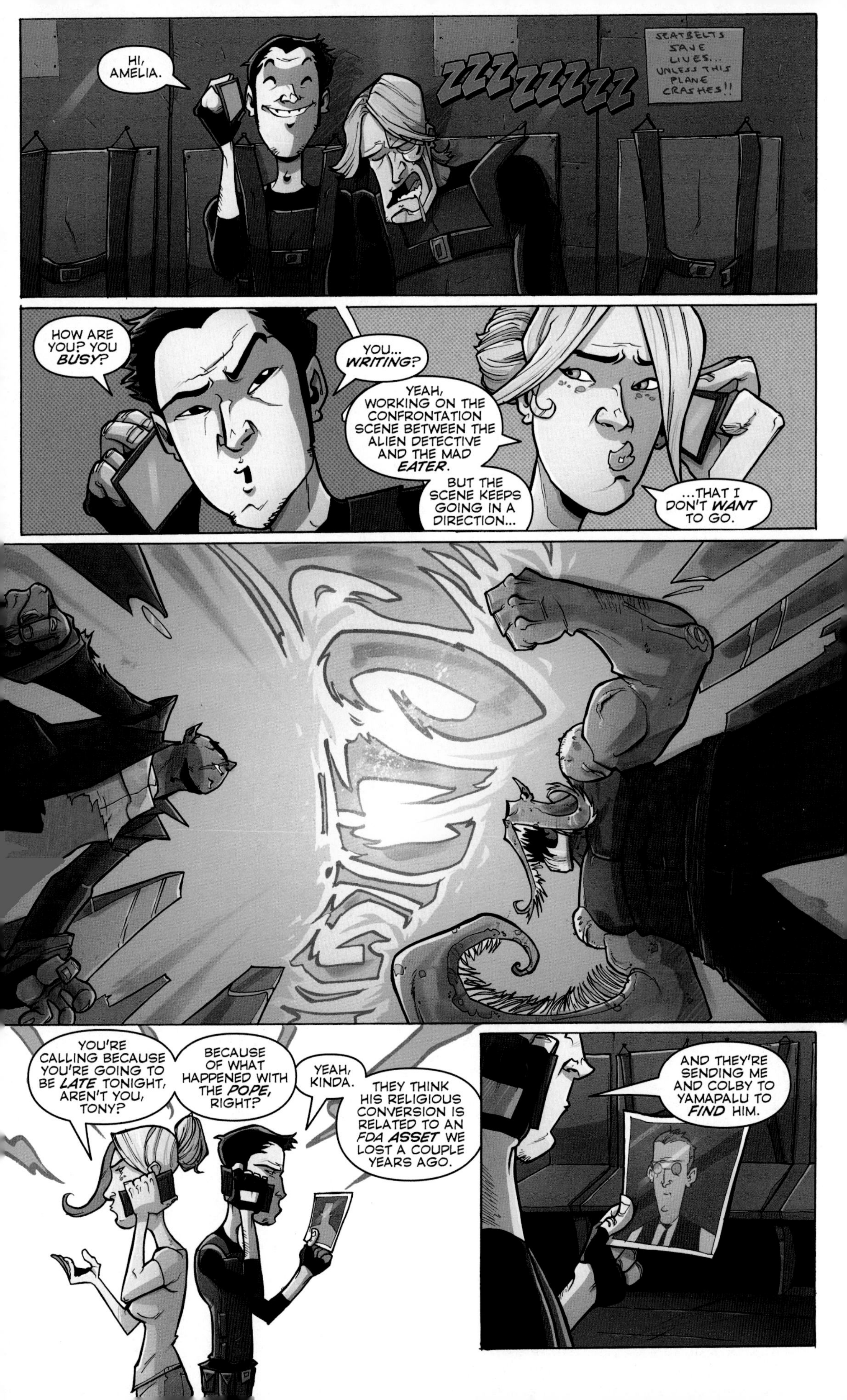
HI, AMELIA.
ZZZZZZZZ
SEATBELTS SAVE LIVES... UNLESS THIS PLANE CRASHES!!
HOW ARE YOU? YOU BUSY?
YOU... WRITING?
YEAH, WORKING ON THE CONFRONTATION SCENE BETWEEN THE ALIEN DETECTIVE AND THE MAD EATER.
BUT THE SCENE KEEPS GOING IN A DIRECTION...
...THAT I DON'T WANT TO GO.
YOU'RE CALLING BECAUSE YOU'RE GOING TO BE LATE TONIGHT, AREN'T YOU, TONY?
BECAUSE OF WHAT HAPPENED WITH THE POPE, RIGHT?
YEAH, KINDA.
THEY THINK HIS RELIGIOUS CONVERSION IS RELATED TO AN FDA ASSET WE LOST A COUPLE YEARS AGO.
AND THEY'RE SENDING ME AND COLBY TO YAMAPALU TO FIND HIM.

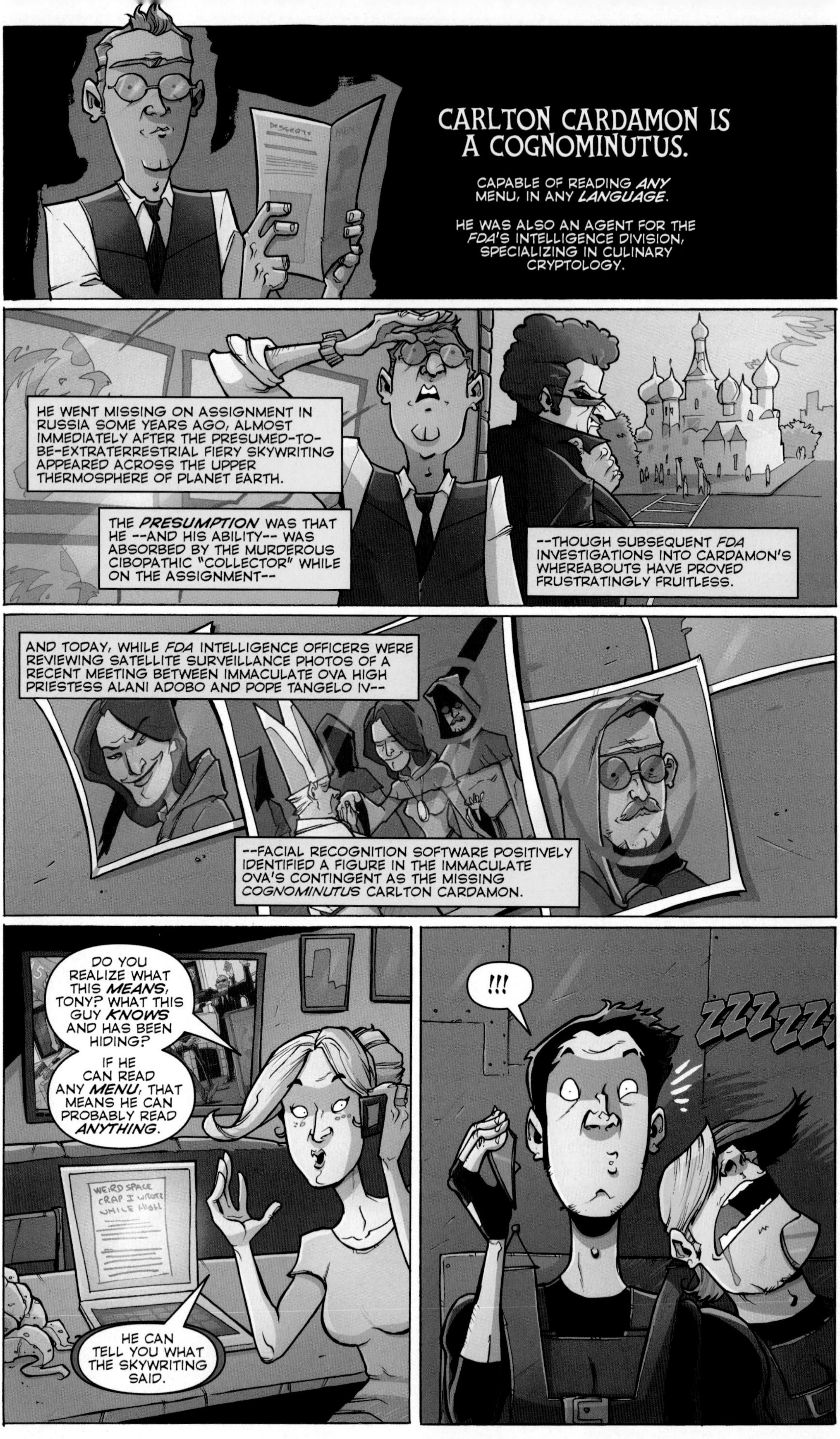
CARLTON CARDAMON IS A COGNOMINUTUS.
CAPABLE OF READING *ANY* MENU, IN ANY *LANGUAGE*.
HE WAS ALSO AN AGENT FOR THE *FDA*'S INTELLIGENCE DIVISION, SPECIALIZING IN CULINARY CRYPTOLOGY.
DESSERTS
MENU
HE WENT MISSING ON ASSIGNMENT IN RUSSIA SOME YEARS AGO, ALMOST IMMEDIATELY AFTER THE PRESUMED-TO-BE-EXTRATERRESTRIAL FIERY SKYWRITING APPEARED ACROSS THE UPPER THERMOSPHERE OF PLANET EARTH.
THE *PRESUMPTION* WAS THAT HE --AND HIS ABILITY-- WAS ABSORBED BY THE MURDEROUS CIBOPATHIC "COLLECTOR" WHILE ON THE ASSIGNMENT--
--THOUGH SUBSEQUENT *FDA* INVESTIGATIONS INTO CARDAMON'S WHEREABOUTS HAVE PROVED FRUSTRATINGLY FRUITLESS.
AND TODAY, WHILE *FDA* INTELLIGENCE OFFICERS WERE REVIEWING SATELLITE SURVEILLANCE PHOTOS OF A RECENT MEETING BETWEEN IMMACULATE OVA HIGH PRIESTESS ALANI ADOBO AND POPE TANGELO IV--
--FACIAL RECOGNITION SOFTWARE POSITIVELY IDENTIFIED A FIGURE IN THE IMMACULATE OVA'S CONTINGENT AS THE MISSING *COGNOMINUTUS* CARLTON CARDAMON.
DO YOU REALIZE WHAT THIS *MEANS*, TONY? WHAT THIS GUY *KNOWS* AND HAS BEEN HIDING?
IF HE CAN READ ANY *MENU*, THAT MEANS HE CAN PROBABLY READ *ANYTHING*.
WEIRD SPACE CRAP I WROTE WHILE HIGH
HE CAN TELL YOU WHAT THE SKYWRITING SAID.
!!!
ZZZ ZZZ

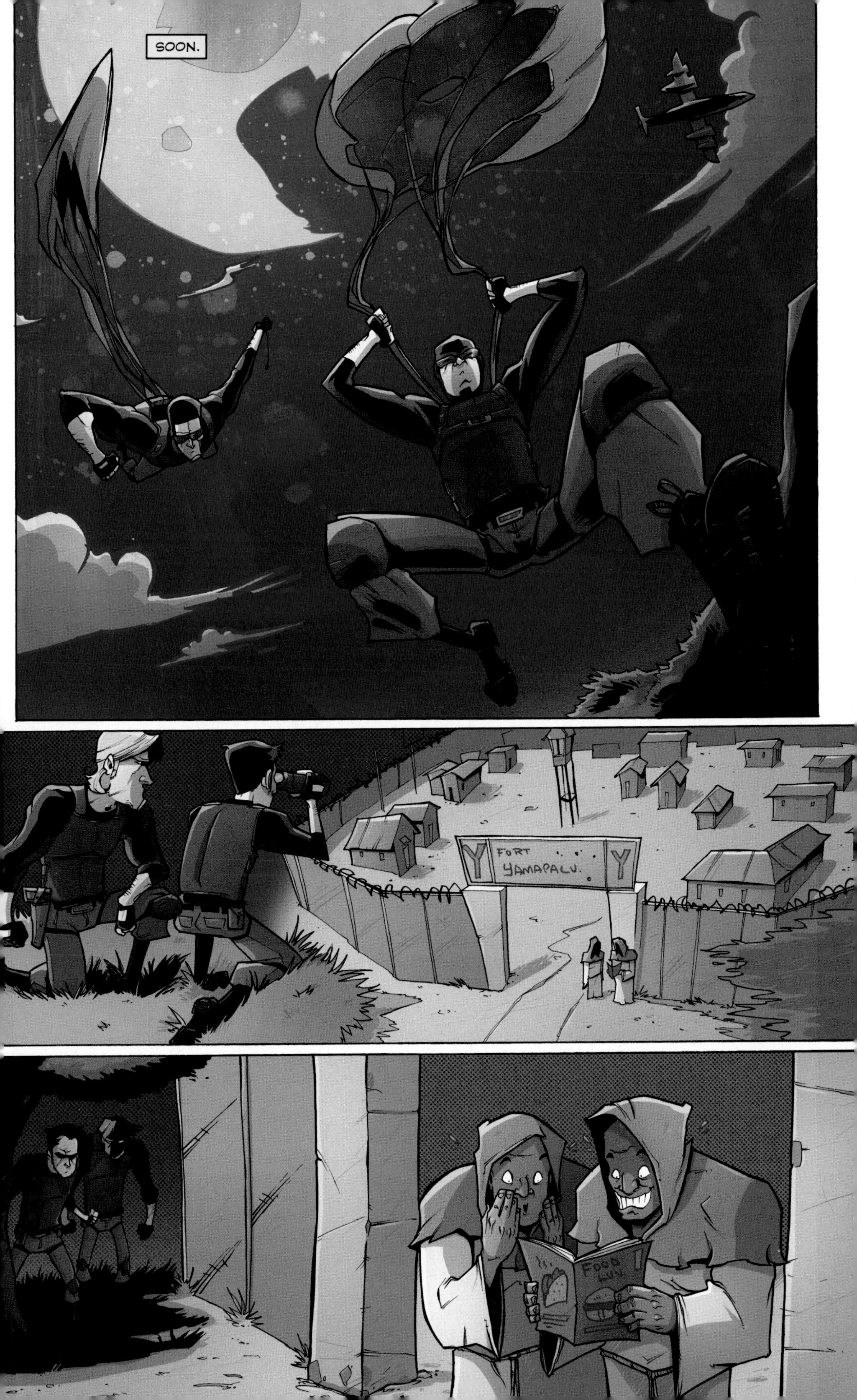
SOON.
FORT YAMAPALU.
FOOD LUV.

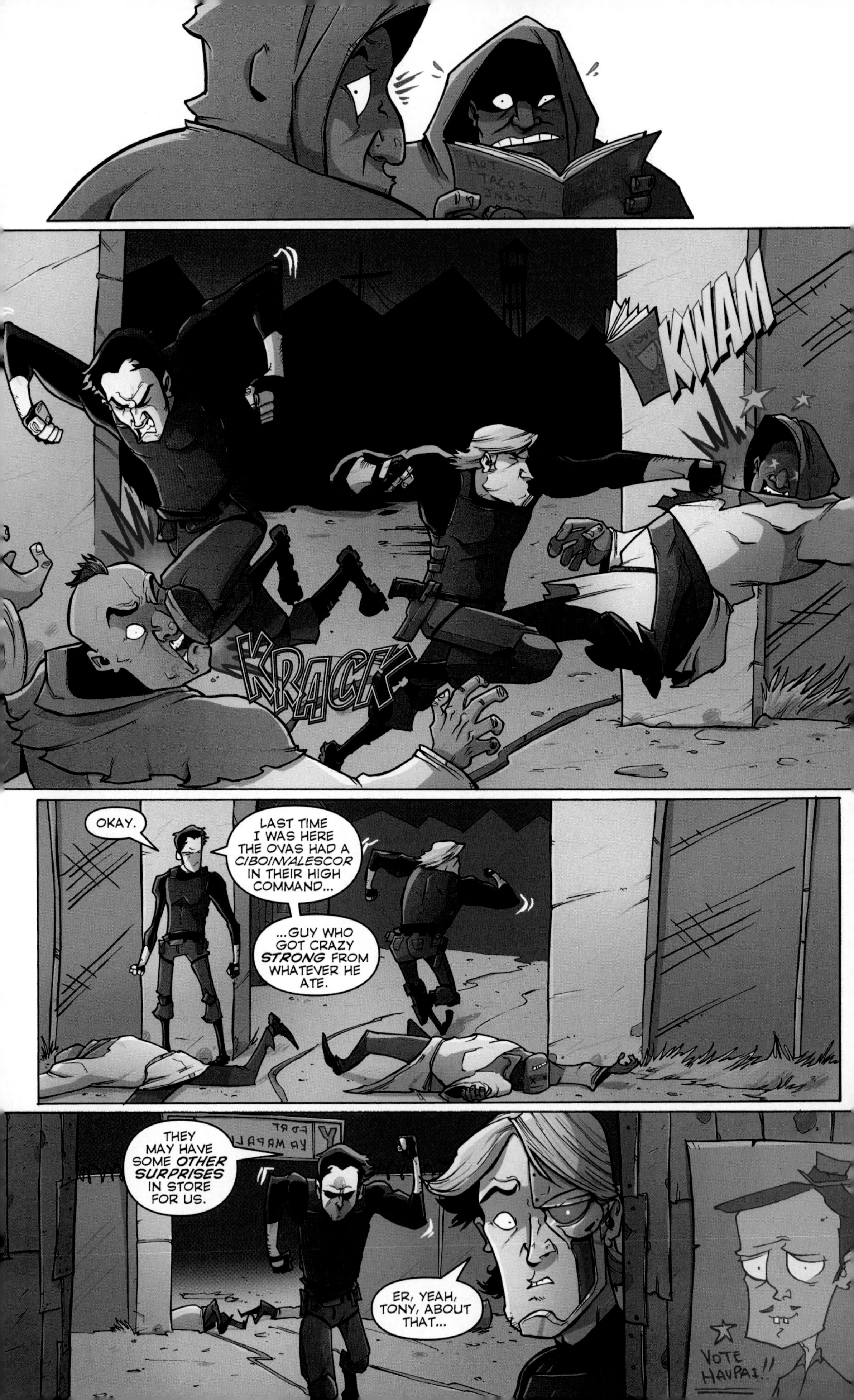
HOT TACOS INSIDE!!
KWAM
KRACK
OKAY.
LAST TIME I WAS HERE THE OVAS HAD A *CIBOINVALESCOR* IN THEIR HIGH COMMAND...
...GUY WHO GOT CRAZY **STRONG** FROM WHATEVER HE ATE.
THEY MAY HAVE SOME ***OTHER SURPRISES*** IN STORE FOR US.
ER, YEAH, TONY, ABOUT THAT...
VOTE HAUPAI!!

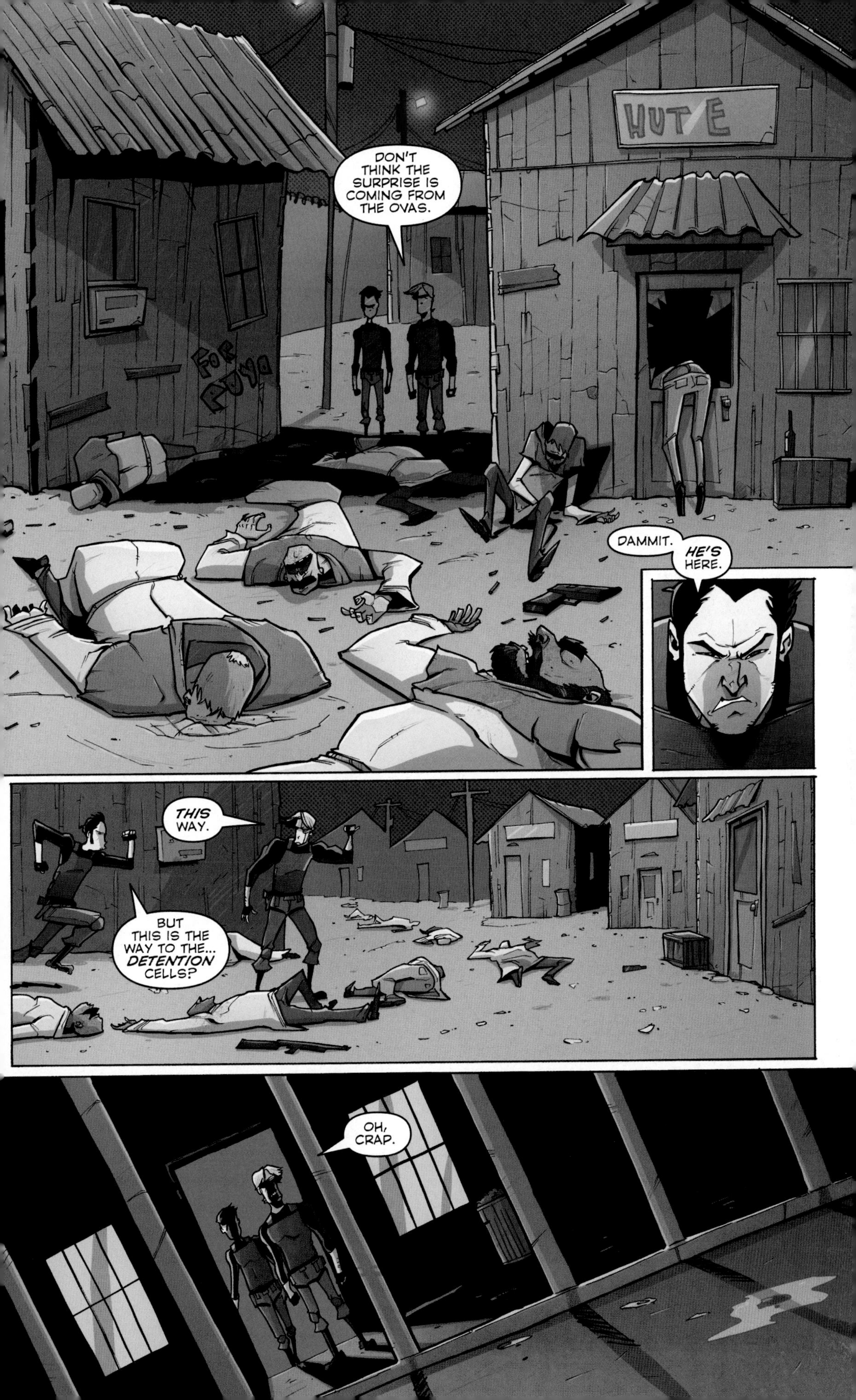
HUT E
DON'T THINK THE SURPRISE IS COMING FROM THE OVAS.
FOR CUYA
DAMMIT. *HE'S* HERE.
THIS WAY.
BUT THIS IS THE WAY TO THE... *DETENTION* CELLS?
OH, CRAP.

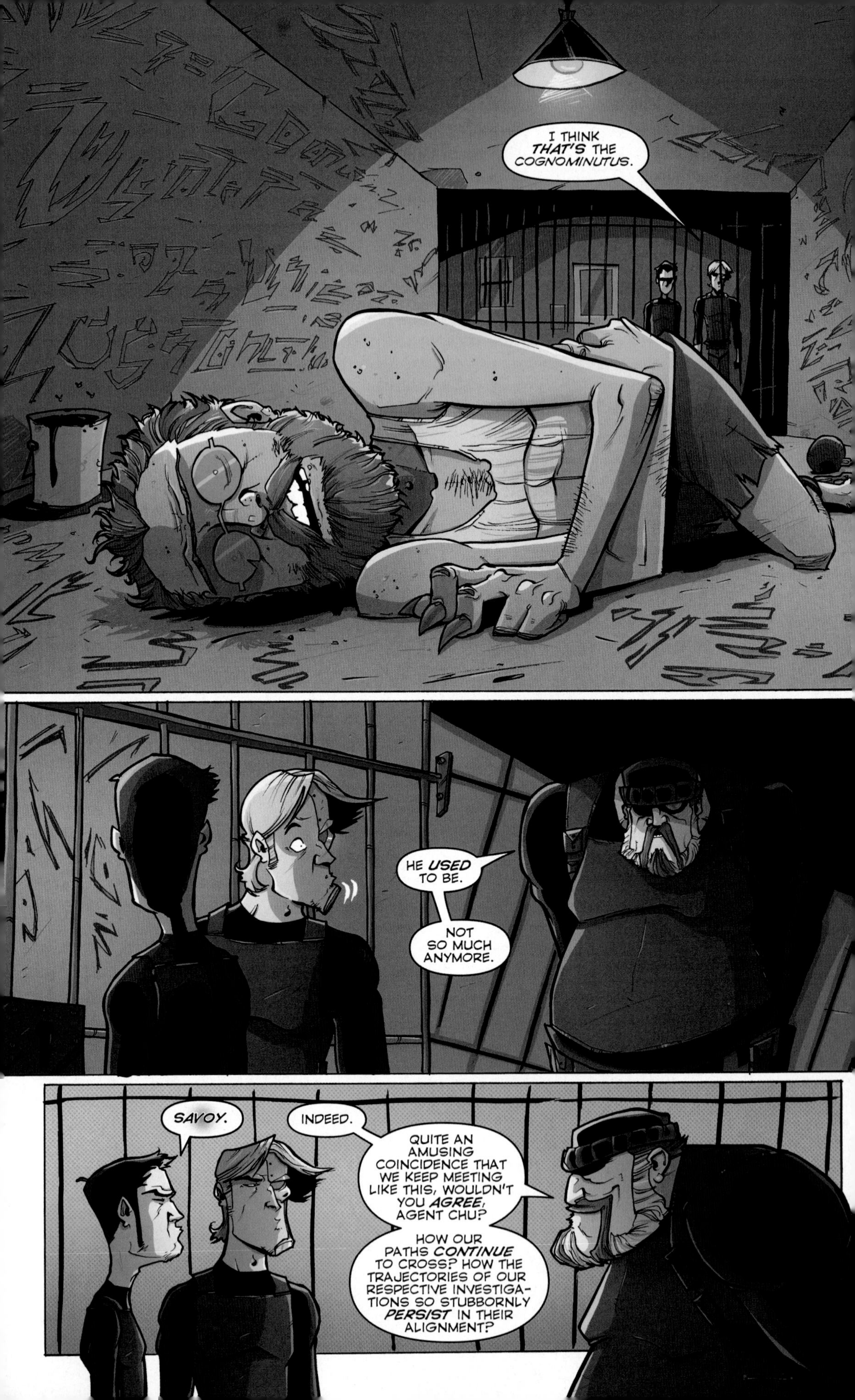
I THINK THAT'S THE COGNOMINUTUS.
HE USED TO BE.
NOT SO MUCH ANYMORE.
SAVOY.
INDEED.
QUITE AN AMUSING COINCIDENCE THAT WE KEEP MEETING LIKE THIS, WOULDN'T YOU AGREE, AGENT CHU?
HOW OUR PATHS CONTINUE TO CROSS? HOW THE TRAJECTORIES OF OUR RESPECTIVE INVESTIGA-TIONS SO STUBBORNLY PERSIST IN THEIR ALIGNMENT?

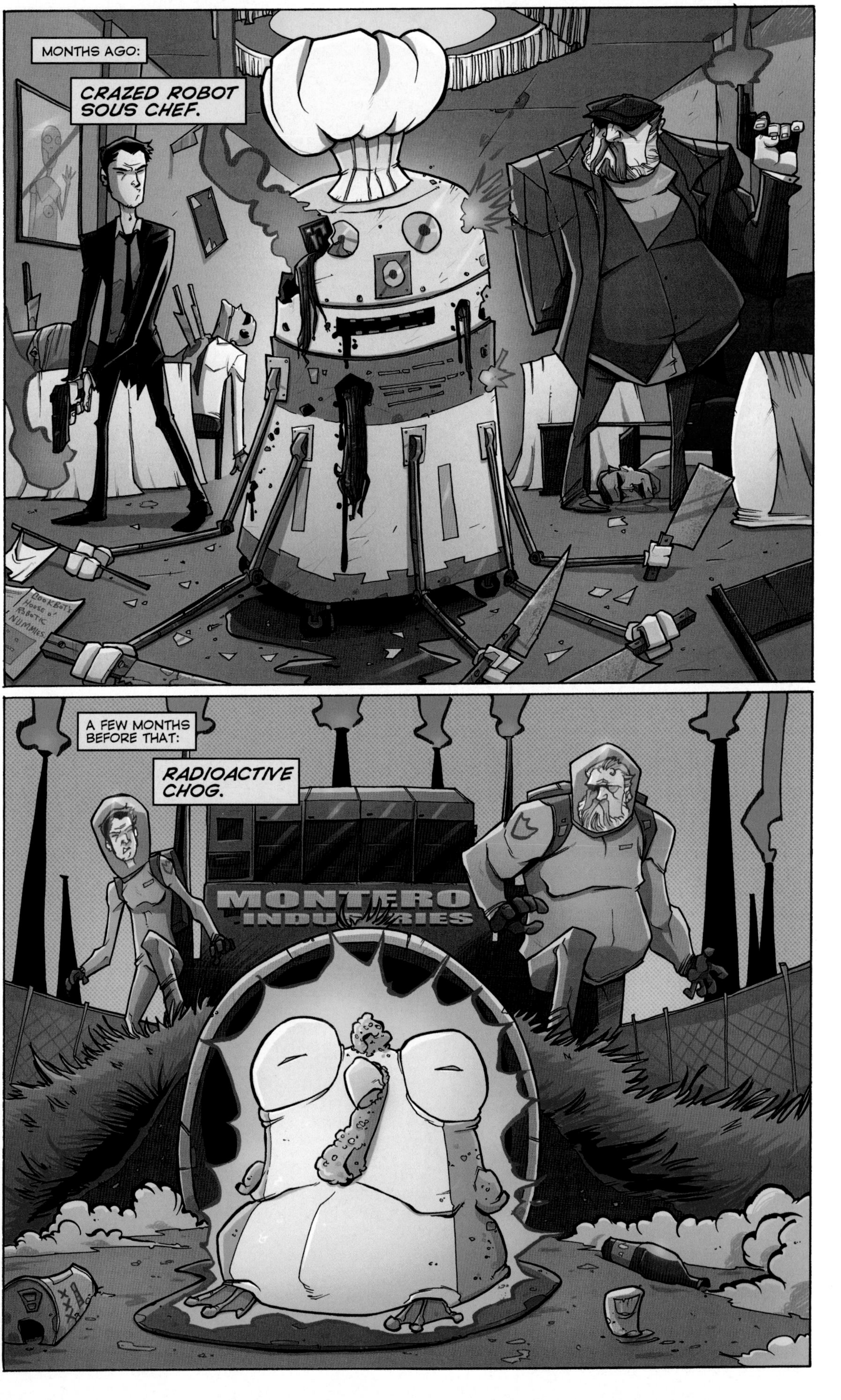
MONTHS AGO:
CRAZED ROBOT SOUS CHEF.
COOKBOT'S HOUSE O' ROBOTIC NUMMIES.
A FEW MONTHS BEFORE THAT:
RADIOACTIVE CHOG.
MONTERO

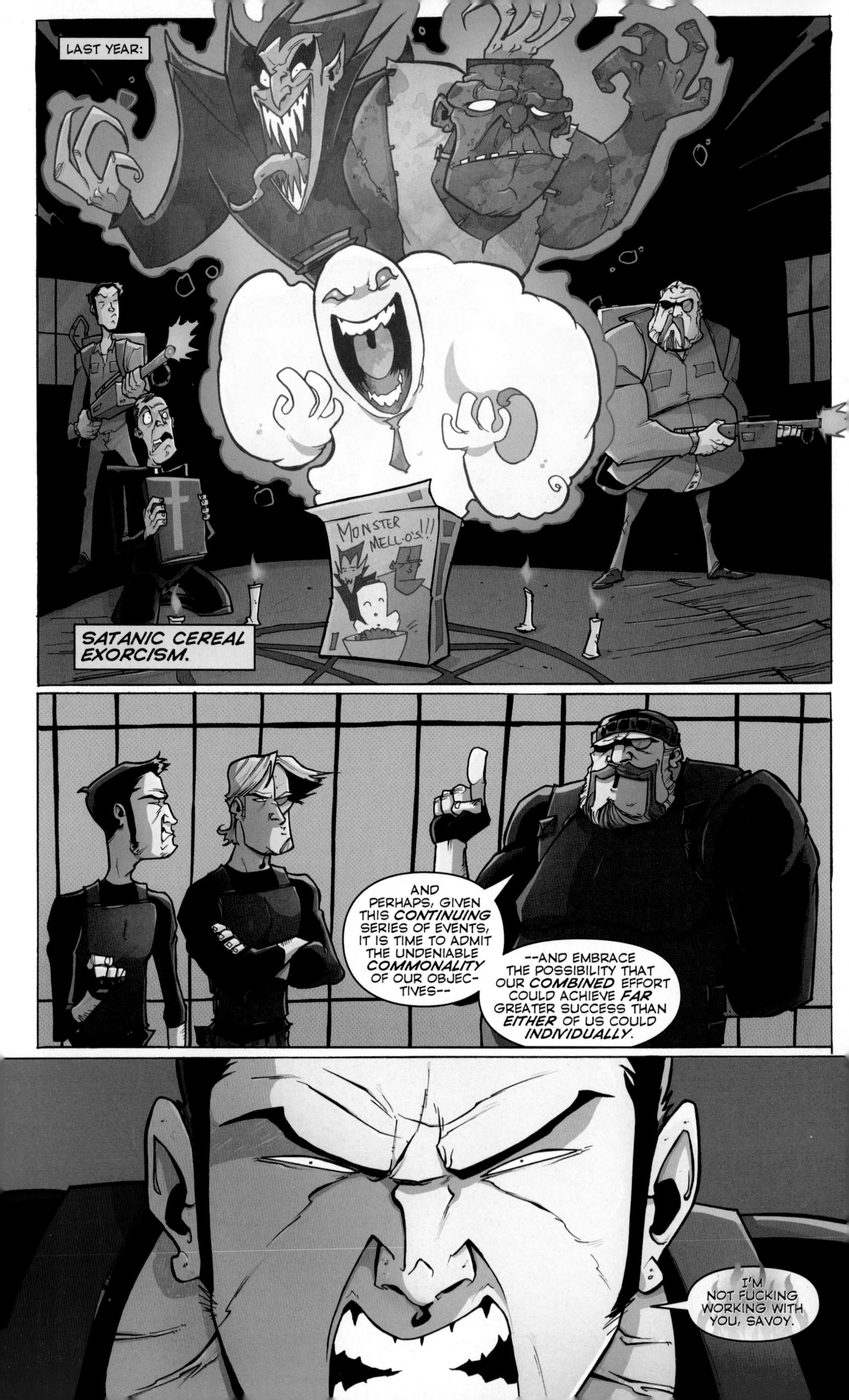
LAST YEAR:
MONSTER MELL-O's!!!
SATANIC CEREAL EXORCISM.
AND PERHAPS, GIVEN THIS CONTINUING SERIES OF EVENTS, IT IS TIME TO ADMIT THE UNDENIABLE COMMONALITY OF OUR OBJECTIVES--
--AND EMBRACE THE POSSIBILITY THAT OUR COMBINED EFFORT COULD ACHIEVE FAR GREATER SUCCESS THAN EITHER OF US COULD INDIVIDUALLY.
I'M NOT FUCKING WORKING WITH YOU, SAVOY.

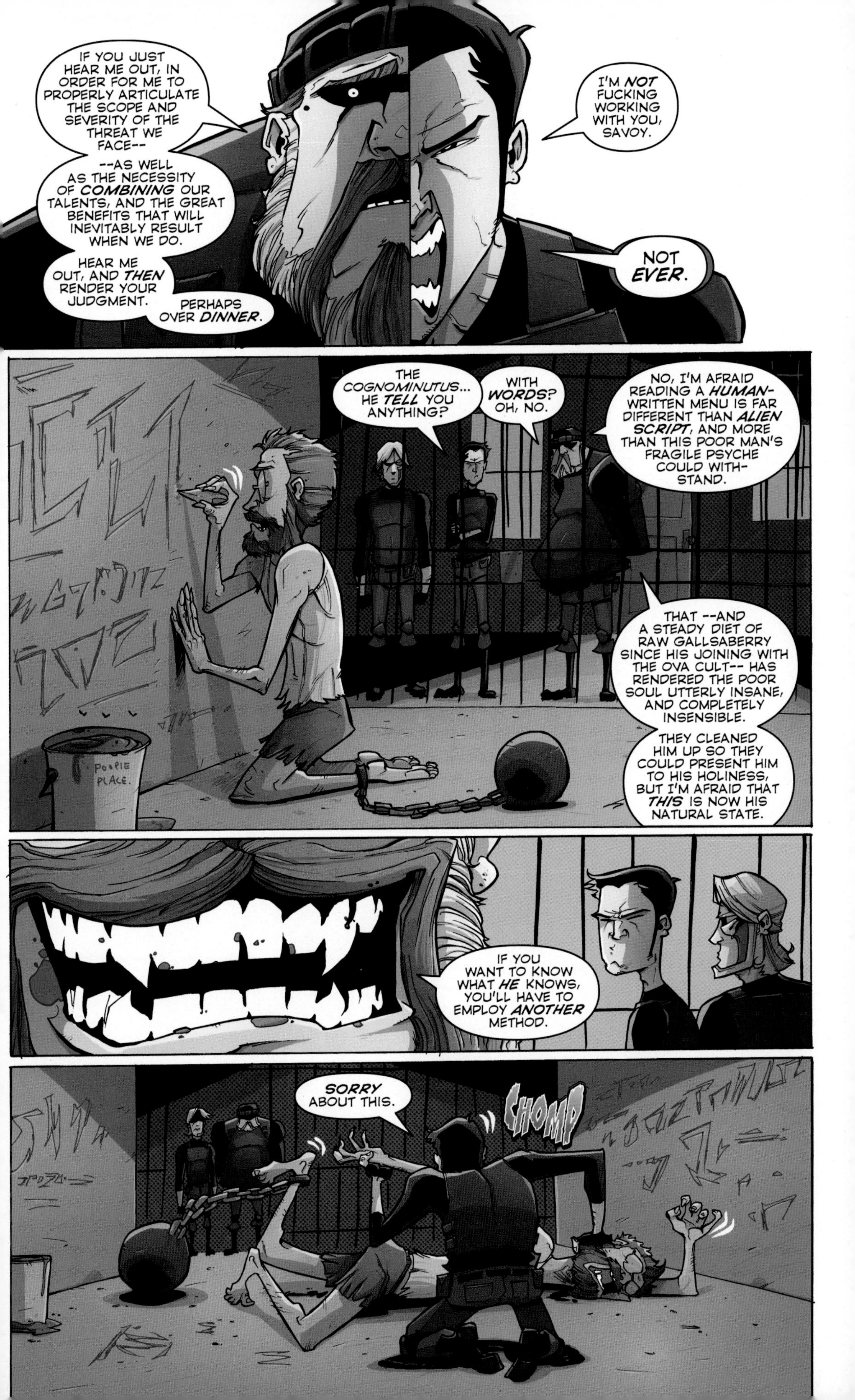
IF YOU JUST HEAR ME OUT, IN ORDER FOR ME TO PROPERLY ARTICULATE THE SCOPE AND SEVERITY OF THE THREAT WE FACE--
I'M NOT FUCKING WORKING WITH YOU, SAVOY.
--AS WELL AS THE NECESSITY OF COMBINING OUR TALENTS, AND THE GREAT BENEFITS THAT WILL INEVITABLY RESULT WHEN WE DO.
HEAR ME OUT, AND THEN RENDER YOUR JUDGMENT.
PERHAPS OVER DINNER.
NOT EVER.
THE COGNOMINUTUS... HE TELL YOU ANYTHING?
WITH WORDS? OH, NO.
NO, I'M AFRAID READING A HUMAN-WRITTEN MENU IS FAR DIFFERENT THAN ALIEN SCRIPT, AND MORE THAN THIS POOR MAN'S FRAGILE PSYCHE COULD WITH-STAND.
THAT --AND A STEADY DIET OF RAW GALLSABERRY SINCE HIS JOINING WITH THE OVA CULT-- HAS RENDERED THE POOR SOUL UTTERLY INSANE, AND COMPLETELY INSENSIBLE.
THEY CLEANED HIM UP SO THEY COULD PRESENT HIM TO HIS HOLINESS, BUT I'M AFRAID THAT THIS IS NOW HIS NATURAL STATE.
POOPIE PLACE.
IF YOU WANT TO KNOW WHAT HE KNOWS, YOU'LL HAVE TO EMPLOY ANOTHER METHOD.
SORRY ABOUT THIS.
CHOMP

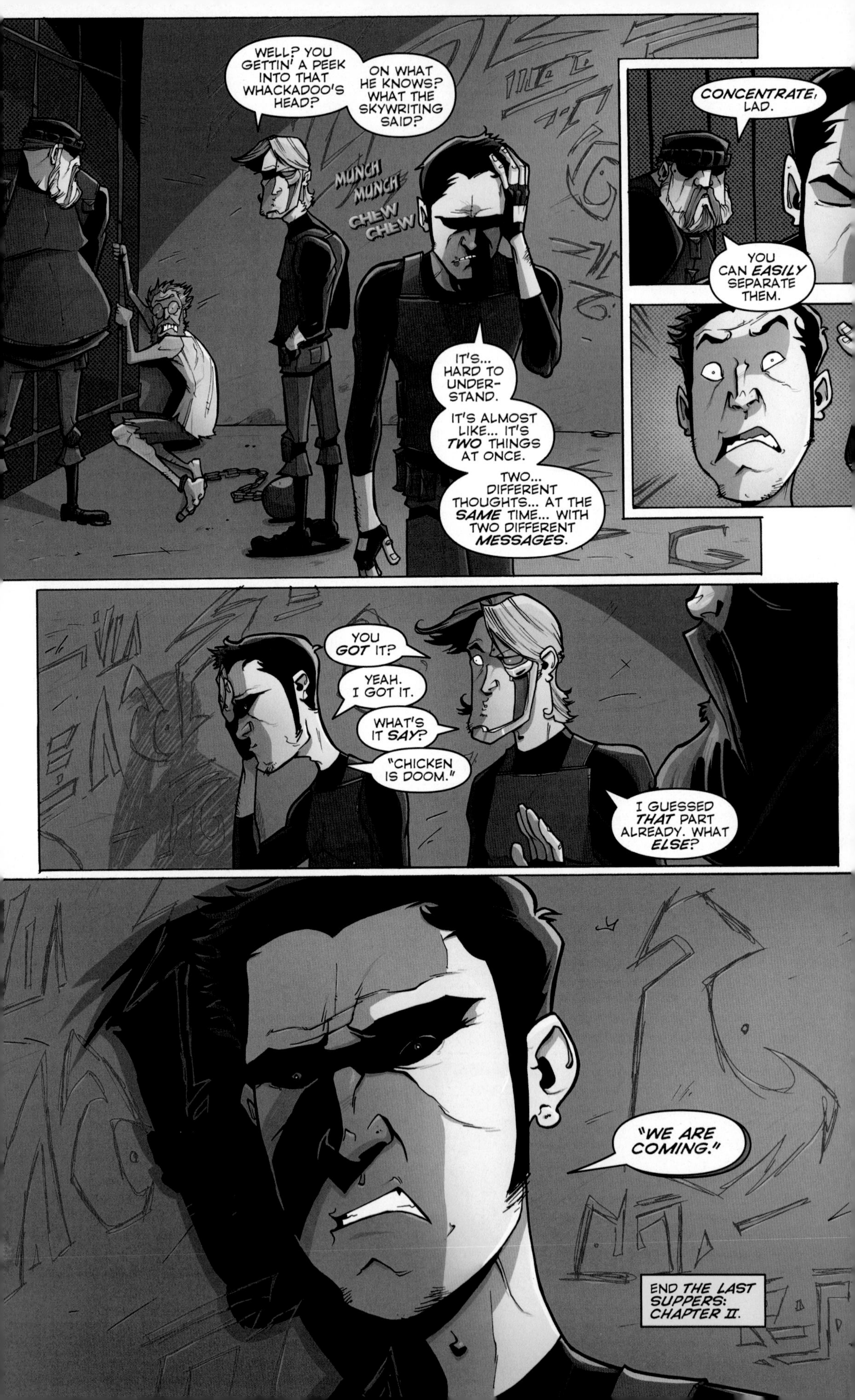
WELL? YOU GETTIN' A PEEK INTO THAT WHACKADOO'S HEAD?
ON WHAT HE KNOWS? WHAT THE SKYWRITING SAID?
MUNCH MUNCH
CHEW CHEW
IT'S... HARD TO UNDER-STAND.
IT'S ALMOST LIKE... IT'S TWO THINGS AT ONCE.
TWO... DIFFERENT THOUGHTS... AT THE SAME TIME... WITH TWO DIFFERENT MESSAGES.
CONCENTRATE, LAD.
YOU CAN EASILY SEPARATE THEM.
YOU GOT IT?
YEAH. I GOT IT.
WHAT'S IT SAY?
"CHICKEN IS DOOM."
I GUESSED THAT PART ALREADY. WHAT ELSE?
"WE ARE COMING."
END THE LAST SUPPERS: CHAPTER II.

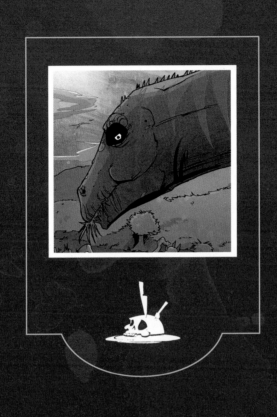

Chapter 3

FDA

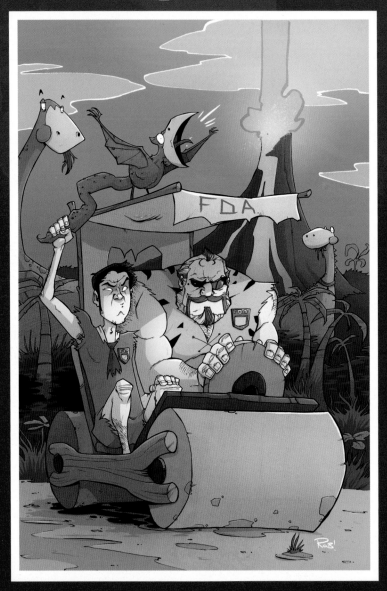

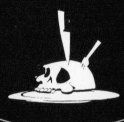

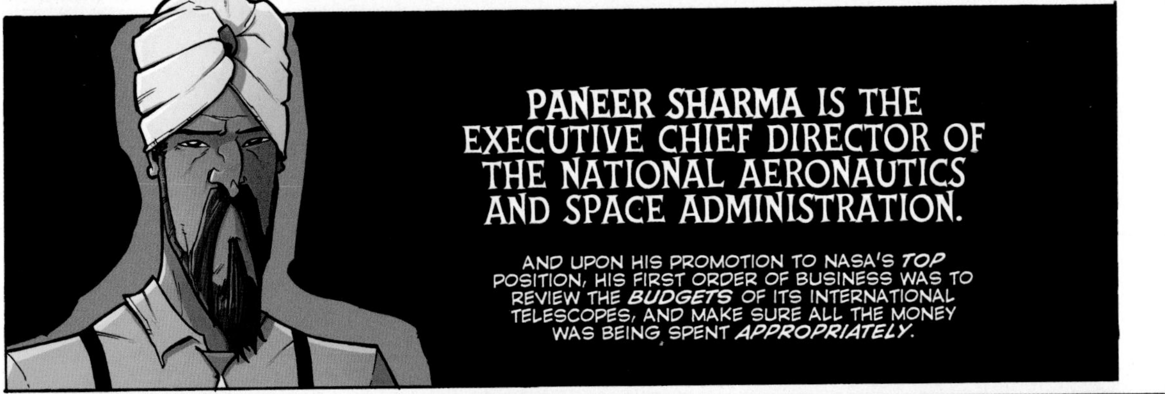
PANEER SHARMA IS THE EXECUTIVE CHIEF DIRECTOR OF THE NATIONAL AERONAUTICS AND SPACE ADMINISTRATION.
AND UPON HIS PROMOTION TO NASA'S *TOP* POSITION, HIS FIRST ORDER OF BUSINESS WAS TO REVIEW THE ***BUDGETS*** OF ITS INTERNATIONAL TELESCOPES, AND MAKE SURE ALL THE MONEY WAS BEING SPENT ***APPROPRIATELY***.

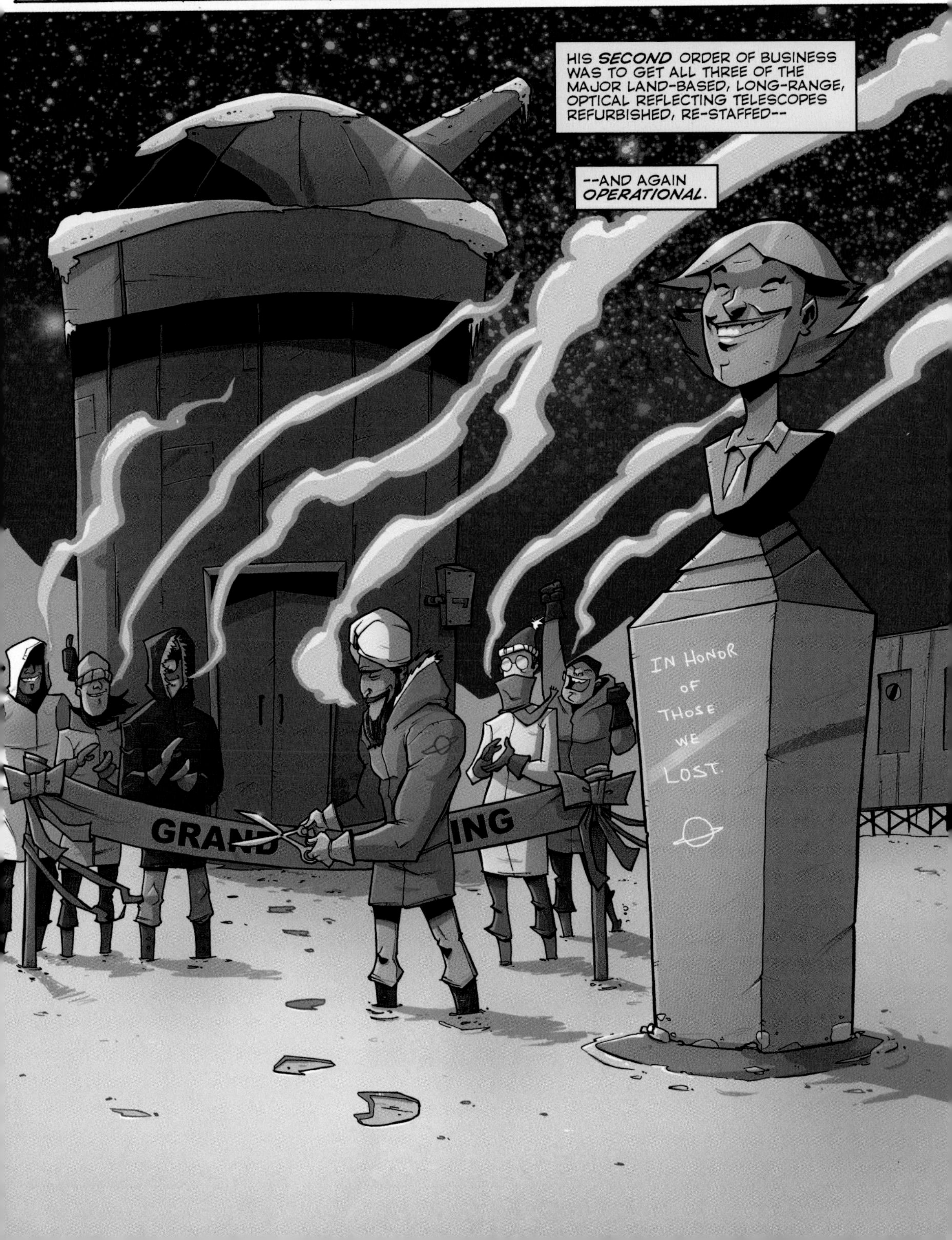
HIS ***SECOND*** ORDER OF BUSINESS WAS TO GET ALL THREE OF THE MAJOR LAND-BASED, LONG-RANGE, OPTICAL REFLECTING TELESCOPES REFURBISHED, RE-STAFFED--
--AND AGAIN ***OPERATIONAL***.
GRAND
ING
IN HONOR OF THOSE WE LOST.

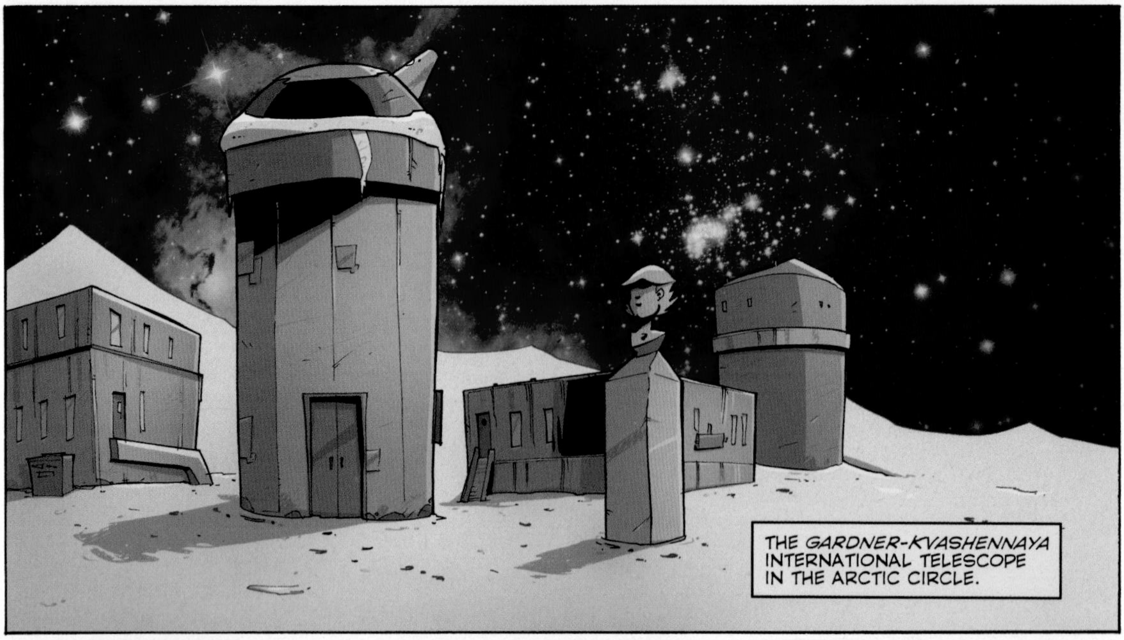
THE GARDNER-KVASHENNAYA INTERNATIONAL TELESCOPE IN THE ARCTIC CIRCLE.

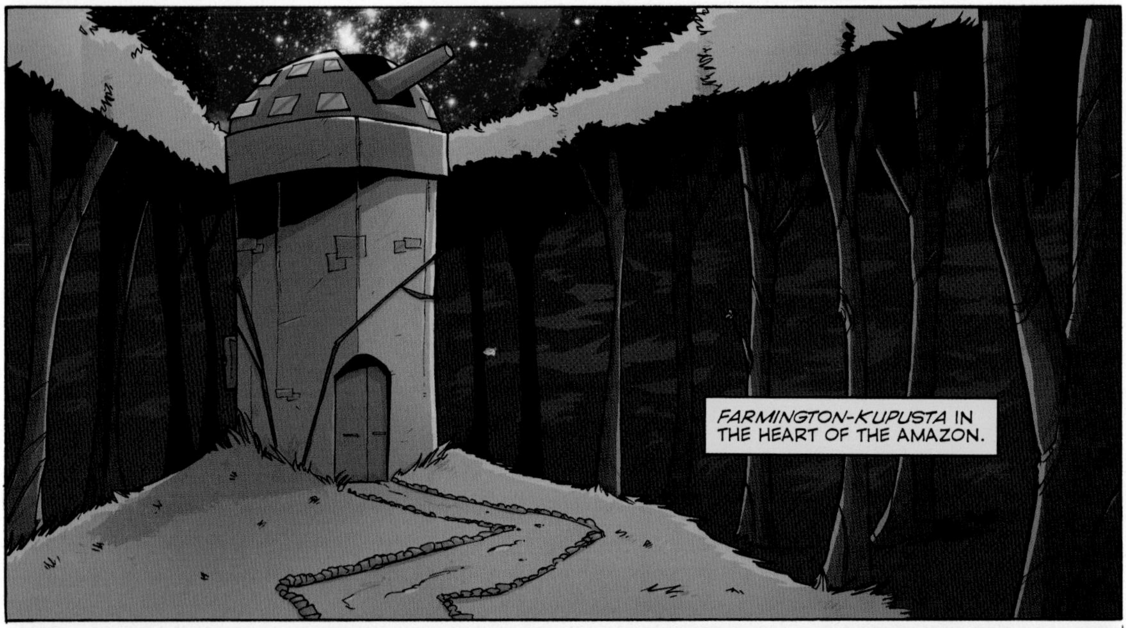
FARMINGTON-KUPUSTA IN THE HEART OF THE AMAZON.

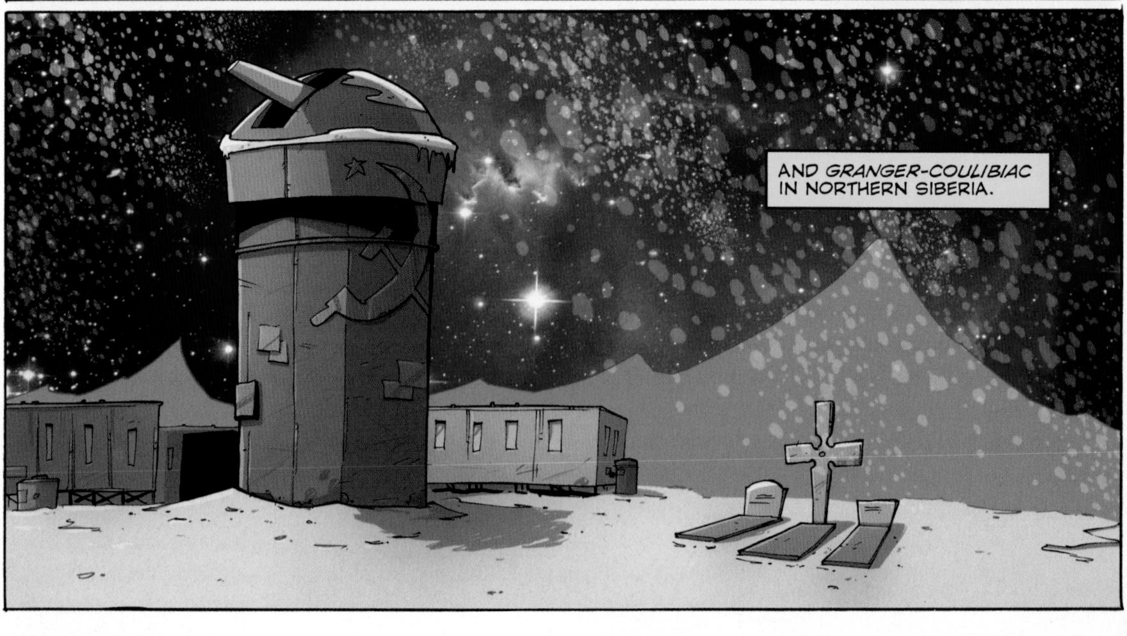
AND GRANGER-COULIBIAC IN NORTHERN SIBERIA.

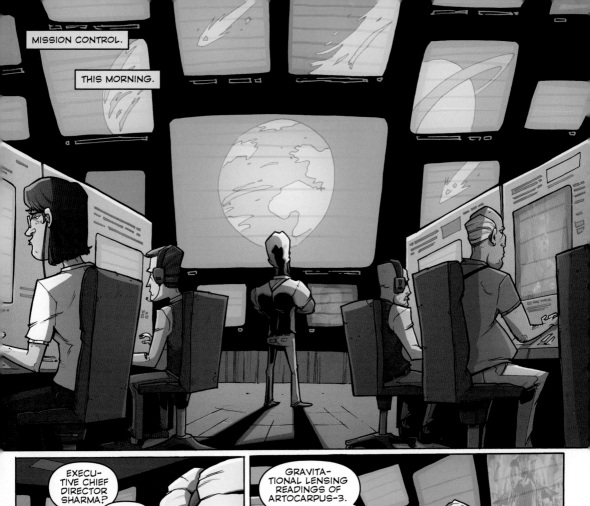

MISSION CONTROL.

THIS MORNING.

EXECUTIVE CHIEF DIRECTOR SHARMA?

HMM?

GOT SOMETHING I THINK YOU SHOULD SEE.

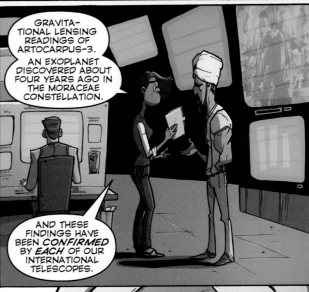

GRAVITATIONAL LENSING READINGS OF ARTOCARPUS-3.

AN EXOPLANET DISCOVERED ABOUT FOUR YEARS AGO IN THE MORACEAE CONSTELLATION.

AND THESE FINDINGS HAVE BEEN *CONFIRMED* BY *EACH* OF OUR INTERNATIONAL TELESCOPES.

HOLY SHIT!!!

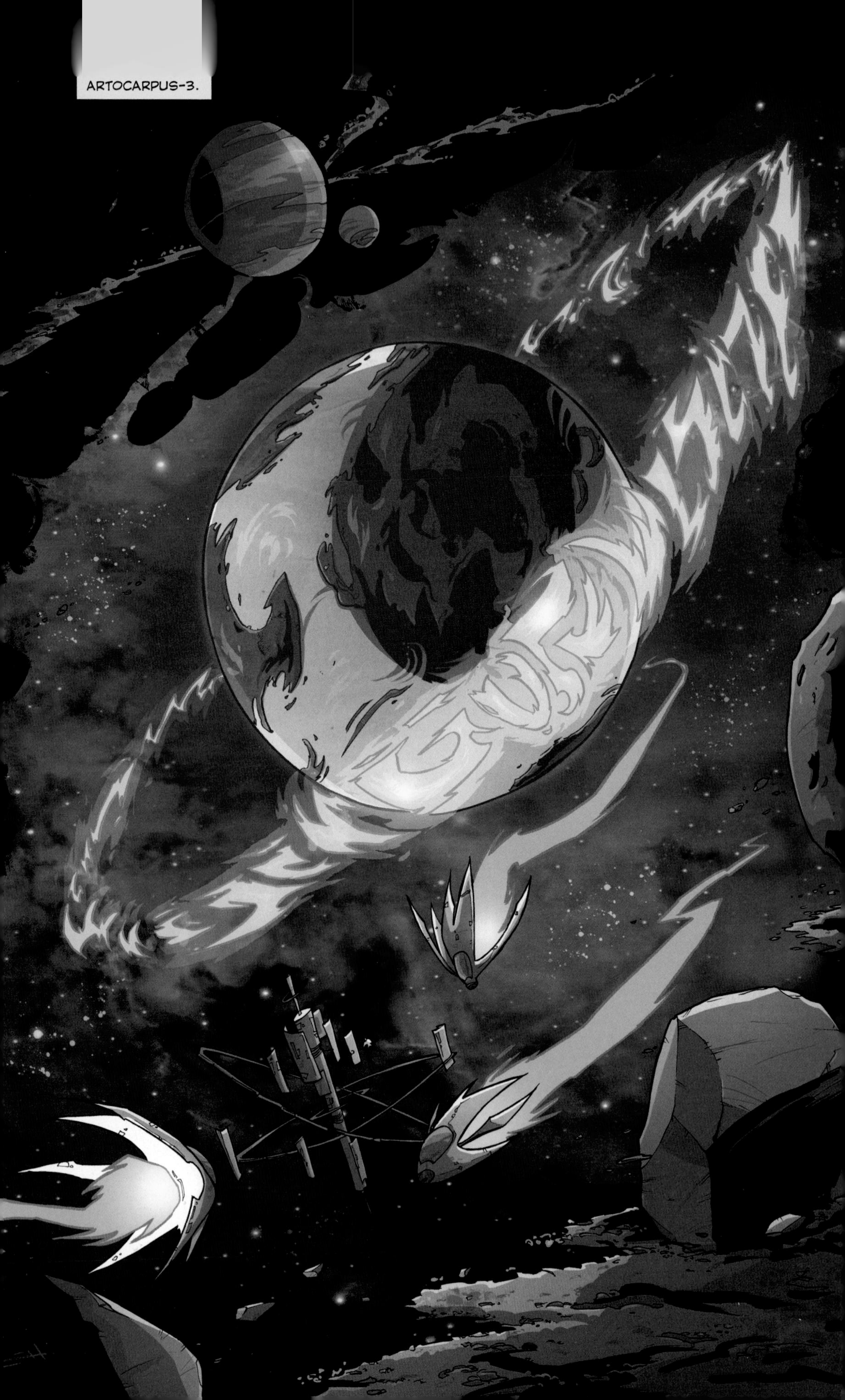
ARTOCARPUS-3.

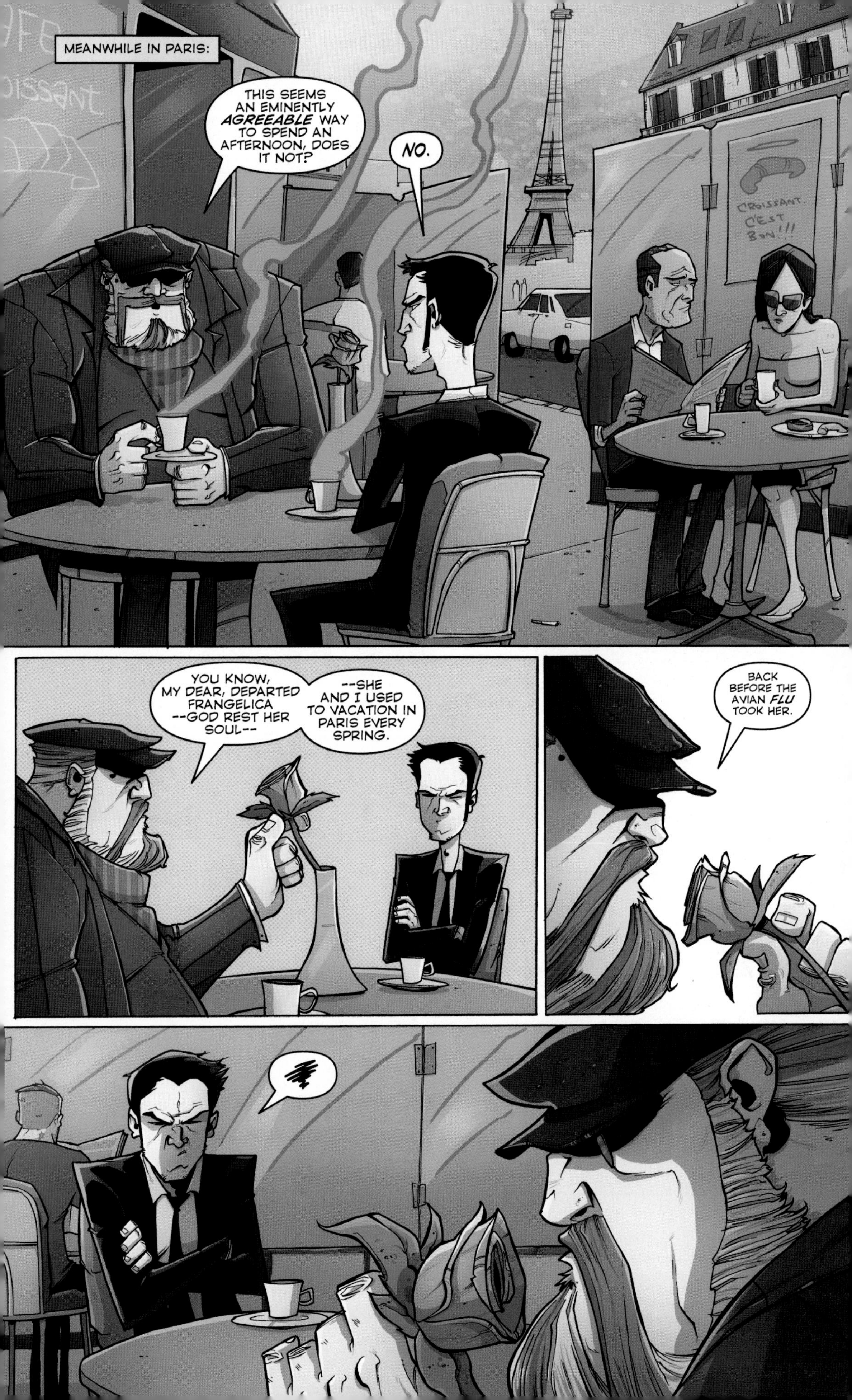
MEANWHILE IN PARIS:
THIS SEEMS AN EMINENTLY AGREEABLE WAY TO SPEND AN AFTERNOON, DOES IT NOT?
NO.
CROISSANT. C'EST BON!!!
YOU KNOW, MY DEAR, DEPARTED FRANGELICA --GOD REST HER SOUL--
--SHE AND I USED TO VACATION IN PARIS EVERY SPRING.
BACK BEFORE THE AVIAN FLU TOOK HER.

PLEASE PASS ALONG MY COMPLIMENTS TO YOUR LOVELY BRIDE ON HER MOST RECENT NOVEL.

AND LET HER KNOW I *FERVENTLY* AWAIT THE *CONCLUSION* OF HER SAGA.

AND I HEAR OUR *OLIVE* IS DOING WELL.

AT THE *TOP* OF HER CLASS AT THE *FDA* TRAINING ACADEMY. ON HER WAY TO A *MOST* IMPRESSIVE LAW ENFORCEMENT CAREER.

AH, SUCH A WONDERFUL, DELIGHTFUL, REMARKABLE YOUNG LADY.

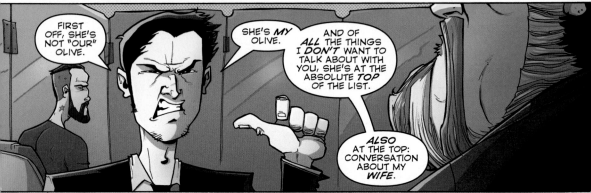

FIRST OFF, SHE'S NOT "OUR" OLIVE.

SHE'S *MY* OLIVE.

AND OF *ALL* THE THINGS I *DON'T* WANT TO TALK ABOUT WITH YOU, SHE'S AT THE ABSOLUTE *TOP* OF THE LIST.

ALSO AT THE TOP: CONVERSATION ABOUT MY *WIFE.*

I DON'T GIVE A FUCK ABOUT MAKING *SMALL TALK* WITH YOU, SAVOY.

YOU SAID YOU HAVE SOMETHING *IMPORTANT* TO SAY. FUCKING *GET TO IT.*

BUT I DON'T GIVE A *FUCK* ABOUT YOUR VACATIONS. AND I DON'T GIVE A *FUCK* ABOUT PARIS.

HMMPH. *FINE.*

MR. ANARI. WHAT *ELSE* DO YOU HAVE FOR AGENT CHU?

EGYPTIAN TEA?

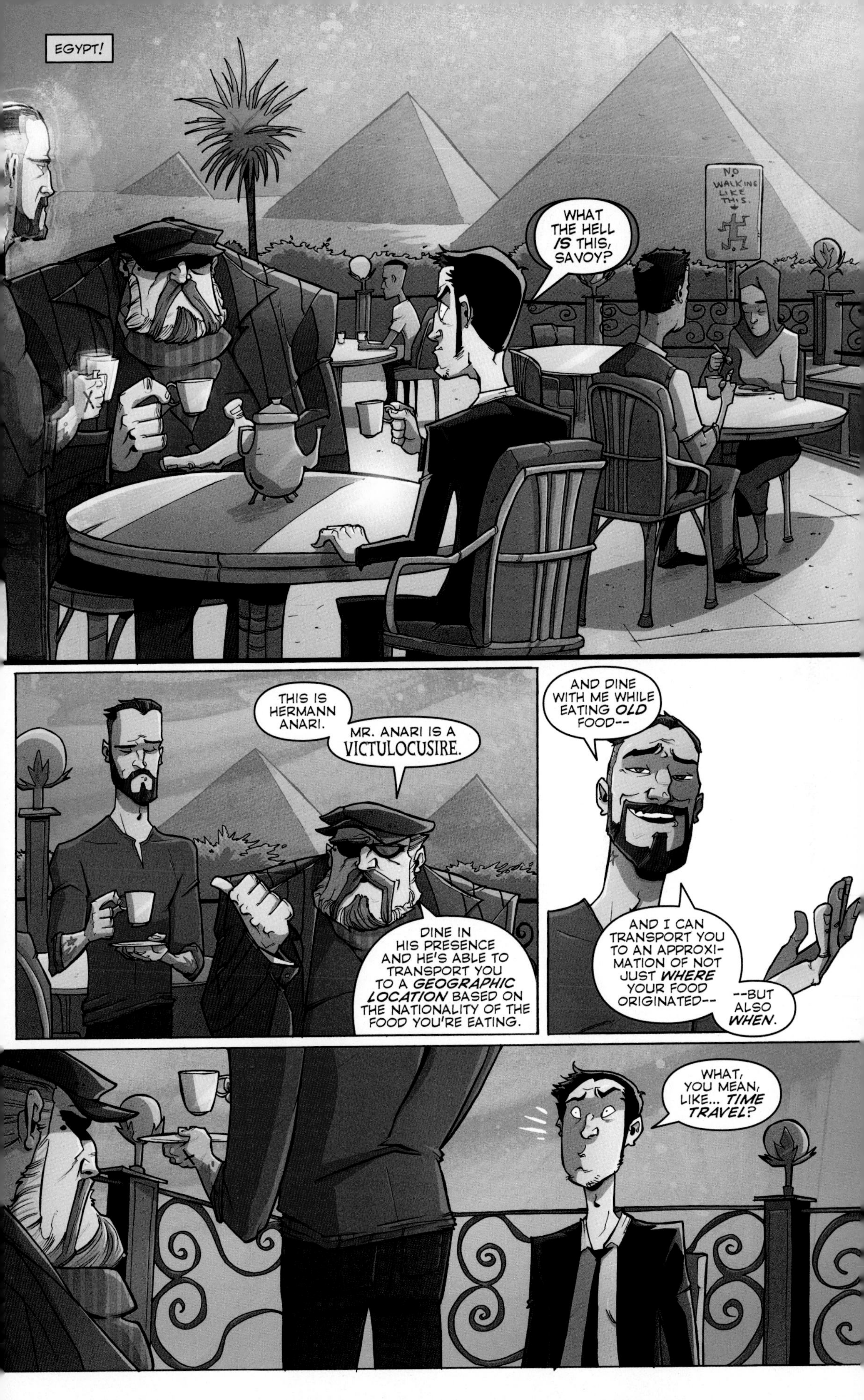
EGYPT!
NO WALKING LIKE THIS.
WHAT THE HELL IS THIS, SAVOY?
THIS IS HERMANN ANARI.
MR. ANARI IS A VICTULOCUSIRE.
DINE IN HIS PRESENCE AND HE'S ABLE TO TRANSPORT YOU TO A GEOGRAPHIC LOCATION BASED ON THE NATIONALITY OF THE FOOD YOU'RE EATING.
AND DINE WITH ME WHILE EATING OLD FOOD--
AND I CAN TRANSPORT YOU TO AN APPROXIMATION OF NOT JUST WHERE YOUR FOOD ORIGINATED--
--BUT ALSO WHEN.
WHAT, YOU MEAN, LIKE... TIME TRAVEL?

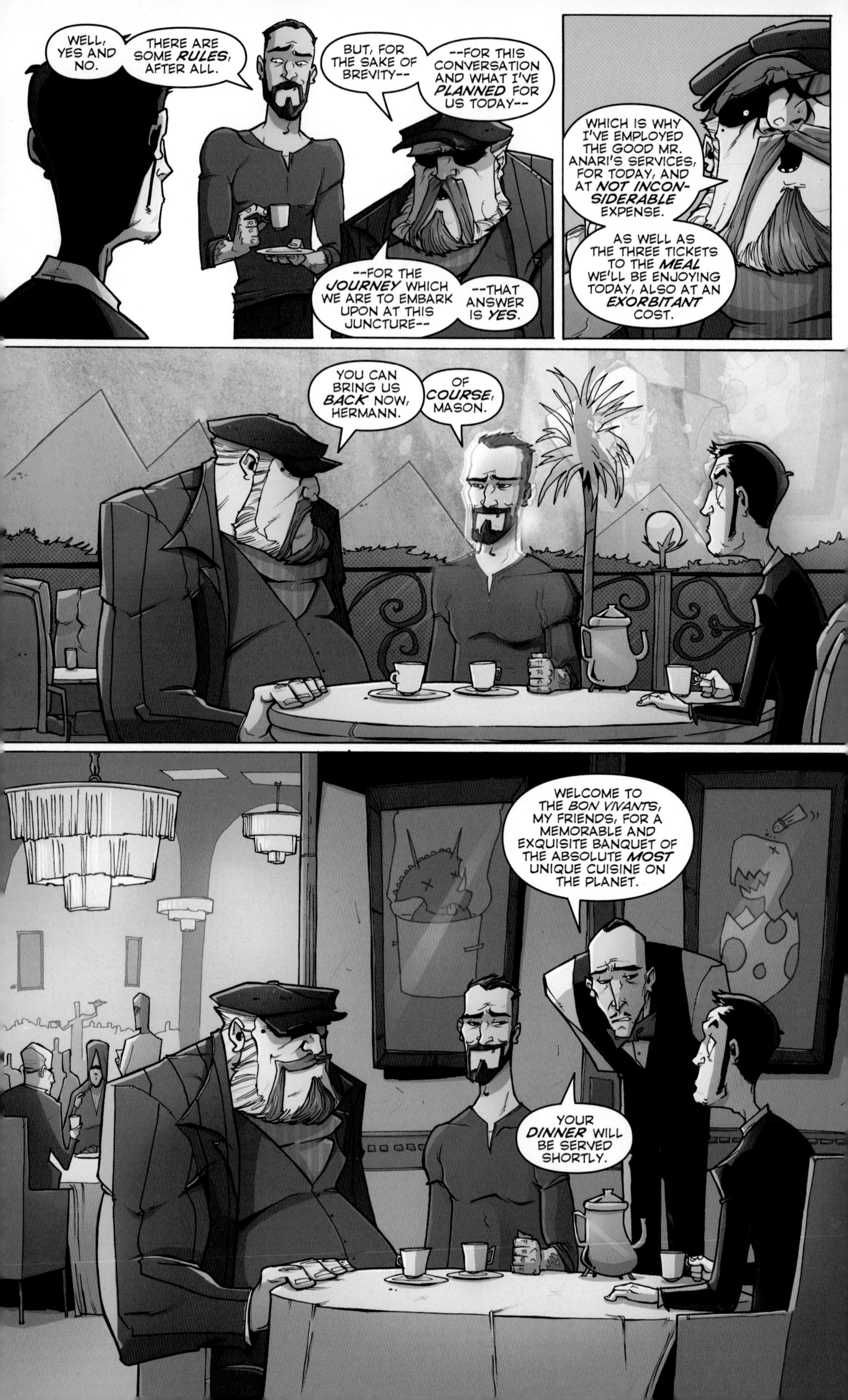
WELL, YES AND NO.
THERE ARE SOME RULES, AFTER ALL.
BUT, FOR THE SAKE OF BREVITY--
--FOR THIS CONVERSATION AND WHAT I'VE PLANNED FOR US TODAY--
--FOR THE JOURNEY WHICH WE ARE TO EMBARK UPON AT THIS JUNCTURE--
--THAT ANSWER IS YES.
WHICH IS WHY I'VE EMPLOYED THE GOOD MR. ANARI'S SERVICES, FOR TODAY, AND AT NOT INCONSIDERABLE EXPENSE.
AS WELL AS THE THREE TICKETS TO THE MEAL WE'LL BE ENJOYING TODAY, ALSO AT AN EXORBITANT COST.
YOU CAN BRING US BACK NOW, HERMANN.
OF COURSE, MASON.
WELCOME TO THE BON VIVANTS, MY FRIENDS, FOR A MEMORABLE AND EXQUISITE BANQUET OF THE ABSOLUTE MOST UNIQUE CUISINE ON THE PLANET.
YOUR DINNER WILL BE SERVED SHORTLY.

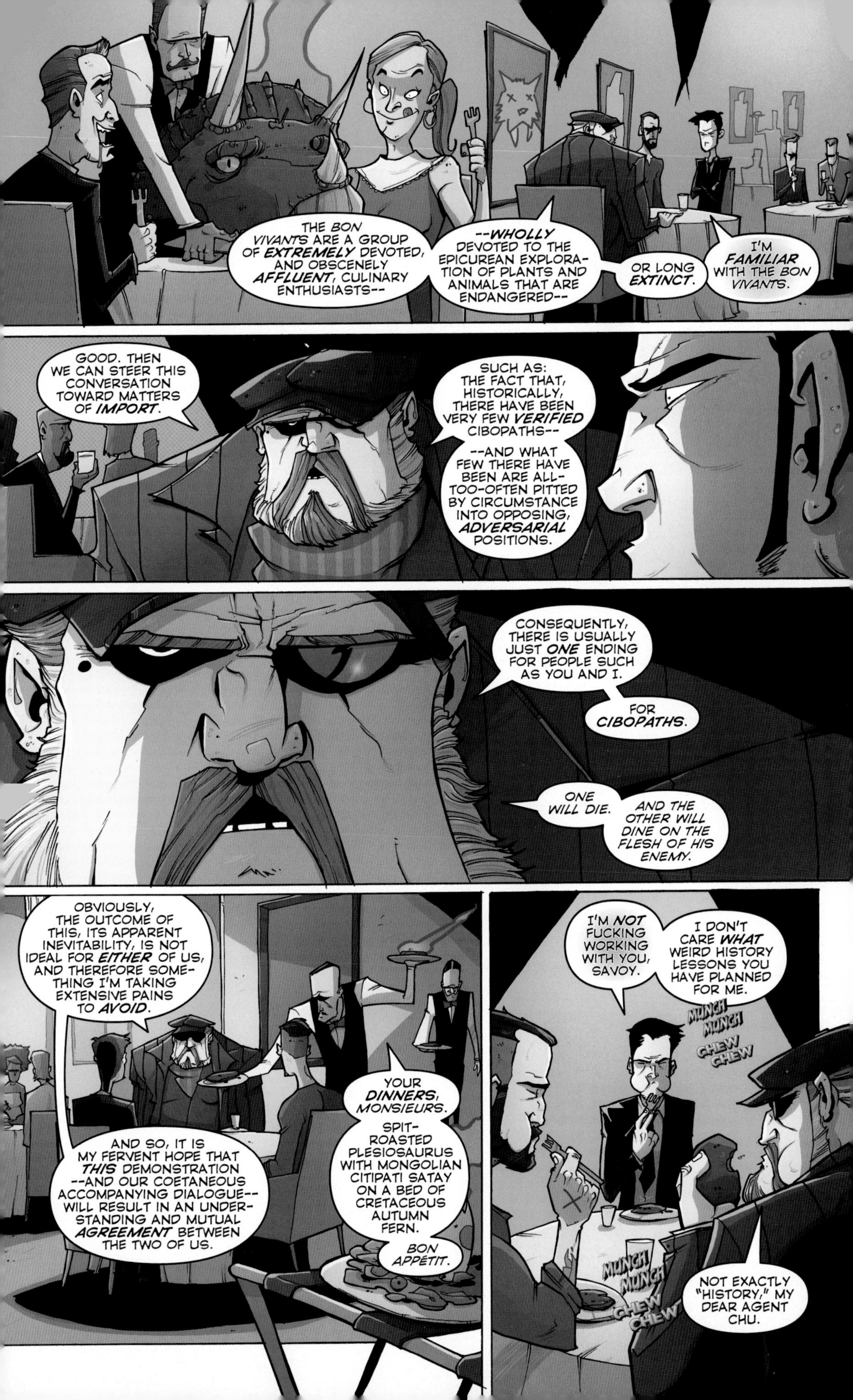

THE BON VIVANTS ARE A GROUP OF EXTREMELY DEVOTED, AND OBSCENELY AFFLUENT, CULINARY ENTHUSIASTS--
--WHOLLY DEVOTED TO THE EPICUREAN EXPLORATION OF PLANTS AND ANIMALS THAT ARE ENDANGERED--
OR LONG EXTINCT.
I'M FAMILIAR WITH THE BON VIVANTS.
GOOD. THEN WE CAN STEER THIS CONVERSATION TOWARD MATTERS OF IMPORT.
SUCH AS: THE FACT THAT, HISTORICALLY, THERE HAVE BEEN VERY FEW VERIFIED CIBOPATHS--
--AND WHAT FEW THERE HAVE BEEN ARE ALL-TOO-OFTEN PITTED BY CIRCUMSTANCE INTO OPPOSING, ADVERSARIAL POSITIONS.
CONSEQUENTLY, THERE IS USUALLY JUST ONE ENDING FOR PEOPLE SUCH AS YOU AND I.
FOR CIBOPATHS.
ONE WILL DIE.
AND THE OTHER WILL DINE ON THE FLESH OF HIS ENEMY.
OBVIOUSLY, THE OUTCOME OF THIS, ITS APPARENT INEVITABILITY, IS NOT IDEAL FOR EITHER OF US, AND THEREFORE SOMETHING I'M TAKING EXTENSIVE PAINS TO AVOID.
AND SO, IT IS MY FERVENT HOPE THAT THIS DEMONSTRATION --AND OUR COETANEOUS ACCOMPANYING DIALOGUE-- WILL RESULT IN AN UNDERSTANDING AND MUTUAL AGREEMENT BETWEEN THE TWO OF US.
YOUR DINNERS, MONSIEURS.
SPIT-ROASTED PLESIOSAURUS WITH MONGOLIAN CITIPATI SATAY ON A BED OF CRETACEOUS AUTUMN FERN.
BON APPÉTIT.
I'M NOT FUCKING WORKING WITH YOU, SAVOY.
I DON'T CARE WHAT WEIRD HISTORY LESSONS YOU HAVE PLANNED FOR ME.
MUNCH MUNCH
CHEW CHEW
MUNCH MUNCH
CHEW CHEW
NOT EXACTLY "HISTORY," MY DEAR AGENT CHU.

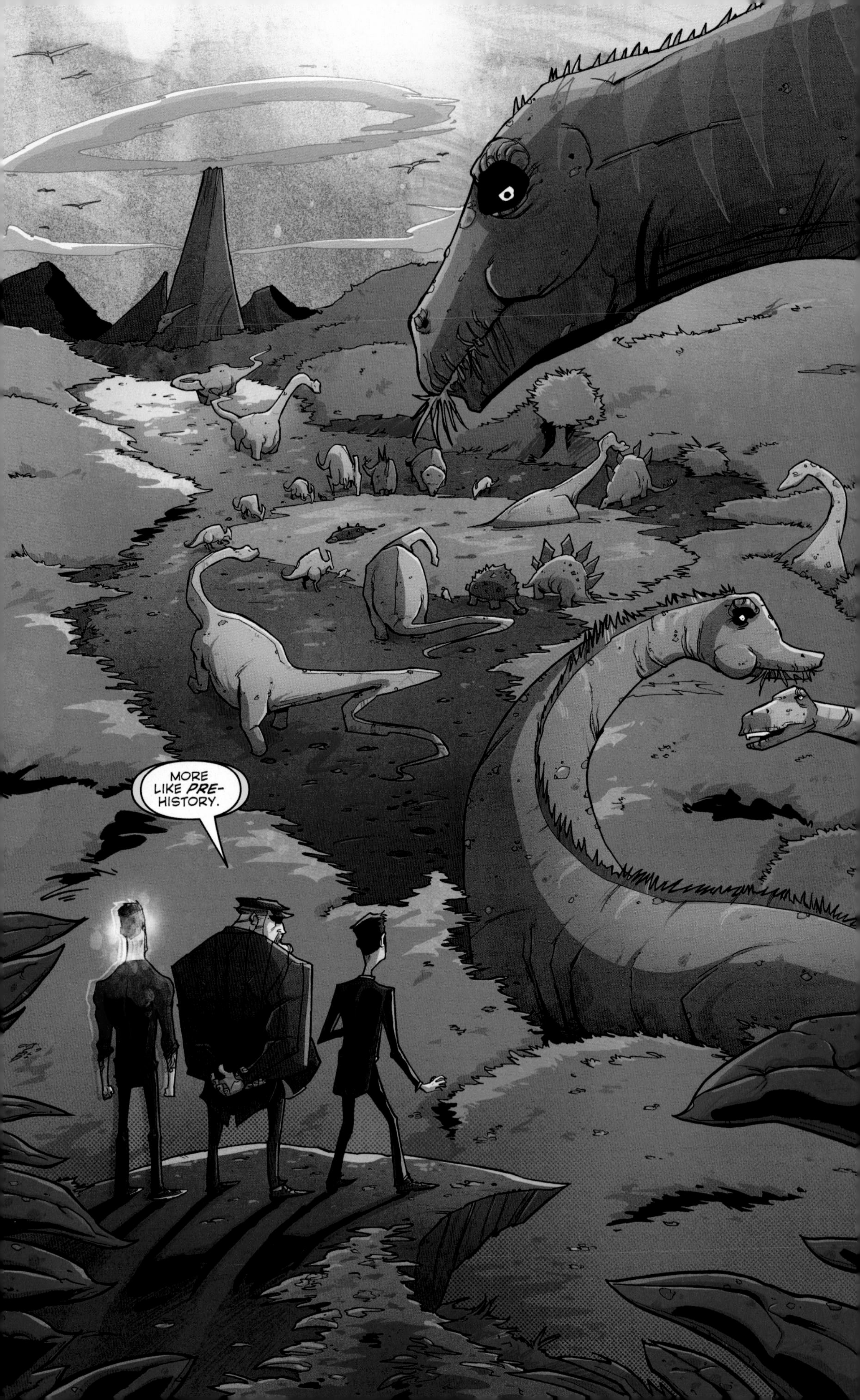
MORE LIKE *PRE*-HISTORY.

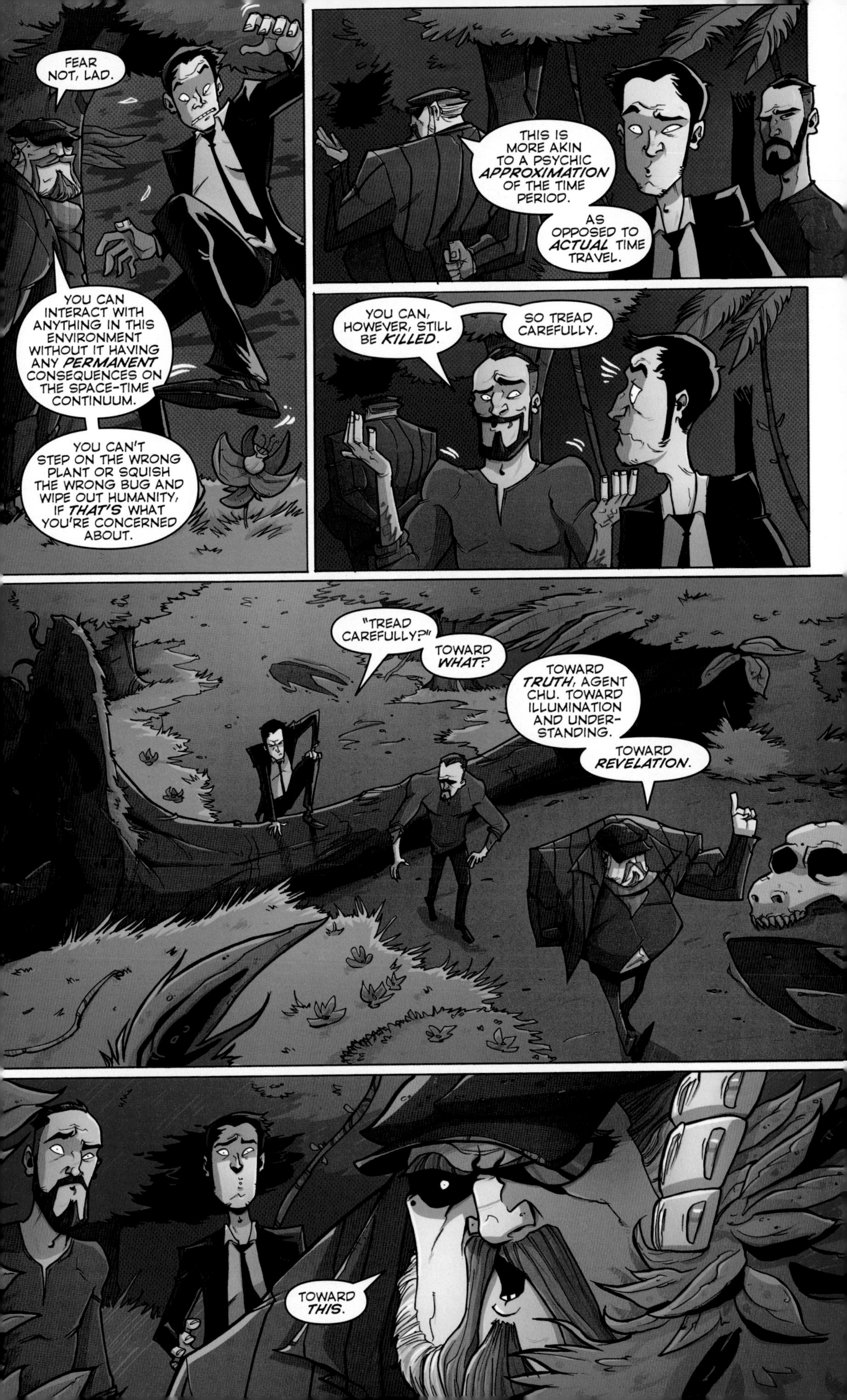
FEAR NOT, LAD.
THIS IS MORE AKIN TO A PSYCHIC *APPROXIMATION* OF THE TIME PERIOD.
AS OPPOSED TO *ACTUAL* TIME TRAVEL.
YOU CAN INTERACT WITH ANYTHING IN THIS ENVIRONMENT WITHOUT IT HAVING ANY *PERMANENT* CONSEQUENCES ON THE SPACE-TIME CONTINUUM.
YOU CAN'T STEP ON THE WRONG PLANT OR SQUISH THE WRONG BUG AND WIPE OUT HUMANITY, IF *THAT'S* WHAT YOU'RE CONCERNED ABOUT.
YOU CAN, HOWEVER, STILL BE *KILLED*.
SO TREAD CAREFULLY.
"TREAD CAREFULLY?"
TOWARD *WHAT*?
TOWARD *TRUTH*, AGENT CHU. TOWARD ILLUMINATION AND UNDER-STANDING.
TOWARD *REVELATION*.
TOWARD *THIS*.

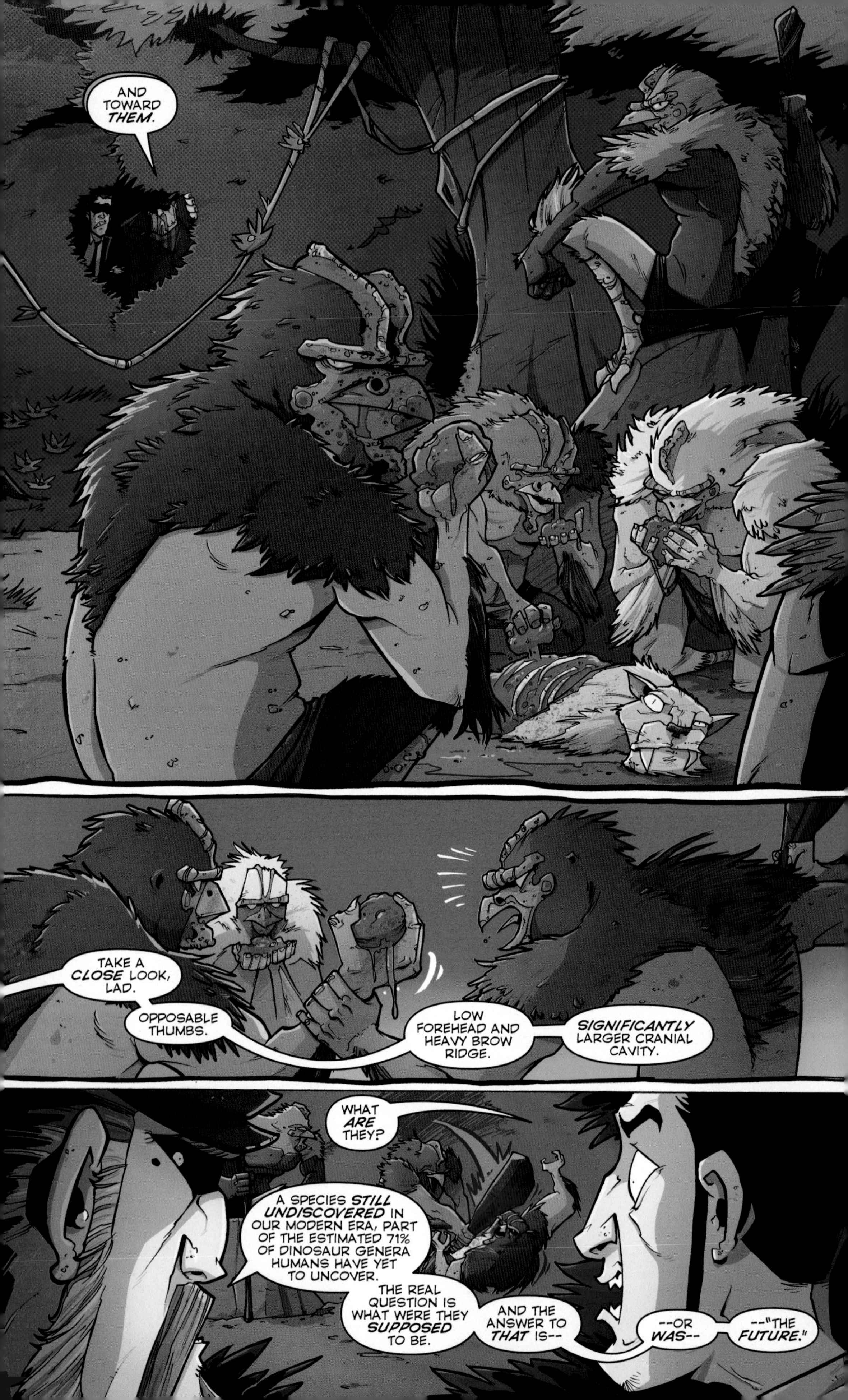
AND TOWARD *THEM*.
TAKE A *CLOSE* LOOK, LAD.
OPPOSABLE THUMBS.
LOW FOREHEAD AND HEAVY BROW RIDGE.
SIGNIFICANTLY LARGER CRANIAL CAVITY.
WHAT *ARE* THEY?
A SPECIES *STILL UNDISCOVERED* IN OUR MODERN ERA, PART OF THE ESTIMATED 71% OF DINOSAUR GENERA HUMANS HAVE YET TO UNCOVER.
THE REAL QUESTION IS WHAT WERE THEY *SUPPOSED* TO BE.
AND THE ANSWER TO *THAT* IS--
--OR *WAS*--
--"THE *FUTURE*."

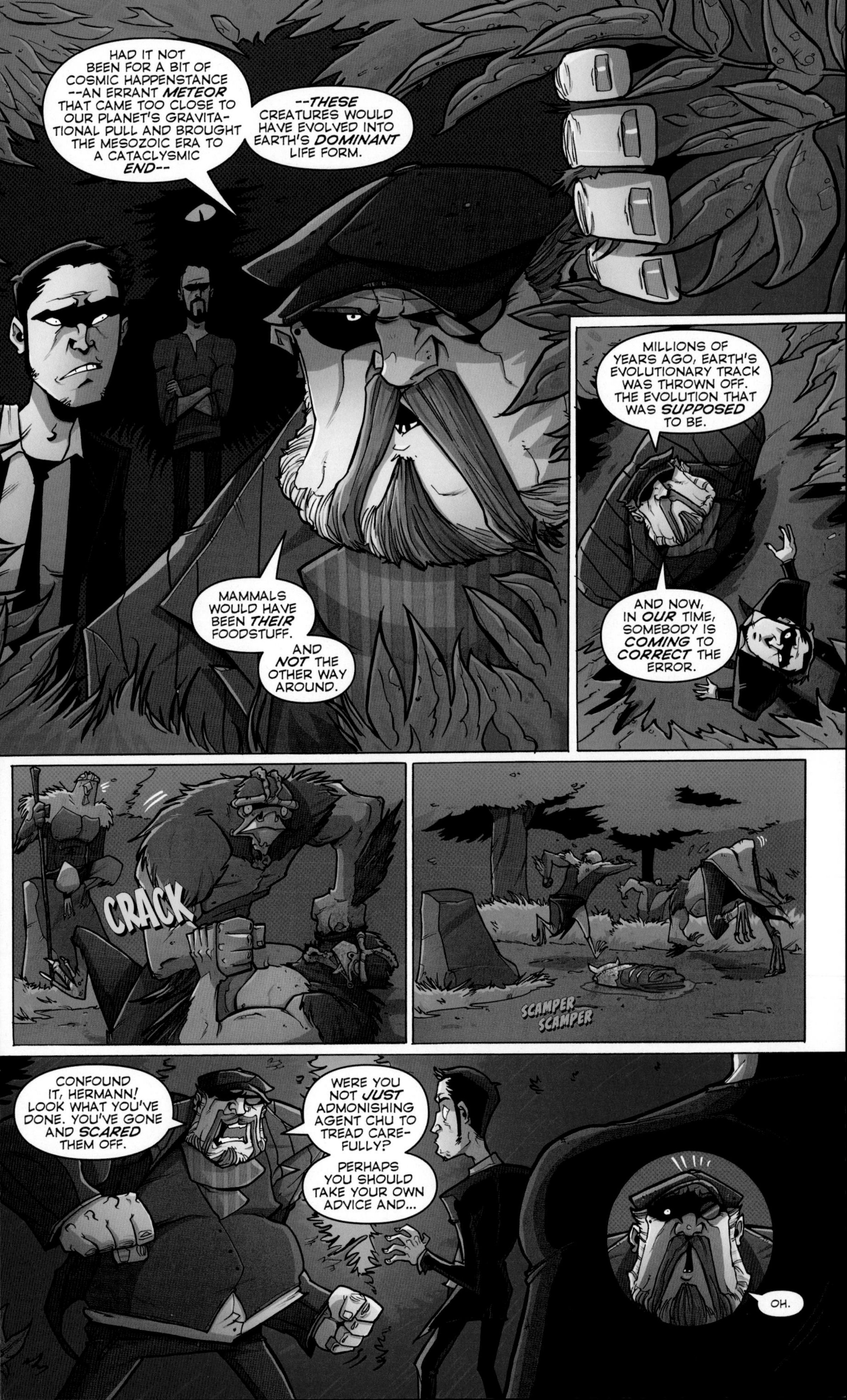
HAD IT NOT BEEN FOR A BIT OF COSMIC HAPPENSTANCE --AN ERRANT METEOR THAT CAME TOO CLOSE TO OUR PLANET'S GRAVITATIONAL PULL AND BROUGHT THE MESOZOIC ERA TO A CATACLYSMIC END--
--THESE CREATURES WOULD HAVE EVOLVED INTO EARTH'S DOMINANT LIFE FORM.
MAMMALS WOULD HAVE BEEN THEIR FOODSTUFF.
AND NOT THE OTHER WAY AROUND.
MILLIONS OF YEARS AGO, EARTH'S EVOLUTIONARY TRACK WAS THROWN OFF. THE EVOLUTION THAT WAS SUPPOSED TO BE.
AND NOW, IN OUR TIME, SOMEBODY IS COMING TO CORRECT THE ERROR.
CRACK
SCAMPER SCAMPER
CONFOUND IT, HERMANN! LOOK WHAT YOU'VE DONE. YOU'VE GONE AND SCARED THEM OFF.
WERE YOU NOT JUST ADMONISHING AGENT CHU TO TREAD CAREFULLY?
PERHAPS YOU SHOULD TAKE YOUR OWN ADVICE AND...
OH.

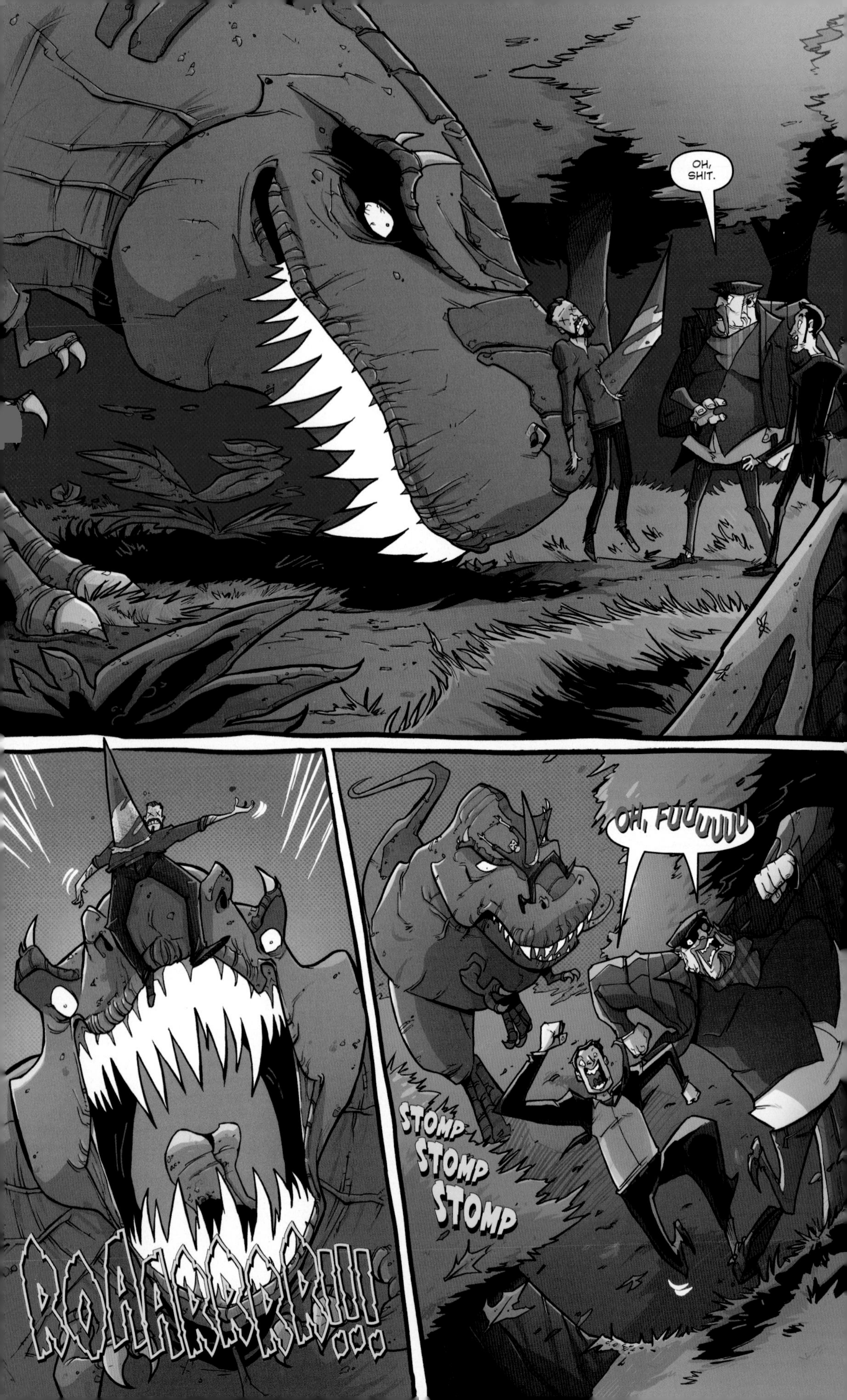
OH, SHIT.
ROARRRR!!!...
OH, FUUUUUU
STOMP
STOMP
STOMP

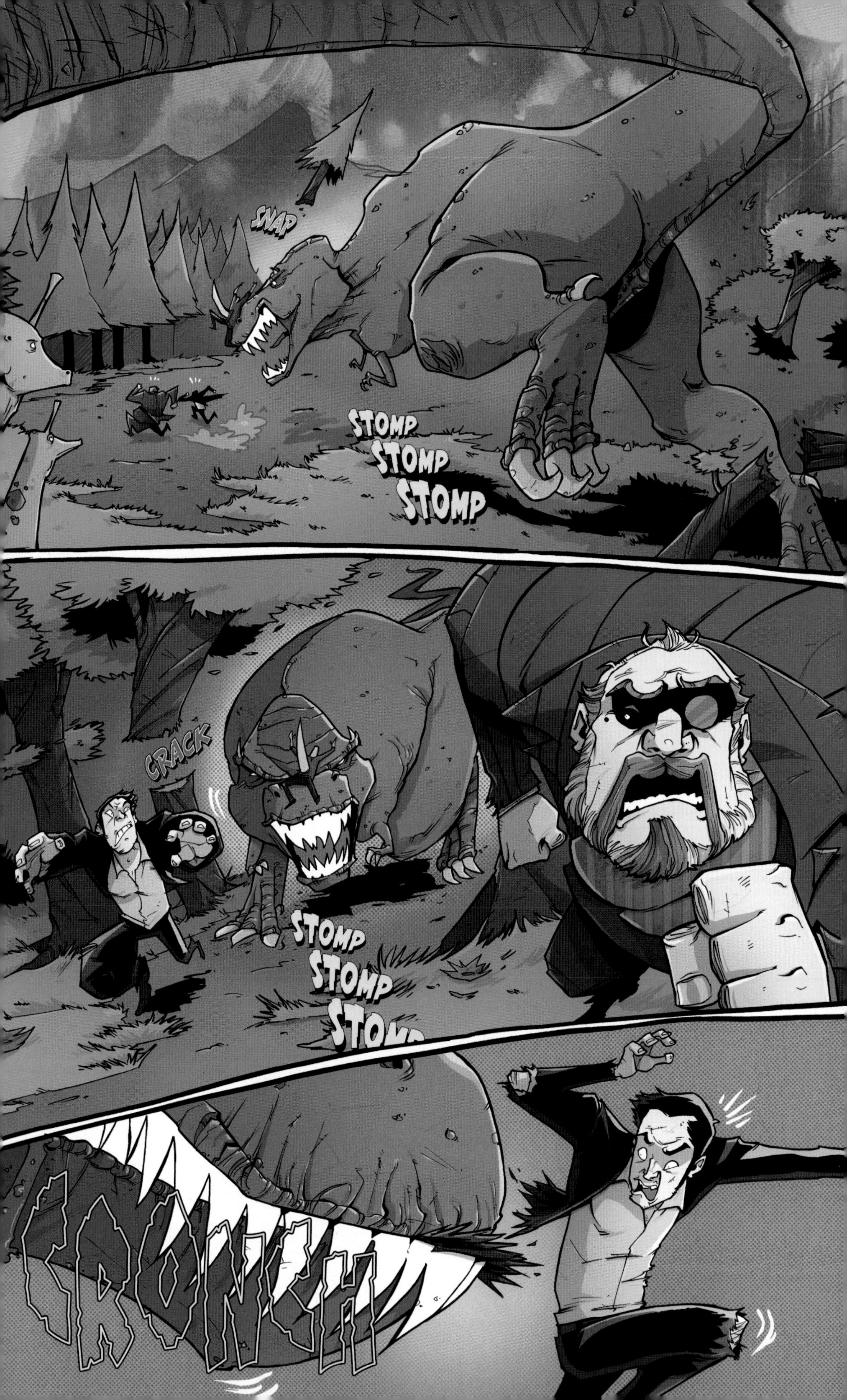
SNAP
STOMP
STOMP
STOMP
CRACK
STOMP
STOMP
CRUNCH

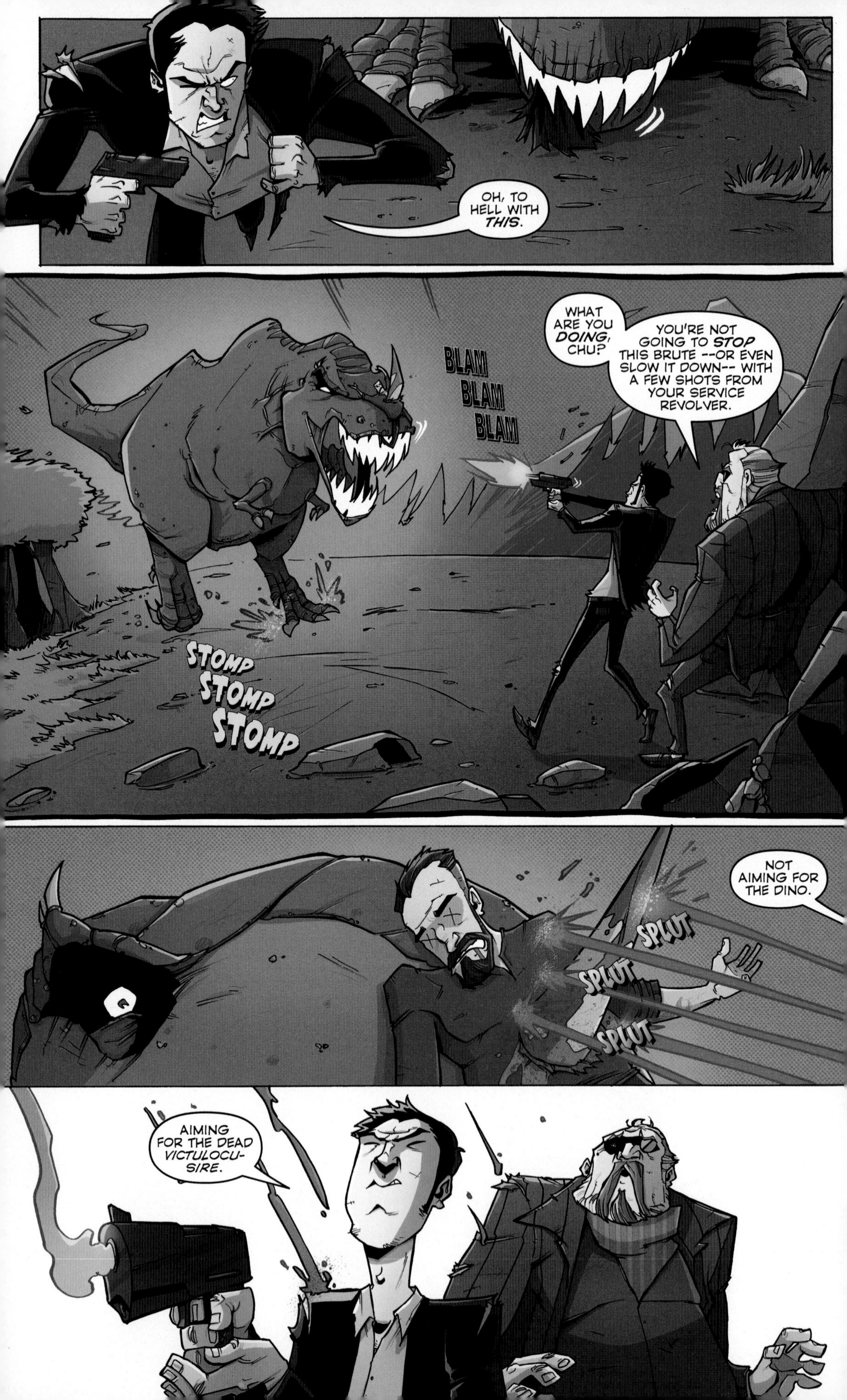
OH, TO HELL WITH *THIS*.
BLAM
BLAM
BLAM
WHAT ARE YOU *DOING*, CHU?
YOU'RE NOT GOING TO *STOP* THIS BRUTE --OR EVEN SLOW IT DOWN-- WITH A FEW SHOTS FROM YOUR SERVICE REVOLVER.
STOMP
STOMP
STOMP
NOT AIMING FOR THE DINO.
SPLUT
SPLUT
SPLUT
AIMING FOR THE DEAD *VICTULOCUSIRE*.

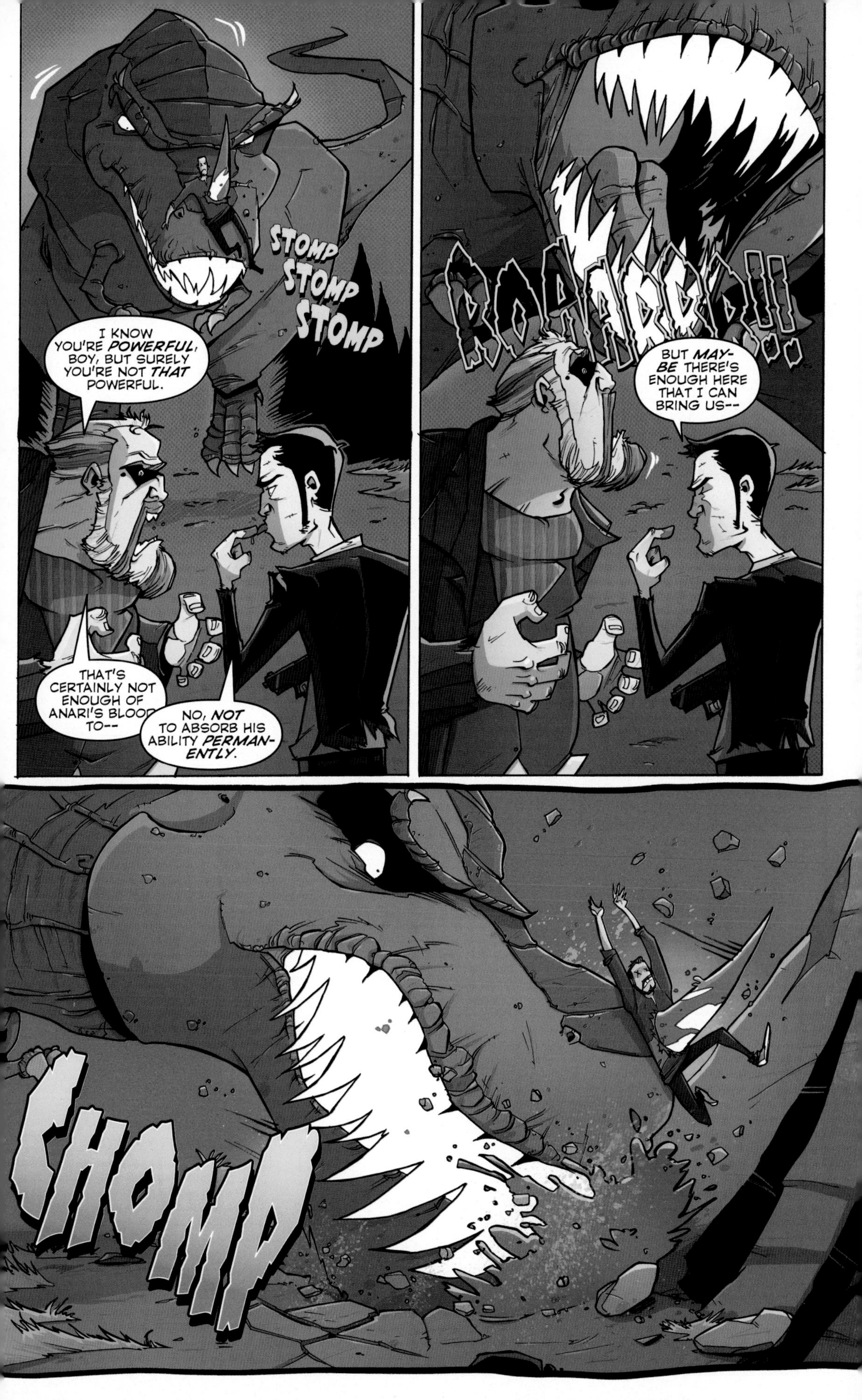
STOMP STOMP STOMP
I KNOW YOU'RE POWERFUL, BOY, BUT SURELY YOU'RE NOT THAT POWERFUL.
THAT'S CERTAINLY NOT ENOUGH OF ANARI'S BLOOD TO--
NO, NOT TO ABSORB HIS ABILITY PERMANENTLY.
ROAARRRR!!
BUT MAYBE THERE'S ENOUGH HERE THAT I CAN BRING US--
CHOMP

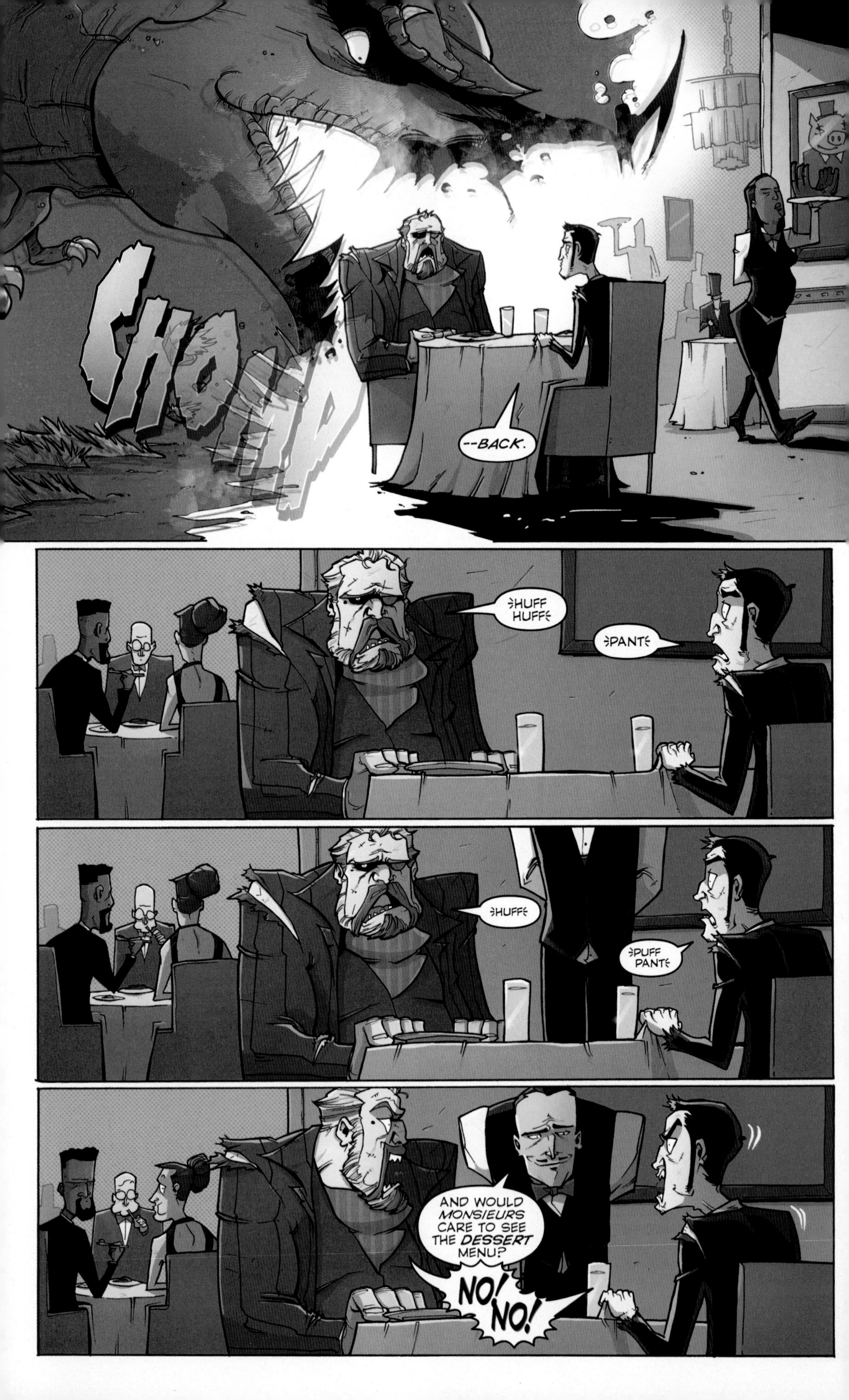
CHOMP
--BACK.
HUFF HUFF
PANT
HUFF
PUFF PANT
AND WOULD MONSIEURS CARE TO SEE THE DESSERT MENU?
NO! NO!

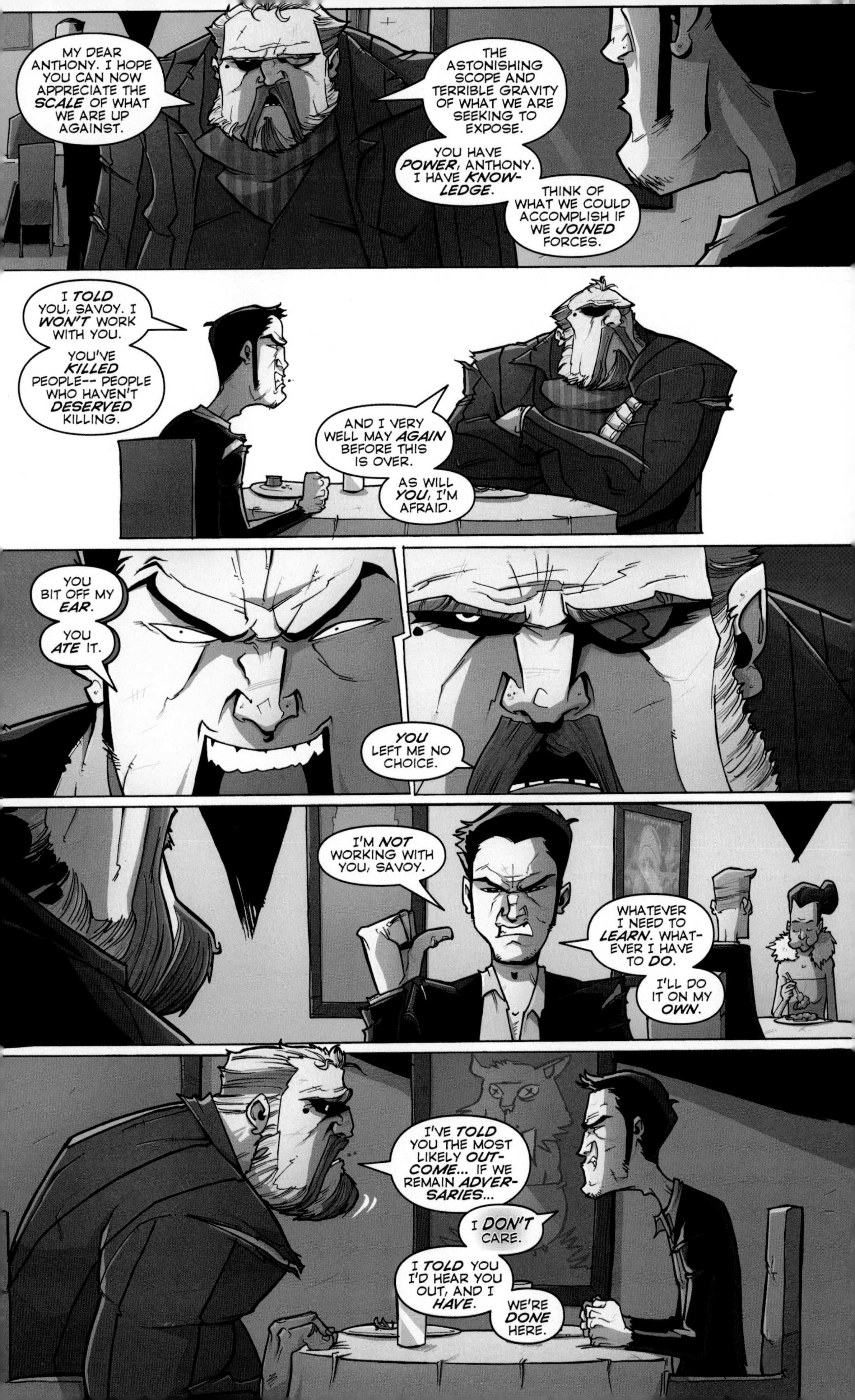

MY DEAR ANTHONY. I HOPE YOU CAN NOW APPRECIATE THE SCALE OF WHAT WE ARE UP AGAINST.
THE ASTONISHING SCOPE AND TERRIBLE GRAVITY OF WHAT WE ARE SEEKING TO EXPOSE.
YOU HAVE POWER, ANTHONY. I HAVE KNOW-LEDGE.
THINK OF WHAT WE COULD ACCOMPLISH IF WE JOINED FORCES.
I TOLD YOU, SAVOY. I WON'T WORK WITH YOU.
YOU'VE KILLED PEOPLE-- PEOPLE WHO HAVEN'T DESERVED KILLING.
AND I VERY WELL MAY AGAIN BEFORE THIS IS OVER.
AS WILL YOU, I'M AFRAID.
YOU BIT OFF MY EAR.
YOU ATE IT.
YOU LEFT ME NO CHOICE.
I'M NOT WORKING WITH YOU, SAVOY.
WHATEVER I NEED TO LEARN. WHAT-EVER I HAVE TO DO.
I'LL DO IT ON MY OWN.
I'VE TOLD YOU THE MOST LIKELY OUT-COME... IF WE REMAIN ADVER-SARIES...
I DON'T CARE.
I TOLD YOU I'D HEAR YOU OUT, AND I HAVE.
WE'RE DONE HERE.

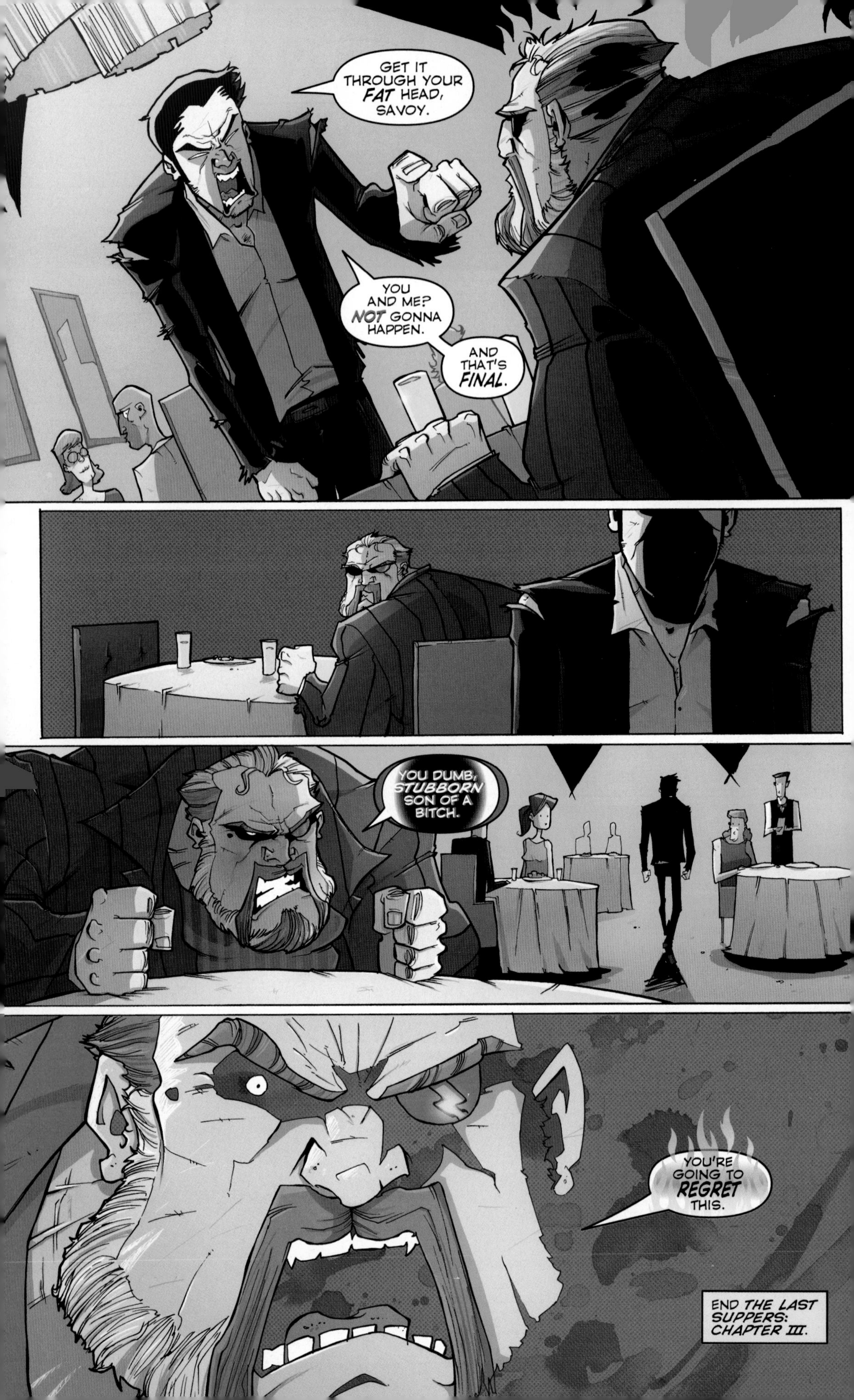
GET IT THROUGH YOUR FAT HEAD, SAVOY.
YOU AND ME? NOT GONNA HAPPEN.
AND THAT'S FINAL.
YOU DUMB, STUBBORN SON OF A BITCH.
YOU'RE GOING TO REGRET THIS.
END THE LAST SUPPERS: CHAPTER III.

Chapter 4

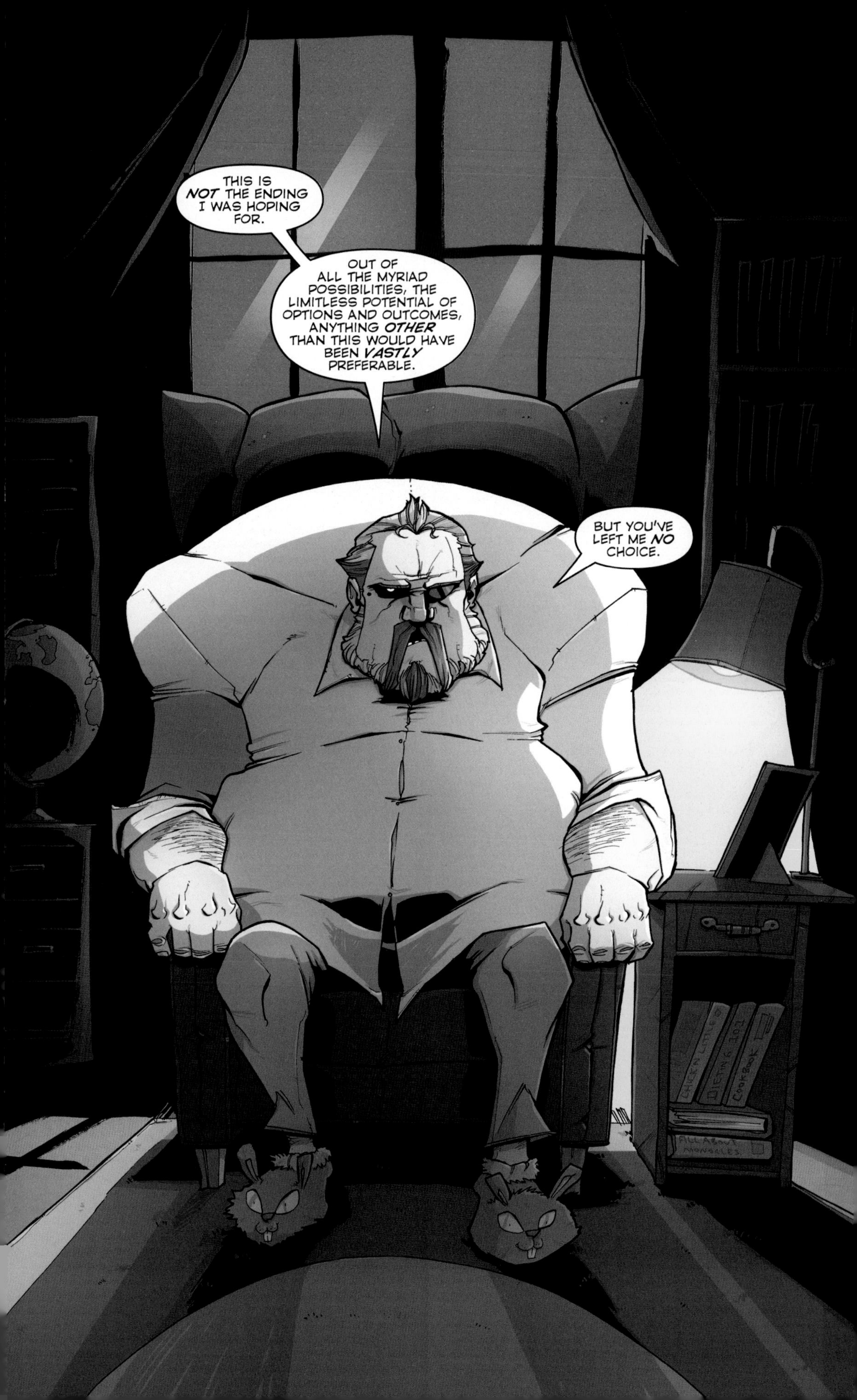
THIS IS *NOT* THE ENDING I WAS HOPING FOR.
OUT OF ALL THE MYRIAD POSSIBILITIES, THE LIMITLESS POTENTIAL OF OPTIONS AND OUTCOMES, ANYTHING *OTHER* THAN THIS WOULD HAVE BEEN *VASTLY* PREFERABLE.
BUT YOU'VE LEFT ME *NO* CHOICE.
CHICKEN LITTLE
DIETING 101
COOKBOOK

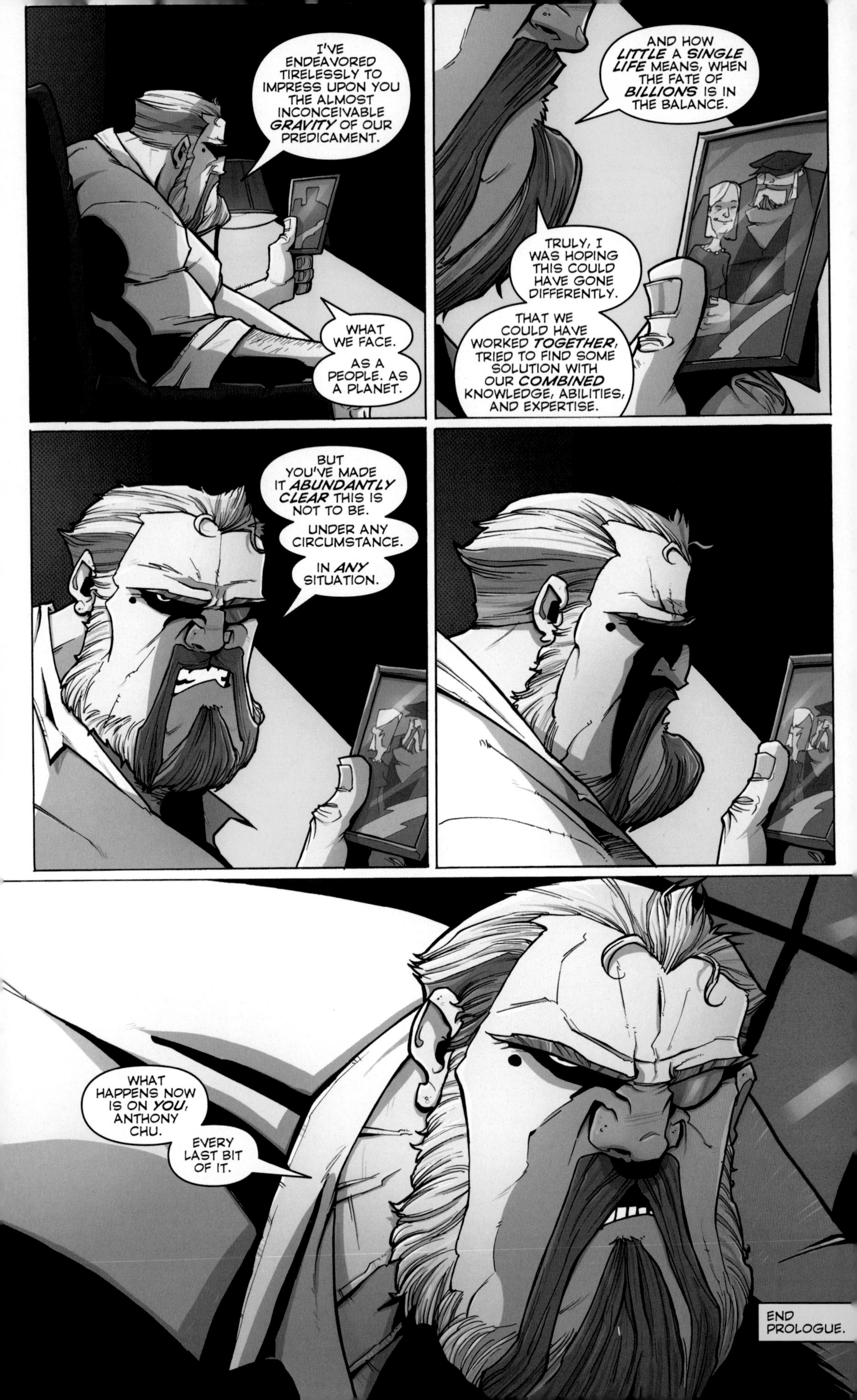
I'VE ENDEAVORED TIRELESSLY TO IMPRESS UPON YOU THE ALMOST INCONCEIVABLE GRAVITY OF OUR PREDICAMENT.
WHAT WE FACE.
AS A PEOPLE. AS A PLANET.
AND HOW LITTLE A SINGLE LIFE MEANS, WHEN THE FATE OF BILLIONS IS IN THE BALANCE.
TRULY, I WAS HOPING THIS COULD HAVE GONE DIFFERENTLY.
THAT WE COULD HAVE WORKED TOGETHER, TRIED TO FIND SOME SOLUTION WITH OUR COMBINED KNOWLEDGE, ABILITIES, AND EXPERTISE.
BUT YOU'VE MADE IT ABUNDANTLY CLEAR THIS IS NOT TO BE.
UNDER ANY CIRCUMSTANCE.
IN ANY SITUATION.
WHAT HAPPENS NOW IS ON YOU, ANTHONY CHU.
EVERY LAST BIT OF IT.
END PROLOGUE.

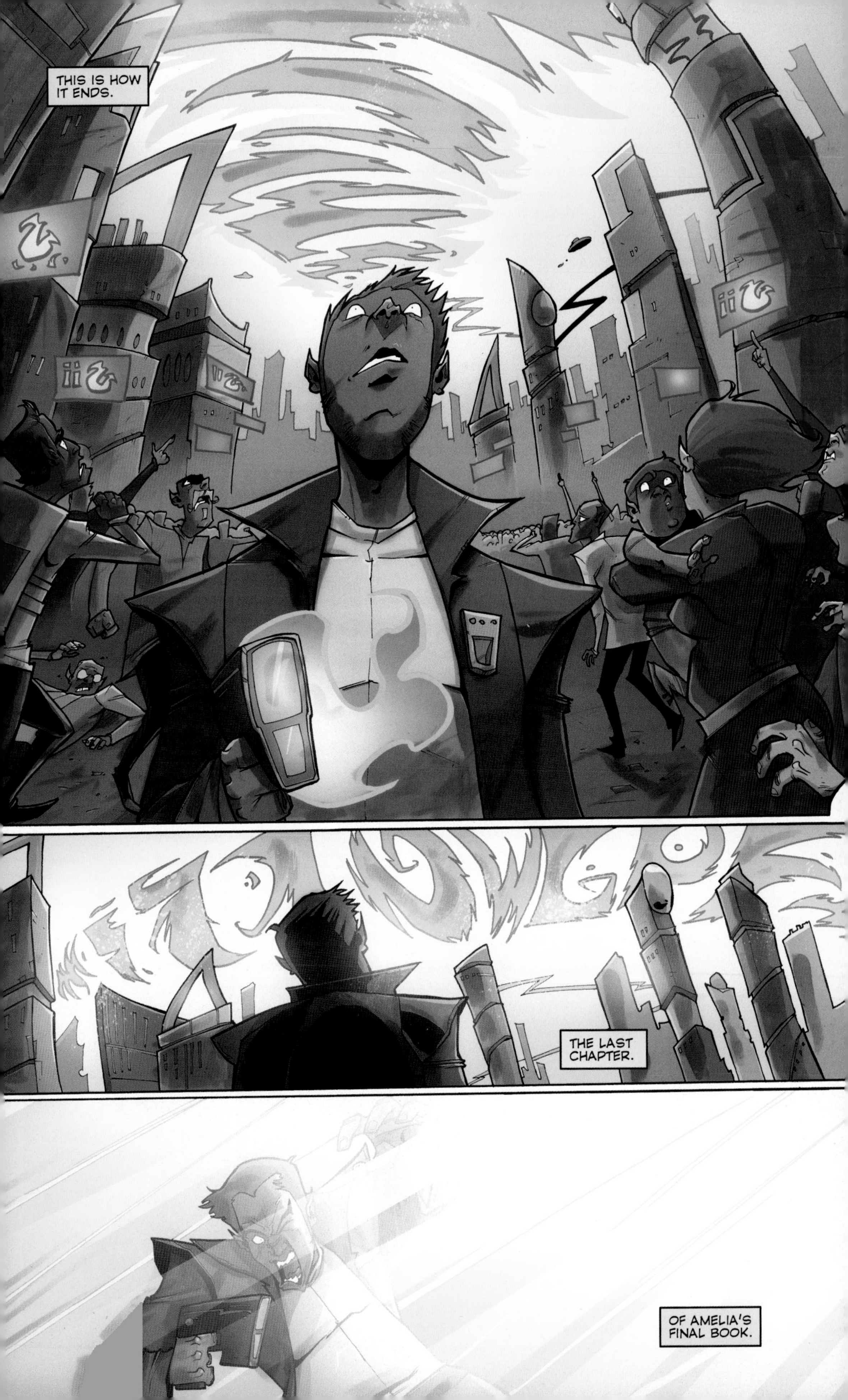
THIS IS HOW IT ENDS.
THE LAST CHAPTER.
OF AMELIA'S FINAL BOOK.

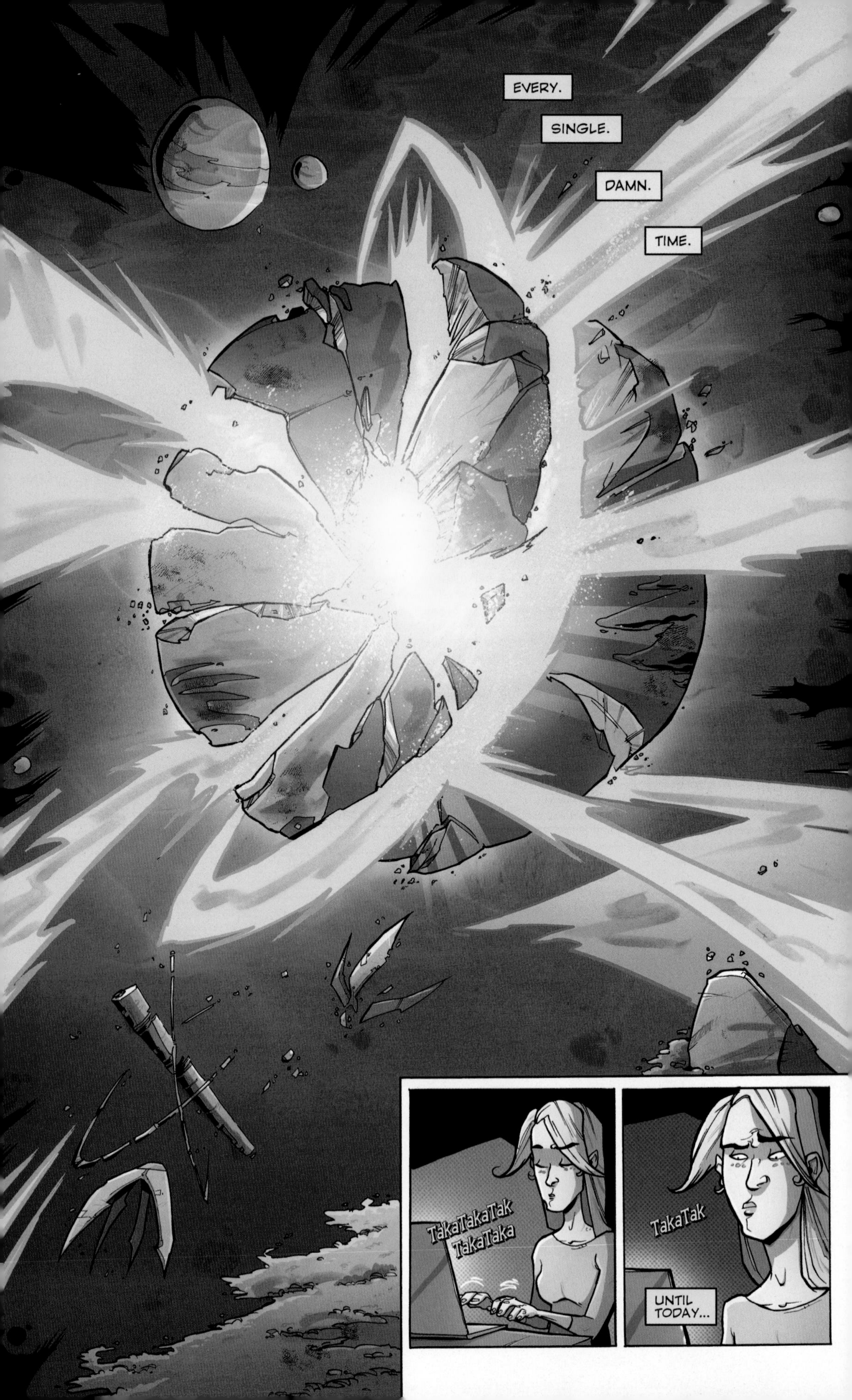
EVERY.
SINGLE.
DAMN.
TIME.
TakaTakaTak
TakaTaka
TakaTak
UNTIL TODAY...

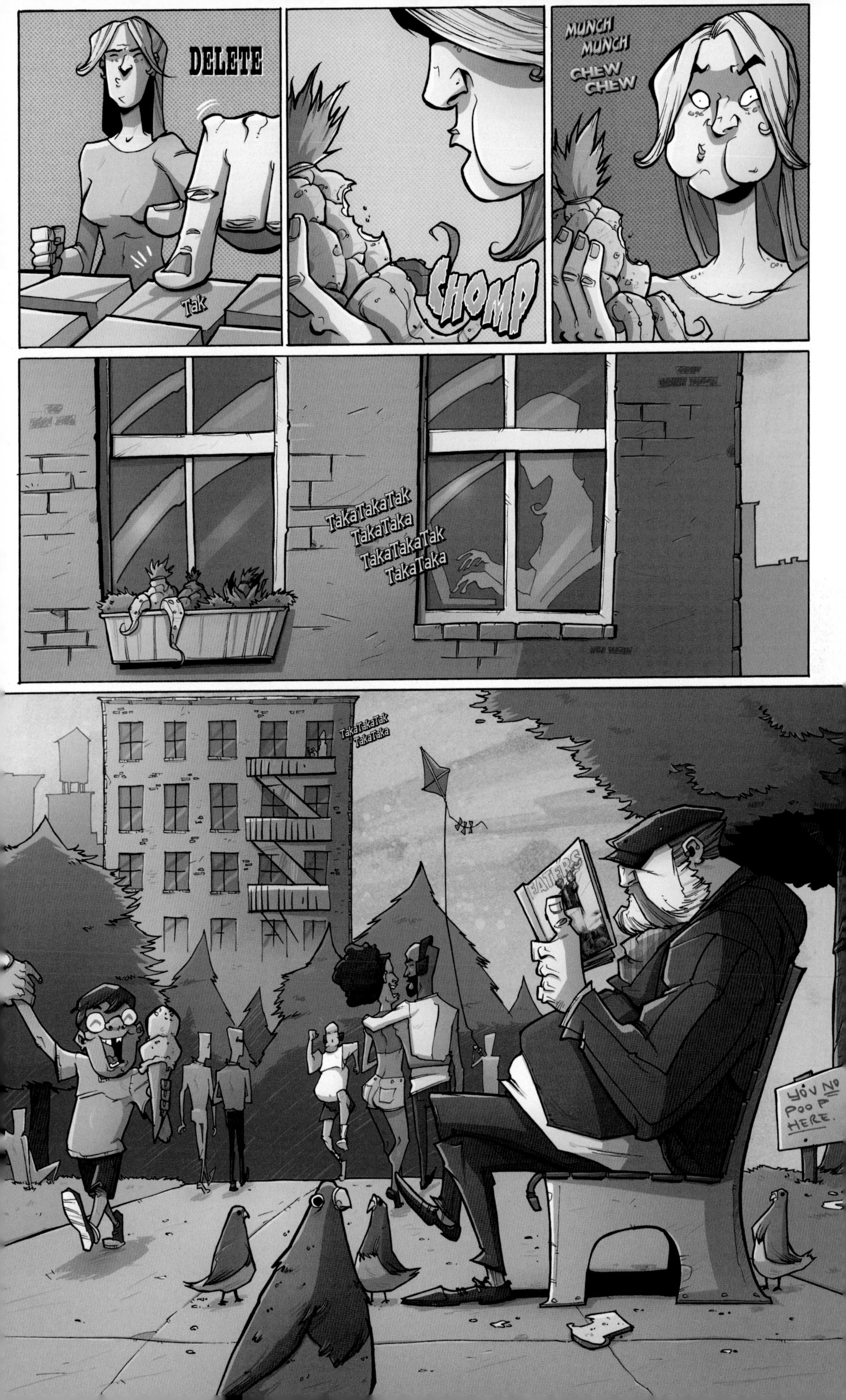
DELETE
Tak
CHOMP
MUNCH
MUNCH
CHEW
CHEW
TakaTakaTak
TakaTaka
TakaTakaTak
TakaTaka
TakaTakaTak
TakaTaka
EATERS
YOU NO POOP HERE.

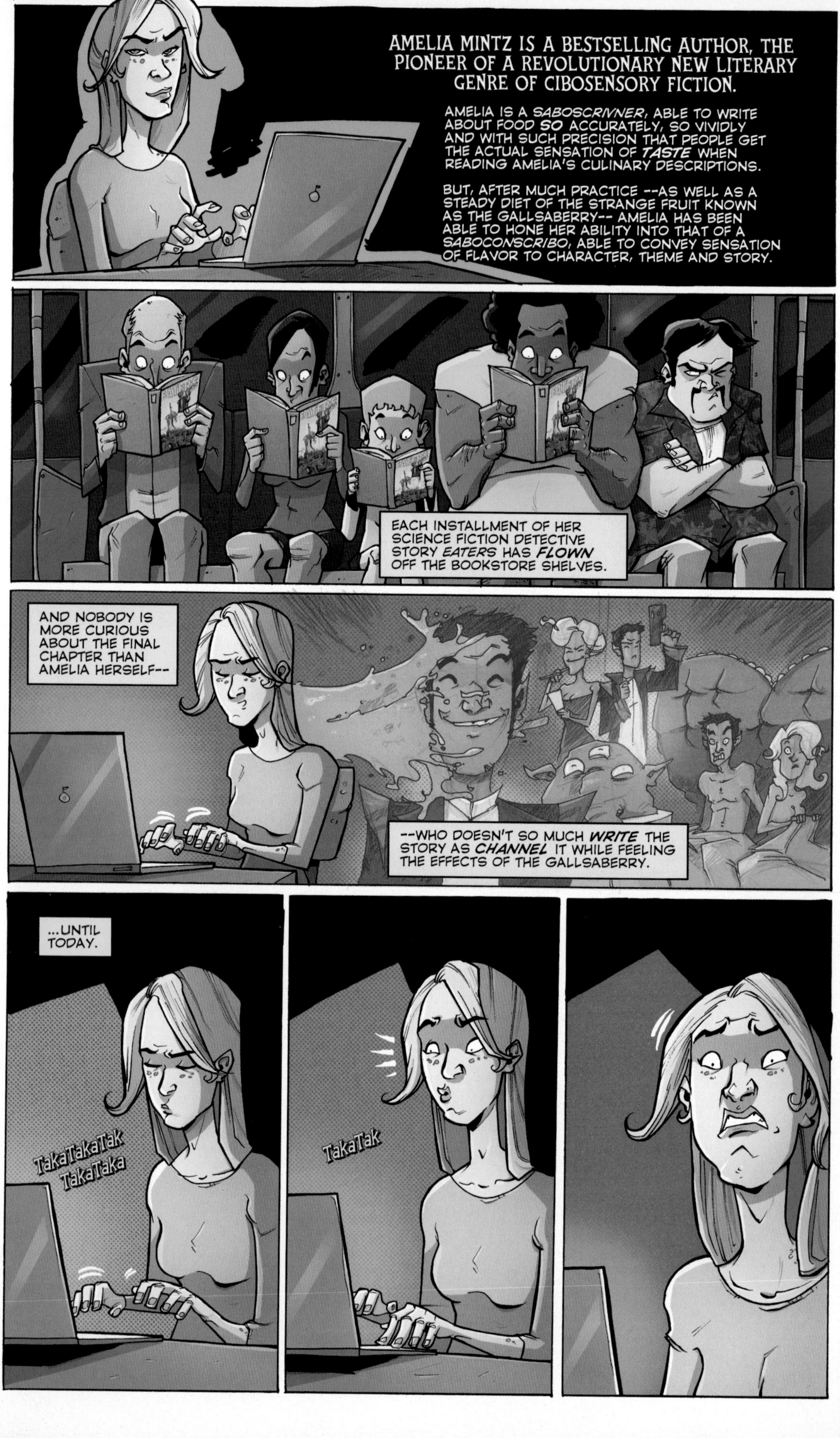
AMELIA MINTZ IS A BESTSELLING AUTHOR, THE PIONEER OF A REVOLUTIONARY NEW LITERARY GENRE OF CIBOSENSORY FICTION.
AMELIA IS A SABOSCRIVNER, ABLE TO WRITE ABOUT FOOD SO ACCURATELY, SO VIVIDLY AND WITH SUCH PRECISION THAT PEOPLE GET THE ACTUAL SENSATION OF TASTE WHEN READING AMELIA'S CULINARY DESCRIPTIONS.
BUT, AFTER MUCH PRACTICE --AS WELL AS A STEADY DIET OF THE STRANGE FRUIT KNOWN AS THE GALLSABERRY-- AMELIA HAS BEEN ABLE TO HONE HER ABILITY INTO THAT OF A SABOCONSCRIBO, ABLE TO CONVEY SENSATION OF FLAVOR TO CHARACTER, THEME AND STORY.
EACH INSTALLMENT OF HER SCIENCE FICTION DETECTIVE STORY EATERS HAS FLOWN OFF THE BOOKSTORE SHELVES.
AND NOBODY IS MORE CURIOUS ABOUT THE FINAL CHAPTER THAN AMELIA HERSELF--
--WHO DOESN'T SO MUCH WRITE THE STORY AS CHANNEL IT WHILE FEELING THE EFFECTS OF THE GALLSABERRY.
...UNTIL TODAY.
TakaTakaTak TakaTaka
TakaTak

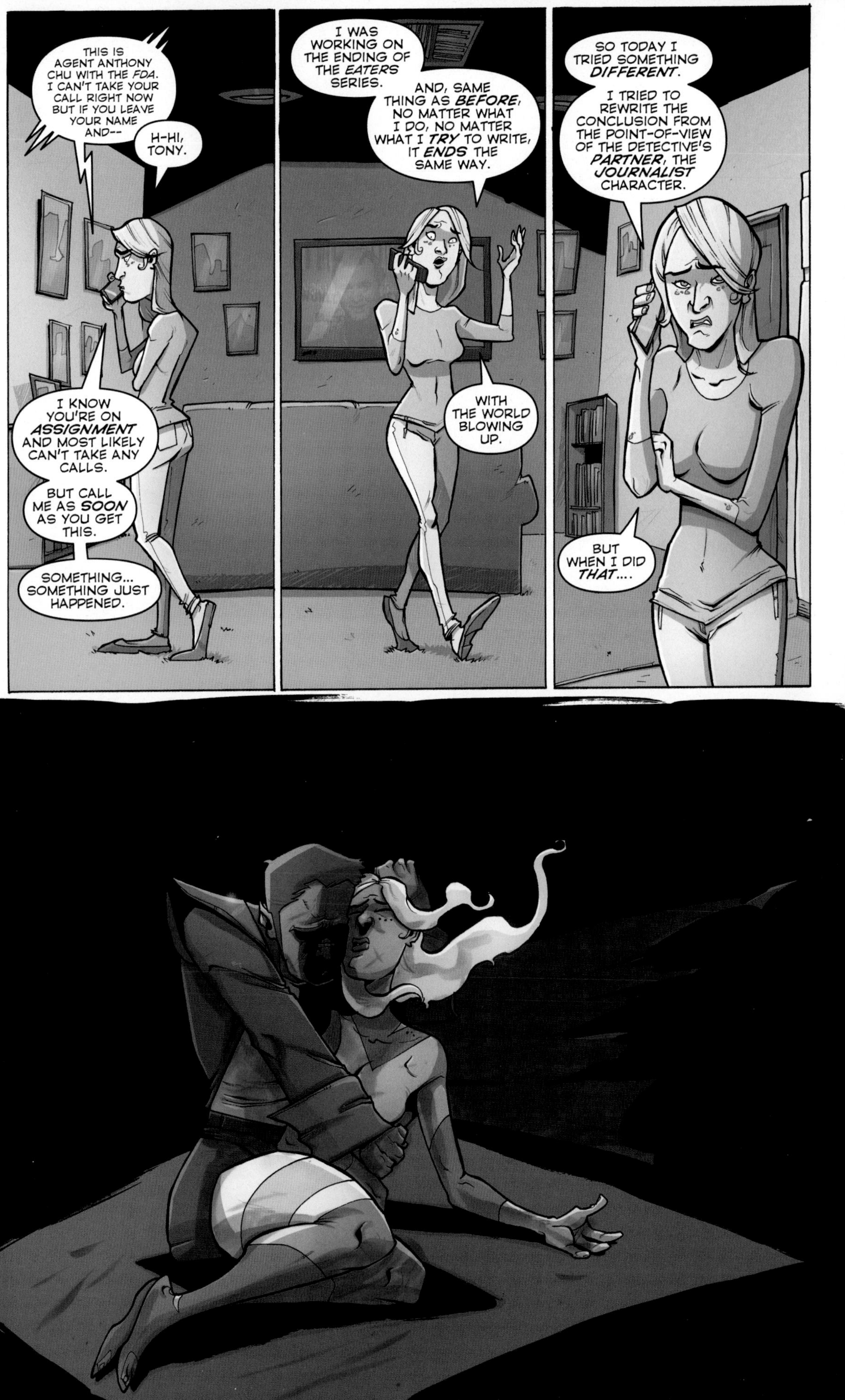
THIS IS AGENT ANTHONY CHU WITH THE FDA. I CAN'T TAKE YOUR CALL RIGHT NOW BUT IF YOU LEAVE YOUR NAME AND--
H-HI, TONY.
I KNOW YOU'RE ON ASSIGNMENT AND MOST LIKELY CAN'T TAKE ANY CALLS.
BUT CALL ME AS SOON AS YOU GET THIS.
SOMETHING... SOMETHING JUST HAPPENED.
I WAS WORKING ON THE ENDING OF THE EATERS SERIES.
AND, SAME THING AS BEFORE, NO MATTER WHAT I DO, NO MATTER WHAT I TRY TO WRITE, IT ENDS THE SAME WAY.
WITH THE WORLD BLOWING UP.
SO TODAY I TRIED SOMETHING DIFFERENT.
I TRIED TO REWRITE THE CONCLUSION FROM THE POINT-OF-VIEW OF THE DETECTIVE'S PARTNER, THE JOURNALIST CHARACTER.
BUT WHEN I DID THAT....

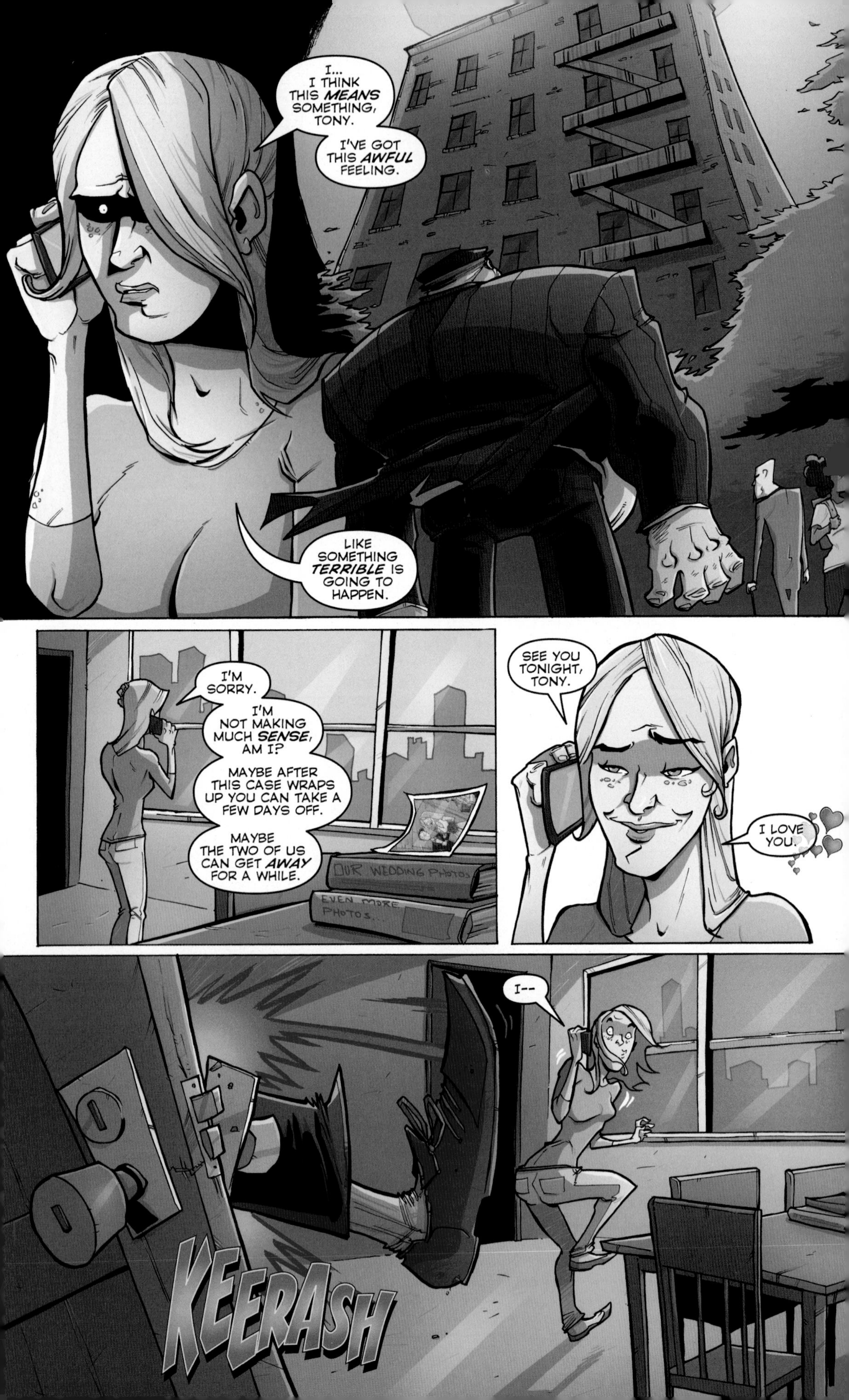
I... I THINK THIS MEANS SOMETHING, TONY.
I'VE GOT THIS AWFUL FEELING.
LIKE SOMETHING TERRIBLE IS GOING TO HAPPEN.
I'M SORRY.
I'M NOT MAKING MUCH SENSE, AM I?
MAYBE AFTER THIS CASE WRAPS UP YOU CAN TAKE A FEW DAYS OFF.
MAYBE THE TWO OF US CAN GET AWAY FOR A WHILE.
OUR WEDDING PHOTOS
EVEN MORE PHOTOS...
SEE YOU TONIGHT, TONY.
I LOVE YOU.
I--
KEERASH

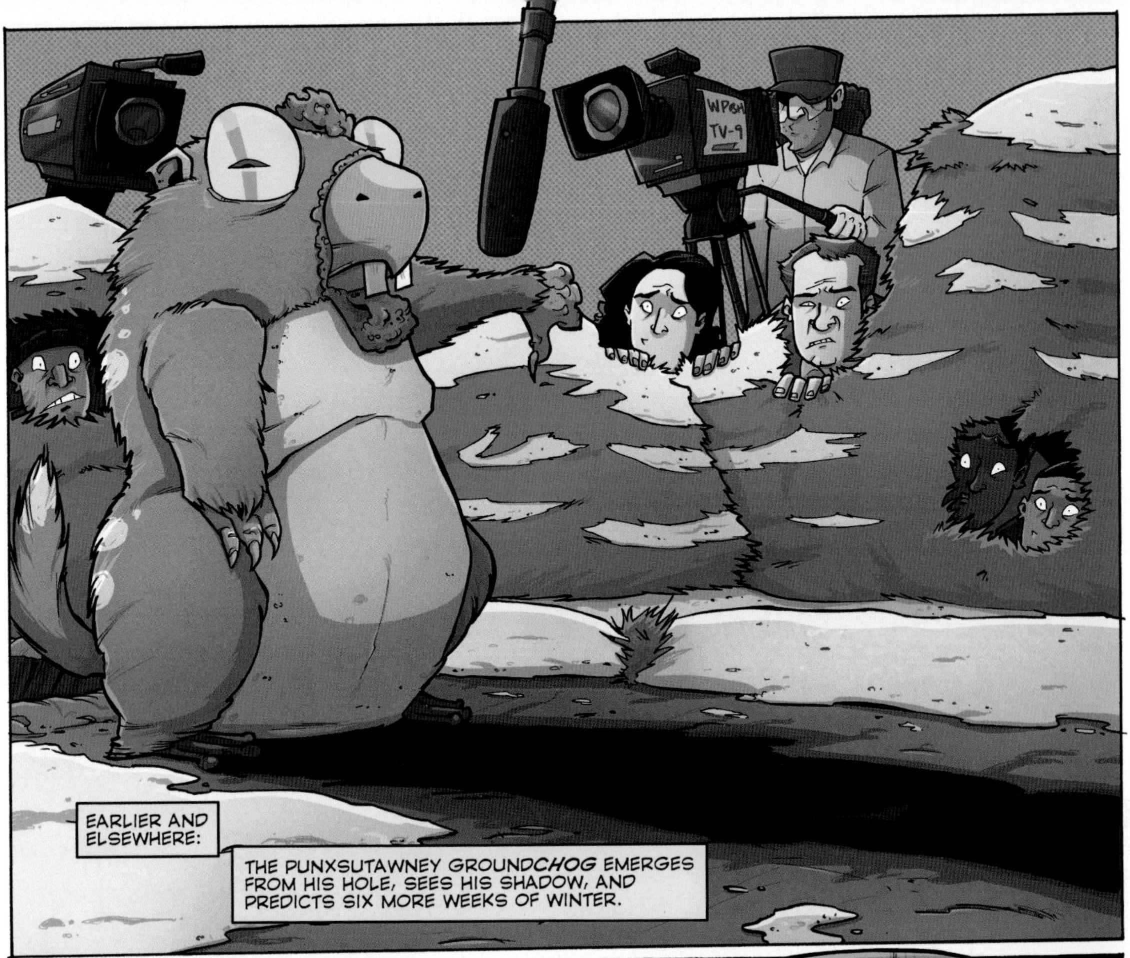
EARLIER AND ELSEWHERE:
THE PUNXSUTAWNEY GROUND*CHOG* EMERGES FROM HIS HOLE, SEES HIS SHADOW, AND PREDICTS SIX MORE WEEKS OF WINTER.

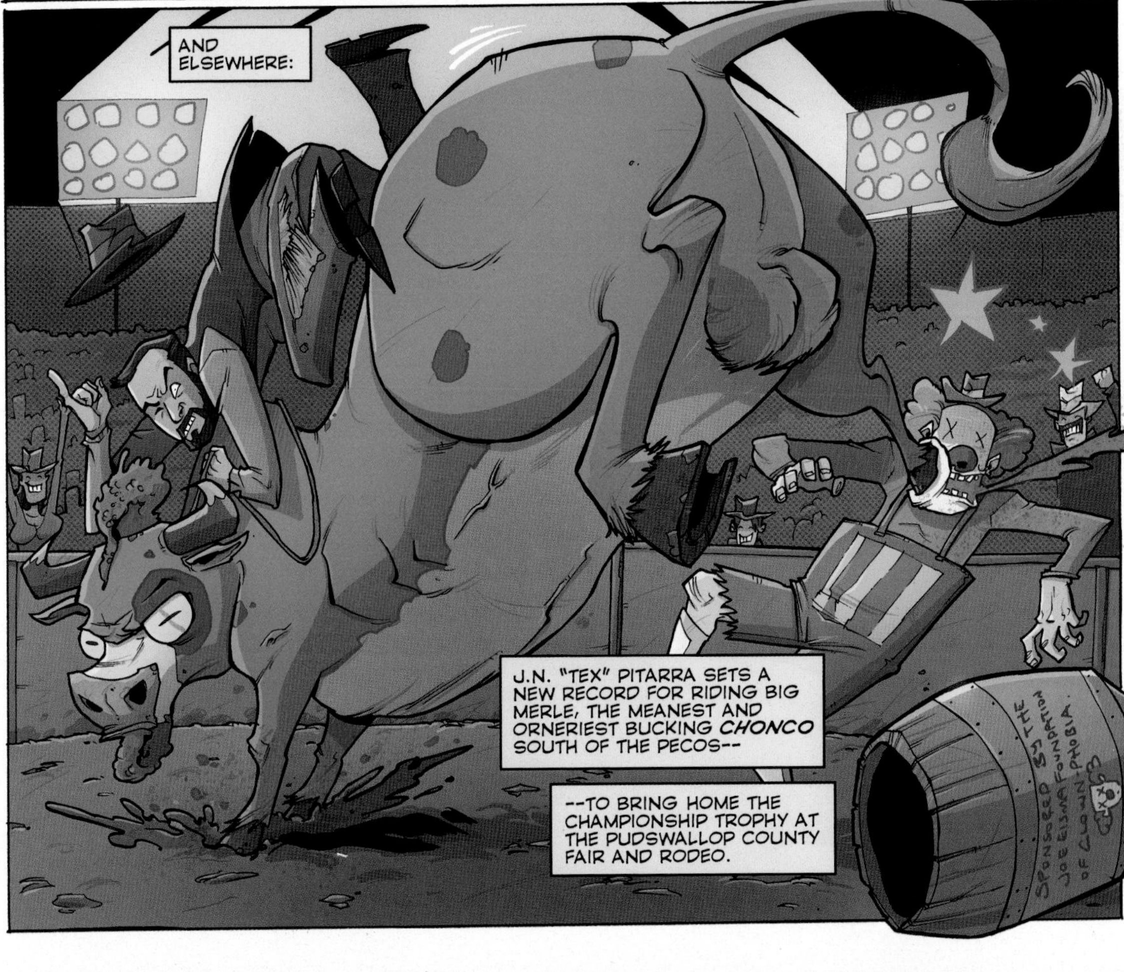
AND ELSEWHERE:
J.N. "TEX" PITARRA SETS A NEW RECORD FOR RIDING BIG MERLE, THE MEANEST AND ORNERIEST BUCKING *CHONCO* SOUTH OF THE PECOS--
--TO BRING HOME THE CHAMPIONSHIP TROPHY AT THE PUDSWALLOP COUNTY FAIR AND RODEO.
SPONSORED BY THE JOE EISMA FOUNDATION OF CLOWN-PHOBIA

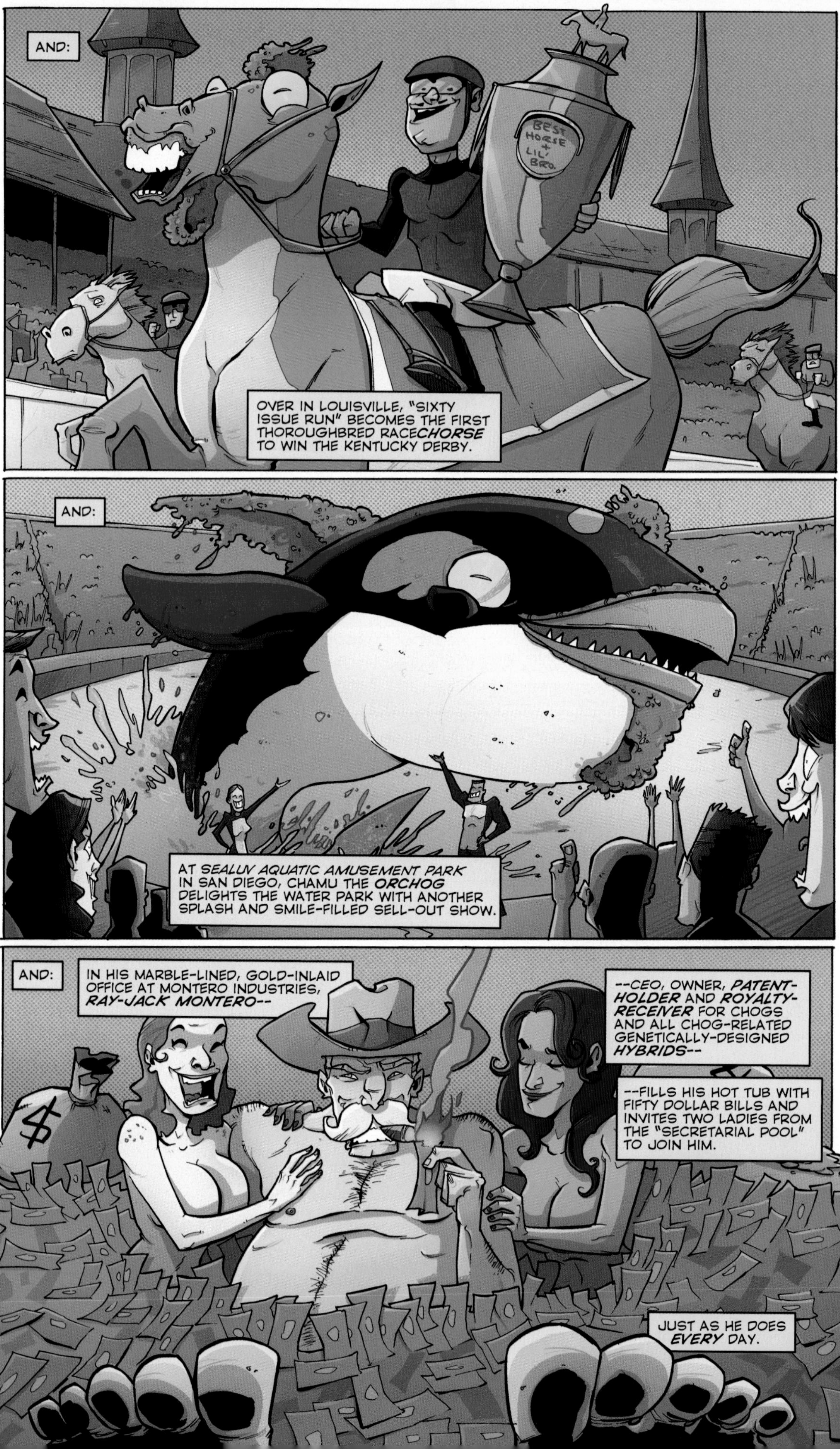
AND:
BEST HORSE + LIL' BRO.
OVER IN LOUISVILLE, "SIXTY ISSUE RUN" BECOMES THE FIRST THOROUGHBRED RACE*CHORSE* TO WIN THE KENTUCKY DERBY.
AND:
AT *SEALUV AQUATIC AMUSEMENT PARK* IN SAN DIEGO, CHAMU THE *ORCHOG* DELIGHTS THE WATER PARK WITH ANOTHER SPLASH AND SMILE-FILLED SELL-OUT SHOW.
AND:
IN HIS MARBLE-LINED, GOLD-INLAID OFFICE AT MONTERO INDUSTRIES, *RAY-JACK MONTERO*--
--CEO, OWNER, *PATENT-HOLDER* AND *ROYALTY-RECEIVER* FOR CHOGS AND ALL CHOG-RELATED GENETICALLY-DESIGNED *HYBRIDS*--
--FILLS HIS HOT TUB WITH FIFTY DOLLAR BILLS AND INVITES TWO LADIES FROM THE "SECRETARIAL POOL" TO JOIN HIM.
JUST AS HE DOES *EVERY* DAY.

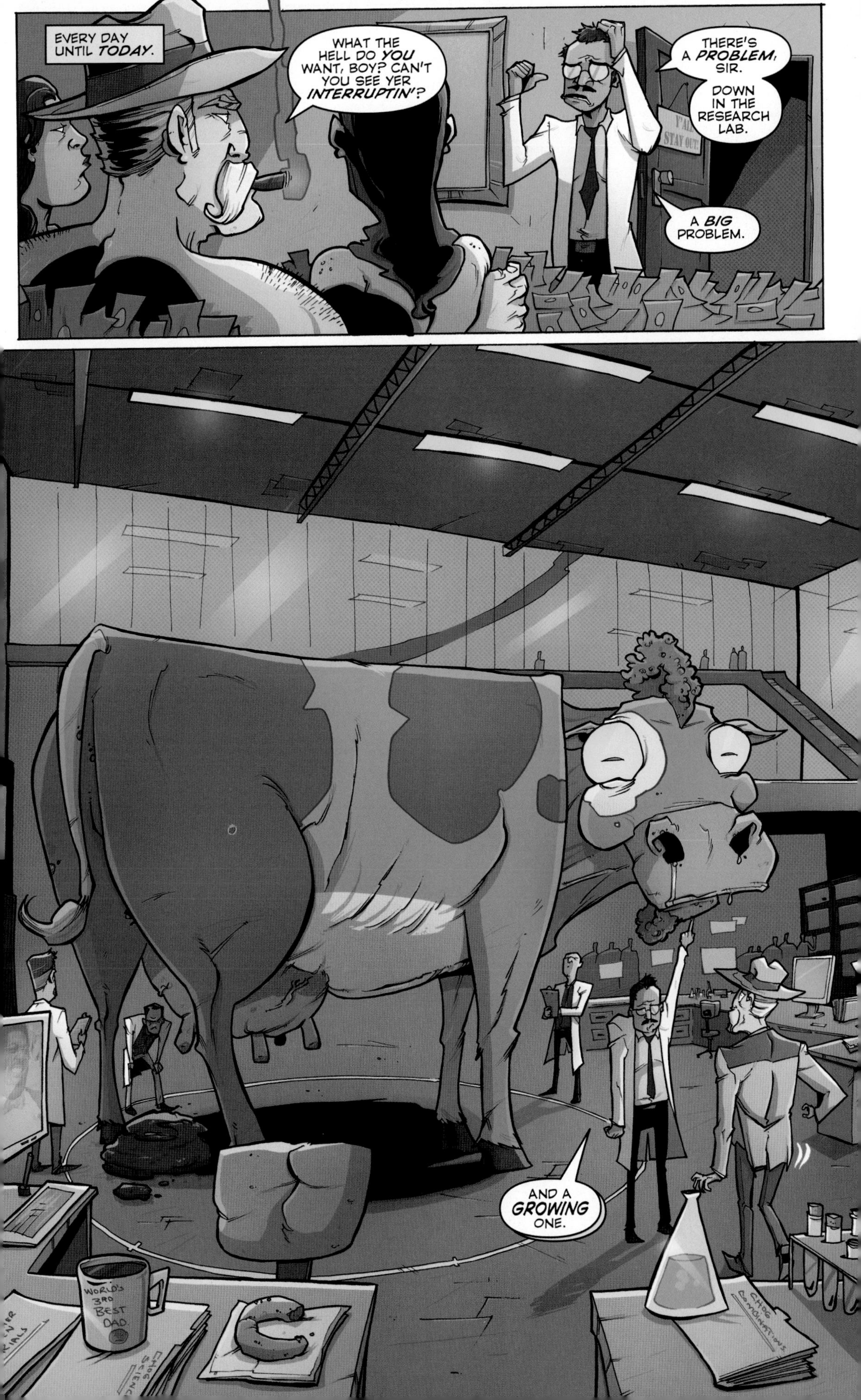
EVERY DAY UNTIL *TODAY*.
WHAT THE HELL DO *YOU* WANT, BOY? CAN'T YOU SEE YER *INTERRUPTIN'*?
THERE'S A *PROBLEM*, SIR.
DOWN IN THE RESEARCH LAB.
STAY OUT!
A *BIG* PROBLEM.
AND A *GROWING* ONE.
WORLD'S 3RD BEST DAD.
CHOG COMBINATIONS

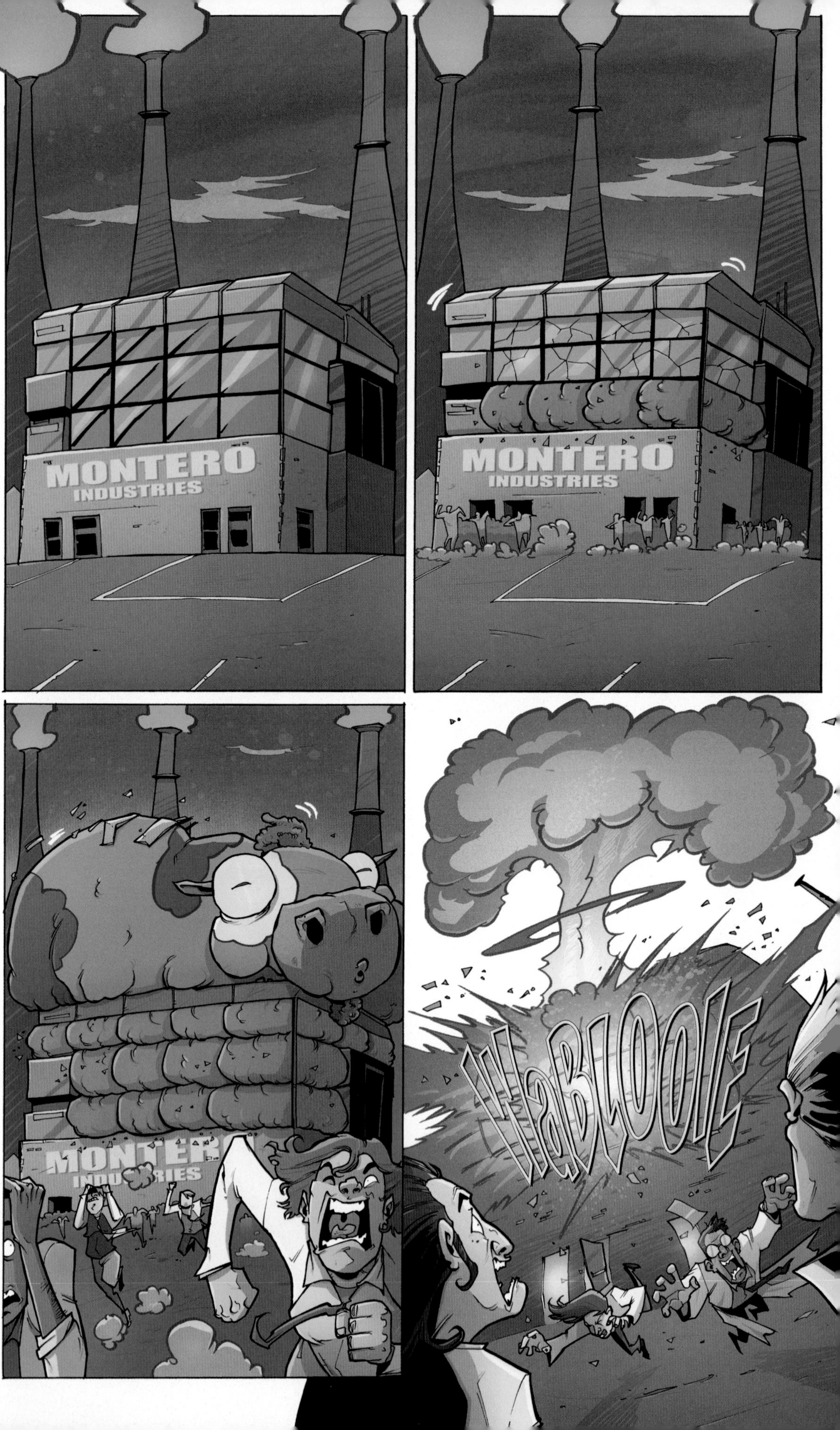
MONTERO
INDUSTRIES
MONTERO
INDUSTRIES
KaBLOOIE

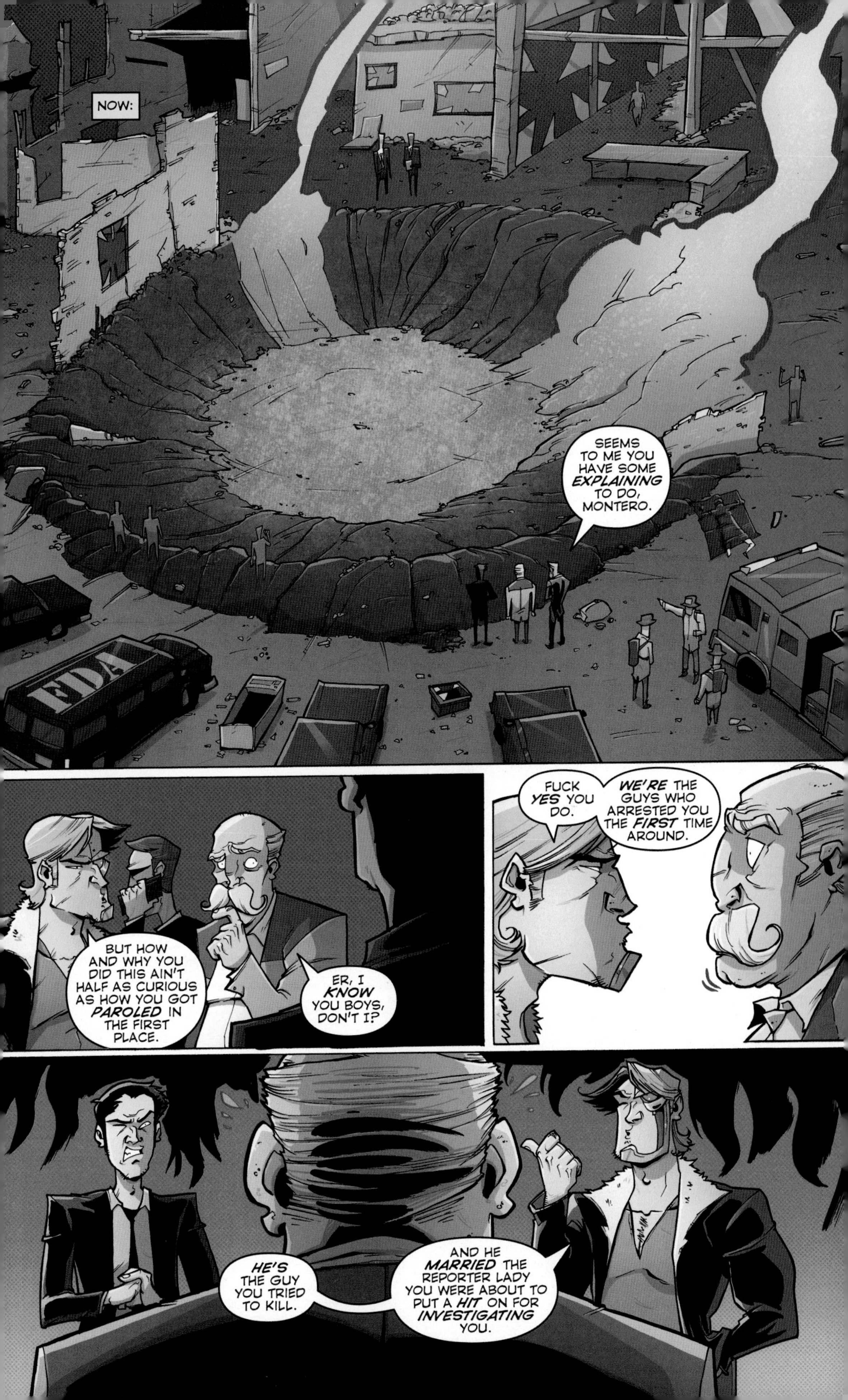
NOW:
SEEMS TO ME YOU HAVE SOME *EXPLAINING* TO DO, MONTERO.
FDA
BUT HOW AND WHY YOU DID THIS AIN'T HALF AS CURIOUS AS HOW YOU GOT *PAROLED* IN THE FIRST PLACE.
ER, I *KNOW* YOU BOYS, DON'T I?
FUCK *YES* YOU DO.
WE'RE THE GUYS WHO ARRESTED YOU THE *FIRST* TIME AROUND.
HE'S THE GUY YOU TRIED TO KILL.
AND HE *MARRIED* THE REPORTER LADY YOU WERE ABOUT TO PUT A *HIT* ON FOR *INVESTIGATING* YOU.

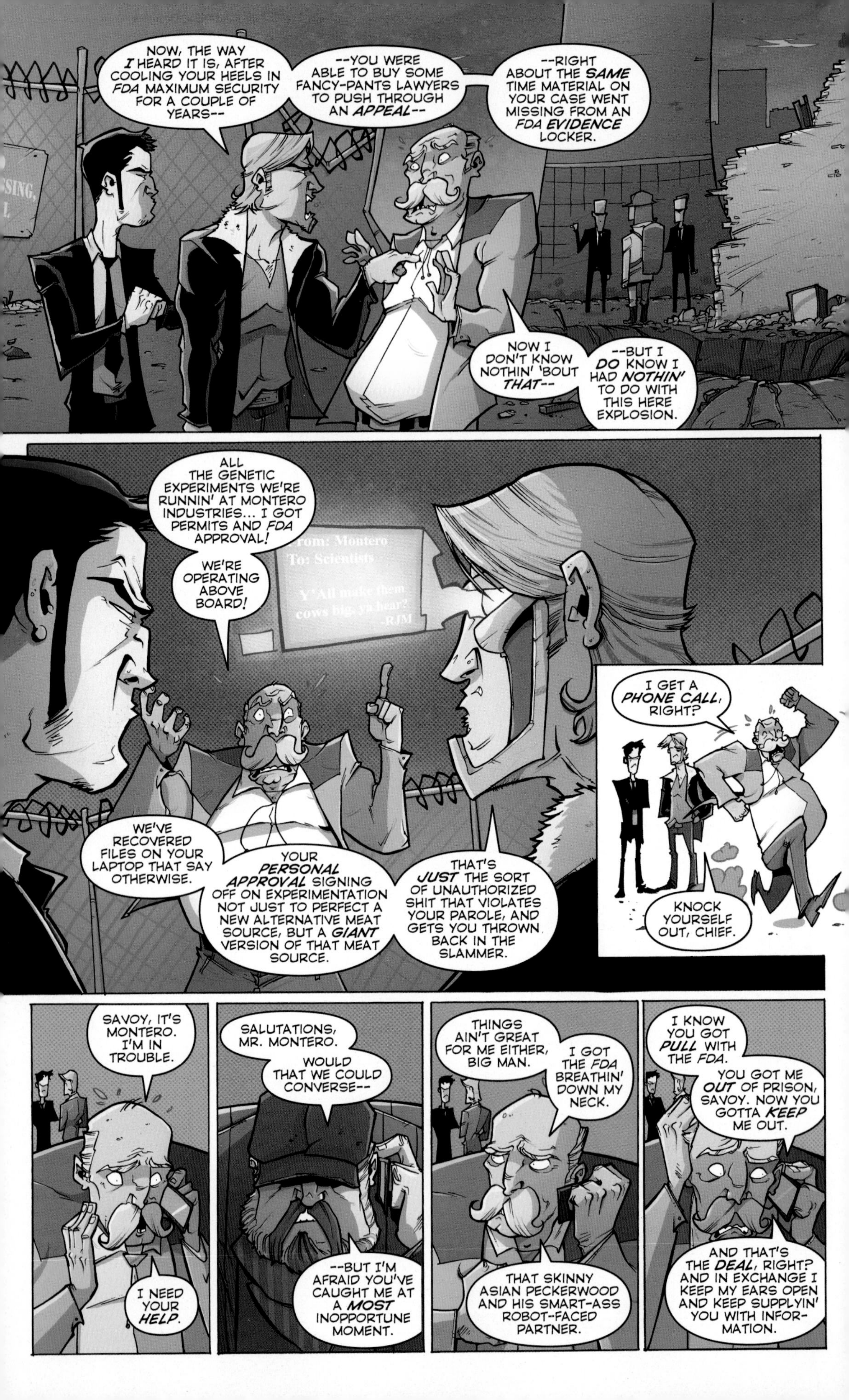
NOW, THE WAY I HEARD IT IS, AFTER COOLING YOUR HEELS IN FDA MAXIMUM SECURITY FOR A COUPLE OF YEARS--
--YOU WERE ABLE TO BUY SOME FANCY-PANTS LAWYERS TO PUSH THROUGH AN APPEAL--
--RIGHT ABOUT THE SAME TIME MATERIAL ON YOUR CASE WENT MISSING FROM AN FDA EVIDENCE LOCKER.
NOW I DON'T KNOW NOTHIN' 'BOUT THAT--
--BUT I DO KNOW I HAD NOTHIN' TO DO WITH THIS HERE EXPLOSION.
ALL THE GENETIC EXPERIMENTS WE'RE RUNNIN' AT MONTERO INDUSTRIES... I GOT PERMITS AND FDA APPROVAL!
WE'RE OPERATING ABOVE BOARD!
To: Scientists
Y'All make them cows big, ya hear?
-RJM
WE'VE RECOVERED FILES ON YOUR LAPTOP THAT SAY OTHERWISE.
YOUR PERSONAL APPROVAL SIGNING OFF ON EXPERIMENTATION NOT JUST TO PERFECT A NEW ALTERNATIVE MEAT SOURCE, BUT A GIANT VERSION OF THAT MEAT SOURCE.
THAT'S JUST THE SORT OF UNAUTHORIZED SHIT THAT VIOLATES YOUR PAROLE, AND GETS YOU THROWN BACK IN THE SLAMMER.
I GET A PHONE CALL, RIGHT?
KNOCK YOURSELF OUT, CHIEF.
SAVOY, IT'S MONTERO. I'M IN TROUBLE.
I NEED YOUR HELP.
SALUTATIONS, MR. MONTERO.
WOULD THAT WE COULD CONVERSE--
--BUT I'M AFRAID YOU'VE CAUGHT ME AT A MOST INOPPORTUNE MOMENT.
THINGS AIN'T GREAT FOR ME EITHER, BIG MAN.
I GOT THE FDA BREATHIN' DOWN MY NECK.
THAT SKINNY ASIAN PECKERWOOD AND HIS SMART-ASS ROBOT-FACED PARTNER.
I KNOW YOU GOT PULL WITH THE FDA.
YOU GOT ME OUT OF PRISON, SAVOY. NOW YOU GOTTA KEEP ME OUT.
AND THAT'S THE DEAL, RIGHT? AND IN EXCHANGE I KEEP MY EARS OPEN AND KEEP SUPPLYIN' YOU WITH INFORMATION.

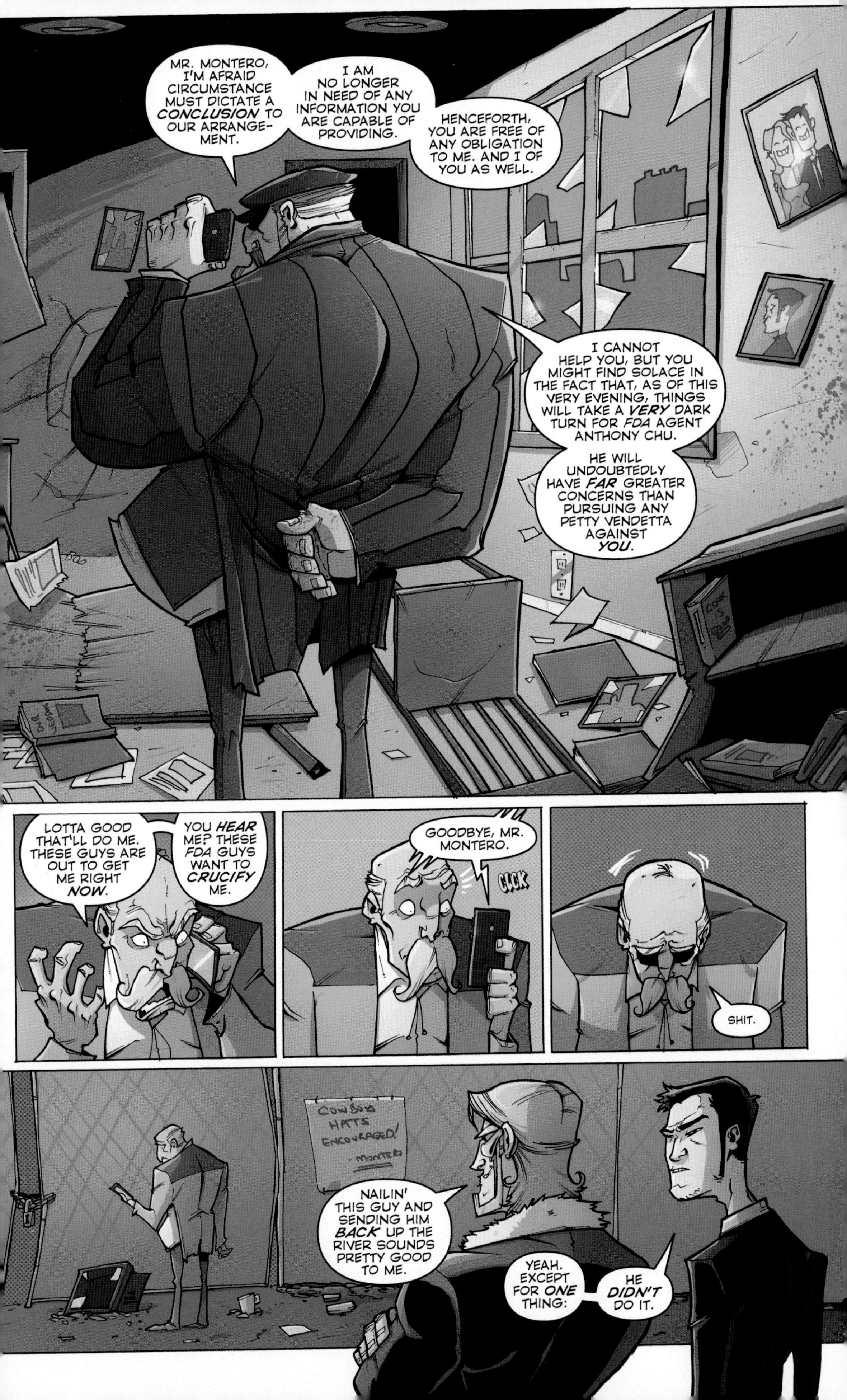
MR. MONTERO, I'M AFRAID CIRCUMSTANCE MUST DICTATE A CONCLUSION TO OUR ARRANGE-MENT.
I AM NO LONGER IN NEED OF ANY INFORMATION YOU ARE CAPABLE OF PROVIDING.
HENCEFORTH, YOU ARE FREE OF ANY OBLIGATION TO ME. AND I OF YOU AS WELL.
COOK IS GOOD
I CANNOT HELP YOU, BUT YOU MIGHT FIND SOLACE IN THE FACT THAT, AS OF THIS VERY EVENING, THINGS WILL TAKE A VERY DARK TURN FOR FDA AGENT ANTHONY CHU.
HE WILL UNDOUBTEDLY HAVE FAR GREATER CONCERNS THAN PURSUING ANY PETTY VENDETTA AGAINST YOU.
OUR WEDDING
LOTTA GOOD THAT'LL DO ME. THESE GUYS ARE OUT TO GET ME RIGHT NOW.
YOU HEAR ME? THESE FDA GUYS WANT TO CRUCIFY ME.
GOODBYE, MR. MONTERO.
CLICK
SHIT.
COWBOY HATS ENCOURAGED! -MONTERO
NAILIN' THIS GUY AND SENDING HIM BACK UP THE RIVER SOUNDS PRETTY GOOD TO ME.
YEAH. EXCEPT FOR ONE THING:
HE DIDN'T DO IT.

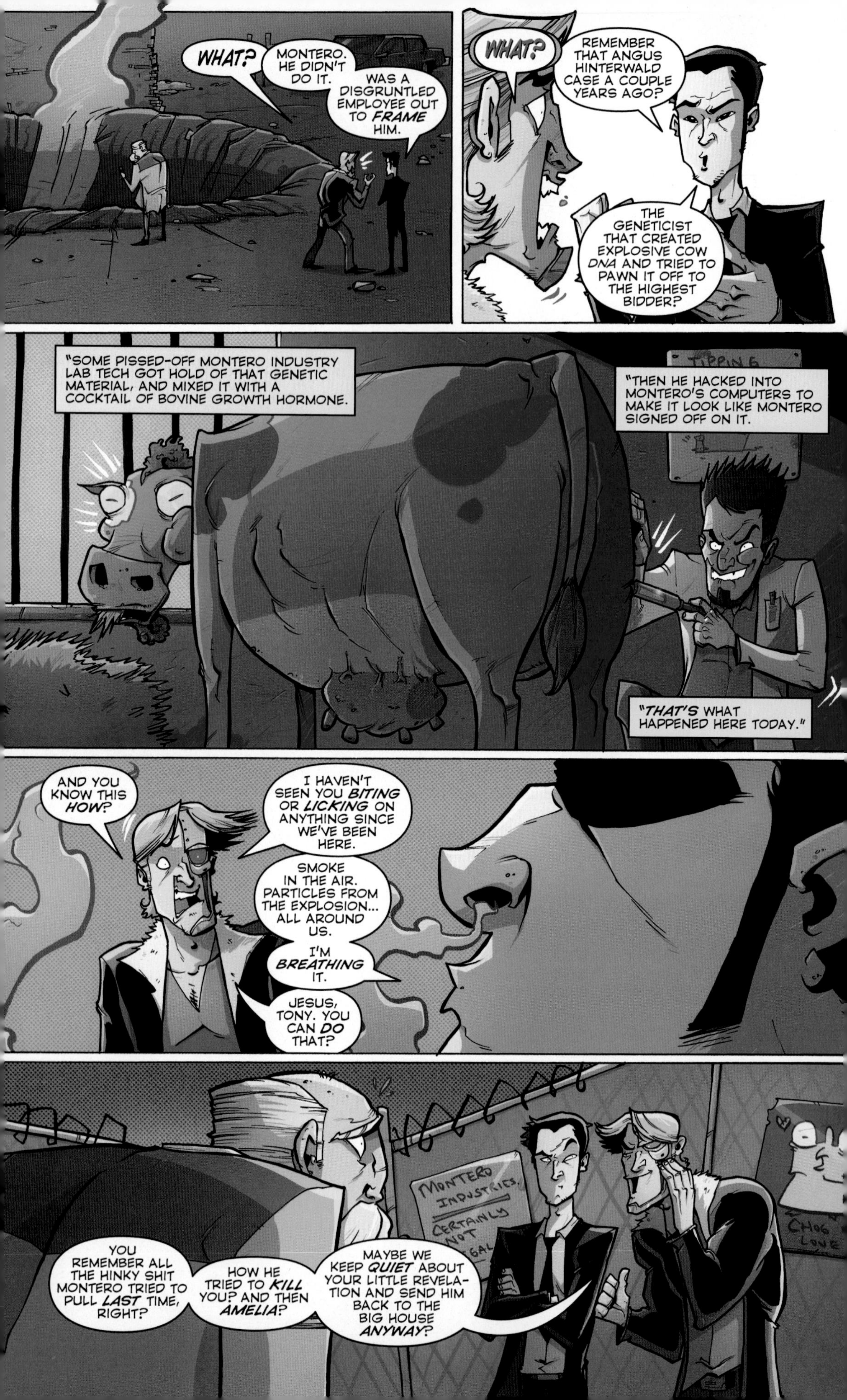
WHAT?
MONTERO. HE DIDN'T DO IT.
WAS A DISGRUNTLED EMPLOYEE OUT TO FRAME HIM.
WHAT?
REMEMBER THAT ANGUS HINTERWALD CASE A COUPLE YEARS AGO?
THE GENETICIST THAT CREATED EXPLOSIVE COW DNA AND TRIED TO PAWN IT OFF TO THE HIGHEST BIDDER?
"SOME PISSED-OFF MONTERO INDUSTRY LAB TECH GOT HOLD OF THAT GENETIC MATERIAL, AND MIXED IT WITH A COCKTAIL OF BOVINE GROWTH HORMONE.
"THEN HE HACKED INTO MONTERO'S COMPUTERS TO MAKE IT LOOK LIKE MONTERO SIGNED OFF ON IT.
TIPPING
"THAT'S WHAT HAPPENED HERE TODAY."
AND YOU KNOW THIS HOW?
I HAVEN'T SEEN YOU BITING OR LICKING ON ANYTHING SINCE WE'VE BEEN HERE.
SMOKE IN THE AIR. PARTICLES FROM THE EXPLOSION... ALL AROUND US.
I'M BREATHING IT.
JESUS, TONY. YOU CAN DO THAT?
MONTERO INDUSTRIES CERTAINLY NOT
CHOG LOVE
YOU REMEMBER ALL THE HINKY SHIT MONTERO TRIED TO PULL LAST TIME, RIGHT?
HOW HE TRIED TO KILL YOU? AND THEN AMELIA?
MAYBE WE KEEP QUIET ABOUT YOUR LITTLE REVELATION AND SEND HIM BACK TO THE BIG HOUSE ANYWAY?

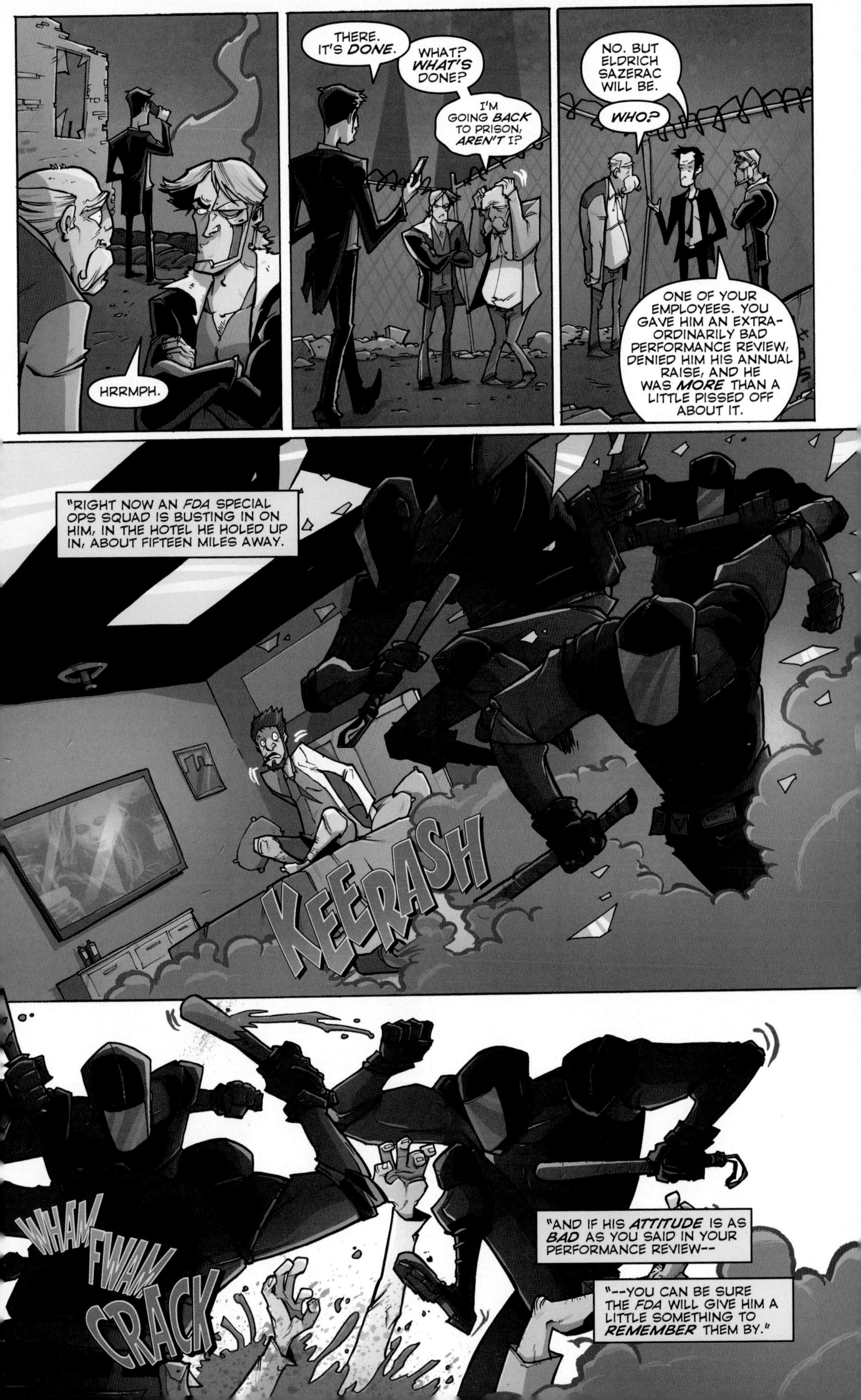
HRRMPH.
THERE. IT'S DONE.
WHAT? WHAT'S DONE?
I'M GOING BACK TO PRISON, AREN'T I?
NO. BUT ELDRICH SAZERAC WILL BE.
WHO?
ONE OF YOUR EMPLOYEES. YOU GAVE HIM AN EXTRA-ORDINARILY BAD PERFORMANCE REVIEW, DENIED HIM HIS ANNUAL RAISE, AND HE WAS MORE THAN A LITTLE PISSED OFF ABOUT IT.
"RIGHT NOW AN FDA SPECIAL OPS SQUAD IS BUSTING IN ON HIM, IN THE HOTEL HE HOLED UP IN, ABOUT FIFTEEN MILES AWAY.
KEERASH
WHAM
FWAM
CRACK
"AND IF HIS ATTITUDE IS AS BAD AS YOU SAID IN YOUR PERFORMANCE REVIEW--
"--YOU CAN BE SURE THE FDA WILL GIVE HIM A LITTLE SOMETHING TO REMEMBER THEM BY."

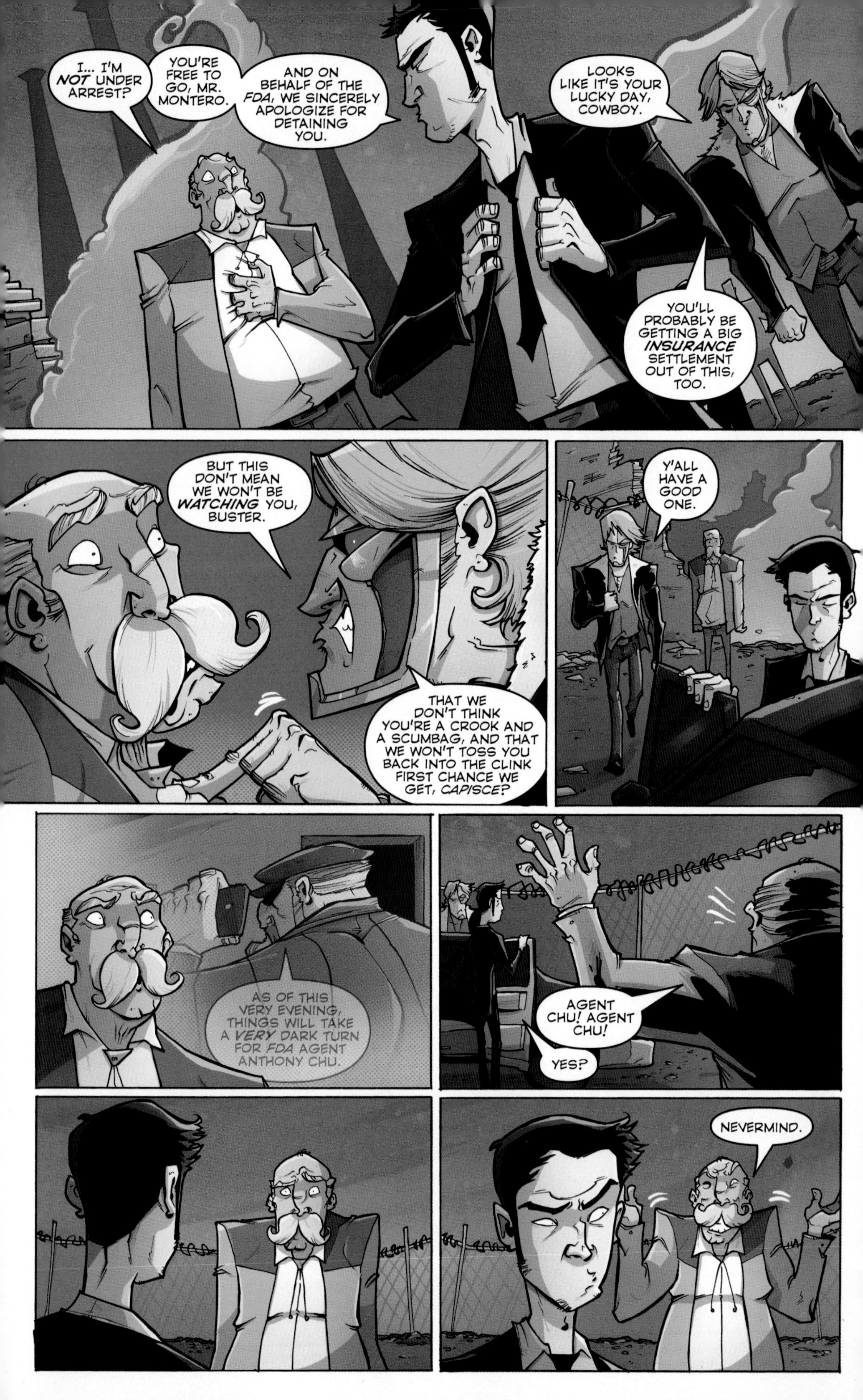
I... I'M NOT UNDER ARREST?
YOU'RE FREE TO GO, MR. MONTERO.
AND ON BEHALF OF THE FDA, WE SINCERELY APOLOGIZE FOR DETAINING YOU.
LOOKS LIKE IT'S YOUR LUCKY DAY, COWBOY.
YOU'LL PROBABLY BE GETTING A BIG INSURANCE SETTLEMENT OUT OF THIS, TOO.
BUT THIS DON'T MEAN WE WON'T BE WATCHING YOU, BUSTER.
THAT WE DON'T THINK YOU'RE A CROOK AND A SCUMBAG, AND THAT WE WON'T TOSS YOU BACK INTO THE CLINK FIRST CHANCE WE GET, CAPISCE?
Y'ALL HAVE A GOOD ONE.
AS OF THIS VERY EVENING, THINGS WILL TAKE A VERY DARK TURN FOR FDA AGENT ANTHONY CHU.
AGENT CHU! AGENT CHU!
YES?
NEVERMIND.

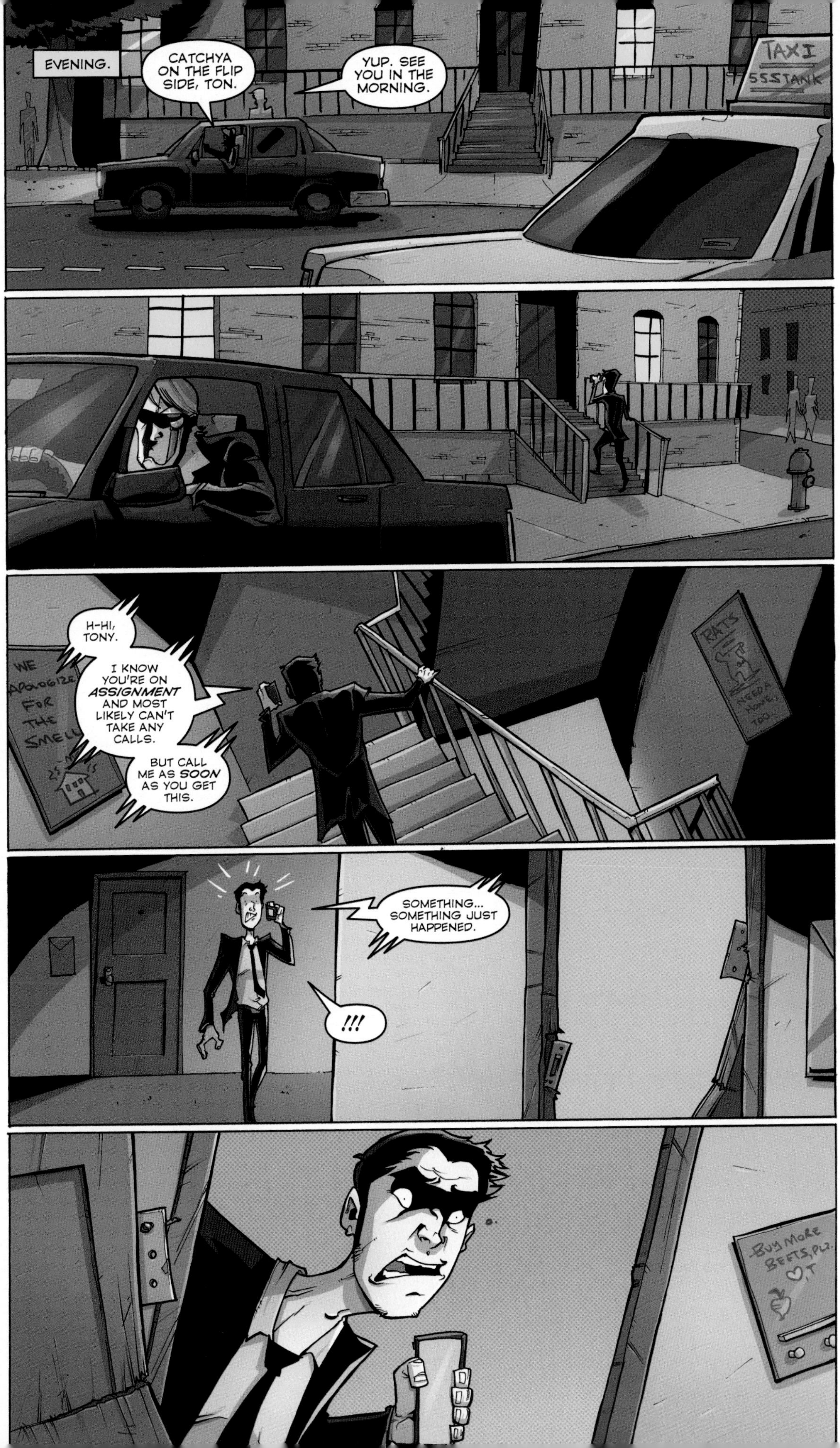
EVENING.
CATCHYA ON THE FLIP SIDE, TON.
YUP. SEE YOU IN THE MORNING.
TAXI
555STANK
WE APOLOGIZE FOR THE SMELL
RATS
NEED A HOME, TOO.
H-HI, TONY.
I KNOW YOU'RE ON *ASSIGNMENT* AND MOST LIKELY CAN'T TAKE ANY CALLS.
BUT CALL ME AS *SOON* AS YOU GET THIS.
SOMETHING... SOMETHING JUST HAPPENED.
!!!
BUY MORE BEETS, PLZ.
♡, T

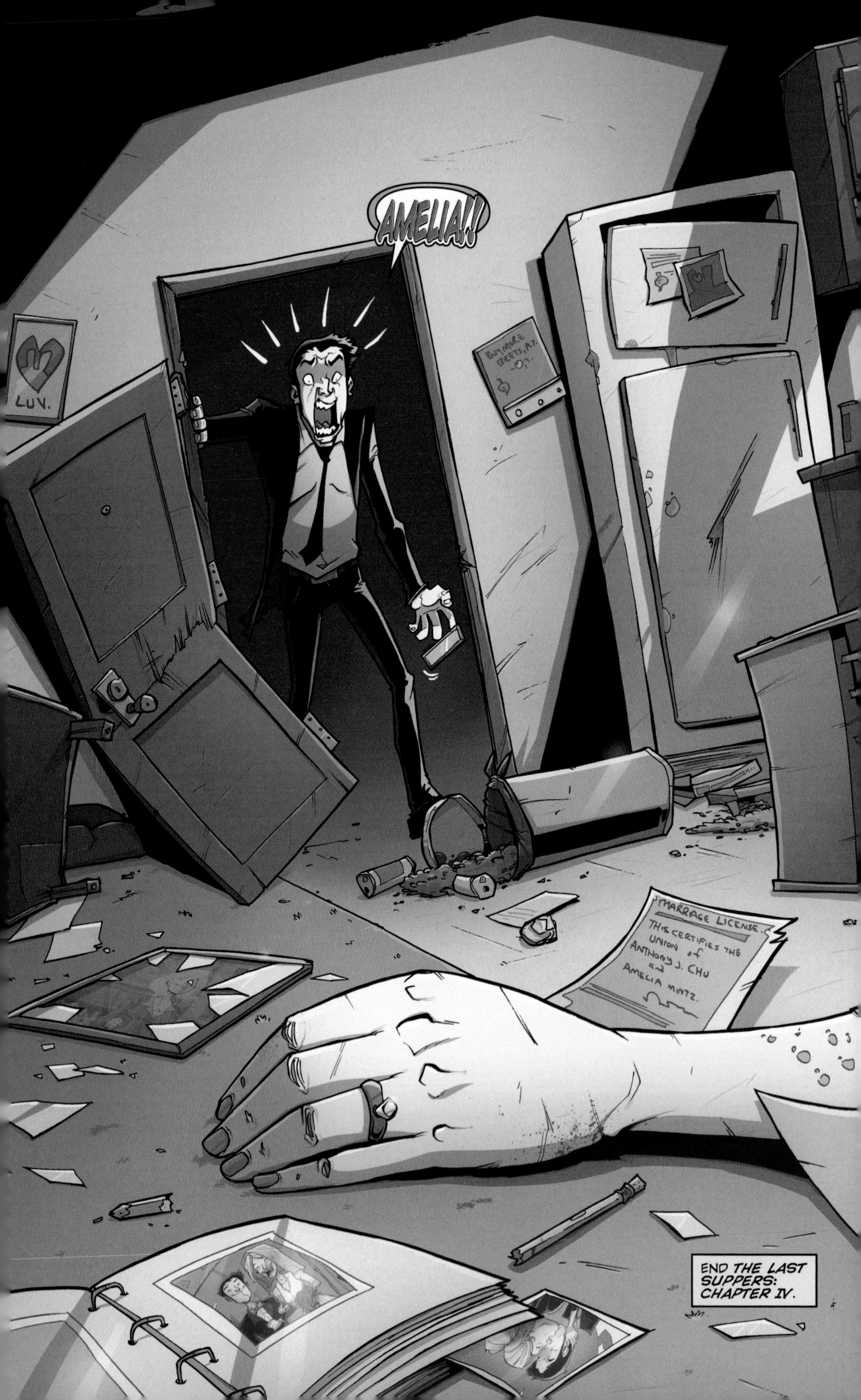
AMELIA!!
LUV.
BUY MORE BEETS,
MARRIAGE LICENSE.
THIS CERTIFIES THE UNION of ANTHONY J. CHU and AMELIA MINTZ.
END THE LAST SUPPERS: CHAPTER IV.

Chapter 5

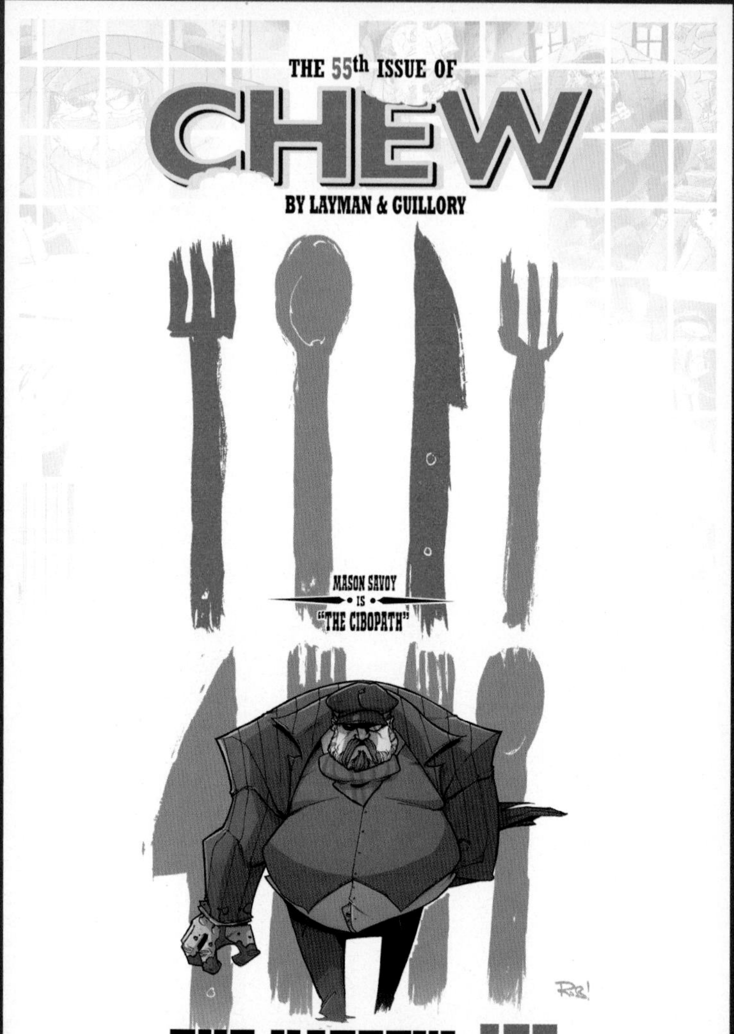

THE 55th ISSUE OF

CHEW

BY LAYMAN & GUILLORY

MASON SAVOY
IS
"THE CIBOPATH"

THE HATEFUL ATE

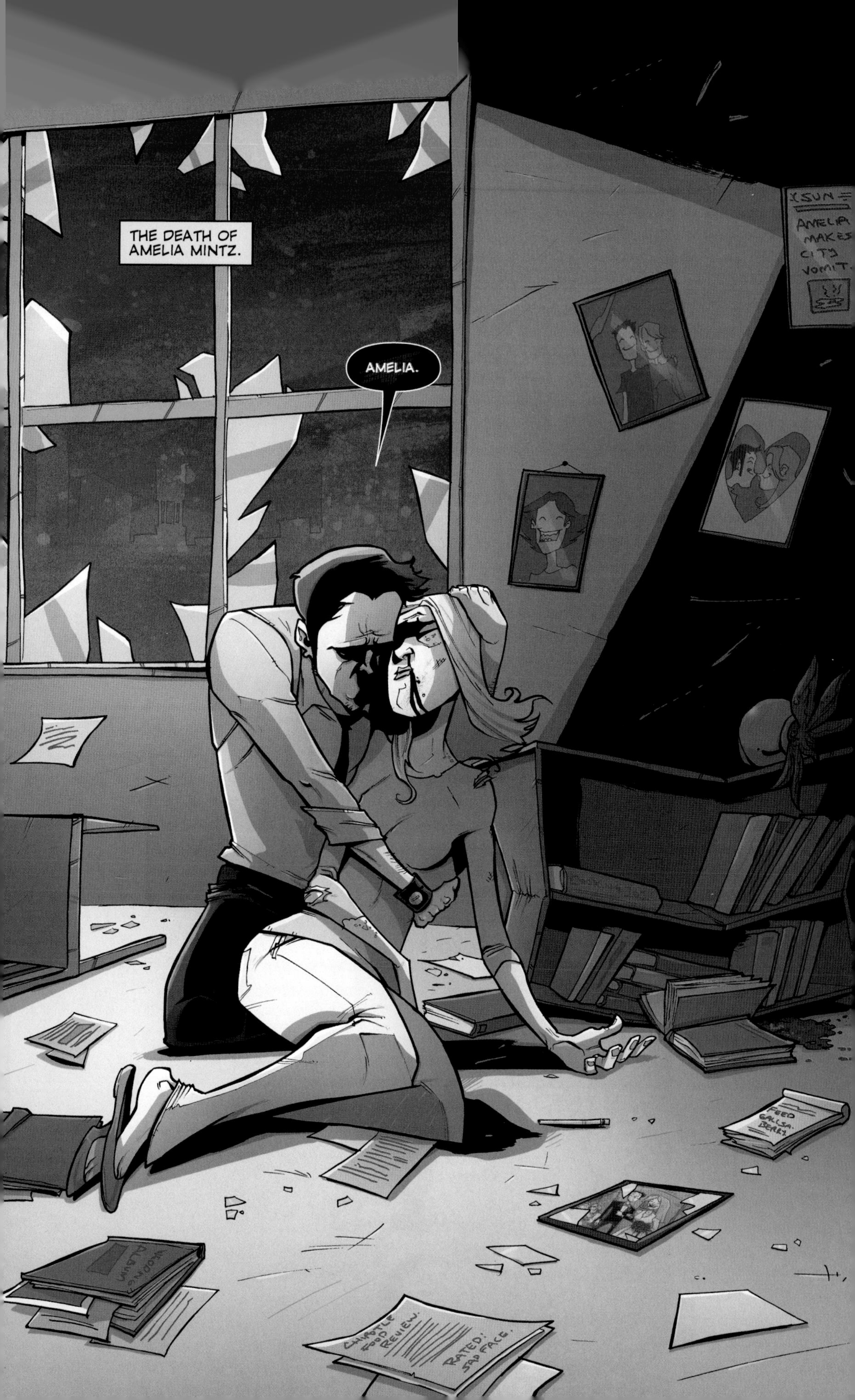
THE DEATH OF AMELIA MINTZ.
AMELIA.
SUN
AMELIA MAKES CITY VOMIT.
FEED GALLSA. BERRY
WEDDING ALBUM
CHIPOTLE FOOD REVIEW.
RATED: SAD FACE.

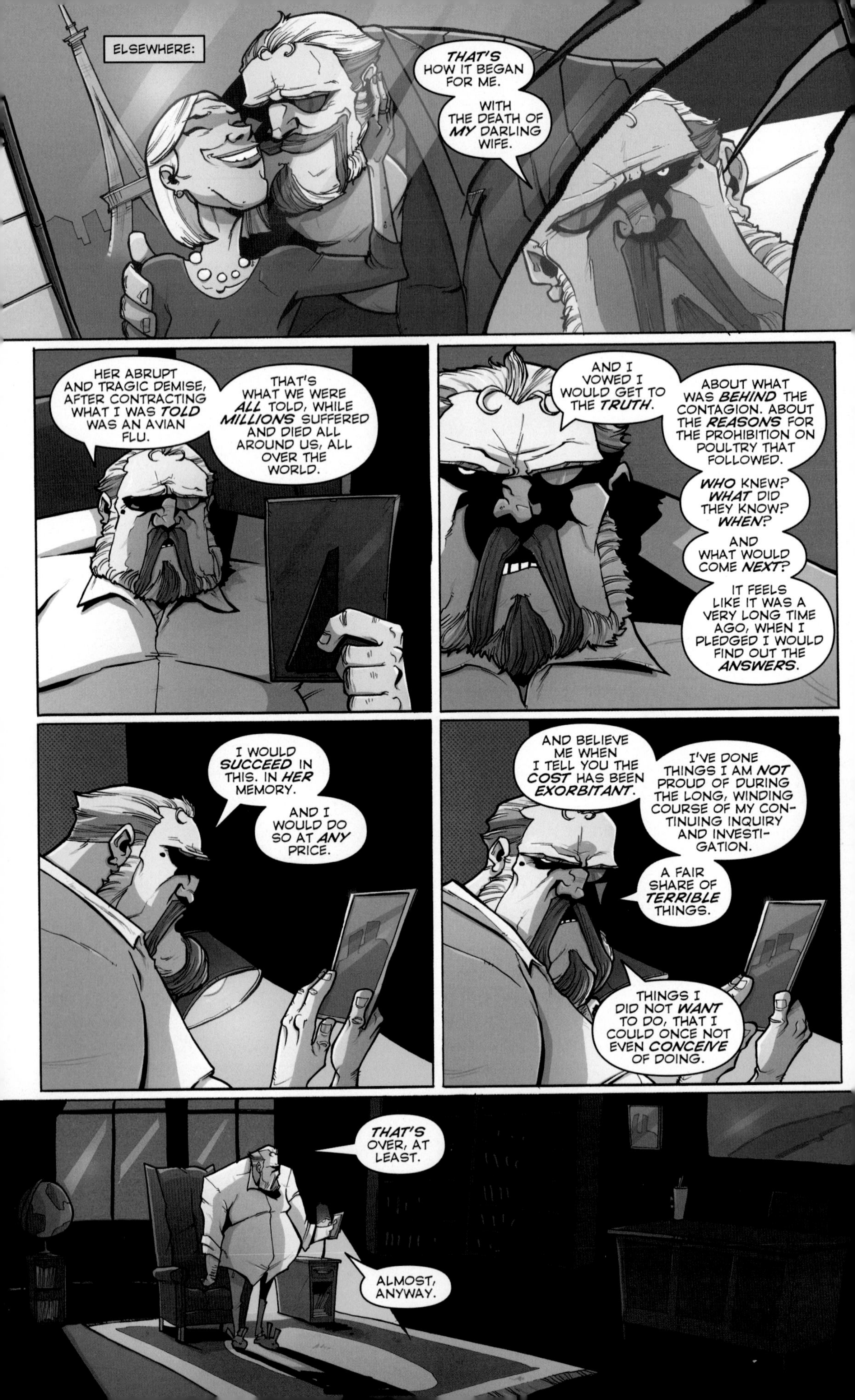
ELSEWHERE:
THAT'S HOW IT BEGAN FOR ME.
WITH THE DEATH OF MY DARLING WIFE.
HER ABRUPT AND TRAGIC DEMISE, AFTER CONTRACTING WHAT I WAS TOLD WAS AN AVIAN FLU.
THAT'S WHAT WE WERE ALL TOLD, WHILE MILLIONS SUFFERED AND DIED ALL AROUND US, ALL OVER THE WORLD.
AND I VOWED I WOULD GET TO THE TRUTH.
ABOUT WHAT WAS BEHIND THE CONTAGION. ABOUT THE REASONS FOR THE PROHIBITION ON POULTRY THAT FOLLOWED.
WHO KNEW? WHAT DID THEY KNOW? WHEN?
AND WHAT WOULD COME NEXT?
IT FEELS LIKE IT WAS A VERY LONG TIME AGO, WHEN I PLEDGED I WOULD FIND OUT THE ANSWERS.
I WOULD SUCCEED IN THIS. IN HER MEMORY.
AND I WOULD DO SO AT ANY PRICE.
AND BELIEVE ME WHEN I TELL YOU THE COST HAS BEEN EXORBITANT.
I'VE DONE THINGS I AM NOT PROUD OF DURING THE LONG, WINDING COURSE OF MY CONTINUING INQUIRY AND INVESTIGATION.
A FAIR SHARE OF TERRIBLE THINGS.
THINGS I DID NOT WANT TO DO, THAT I COULD ONCE NOT EVEN CONCEIVE OF DOING.
THAT'S OVER, AT LEAST.
ALMOST, ANYWAY.

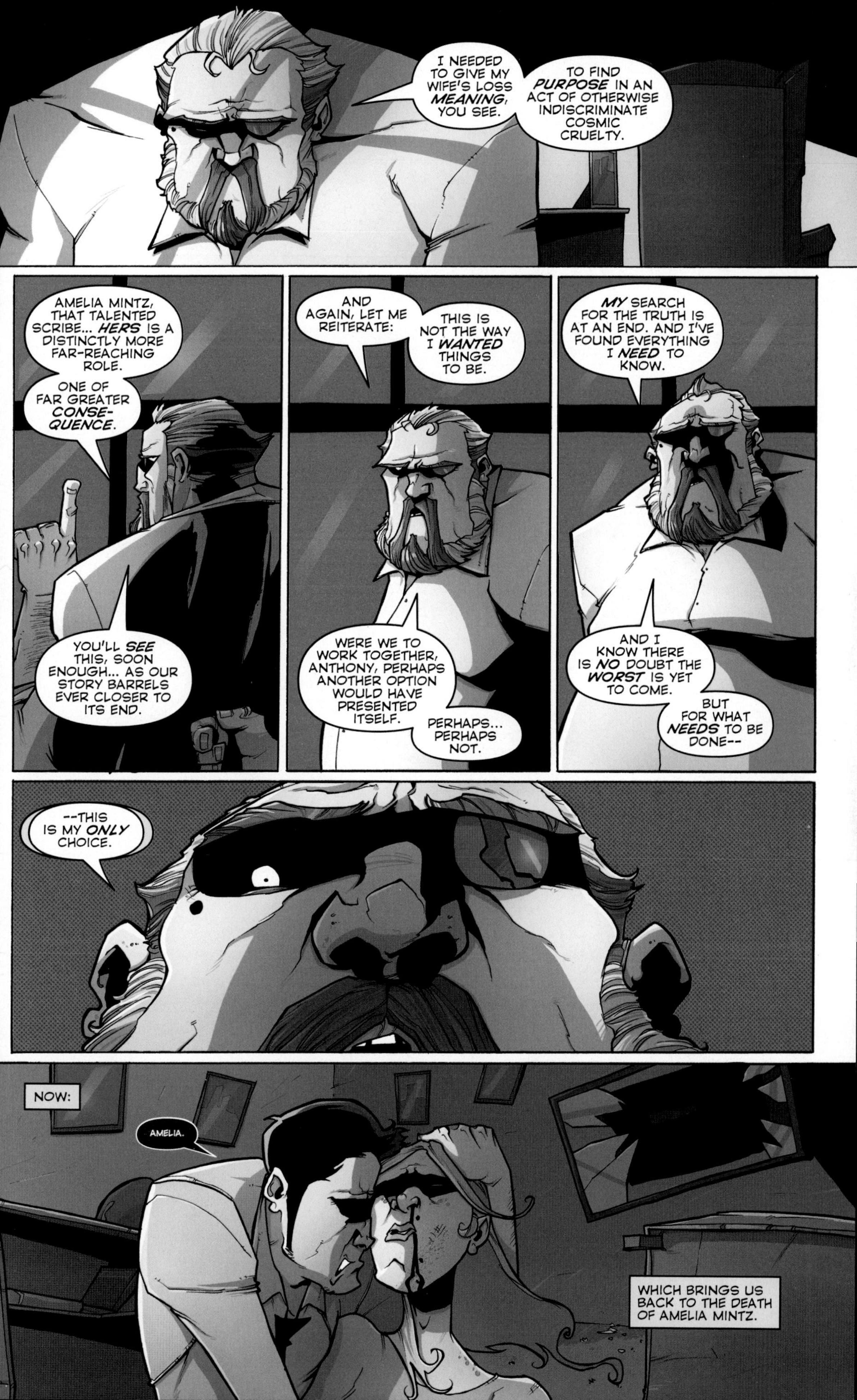
I NEEDED TO GIVE MY WIFE'S LOSS MEANING, YOU SEE.
TO FIND PURPOSE IN AN ACT OF OTHERWISE INDISCRIMINATE COSMIC CRUELTY.
AMELIA MINTZ, THAT TALENTED SCRIBE... HERS IS A DISTINCTLY MORE FAR-REACHING ROLE.
ONE OF FAR GREATER CONSE-QUENCE.
YOU'LL SEE THIS, SOON ENOUGH... AS OUR STORY BARRELS EVER CLOSER TO ITS END.
AND AGAIN, LET ME REITERATE:
THIS IS NOT THE WAY I WANTED THINGS TO BE.
WERE WE TO WORK TOGETHER, ANTHONY, PERHAPS ANOTHER OPTION WOULD HAVE PRESENTED ITSELF.
PERHAPS... PERHAPS NOT.
MY SEARCH FOR THE TRUTH IS AT AN END. AND I'VE FOUND EVERYTHING I NEED TO KNOW.
AND I KNOW THERE IS NO DOUBT THE WORST IS YET TO COME.
BUT FOR WHAT NEEDS TO BE DONE--
--THIS IS MY ONLY CHOICE.
NOW:
AMELIA.
WHICH BRINGS US BACK TO THE DEATH OF AMELIA MINTZ.

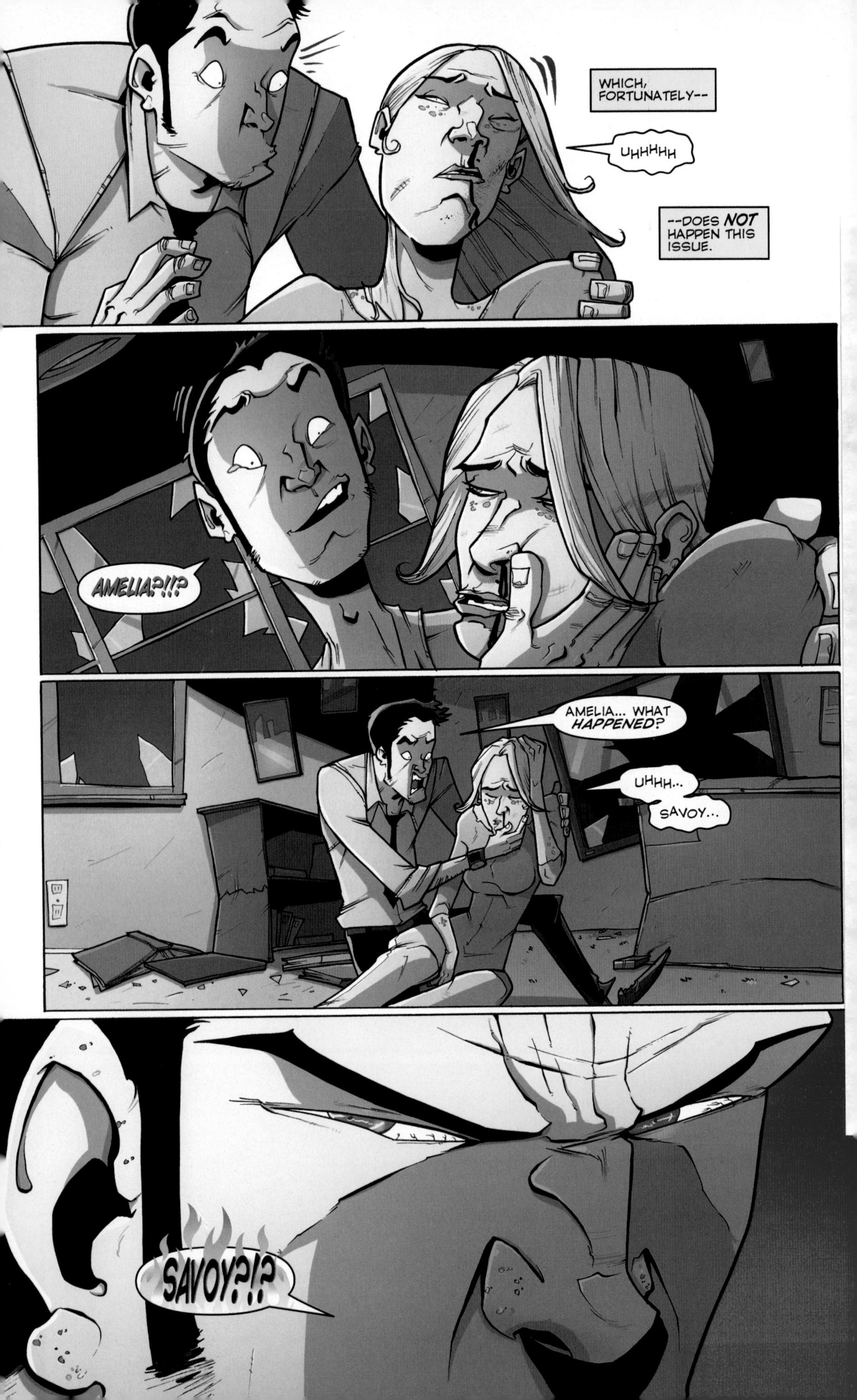
WHICH, FORTUNATELY--
UHHHHH
--DOES NOT HAPPEN THIS ISSUE.
AMELIA?!!?
AMELIA... WHAT HAPPENED?
UHHH...
SAVOY...
SAVOY?!?

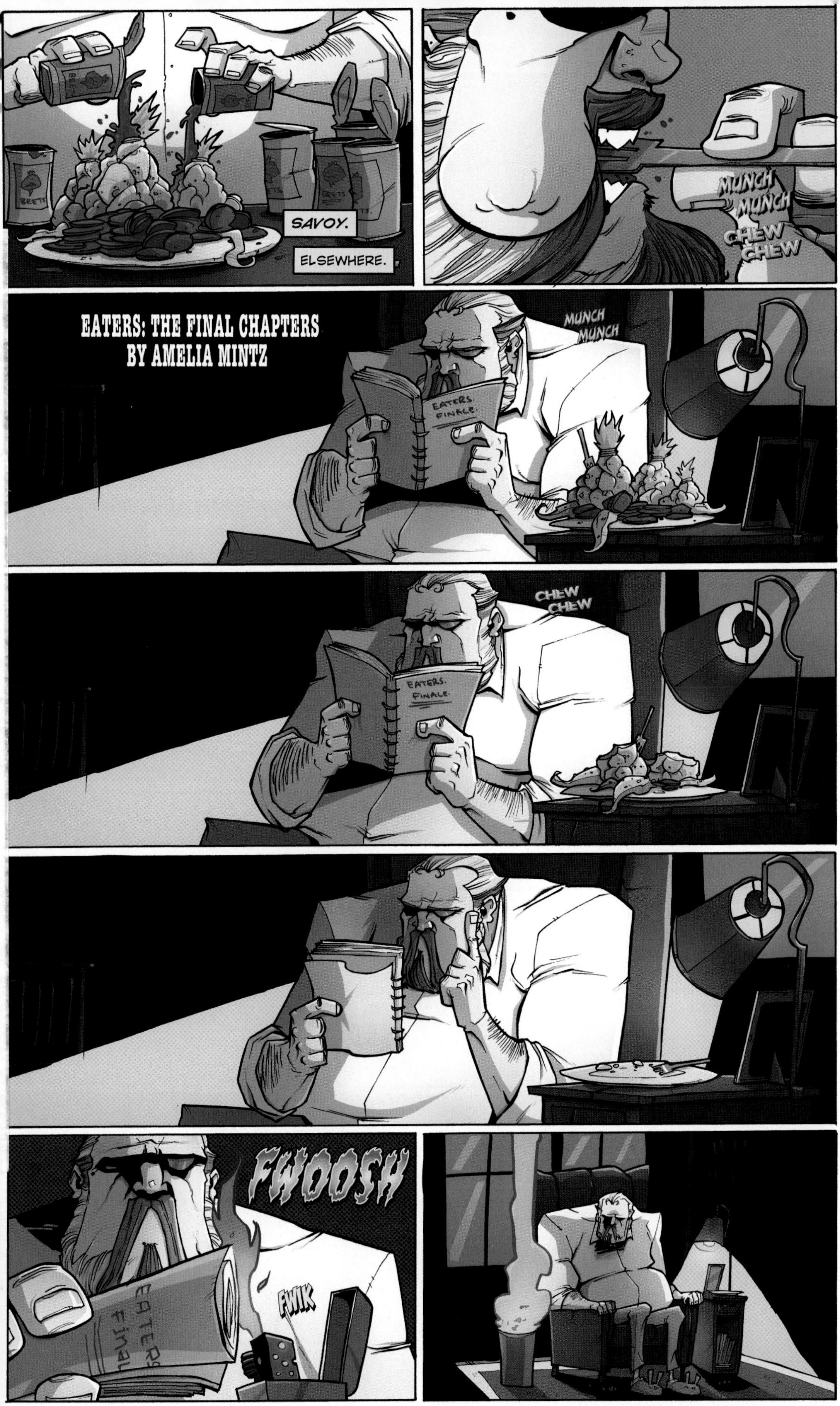
SAVOY.
ELSEWHERE.
BEETS
MUNCH MUNCH
CHEW CHEW
EATERS: THE FINAL CHAPTERS
BY AMELIA MINTZ
MUNCH MUNCH
EATERS. FINALE.
CHEW CHEW
EATERS. FINALE.
FWOOSH
FWIK
EATERS FINALE

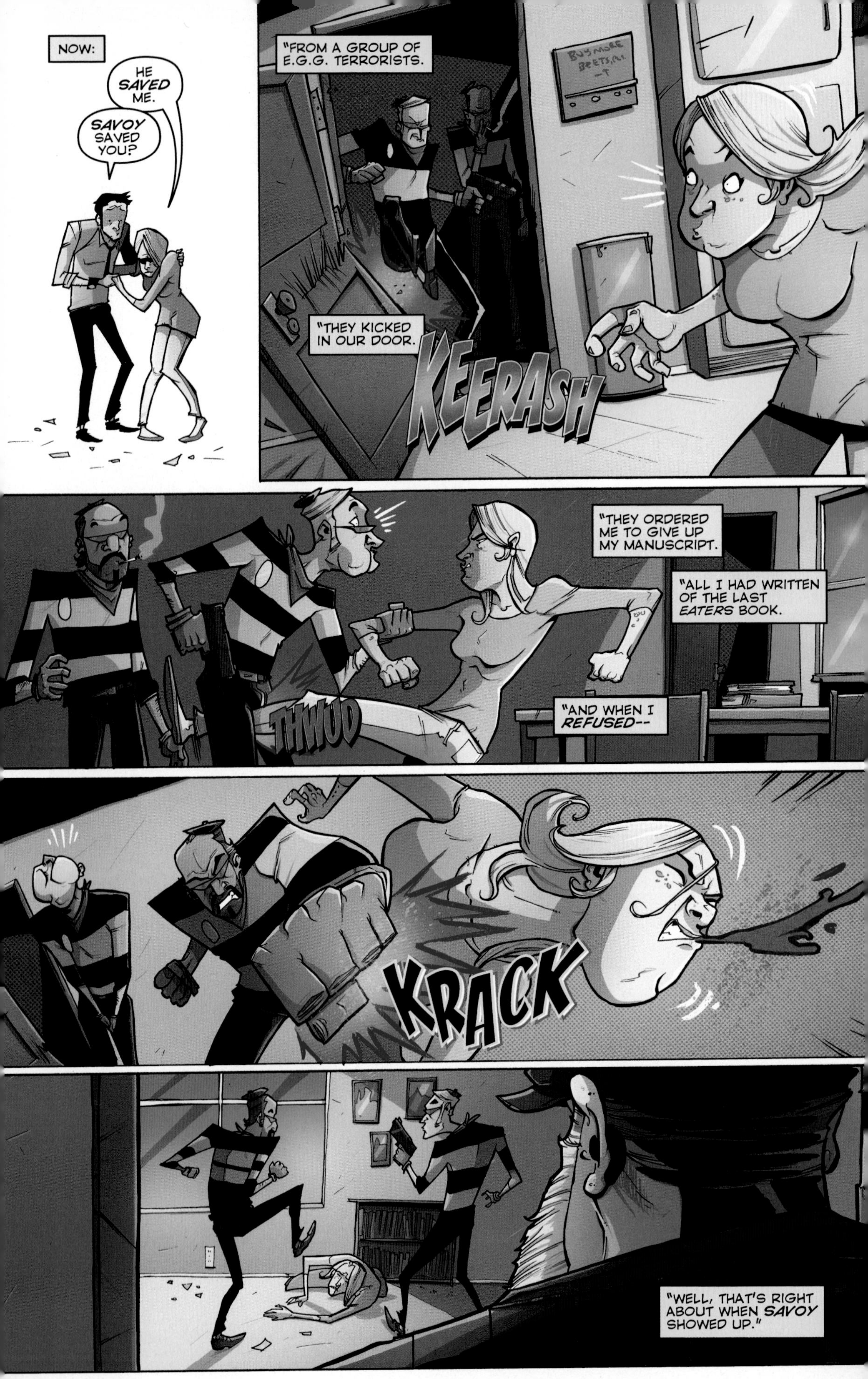
NOW:
HE SAVED ME.
SAVOY SAVED YOU?
"FROM A GROUP OF E.G.G. TERRORISTS.
"THEY KICKED IN OUR DOOR.
KEERASH
"THEY ORDERED ME TO GIVE UP MY MANUSCRIPT.
"ALL I HAD WRITTEN OF THE LAST EATERS BOOK.
"AND WHEN I REFUSED--
THWUD
KRACK
"WELL, THAT'S RIGHT ABOUT WHEN SAVOY SHOWED UP."

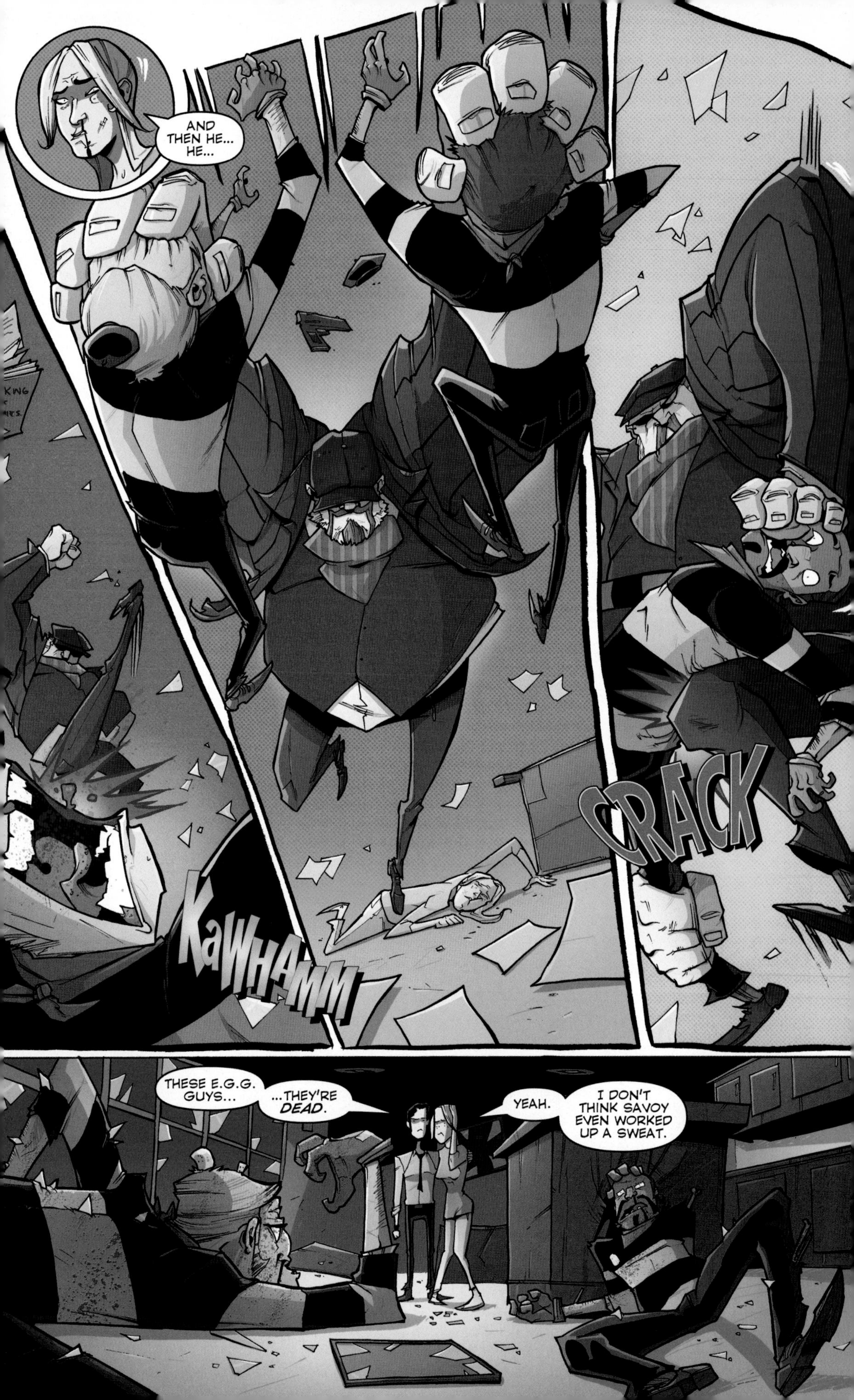
AND THEN HE... HE...
KaWHAMM
CRACK
THESE E.G.G. GUYS...
...THEY'RE DEAD.
YEAH.
I DON'T THINK SAVOY EVEN WORKED UP A SWEAT.

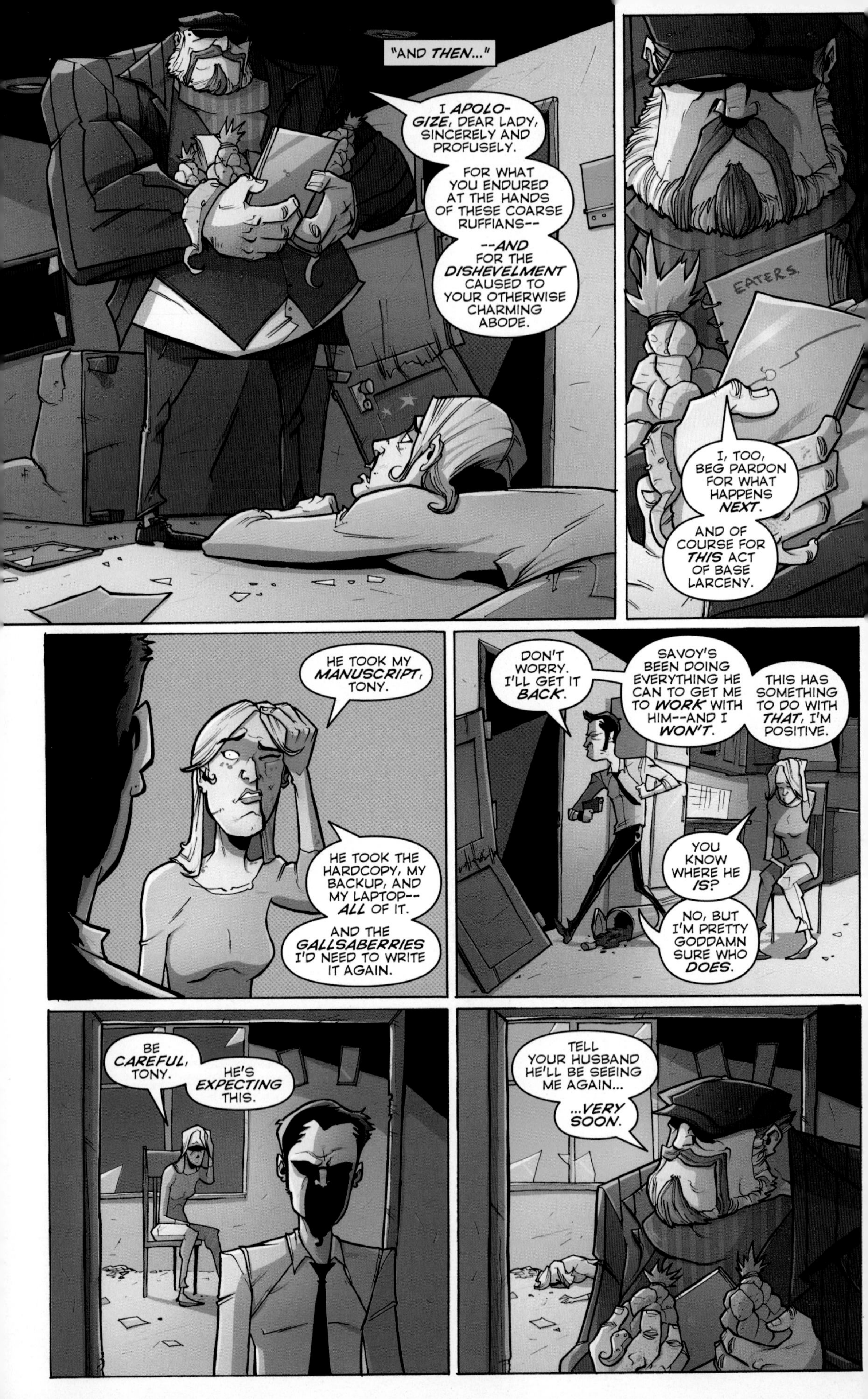
"AND THEN..."
I APOLOGIZE, DEAR LADY, SINCERELY AND PROFUSELY.
FOR WHAT YOU ENDURED AT THE HANDS OF THESE COARSE RUFFIANS--
--AND FOR THE DISHEVELMENT CAUSED TO YOUR OTHERWISE CHARMING ABODE.
EATERS.
I, TOO, BEG PARDON FOR WHAT HAPPENS NEXT.
AND OF COURSE FOR THIS ACT OF BASE LARCENY.
HE TOOK MY MANUSCRIPT, TONY.
HE TOOK THE HARDCOPY, MY BACKUP, AND MY LAPTOP--ALL OF IT.
AND THE GALLSABERRIES I'D NEED TO WRITE IT AGAIN.
DON'T WORRY. I'LL GET IT BACK.
SAVOY'S BEEN DOING EVERYTHING HE CAN TO GET ME TO WORK WITH HIM--AND I WON'T.
THIS HAS SOMETHING TO DO WITH THAT, I'M POSITIVE.
YOU KNOW WHERE HE IS?
NO, BUT I'M PRETTY GODDAMN SURE WHO DOES.
BE CAREFUL, TONY.
HE'S EXPECTING THIS.
TELL YOUR HUSBAND HE'LL BE SEEING ME AGAIN...
...VERY SOON.

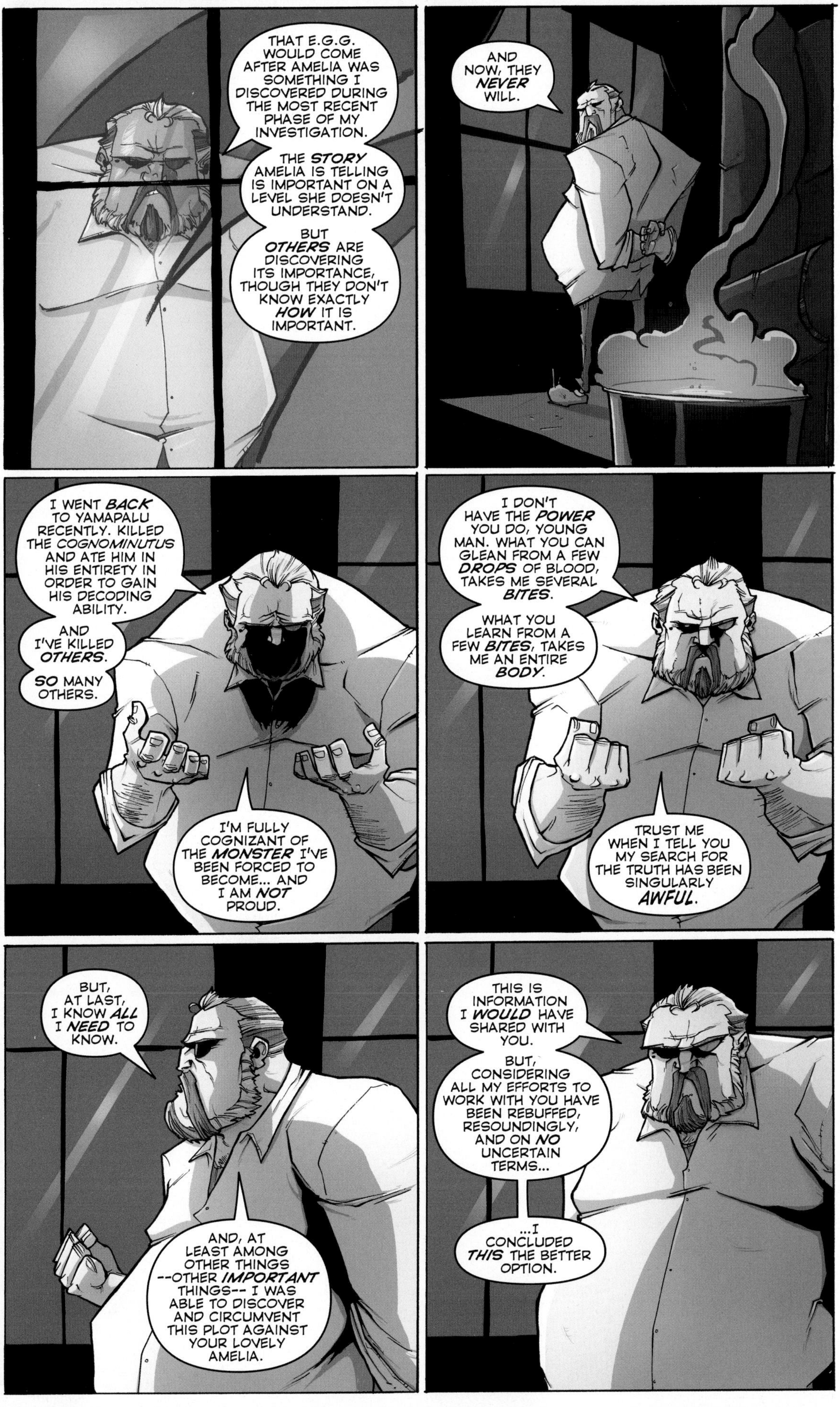
THAT E.G.G. WOULD COME AFTER AMELIA WAS SOMETHING I DISCOVERED DURING THE MOST RECENT PHASE OF MY INVESTIGATION.
THE STORY AMELIA IS TELLING IS IMPORTANT ON A LEVEL SHE DOESN'T UNDERSTAND.
BUT OTHERS ARE DISCOVERING ITS IMPORTANCE, THOUGH THEY DON'T KNOW EXACTLY HOW IT IS IMPORTANT.
AND NOW, THEY NEVER WILL.
I WENT BACK TO YAMAPALU RECENTLY. KILLED THE COGNOMINUTUS AND ATE HIM IN HIS ENTIRETY IN ORDER TO GAIN HIS DECODING ABILITY.
AND I'VE KILLED OTHERS.
SO MANY OTHERS.
I'M FULLY COGNIZANT OF THE MONSTER I'VE BEEN FORCED TO BECOME... AND I AM NOT PROUD.
I DON'T HAVE THE POWER YOU DO, YOUNG MAN. WHAT YOU CAN GLEAN FROM A FEW DROPS OF BLOOD, TAKES ME SEVERAL BITES.
WHAT YOU LEARN FROM A FEW BITES, TAKES ME AN ENTIRE BODY.
TRUST ME WHEN I TELL YOU MY SEARCH FOR THE TRUTH HAS BEEN SINGULARLY AWFUL.
BUT, AT LAST, I KNOW ALL I NEED TO KNOW.
AND, AT LEAST AMONG OTHER THINGS --OTHER IMPORTANT THINGS-- I WAS ABLE TO DISCOVER AND CIRCUMVENT THIS PLOT AGAINST YOUR LOVELY AMELIA.
THIS IS INFORMATION I WOULD HAVE SHARED WITH YOU.
BUT, CONSIDERING ALL MY EFFORTS TO WORK WITH YOU HAVE BEEN REBUFFED, RESOUNDINGLY, AND ON NO UNCERTAIN TERMS...
...I CONCLUDED THIS THE BETTER OPTION.

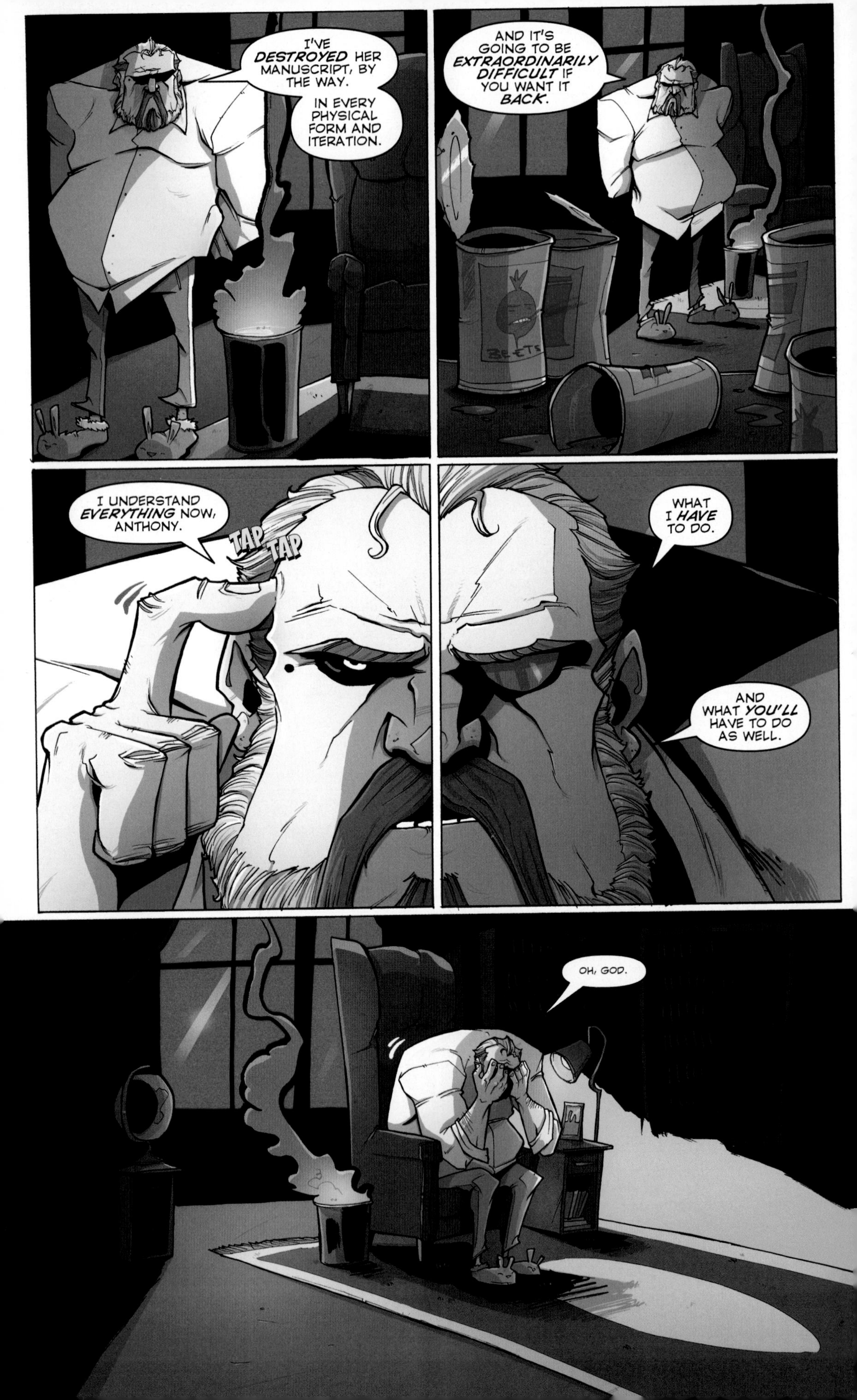
I'VE DESTROYED HER MANUSCRIPT, BY THE WAY.
IN EVERY PHYSICAL FORM AND ITERATION.
AND IT'S GOING TO BE EXTRAORDINARILY DIFFICULT IF YOU WANT IT BACK.
BEETS
I UNDERSTAND EVERYTHING NOW, ANTHONY.
TAP TAP
WHAT I HAVE TO DO.
AND WHAT YOU'LL HAVE TO DO AS WELL.
OH, GOD.

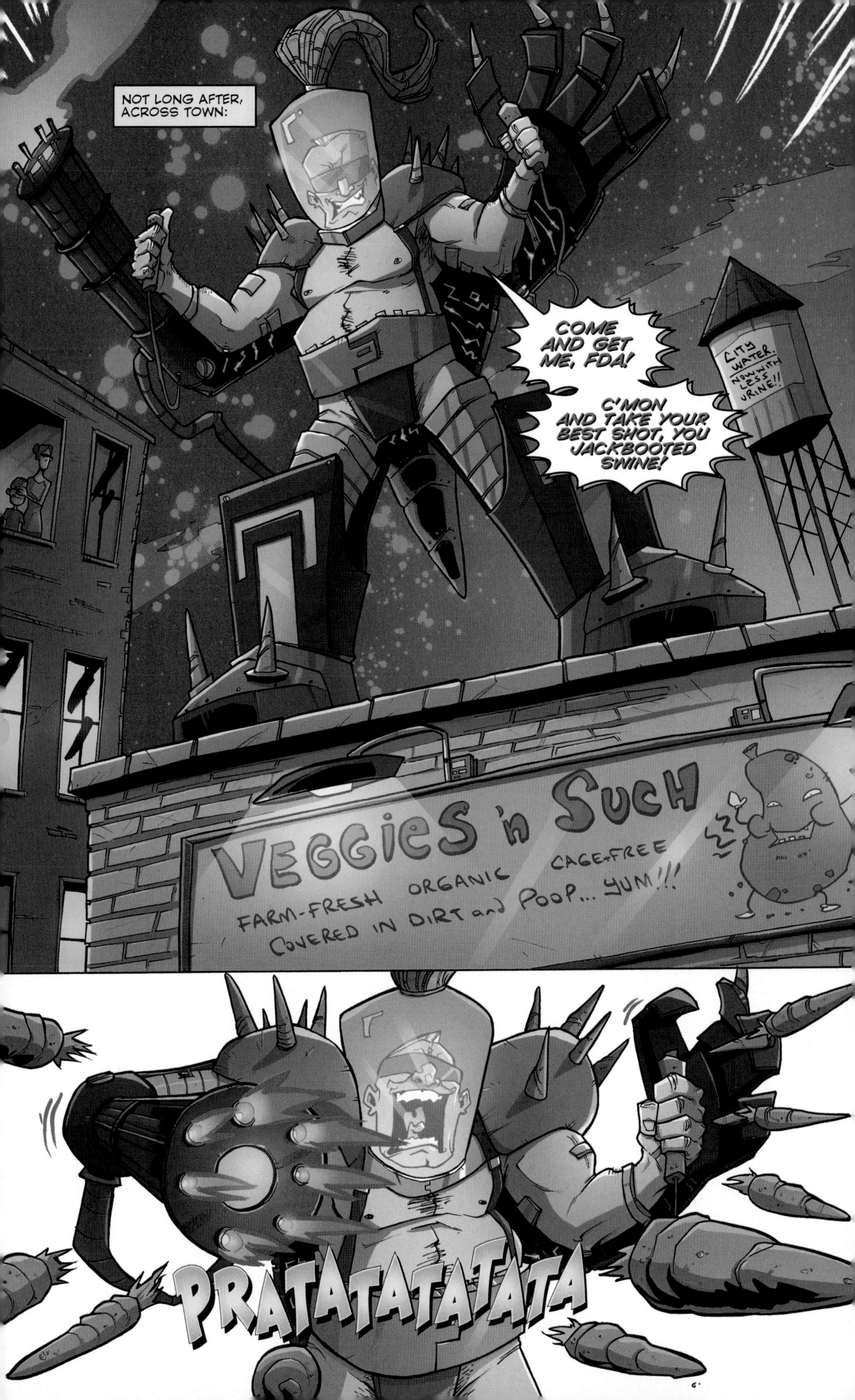
NOT LONG AFTER, ACROSS TOWN:
COME AND GET ME, FDA!
C'MON AND TAKE YOUR BEST SHOT, YOU JACKBOOTED SWINE!
CITY WATER. NOW WITH LESS URINE!!
VEGGIES 'n SUCH
FARM-FRESH ORGANIC CAGE-FREE COVERED IN DIRT and POOP... YUM!!!
PRATATATATATATA

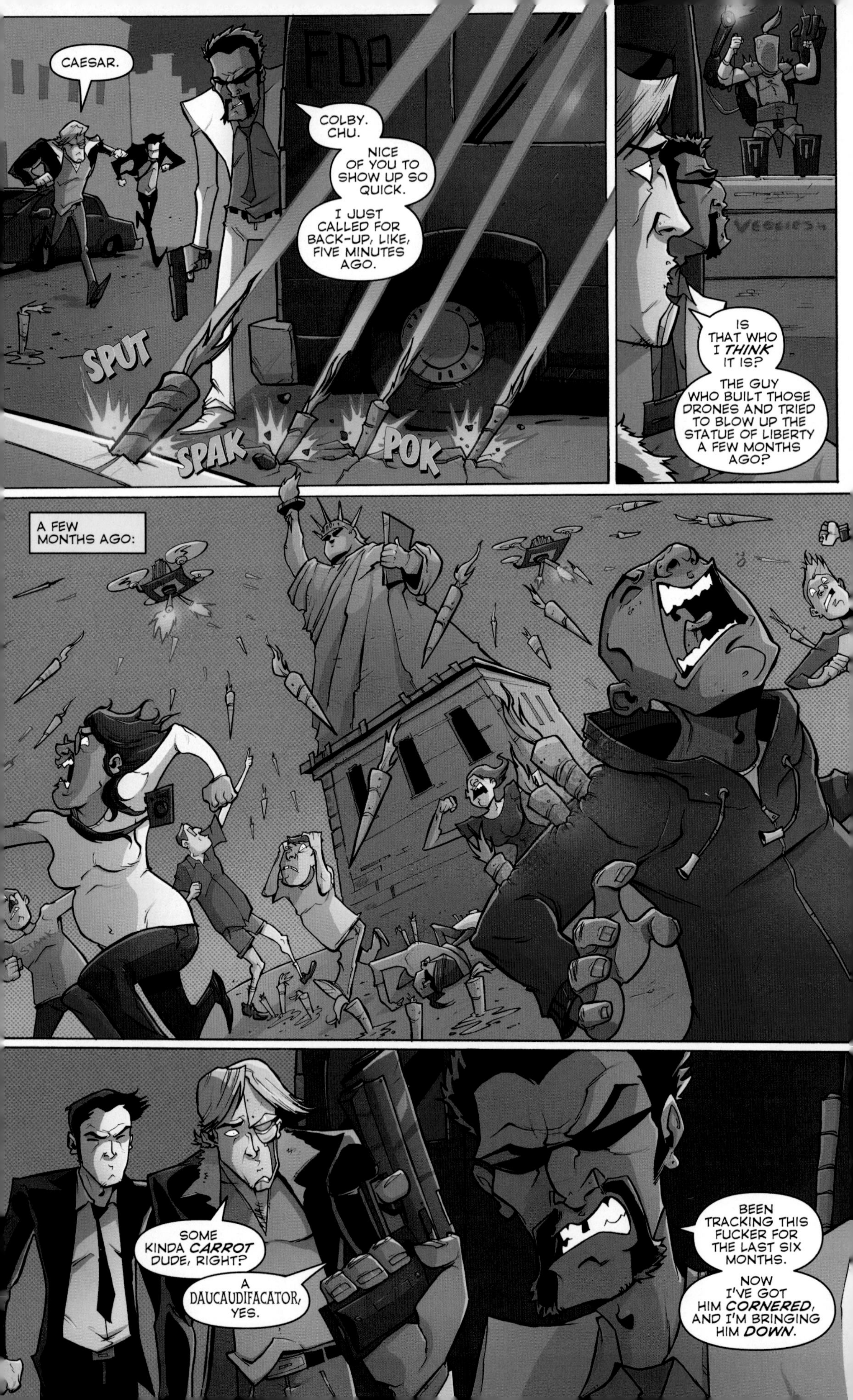
CAESAR.
COLBY. CHU.
NICE OF YOU TO SHOW UP SO QUICK.
I JUST CALLED FOR BACK-UP, LIKE, FIVE MINUTES AGO.
FDA
SPUT
SPAK
POK
IS THAT WHO I THINK IT IS?
THE GUY WHO BUILT THOSE DRONES AND TRIED TO BLOW UP THE STATUE OF LIBERTY A FEW MONTHS AGO?
A FEW MONTHS AGO:
SOME KINDA CARROT DUDE, RIGHT?
A DAUCAUDIFACATOR, YES.
BEEN TRACKING THIS FUCKER FOR THE LAST SIX MONTHS.
NOW I'VE GOT HIM CORNERED, AND I'M BRINGING HIM DOWN.

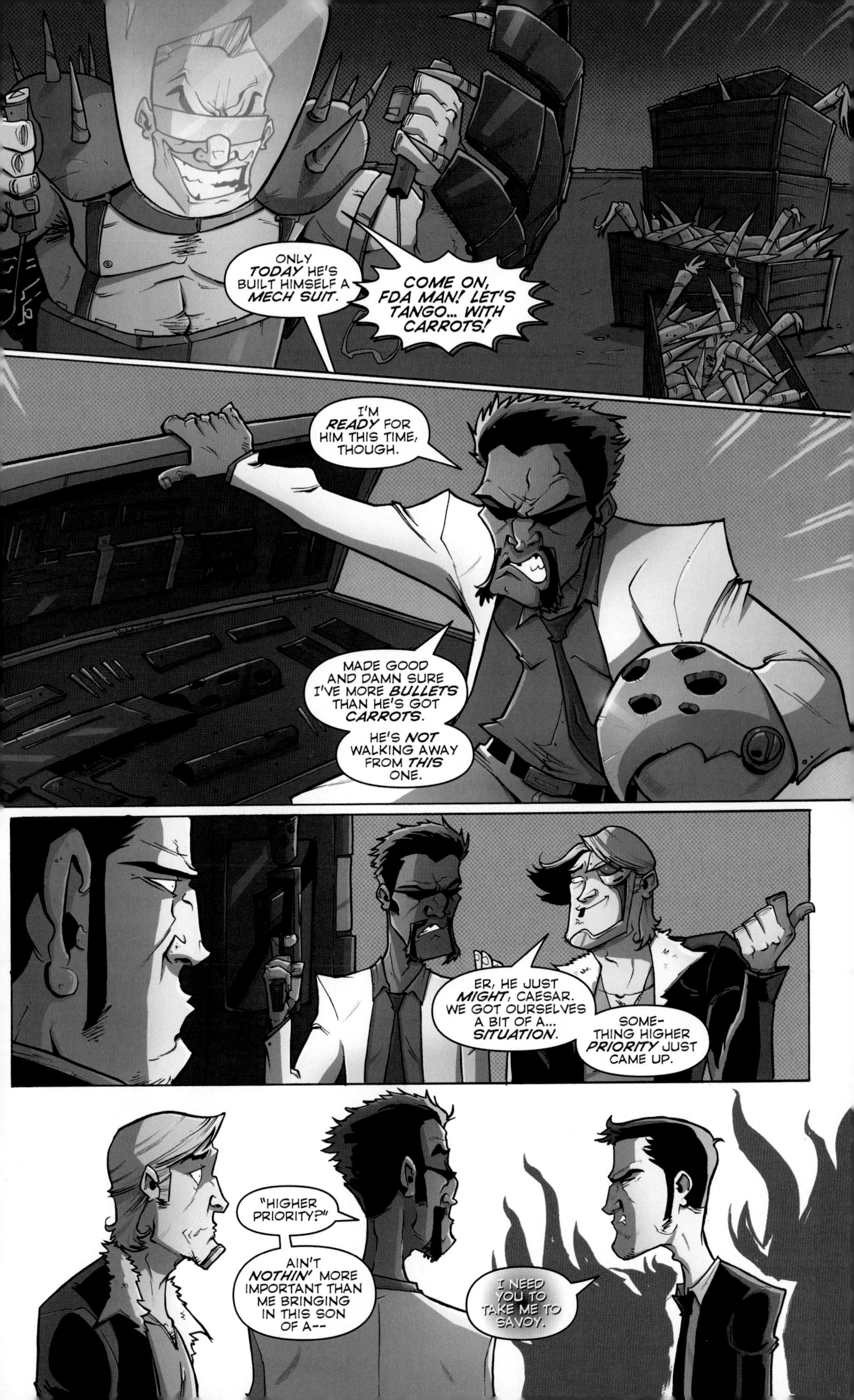
ONLY TODAY HE'S BUILT HIMSELF A MECH SUIT.
COME ON, FDA MAN! LET'S TANGO... WITH CARROTS!
I'M READY FOR HIM THIS TIME, THOUGH.
MADE GOOD AND DAMN SURE I'VE MORE BULLETS THAN HE'S GOT CARROTS.
HE'S NOT WALKING AWAY FROM THIS ONE.
ER, HE JUST MIGHT, CAESAR. WE GOT OURSELVES A BIT OF A... SITUATION.
SOME-THING HIGHER PRIORITY JUST CAME UP.
"HIGHER PRIORITY?"
AIN'T NOTHIN' MORE IMPORTANT THAN ME BRINGING IN THIS SON OF A--
I NEED YOU TO TAKE ME TO SAVOY.

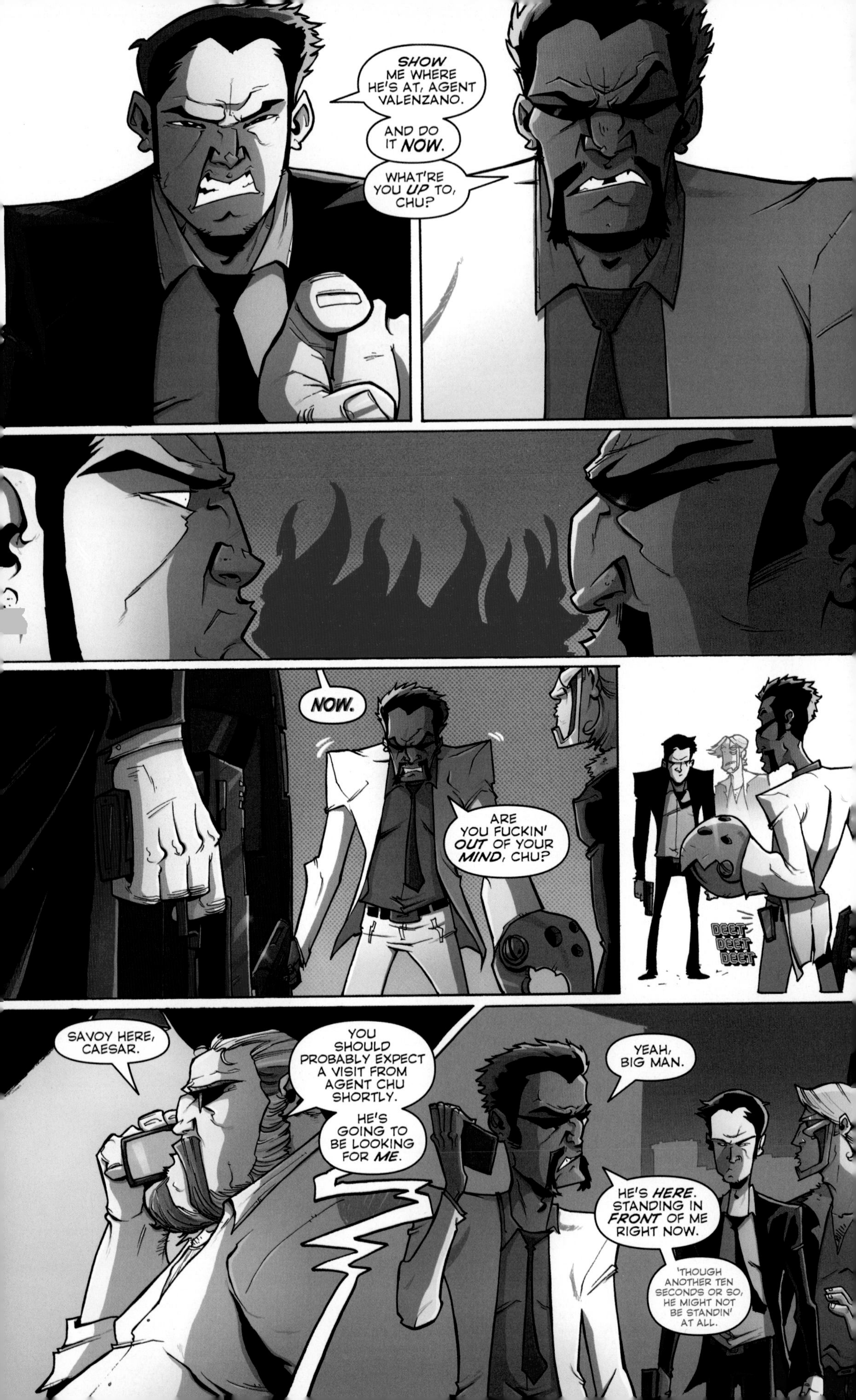
SHOW ME WHERE HE'S AT, AGENT VALENZANO.
AND DO IT NOW.
WHAT'RE YOU UP TO, CHU?
NOW.
ARE YOU FUCKIN' OUT OF YOUR MIND, CHU?
DEET DEET DEET
SAVOY HERE, CAESAR.
YOU SHOULD PROBABLY EXPECT A VISIT FROM AGENT CHU SHORTLY.
HE'S GOING TO BE LOOKING FOR ME.
YEAH, BIG MAN.
HE'S HERE. STANDING IN FRONT OF ME RIGHT NOW.
'THOUGH ANOTHER TEN SECONDS OR SO, HE MIGHT NOT BE STANDIN' AT ALL.

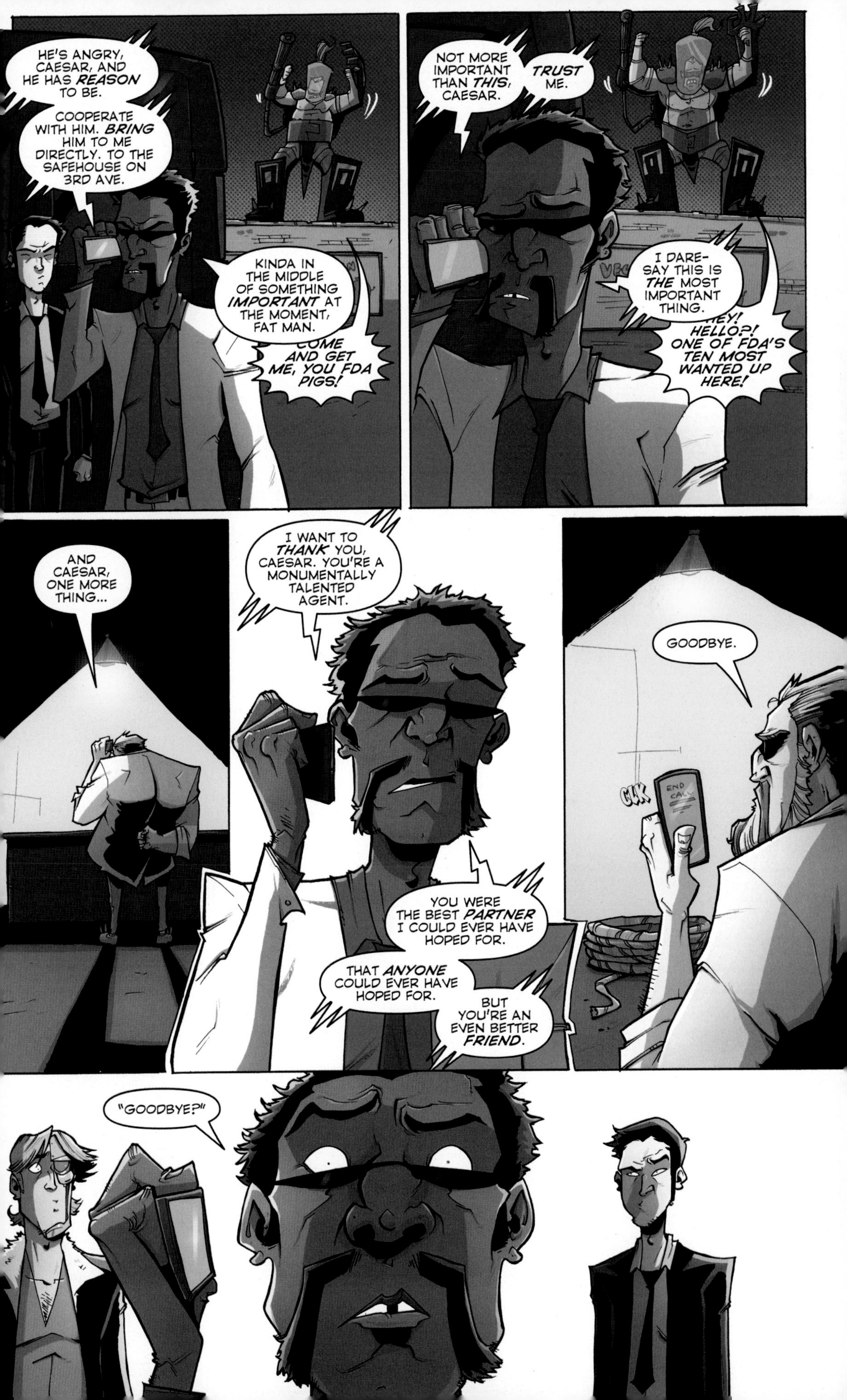
HE'S ANGRY, CAESAR, AND HE HAS REASON TO BE.
COOPERATE WITH HIM. BRING HIM TO ME DIRECTLY. TO THE SAFEHOUSE ON 3RD AVE.
KINDA IN THE MIDDLE OF SOMETHING IMPORTANT AT THE MOMENT, FAT MAN.
COME AND GET ME, YOU FDA PIGS!
NOT MORE IMPORTANT THAN THIS, CAESAR.
TRUST ME.
I DARE-SAY THIS IS THE MOST IMPORTANT THING.
HEY! HELLO?! ONE OF FDA'S TEN MOST WANTED UP HERE!
AND CAESAR, ONE MORE THING...
I WANT TO THANK YOU, CAESAR. YOU'RE A MONUMENTALLY TALENTED AGENT.
YOU WERE THE BEST PARTNER I COULD EVER HAVE HOPED FOR.
THAT ANYONE COULD EVER HAVE HOPED FOR.
BUT YOU'RE AN EVEN BETTER FRIEND.
GOODBYE.
CLIK
END CALL
"GOODBYE?"

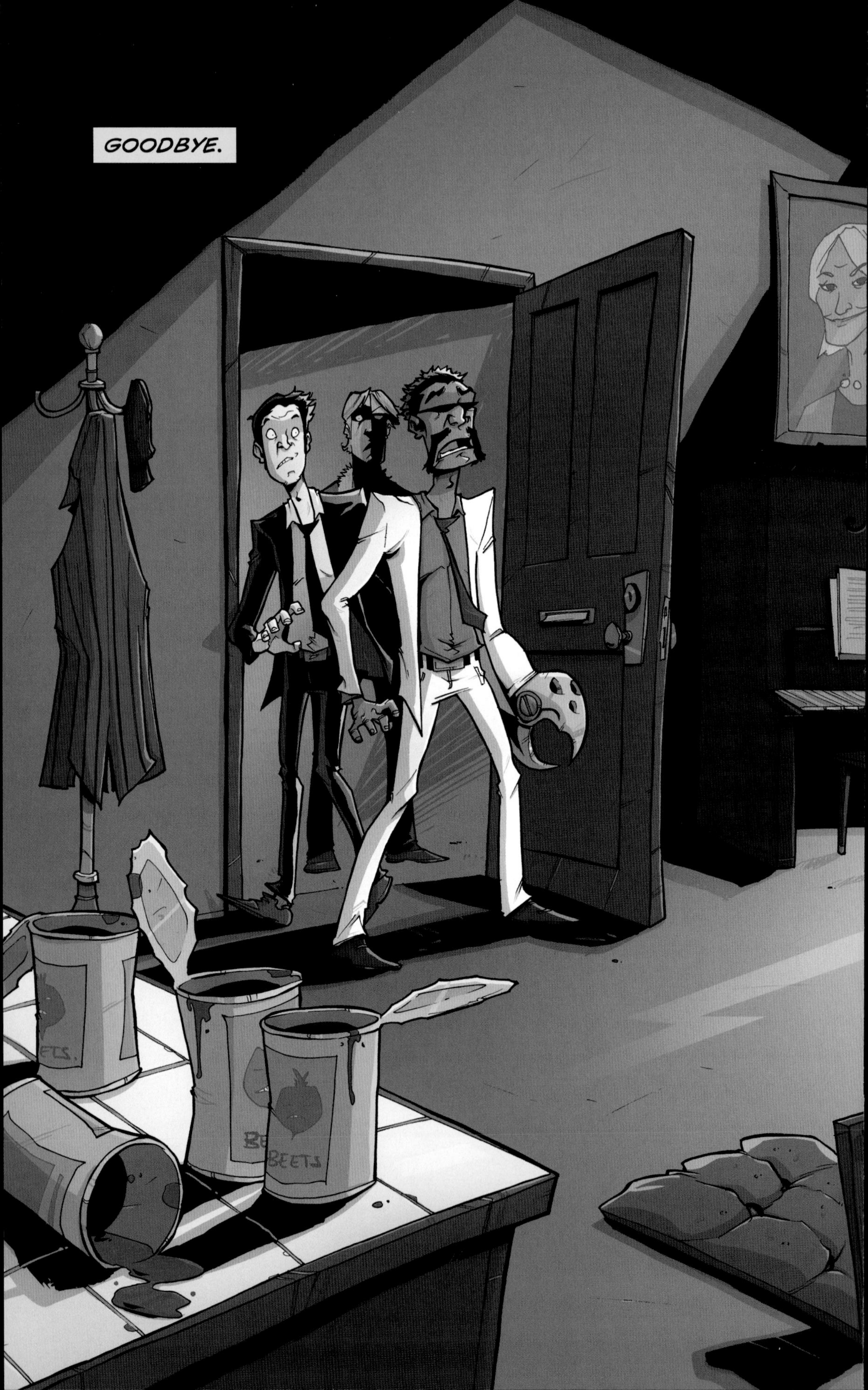
GOODBYE.
BEETS

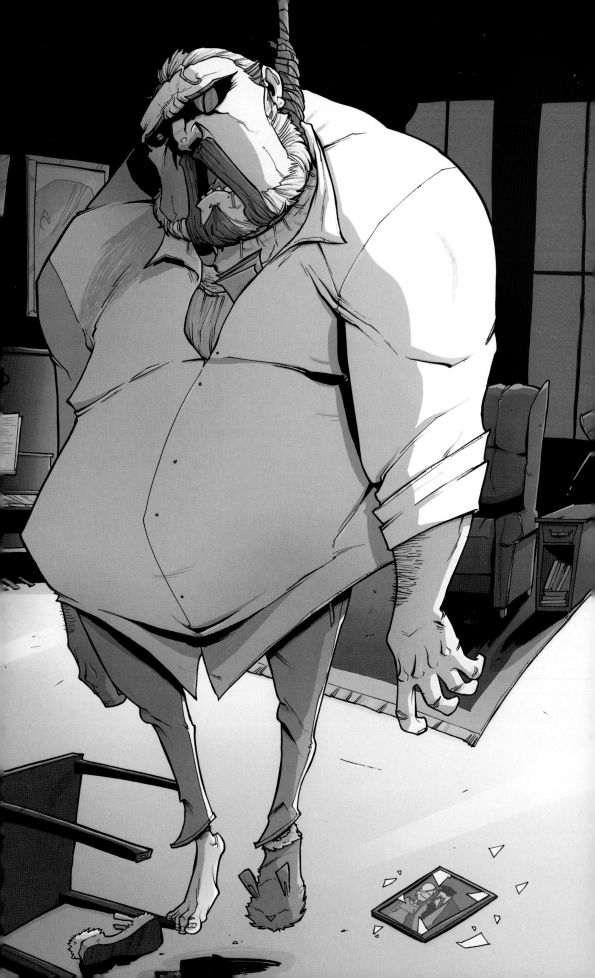

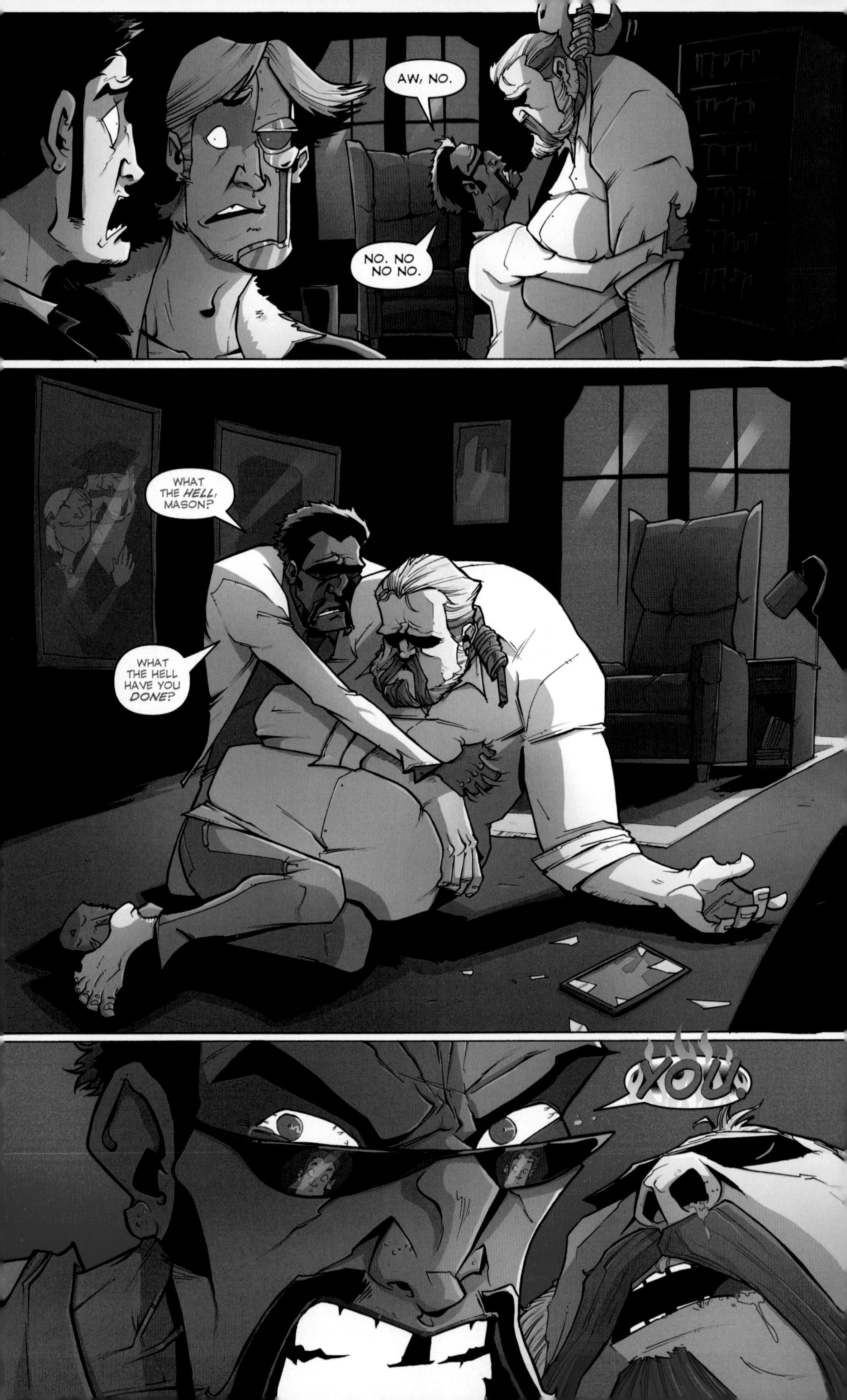
AW, NO.
NO. NO NO NO.
WHAT THE *HELL*, MASON?
WHAT THE HELL HAVE YOU *DONE*?
YOU!

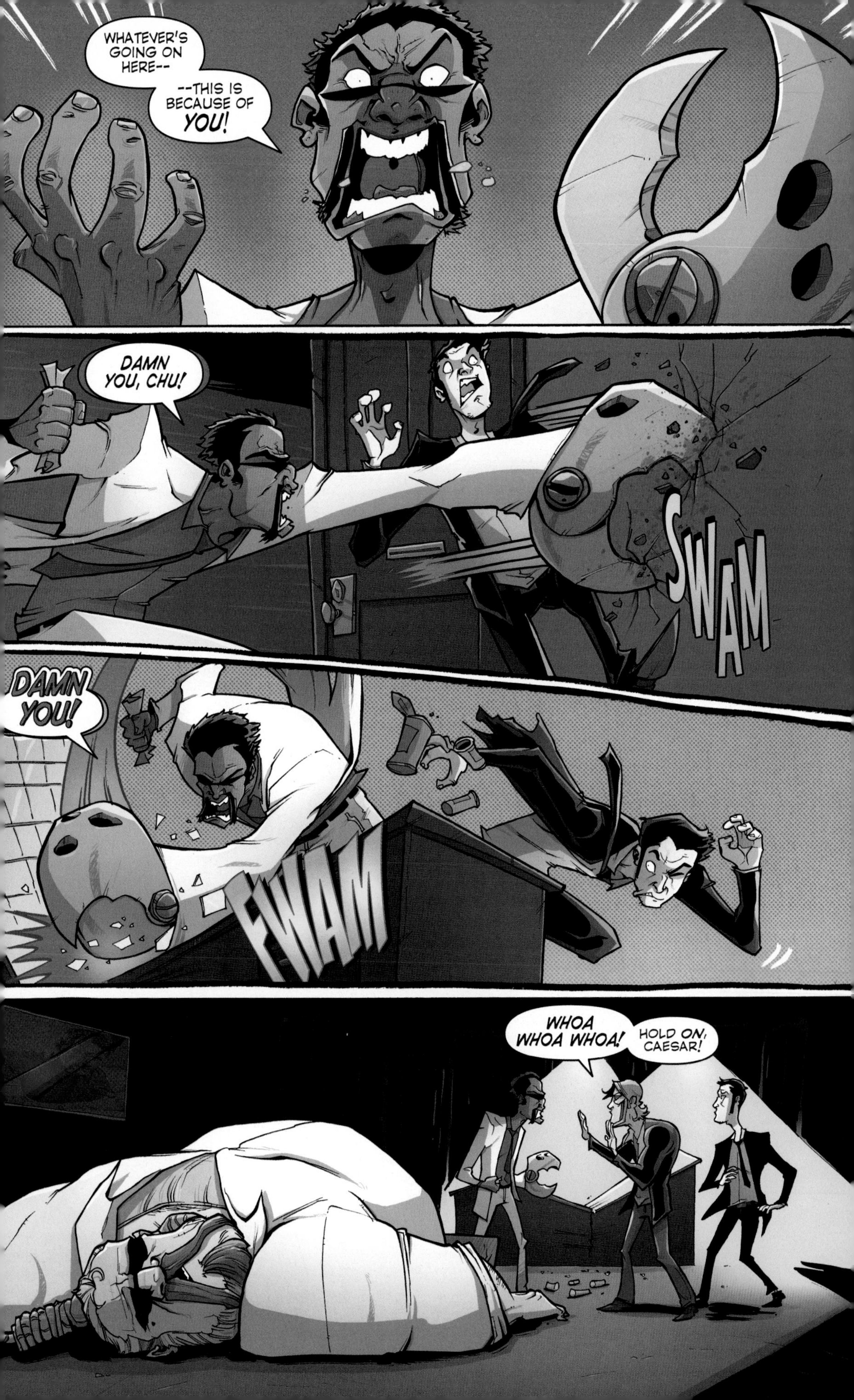
WHATEVER'S GOING ON HERE--
--THIS IS BECAUSE OF YOU!
DAMN YOU, CHU!
SWAM
DAMN YOU!
FWAM
WHOA WHOA WHOA!
HOLD ON, CAESAR!

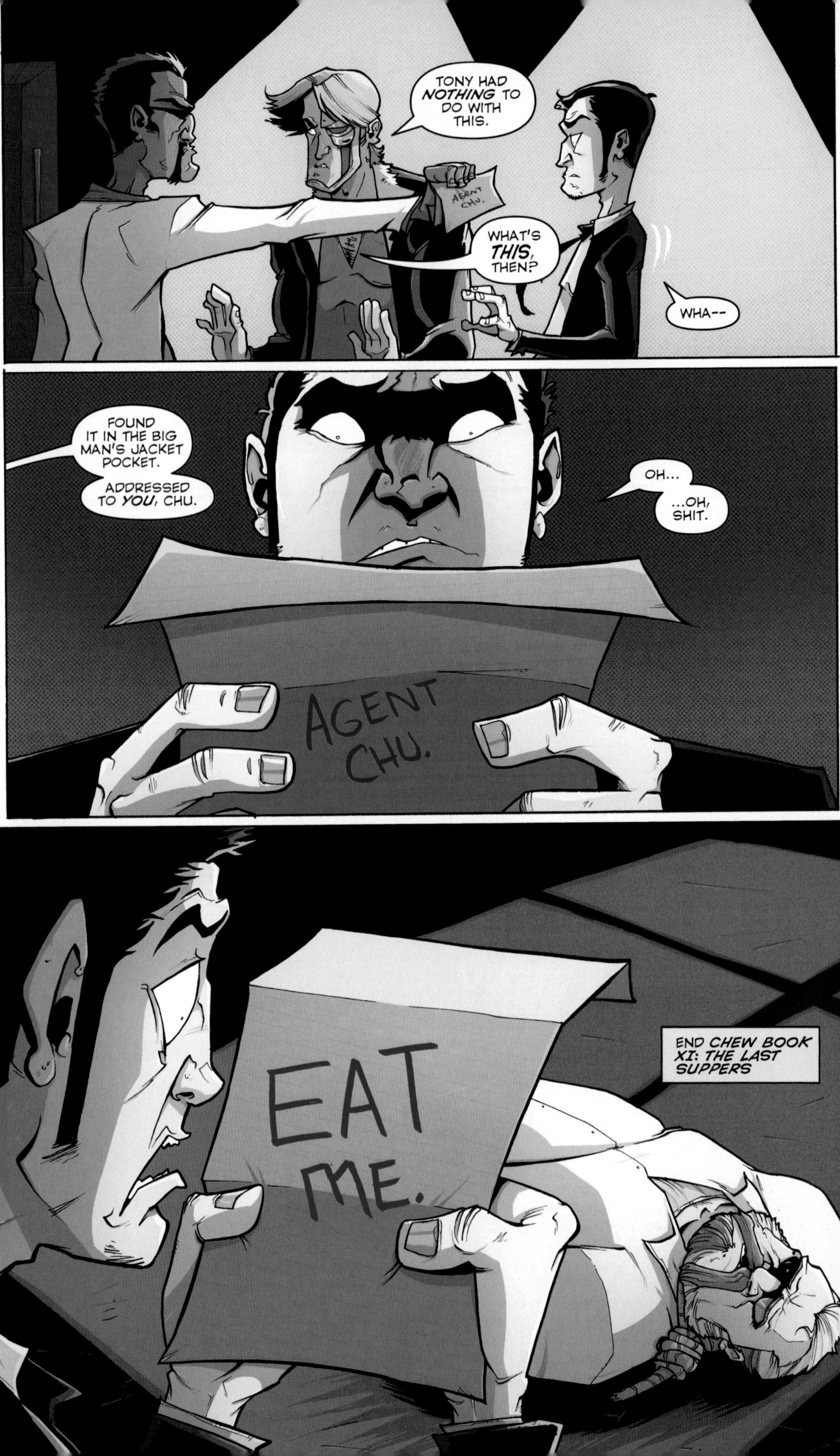

TONY HAD *NOTHING* TO DO WITH THIS.
AGENT CHU.
WHAT'S *THIS*, THEN?
WHA--
FOUND IT IN THE BIG MAN'S JACKET POCKET.
ADDRESSED TO *YOU*, CHU.
OH...
...OH, SHIT.
AGENT CHU.
EAT ME.
END *CHEW BOOK XI: THE LAST SUPPERS*

Bonus

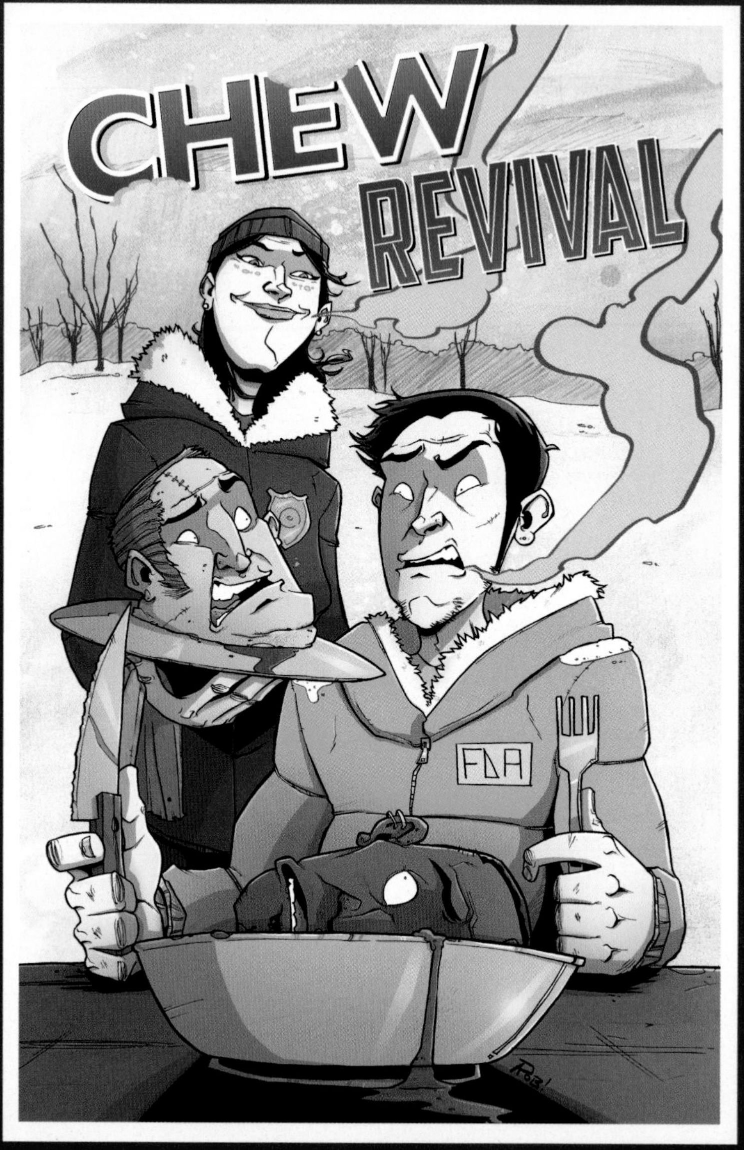
CHEW
REVIVAL
FDA

In May 2014, we published a cross-over flip book where the world of CHEW intersected with REVIVAL, a rural noir by Tim Seeley and Mike Norton. REVIVAL is set in a small town in Wisconsin, where the dead have come back to life. Local law enforcement officer Dana Cypress investigates "Reviver"-related crimes.. Presented here is our half of the flip book, a stand-alone story by Layman and Rob.

Also: REVIVAL is highly recommended and totally awesome. Check it out!

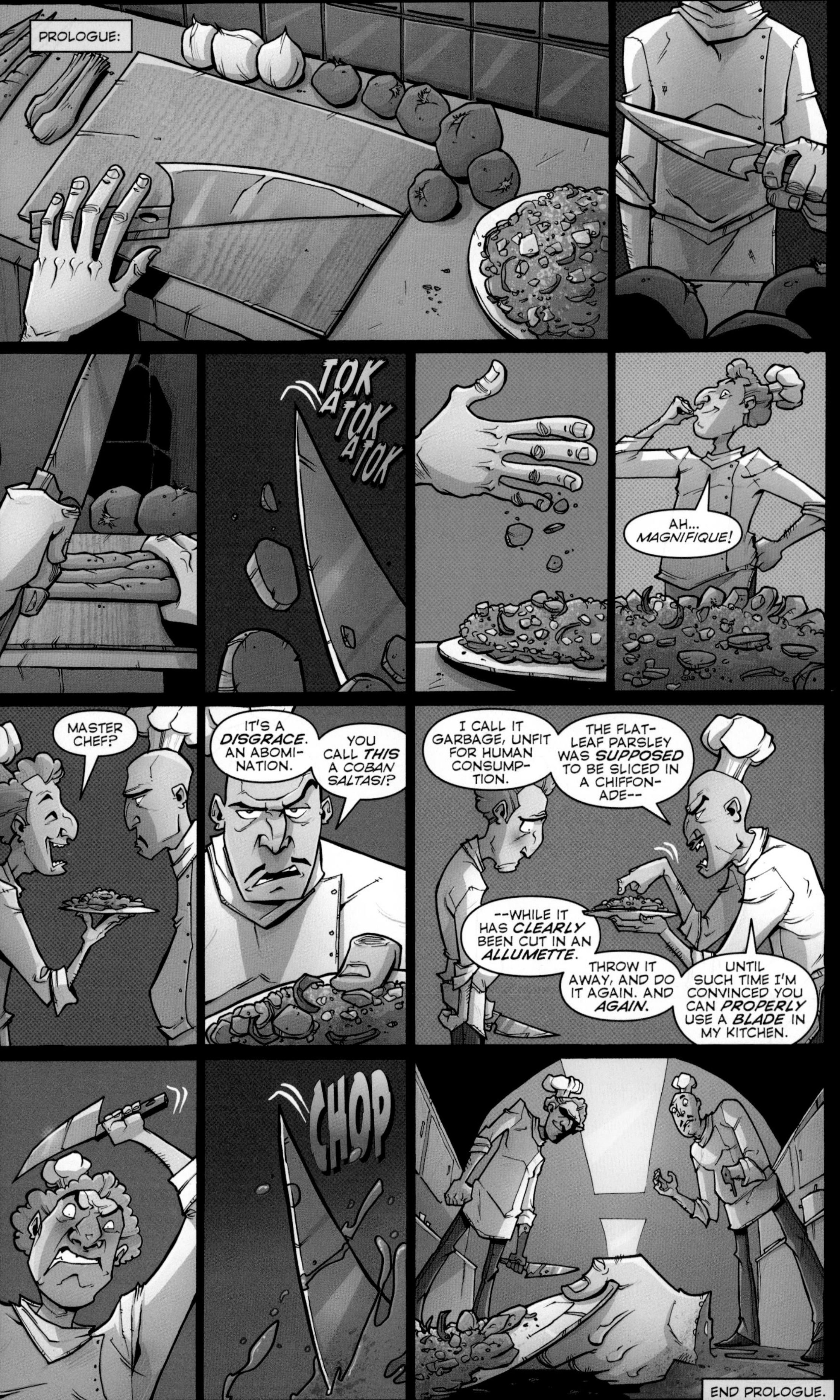
PROLOGUE:
TOK A TOK A TOK
AH... MAGNIFIQUE!
MASTER CHEF?
IT'S A DISGRACE. AN ABOMINATION.
YOU CALL THIS A COBAN SALTASI?
I CALL IT GARBAGE, UNFIT FOR HUMAN CONSUMPTION.
THE FLAT-LEAF PARSLEY WAS SUPPOSED TO BE SLICED IN A CHIFFONADE--
--WHILE IT HAS CLEARLY BEEN CUT IN AN ALLUMETTE.
THROW IT AWAY, AND DO IT AGAIN. AND AGAIN.
UNTIL SUCH TIME I'M CONVINCED YOU CAN PROPERLY USE A BLADE IN MY KITCHEN.
CHOP
END PROLOGUE.

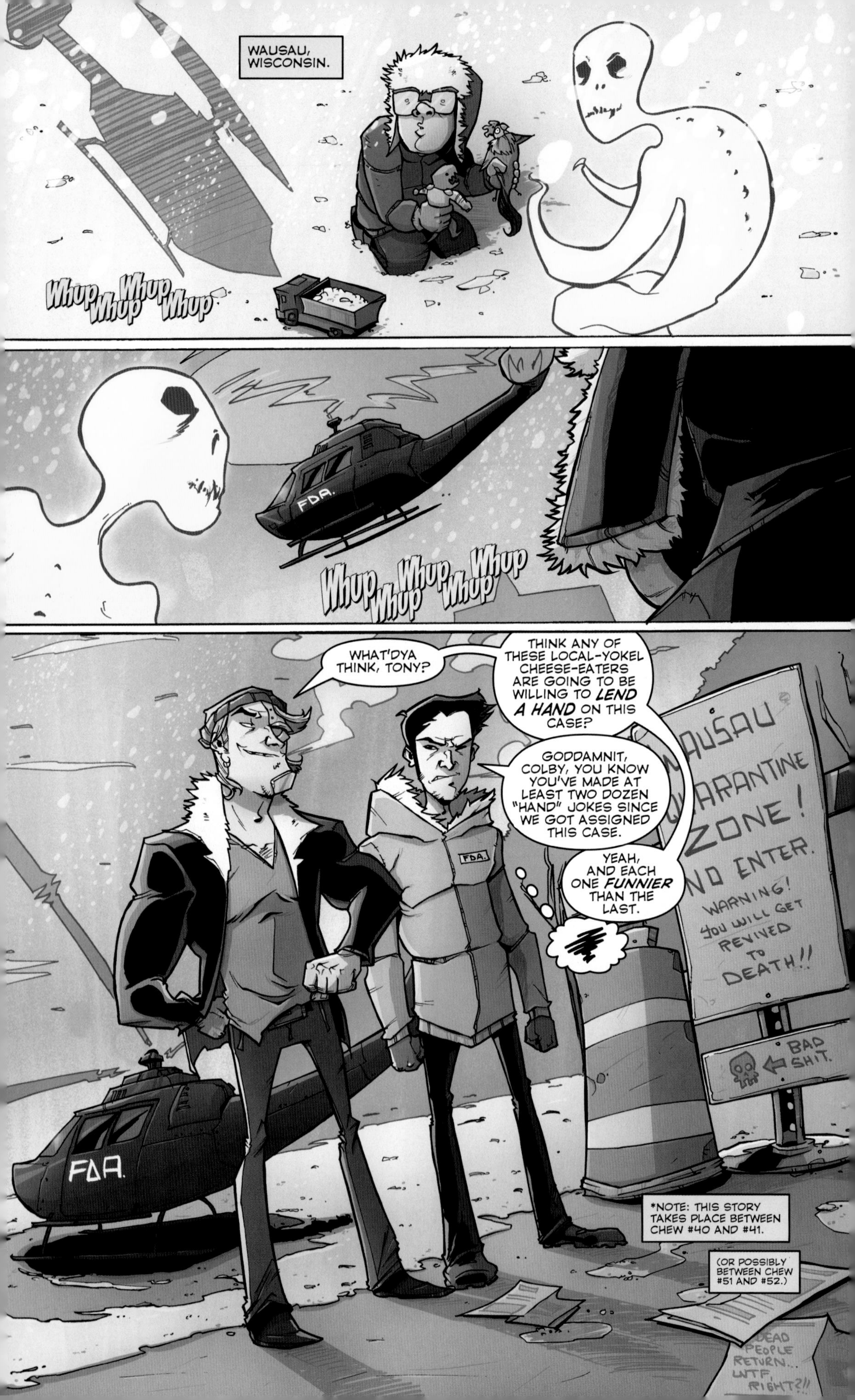
WAUSAU, WISCONSIN.
Whup Whup Whup Whup
FDA.
Whup Whup Whup Whup Whup
WHAT'DYA THINK, TONY?
THINK ANY OF THESE LOCAL-YOKEL CHEESE-EATERS ARE GOING TO BE WILLING TO LEND A HAND ON THIS CASE?
GODDAMNIT, COLBY, YOU KNOW YOU'VE MADE AT LEAST TWO DOZEN "HAND" JOKES SINCE WE GOT ASSIGNED THIS CASE.
YEAH, AND EACH ONE FUNNIER THAN THE LAST.
FDA.
WAUSAU
QUARANTINE ZONE!
NO ENTER
WARNING! YOU WILL GET REVIVED TO DEATH!!
BAD SHIT.
FDA.
*NOTE: THIS STORY TAKES PLACE BETWEEN CHEW #40 AND #41.
(OR POSSIBLY BETWEEN CHEW #51 AND #52.)
DEAD PEOPLE RETURN.. WTF, RIGHT?!!

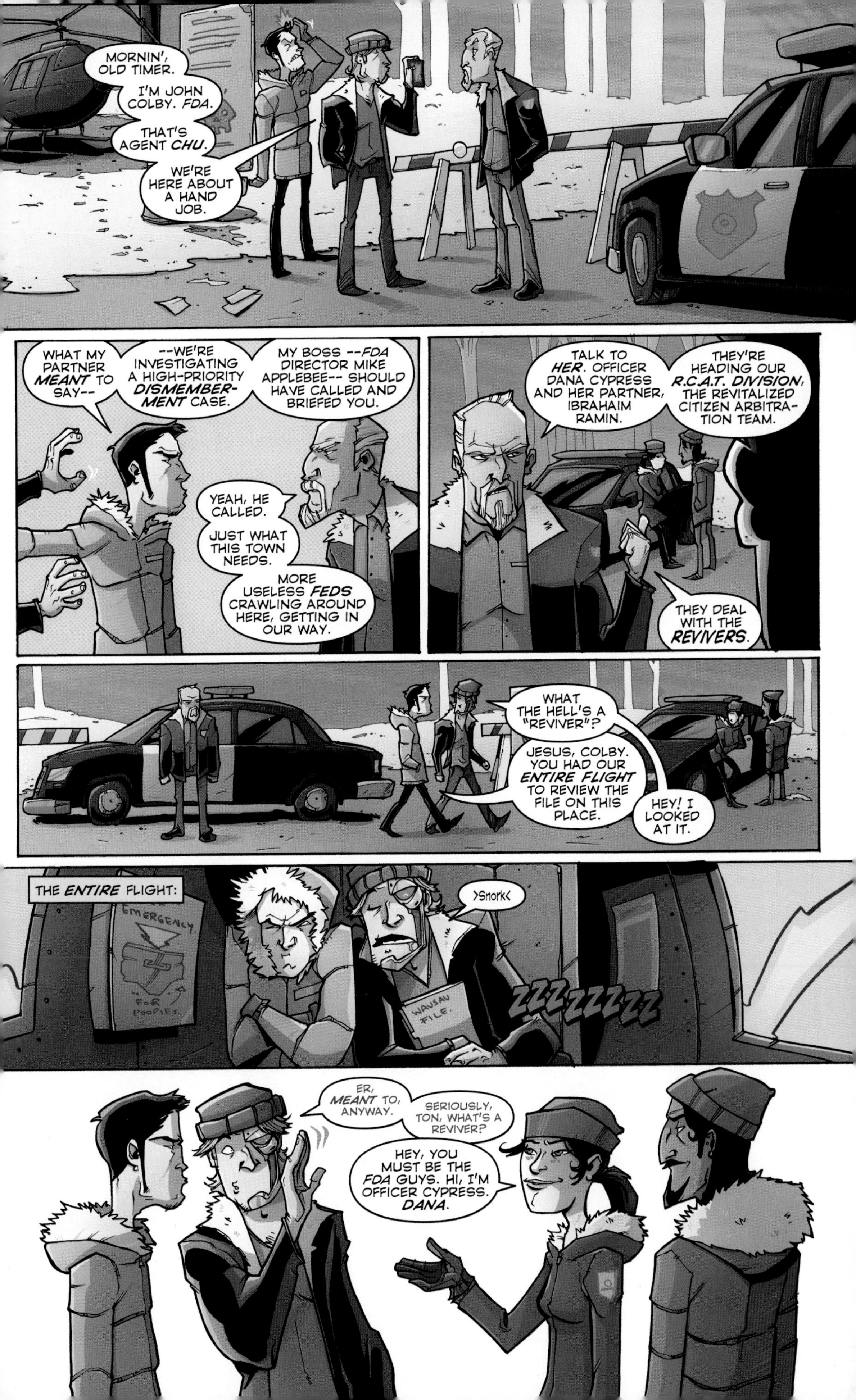
MORNIN', OLD TIMER.
I'M JOHN COLBY. FDA.
THAT'S AGENT CHU.
WE'RE HERE ABOUT A HAND JOB.
WHAT MY PARTNER MEANT TO SAY--
--WE'RE INVESTIGATING A HIGH-PRIORITY DISMEMBERMENT CASE.
MY BOSS --FDA DIRECTOR MIKE APPLEBEE-- SHOULD HAVE CALLED AND BRIEFED YOU.
YEAH, HE CALLED.
JUST WHAT THIS TOWN NEEDS.
MORE USELESS FEDS CRAWLING AROUND HERE, GETTING IN OUR WAY.
TALK TO HER. OFFICER DANA CYPRESS AND HER PARTNER, IBRAHAIM RAMIN.
THEY'RE HEADING OUR R.C.A.T. DIVISION, THE REVITALIZED CITIZEN ARBITRATION TEAM.
THEY DEAL WITH THE REVIVERS.
WHAT THE HELL'S A "REVIVER"?
JESUS, COLBY. YOU HAD OUR ENTIRE FLIGHT TO REVIEW THE FILE ON THIS PLACE.
HEY! I LOOKED AT IT.
THE ENTIRE FLIGHT:
EMERGENCY
FOR POOPIES.
WAUSAU FILE.
>Snork<
ZZZZZZZZZ
ER, MEANT TO, ANYWAY.
SERIOUSLY, TON, WHAT'S A REVIVER?
HEY, YOU MUST BE THE FDA GUYS. HI, I'M OFFICER CYPRESS. DANA.

MEET DANA CYPRESS.

FOR ONE DAY IN RURAL WISCONSIN, THE *DEAD CAME BACK TO LIFE*. NOW IT'S UP TO HER TO DEAL WITH THE MEDIA SCRUTINY, RELIGIOUS ZEALOTS, GOVERNMENT QUARANTINE, AND ASSORTED OTHER CRAZINESS THAT HAS COME WITH THEM.

PLEASURE TO MEET YOU, AGENT CHU.

HOW'S IT HANGIN', FELLA?

LIKEWISE, OFFICER CYPRESS.

DAPS!

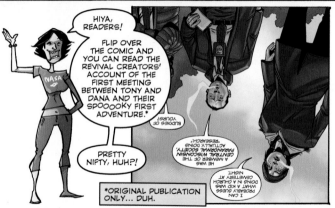

HIYA, READERS!

FLIP OVER THE COMIC AND YOU CAN READ THE REVIVAL CREATORS' ACCOUNT OF THE FIRST MEETING BETWEEN TONY AND DANA AND THEIR SPOOOOKY FIRST ADVENTURE.*

PRETTY NIFTY, HUH?!

*ORIGINAL PUBLICATION ONLY... DUH.

BUDDIES OF YOURS?

I CAN PROBABLY GUESS WHAT A KID WAS DOING IN A CHURCH CEMETERY AT NIGHT.

HE WAS A MEMBER OF THE CENTRAL WISCONSIN PARANORMAL SOCIETY, ACTUALLY DOING "RESEARCH."

THOSE NUTTY *REVIVAL* CREATORS THINK *THEIR* STORY COMES FIRST IN CONTINUITY.

BUT THIS ONE *REALLY* DOES.

SHHH!

DON'T TELL THEM. THEY'RE *SENSITIVE!*

YOU'RE THE *FDA* EATING GUY, RIGHT, THE... THE...

CIBOPATH.

ER, I'M SORTA UNCLEAR ABOUT--

GETS PSYCHIC IMPRESSIONS FROM WHAT HE EATS.

BITES AN APPLE, AN' GETS A FEELING IN HIS HEAD ABOUT WHAT TREE IT GREW FROM, WHAT PESTICIDES WERE USED ON THE CROPS, WHEN IT WAS HARVESTED, ETCETERA, ETCETERA.

OR... YOU COULD TAKE A BITE OF REANIMATED NECROTIC HUMAN TISSUE AND DETERMINE...

... EW.

YEAH, IT'S A BIT *DISTASTEFUL*, BUT OCCASIONALLY IT COMES IN *HANDY.*

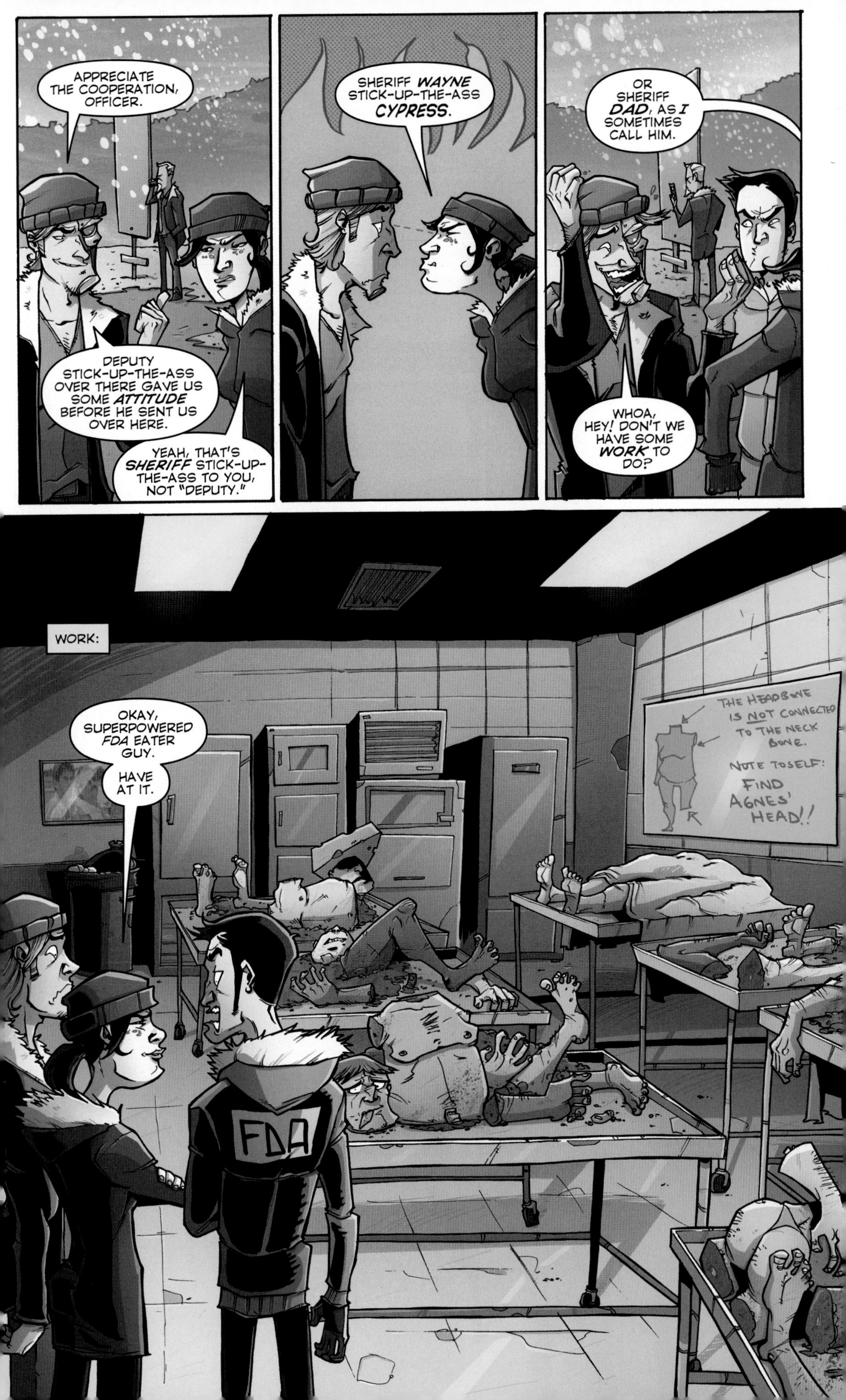

APPRECIATE THE COOPERATION, OFFICER.
DEPUTY STICK-UP-THE-ASS OVER THERE GAVE US SOME ATTITUDE BEFORE HE SENT US OVER HERE.
YEAH, THAT'S SHERIFF STICK-UP-THE-ASS TO YOU, NOT "DEPUTY."
SHERIFF WAYNE STICK-UP-THE-ASS CYPRESS.
OR SHERIFF DAD, AS I SOMETIMES CALL HIM.
WHOA, HEY! DON'T WE HAVE SOME WORK TO DO?
WORK:
OKAY, SUPERPOWERED FDA EATER GUY.
HAVE AT IT.
THE HEADBONE IS NOT CONNECTED TO THE NECK BONE.
NOTE TOSELF: FIND AGNES' HEAD!!
FDA

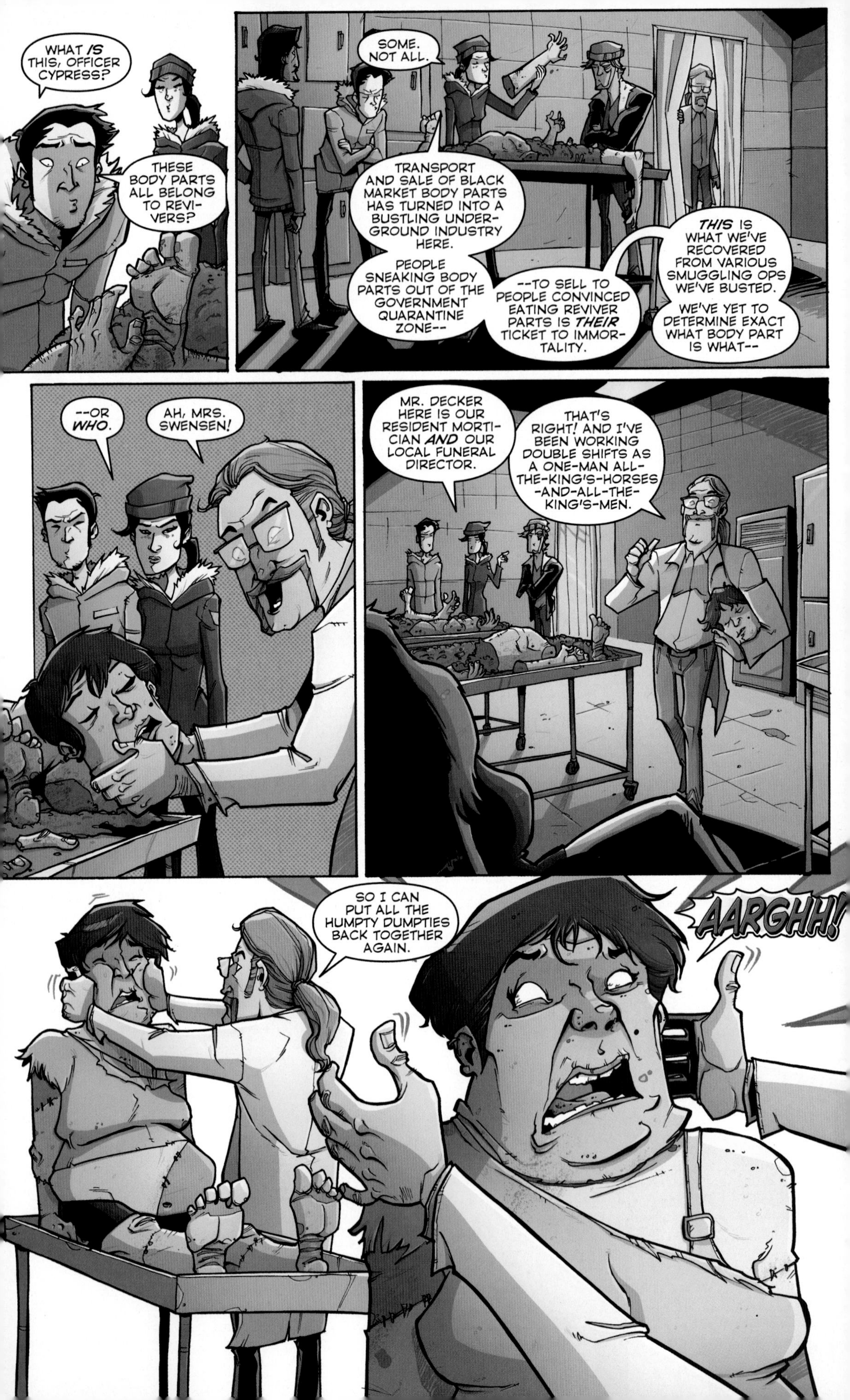
WHAT *IS* THIS, OFFICER CYPRESS?
THESE BODY PARTS ALL BELONG TO REVIVERS?
SOME. NOT ALL.
TRANSPORT AND SALE OF BLACK MARKET BODY PARTS HAS TURNED INTO A BUSTLING UNDERGROUND INDUSTRY HERE.
PEOPLE SNEAKING BODY PARTS OUT OF THE GOVERNMENT QUARANTINE ZONE--
--TO SELL TO PEOPLE CONVINCED EATING REVIVER PARTS IS *THEIR* TICKET TO IMMORTALITY.
THIS IS WHAT WE'VE RECOVERED FROM VARIOUS SMUGGLING OPS WE'VE BUSTED.
WE'VE YET TO DETERMINE EXACT WHAT BODY PART IS WHAT--
--OR *WHO*.
AH, MRS. SWENSEN!
MR. DECKER HERE IS OUR RESIDENT MORTICIAN *AND* OUR LOCAL FUNERAL DIRECTOR.
THAT'S RIGHT! AND I'VE BEEN WORKING DOUBLE SHIFTS AS A ONE-MAN ALL-THE-KING'S-HORSES-AND-ALL-THE-KING'S-MEN.
SO I CAN PUT ALL THE HUMPTY DUMPTIES BACK TOGETHER AGAIN.
AARGHH!

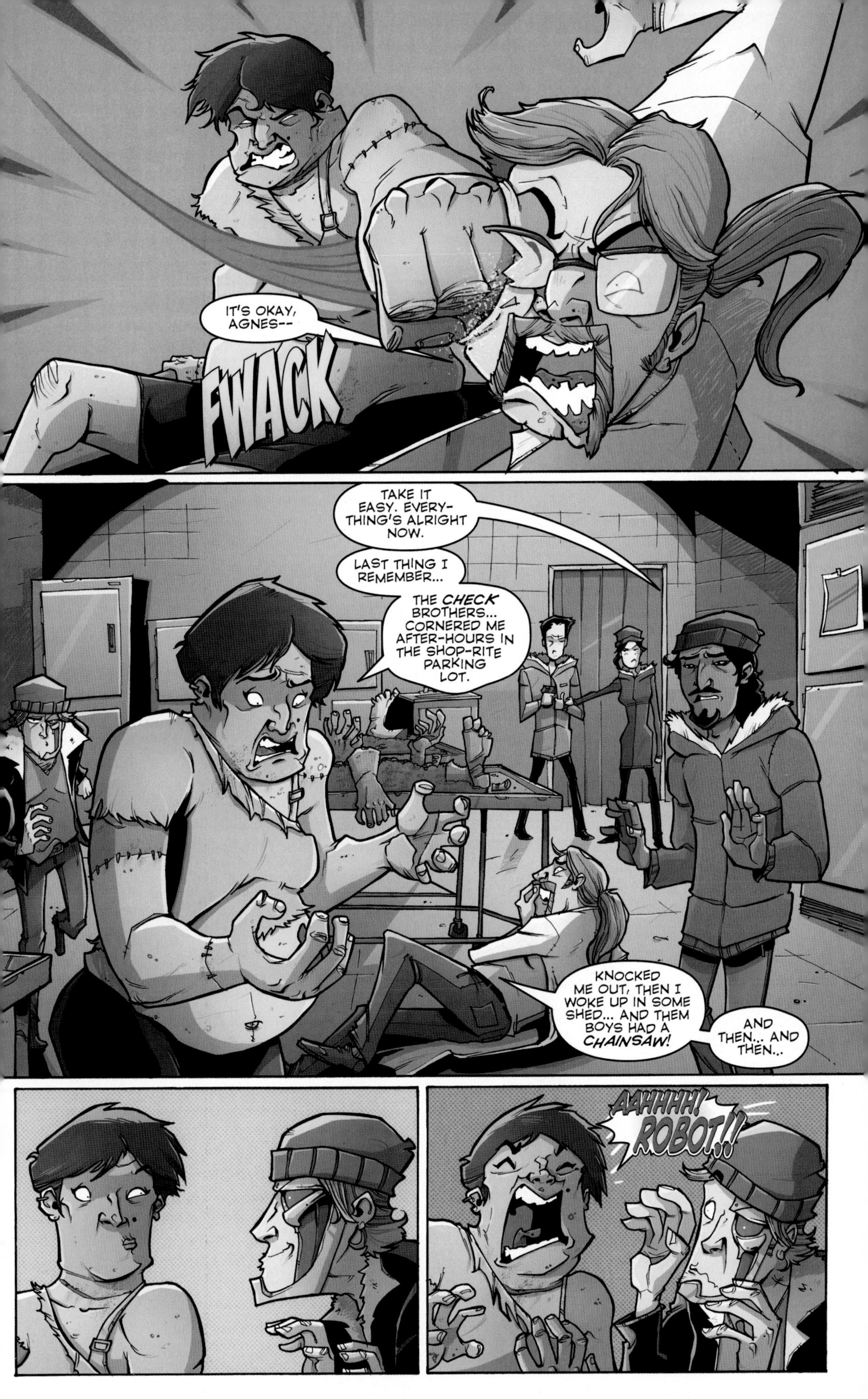
IT'S OKAY, AGNES--
FWACK
TAKE IT EASY. EVERY-THING'S ALRIGHT NOW.
LAST THING I REMEMBER...
THE CHECK BROTHERS... CORNERED ME AFTER-HOURS IN THE SHOP-RITE PARKING LOT.
KNOCKED ME OUT, THEN I WOKE UP IN SOME SHED... AND THEM BOYS HAD A CHAINSAW!
AND THEN... AND THEN...
AAHHHH! ROBOT!!

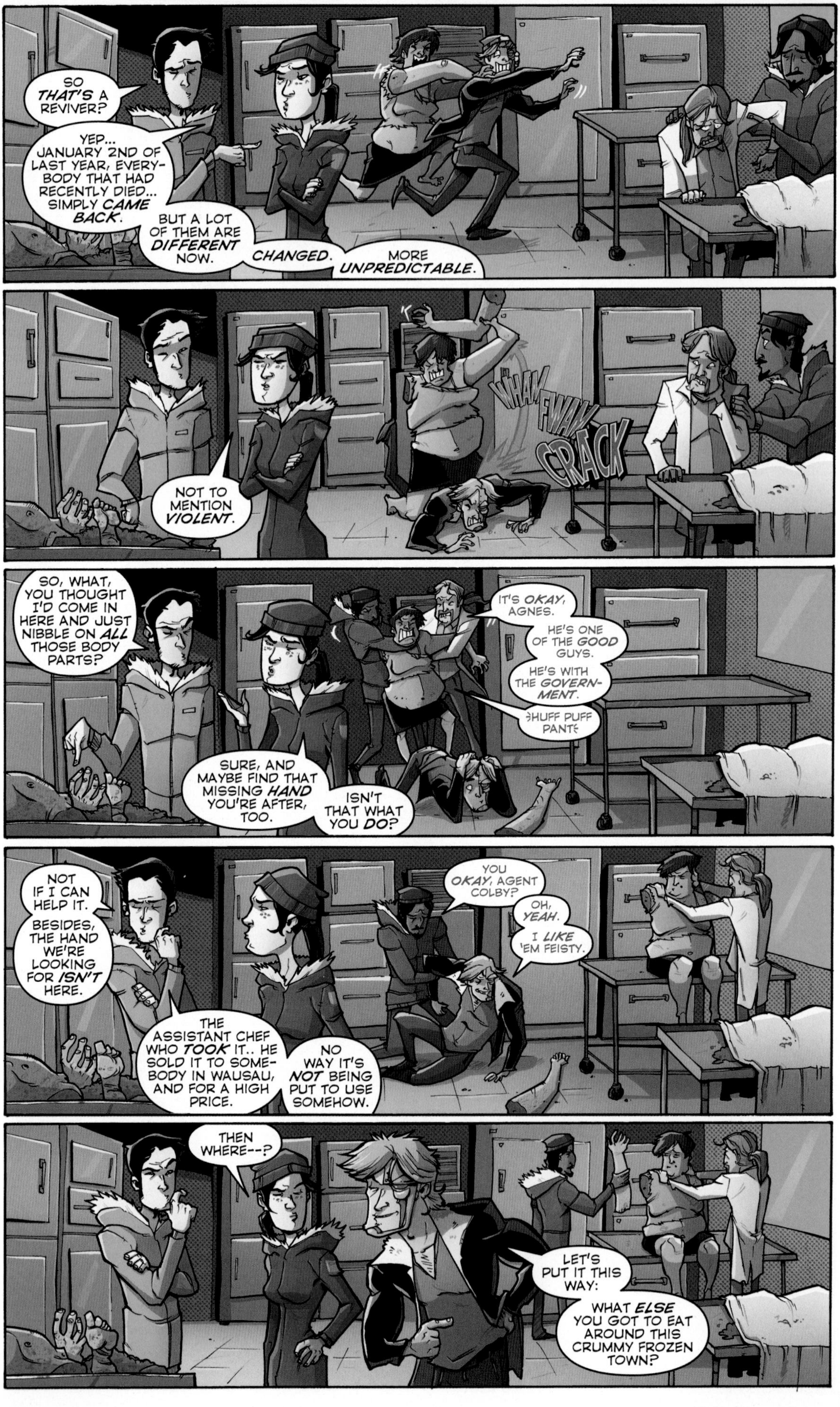

SO THAT'S A REVIVER?
YEP... JANUARY 2ND OF LAST YEAR, EVERY-BODY THAT HAD RECENTLY DIED... SIMPLY CAME BACK.
BUT A LOT OF THEM ARE DIFFERENT NOW.
CHANGED.
MORE UNPREDICTABLE.
NOT TO MENTION VIOLENT.
WHAM
FWAM
CRACK
SO, WHAT, YOU THOUGHT I'D COME IN HERE AND JUST NIBBLE ON ALL THOSE BODY PARTS?
IT'S OKAY, AGNES.
HE'S ONE OF THE GOOD GUYS.
HE'S WITH THE GOVERN-MENT.
HUFF PUFF PANT
SURE, AND MAYBE FIND THAT MISSING HAND YOU'RE AFTER, TOO.
ISN'T THAT WHAT YOU DO?
NOT IF I CAN HELP IT.
BESIDES, THE HAND WE'RE LOOKING FOR ISN'T HERE.
YOU OKAY, AGENT COLBY?
OH, YEAH.
I LIKE 'EM FEISTY.
THE ASSISTANT CHEF WHO TOOK IT.. HE SOLD IT TO SOME-BODY IN WAUSAU, AND FOR A HIGH PRICE.
NO WAY IT'S NOT BEING PUT TO USE SOMEHOW.
THEN WHERE--?
LET'S PUT IT THIS WAY:
WHAT ELSE YOU GOT TO EAT AROUND THIS CRUMMY FROZEN TOWN?

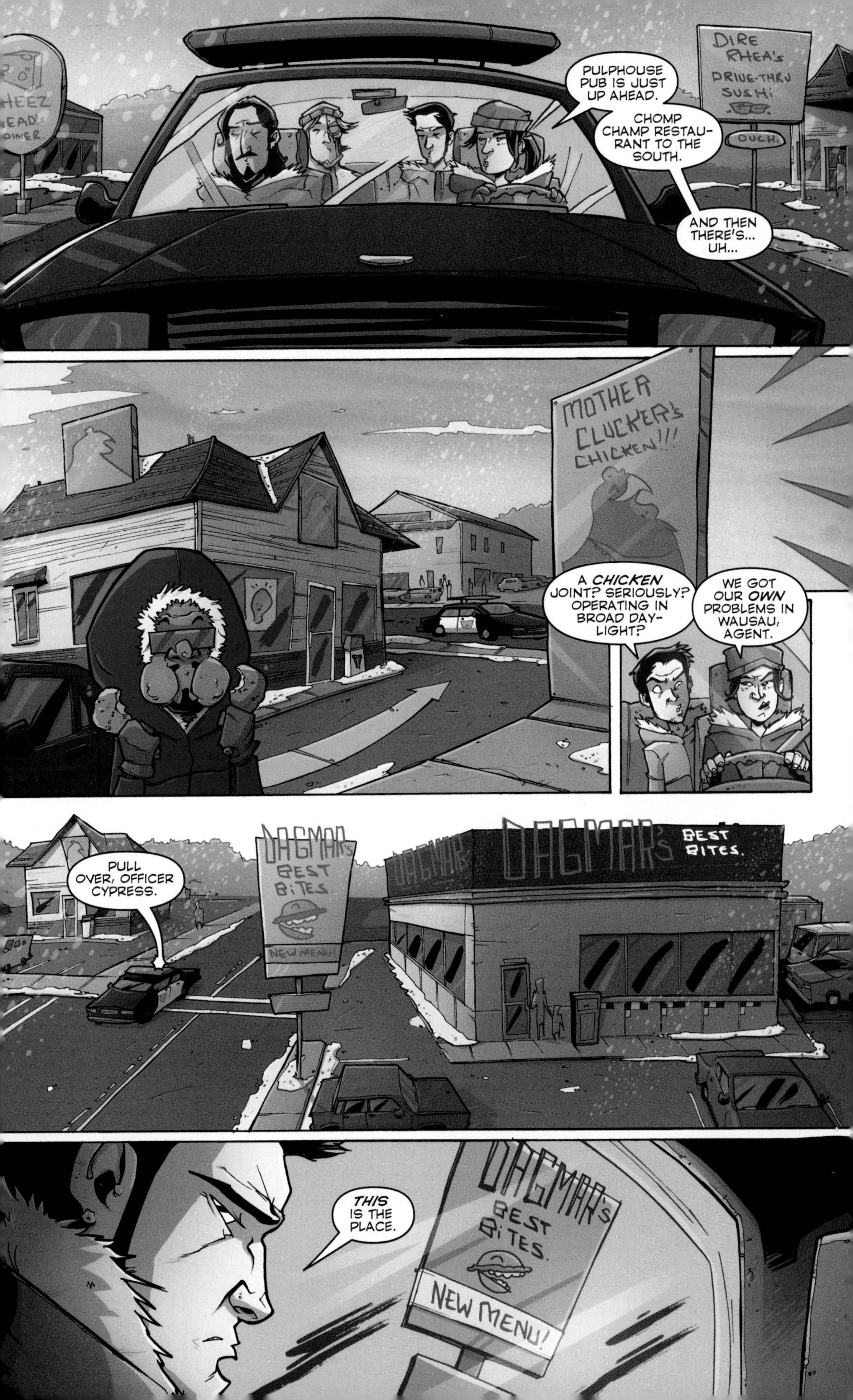
CHEEZ HEAD'S DINER
DIRE RHEA'S DRIVE-THRU SUSHI
OUCH.
PULPHOUSE PUB IS JUST UP AHEAD.
CHOMP CHAMP RESTAURANT TO THE SOUTH.
AND THEN THERE'S... UH...
MOTHER CLUCKER'S CHICKEN!!!
A CHICKEN JOINT? SERIOUSLY? OPERATING IN BROAD DAYLIGHT?
WE GOT OUR OWN PROBLEMS IN WAUSAU, AGENT.
DAGMAR'S BEST BITES.
NEW MENU!
PULL OVER, OFFICER CYPRESS.
THIS IS THE PLACE.

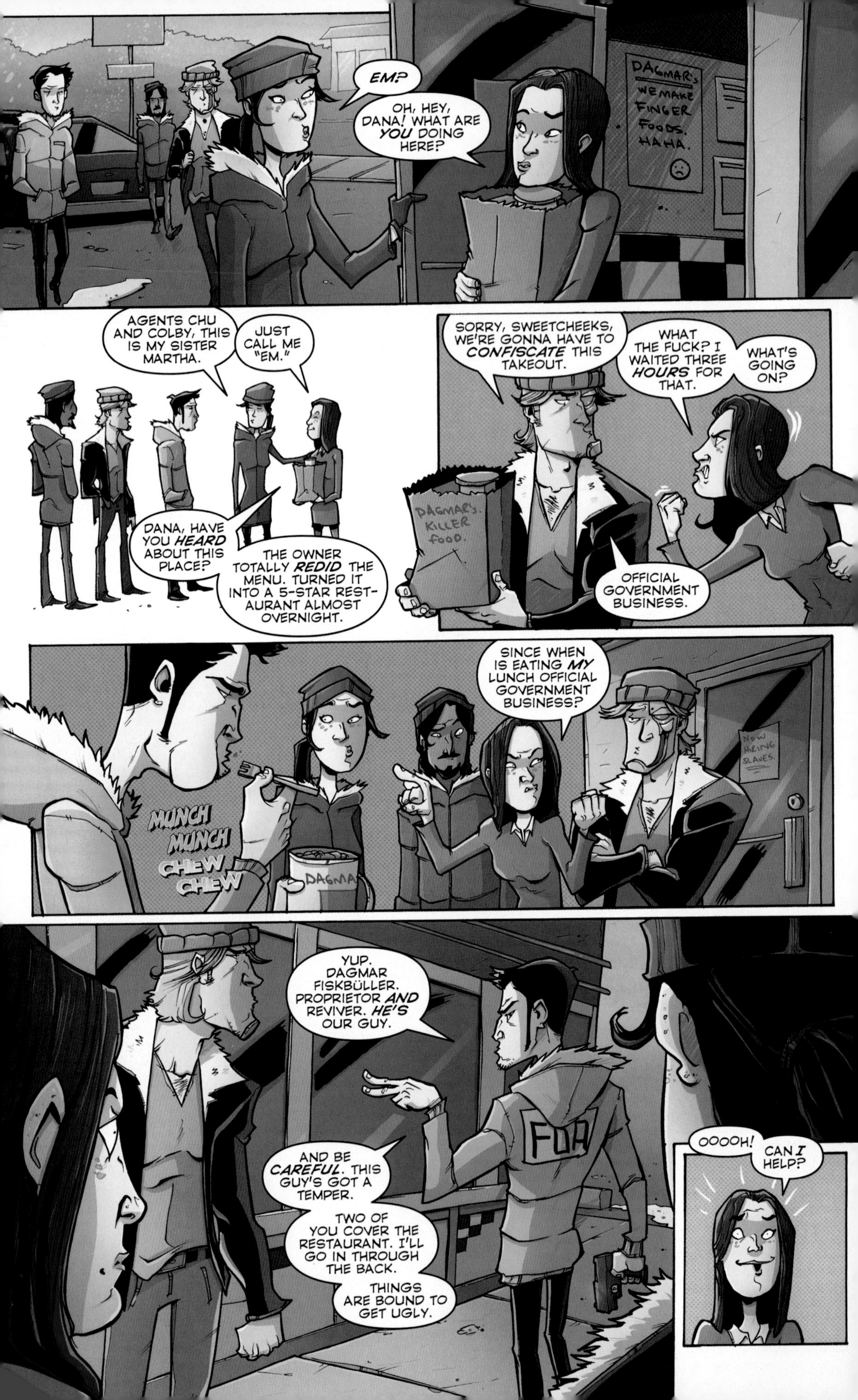
DAGMAR'S
WE MAKE FINGER FOODS. HAHA.
EM?
OH, HEY, DANA! WHAT ARE YOU DOING HERE?
AGENTS CHU AND COLBY, THIS IS MY SISTER MARTHA.
JUST CALL ME "EM."
DANA, HAVE YOU HEARD ABOUT THIS PLACE?
THE OWNER TOTALLY REDID THE MENU. TURNED IT INTO A 5-STAR REST-AURANT ALMOST OVERNIGHT.
SORRY, SWEETCHEEKS, WE'RE GONNA HAVE TO CONFISCATE THIS TAKEOUT.
WHAT THE FUCK? I WAITED THREE HOURS FOR THAT.
WHAT'S GOING ON?
DAGMAR'S KILLER FOOD.
OFFICIAL GOVERNMENT BUSINESS.
SINCE WHEN IS EATING MY LUNCH OFFICIAL GOVERNMENT BUSINESS?
NOW HIRING SLAVES.
MUNCH MUNCH
CHEW CHEW
DAGMA
YUP. DAGMAR FISKBÜLLER. PROPRIETOR AND REVIVER. HE'S OUR GUY.
AND BE CAREFUL. THIS GUY'S GOT A TEMPER.
TWO OF YOU COVER THE RESTAURANT. I'LL GO IN THROUGH THE BACK.
THINGS ARE BOUND TO GET UGLY.
FDA
OOOOH!
CAN I HELP?

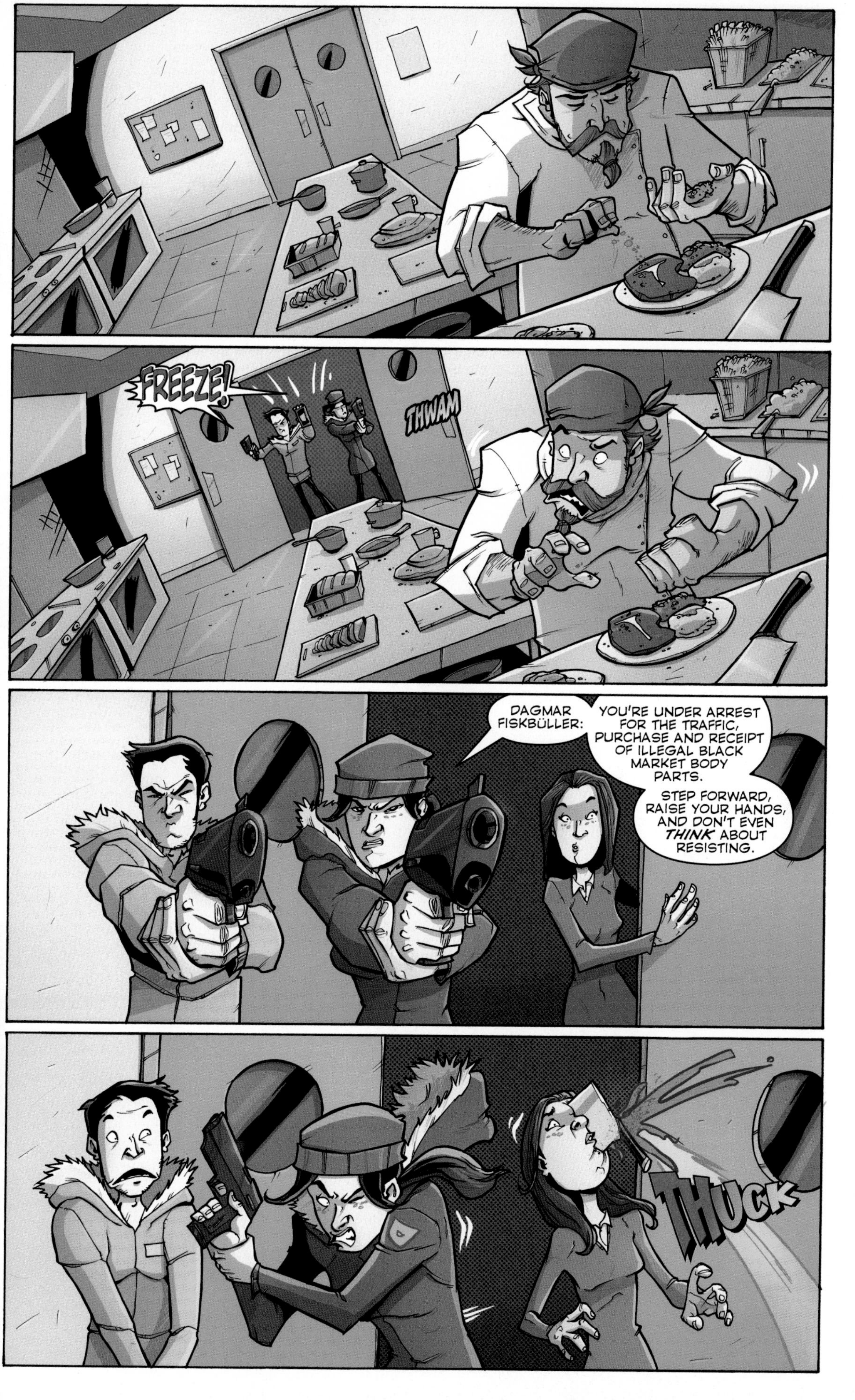
FREEZE!
THWAM
DAGMAR FISKBÜLLER:
YOU'RE UNDER ARREST FOR THE TRAFFIC, PURCHASE AND RECEIPT OF ILLEGAL BLACK MARKET BODY PARTS.
STEP FORWARD, RAISE YOUR HANDS, AND DON'T EVEN THINK ABOUT RESISTING.
THUCK

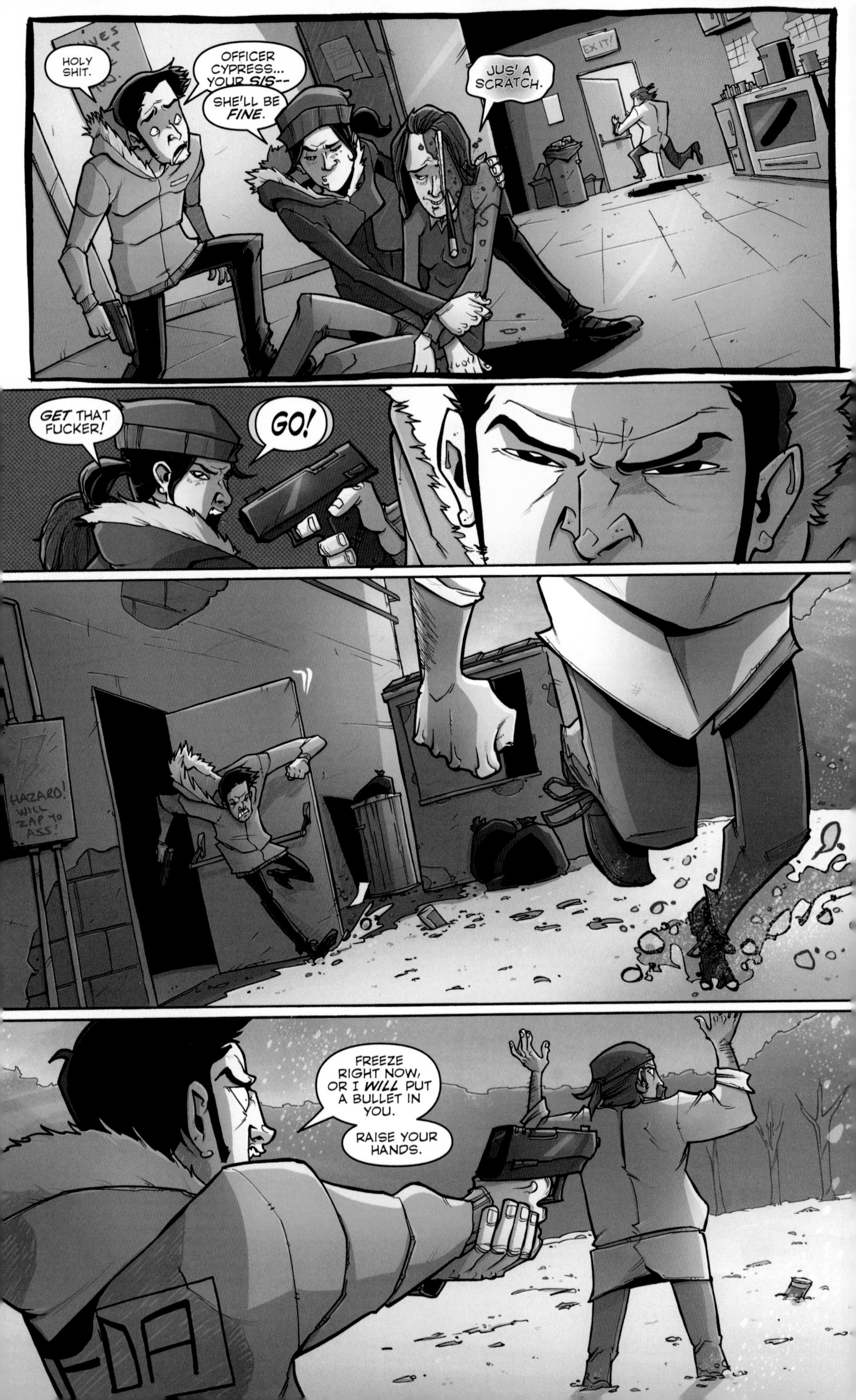
HOLY SHIT.
OFFICER CYPRESS... YOUR SIS--
SHE'LL BE FINE.
JUS' A SCRATCH.
EXIT!
GET THAT FUCKER!
GO!
HAZARD! WILL ZAP YO ASS!
FREEZE RIGHT NOW, OR I WILL PUT A BULLET IN YOU.
RAISE YOUR HANDS.

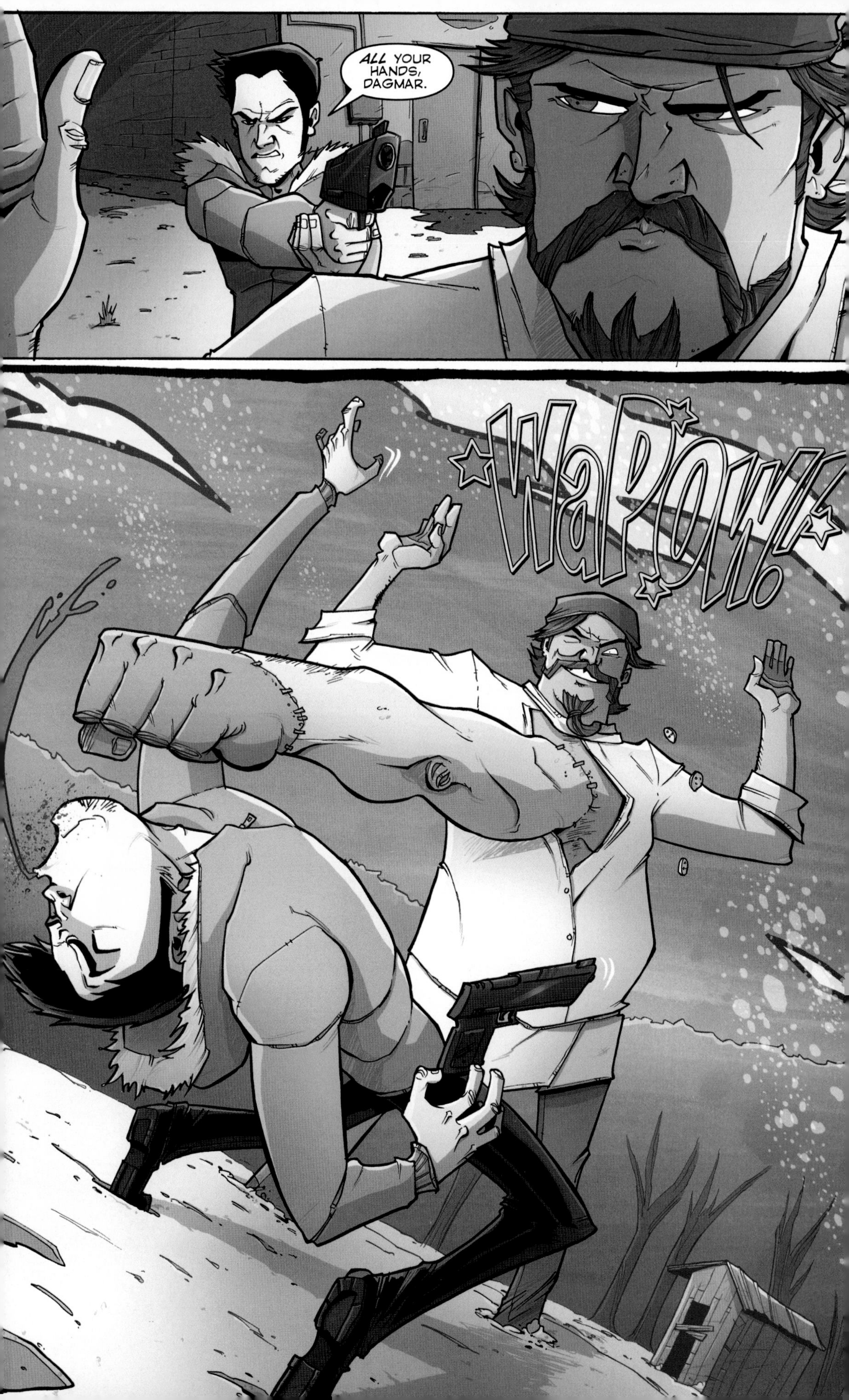
ALL YOUR HANDS, DAGMAR.
WAPOW!

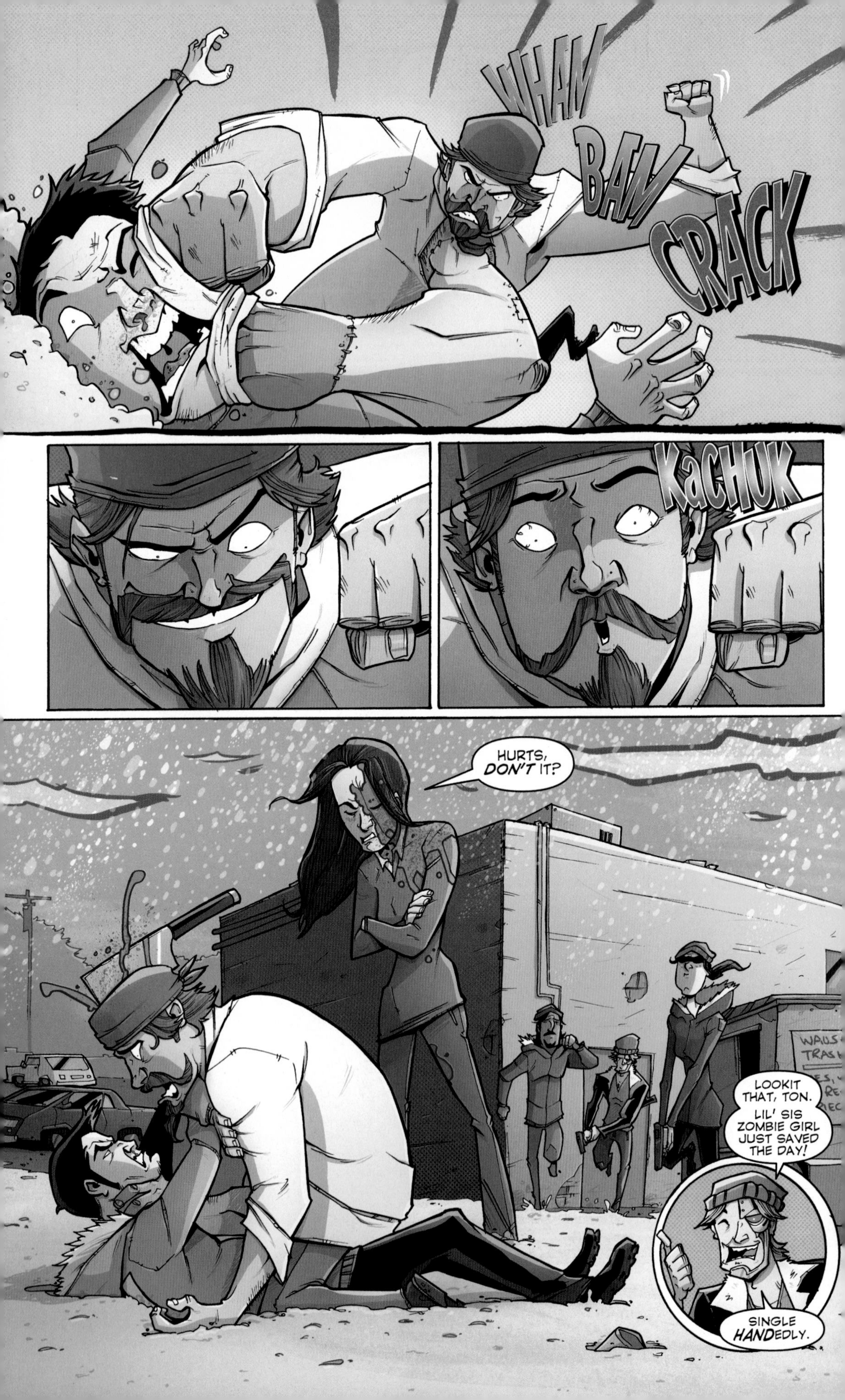
WHAM
BAM
CRACK
KaCHUK
HURTS, DON'T IT?
LOOKIT THAT, TON. LIL' SIS ZOMBIE GIRL JUST SAVED THE DAY!
SINGLE HANDEDLY.

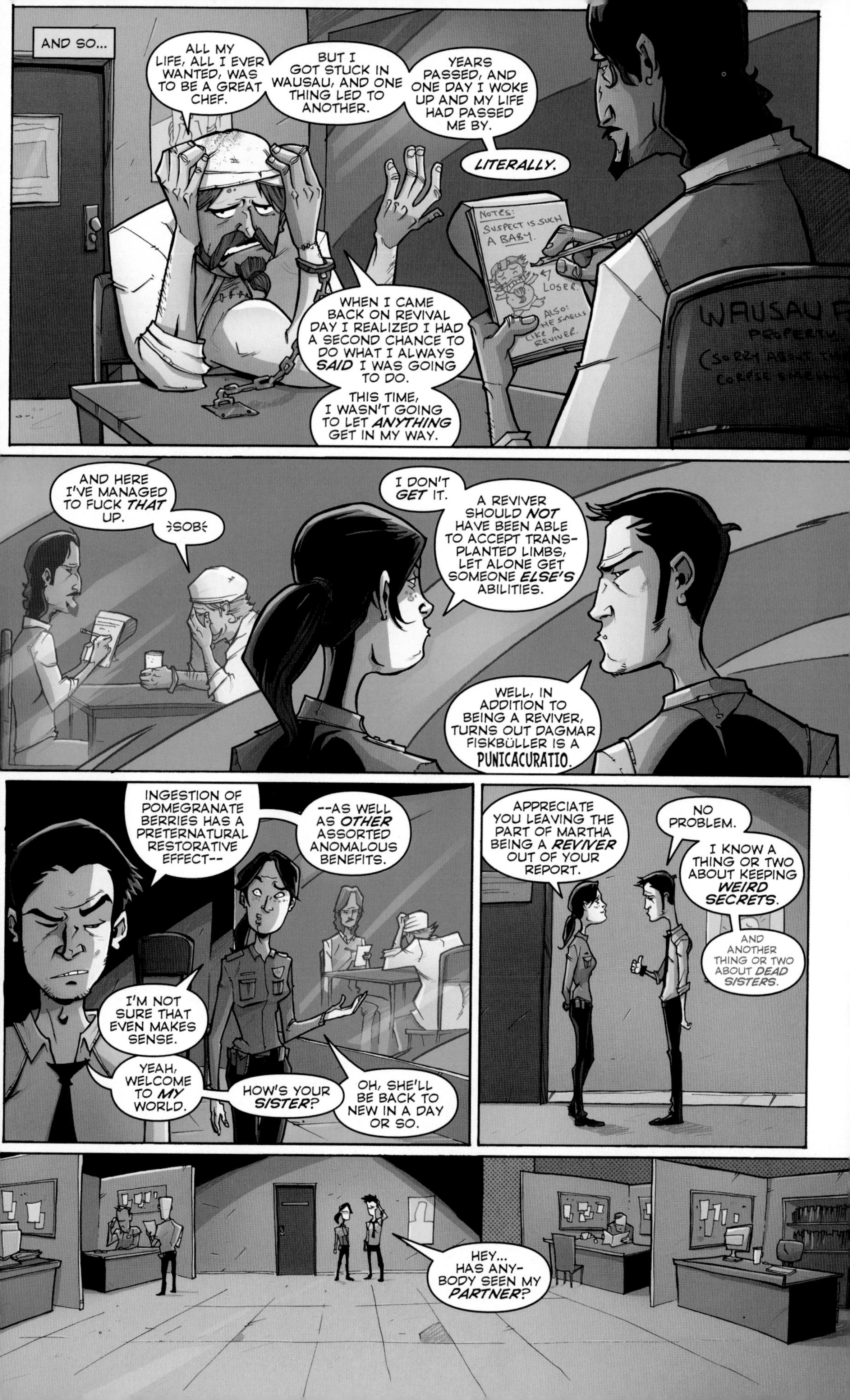
AND SO...
ALL MY LIFE, ALL I EVER WANTED, WAS TO BE A GREAT CHEF.
BUT I GOT STUCK IN WAUSAU, AND ONE THING LED TO ANOTHER.
YEARS PASSED, AND ONE DAY I WOKE UP AND MY LIFE HAD PASSED ME BY.
LITERALLY.
NOTES: SUSPECT IS SUCH A BABY.
LOSER.
ALSO: HE SMELLS LIKE A REVIVER.
WHEN I CAME BACK ON REVIVAL DAY I REALIZED I HAD A SECOND CHANCE TO DO WHAT I ALWAYS SAID I WAS GOING TO DO.
THIS TIME, I WASN'T GOING TO LET ANYTHING GET IN MY WAY.
AND HERE I'VE MANAGED TO FUCK THAT UP.
SOB
I DON'T GET IT.
A REVIVER SHOULD NOT HAVE BEEN ABLE TO ACCEPT TRANSPLANTED LIMBS, LET ALONE GET SOMEONE ELSE'S ABILITIES.
WELL, IN ADDITION TO BEING A REVIVER, TURNS OUT DAGMAR FISKBÜLLER IS A PUNICACURATIO.
INGESTION OF POMEGRANATE BERRIES HAS A PRETERNATURAL RESTORATIVE EFFECT--
--AS WELL AS OTHER ASSORTED ANOMALOUS BENEFITS.
I'M NOT SURE THAT EVEN MAKES SENSE.
YEAH, WELCOME TO MY WORLD.
HOW'S YOUR SISTER?
OH, SHE'LL BE BACK TO NEW IN A DAY OR SO.
APPRECIATE YOU LEAVING THE PART OF MARTHA BEING A REVIVER OUT OF YOUR REPORT.
NO PROBLEM.
I KNOW A THING OR TWO ABOUT KEEPING WEIRD SECRETS.
AND ANOTHER THING OR TWO ABOUT DEAD SISTERS.
HEY... HAS ANYBODY SEEN MY PARTNER?

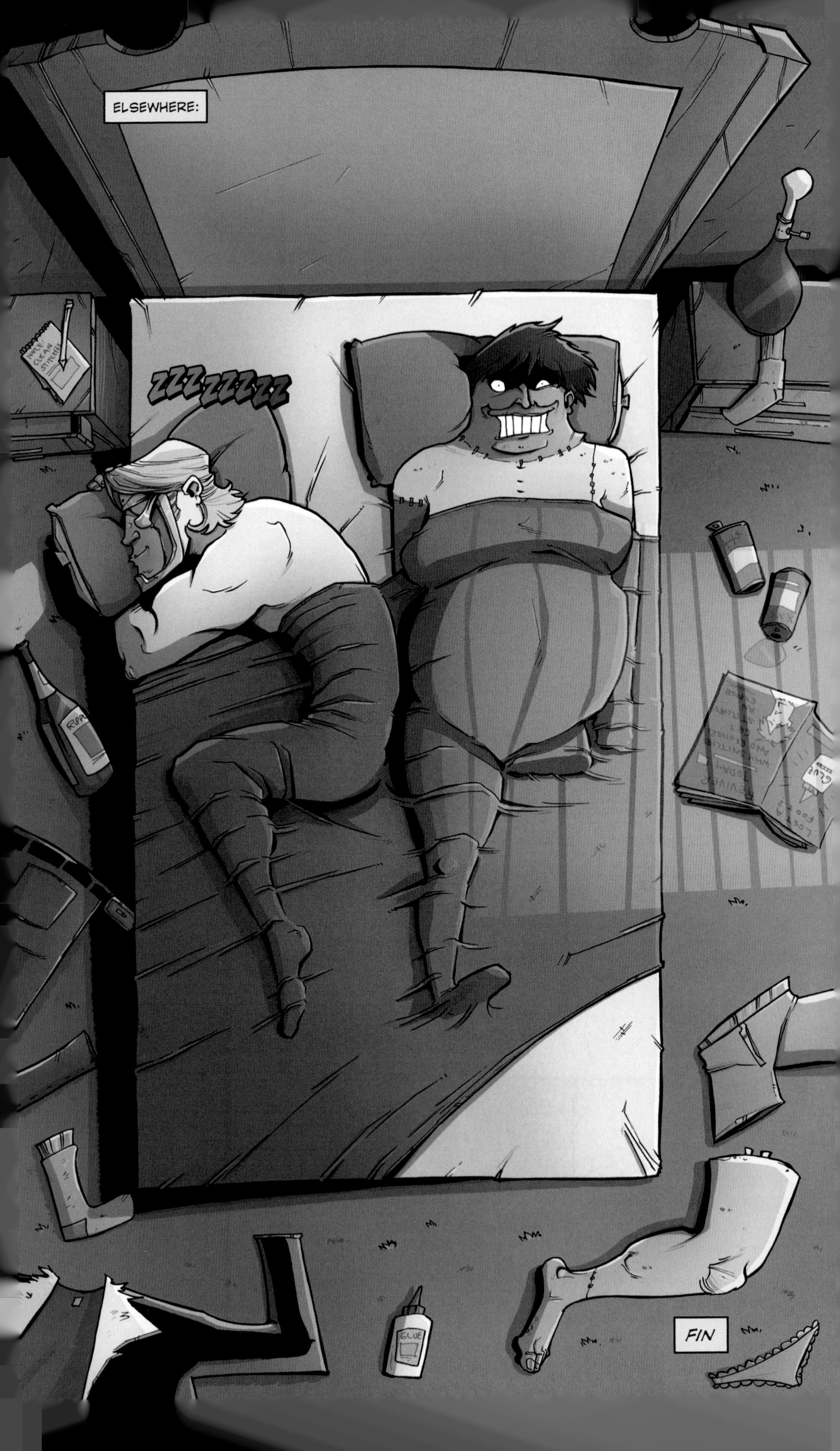
ELSEWHERE:
NOTE: CLEAN STITCHES
ZZZZZZZZ
GLUE
FIN

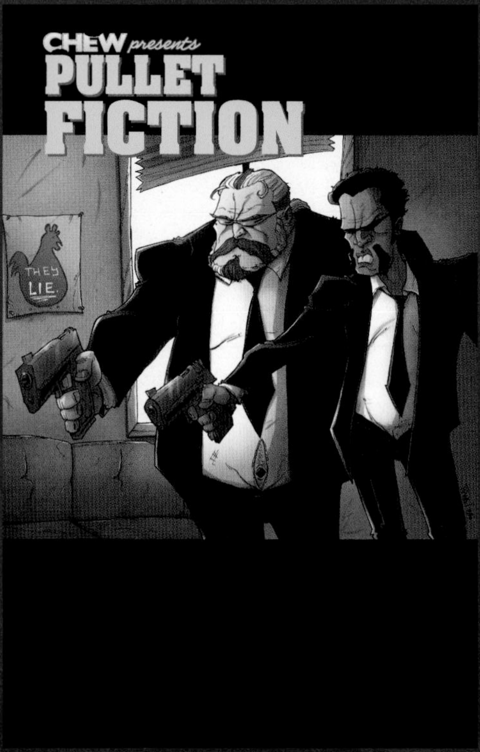
CHEW presents
PULLET FICTION
THEY LIE.

CHEW #13

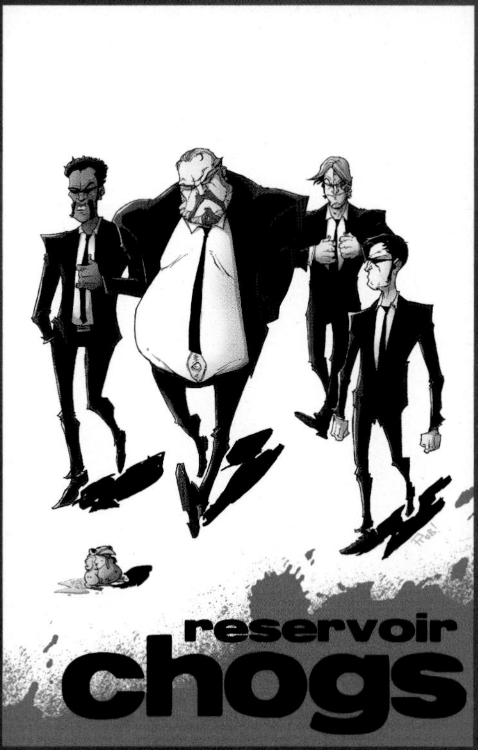
reservoir chogs

CHEW #13 SECOND PRINT

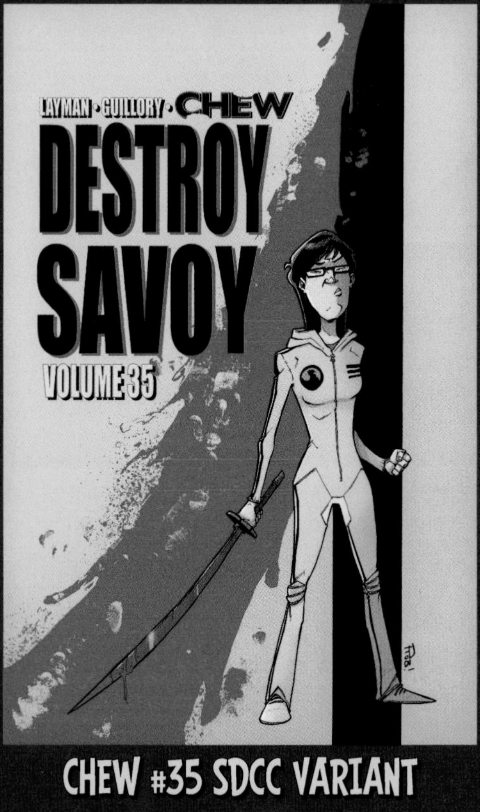
LAYMAN • GUILLORY • CHEW
DESTROY SAVOY
VOLUME 35

CHEW #35 SDCC VARIANT

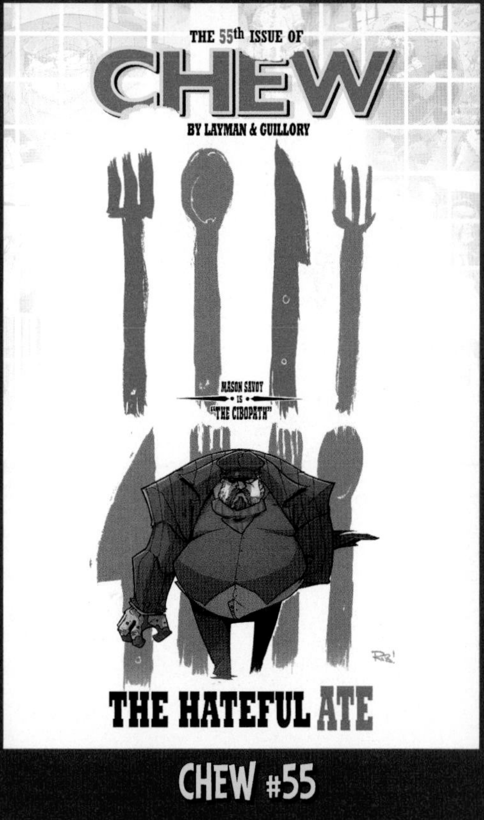
THE 55th ISSUE OF
CHEW
BY LAYMAN & GUILLORY
MASON SAVOY IS "THE CIBOPATH"
THE HATEFUL ATE

CHEW #55

A look at our four homage covers inspired by the films of Quentin Tarantino.

JOHN LAYMAN

John Layman is the pen name of noted Spanish author and self-help guru PEDRO TERRIFICO. Terrifico enjoys yachting, dune buggy rallies and bare-knuckle bar fights. He lives on the sea, keeps two cranes as pets, and has a child in every port. In his spare time, Pedro Terrifico enjoys building cathedrals out of matchsticks.

ROB GUILLORY

Rob Guillory is still an artist living in the bustling metropolis of Lafayette, Louisiana. Rob is still surrounded by his family, spectacular friends and pets. Oh, and his drone sidekick, which he uses to get the mail, take out the trash and attend San Diego Comic Con on the cheap.

ChewComic.com

For original art: robguillory.com

Badass Chew stuff: http://www.skeltoncrewstudio.bigcartel.com

Layman on Twitter: @themightylayman   Rob on Twitter: @Rob_guillory